Always Remembering

KATHY KASUNICH
WONDERFUL WORLD PUBLISHING

KATHY KASUNICH
WONDERFUL WORLD PUBLISHING

Printed in the United States of America
First Printing 2022
First Edition 2022

10 9 8 7 6 5 4 3 2 1

Library of Congress Control Number: 2022903752
ISBN 979-8-9850103-0-5

Dedication

This is dedicated to Mike and Helen, who had a time to love, a time of war, and a time of peace. He fought the battles overseas, while she endured the struggles stateside. And to the men and the women of the armed services, especially the 42nd Rainbow Division, and their families, who understand and fight the pains of war and grapple with the distance it puts between loved ones.

The army can take a lot of things from you, but they can't take our memories. These are the things that give you hope and the feeling of security. Once the memories are taken from you there isn't much you can rely on. —Mike Wozniak

PART I

Love Begins

Chapter One

Helen staggered toward the window, her nightgown damp with sweat and her heart pounding. Standing alone in the moonlight, she shivered as the breeze swept through the old single pane of glass and across her skin. Yet she hardly noticed the chill, for her mind still reeled from the image of Mike standing in a snowy field, his arm dangling from his shoulder, and blood oozing from a gigantic hole in his chest.

Her heart throbbed like war drums, echoing in her ears, and her face grew paler as the vision permeated her mind. Her anguish spread through her torso into her arms and her trembling hands. She stared at her palms, then clenched her hands, struggling to bury the thoughts of blood and death that bombarded her mind. Without warning, her emotions exploded as fast as the bombs descending upon Pearl Harbor almost a year ago. Tears, no longer contained, broke free like a dam weakened by the tides of change and fell like steady rain to the floor.

In a few short hours, the man she had surrendered her soul to would be torn from her and tossed into a turmoil she barely understood. A war fought by men just starting their lives, brimming with love and dreams; a war fought by men like Mike. During the last year, neighbors, shop owners, and friends had disappeared as the war reached in and plucked them, one by one, from her peaceful existence. Faces once familiar and safe, instantly gone, swept into the battle of the nations. Would Mike also be expunged from her life in a flash, as though he'd never been there at all?

Chilled, she pulled her mother's threadbare chenille blanket over her shoulders and peeked out the wavy glass window of the slouching row house on Pittsburgh's South Side. In the glow of the moon, her face, wrought with apprehension, appeared considerably older than her twenty-one years. Her reddened eyes glazed over as she stared into the dark night, unaware of snowflakes dancing in the November breeze. The wind roared harder and rattled the shutters with a loud bang. Helen yelped and sprang backward. Her slipper flew off and landed on the bed as her blanket slipped to the wool area rug. Teetering, Helen peered over her shoulder, relieved to see her younger sister Flo undisturbed by her restlessness.

Quietly, Helen gathered the blanket, ambled toward her bed, and knelt. She asked God to guard Mike and erase the horridness from her head. Gradually, her mind brimmed over with exhilaration as she remembered dancing with Mike, moments of laughter and love, and long, intimate walks. The weight of anxiety melted away, her tears subsided, and a smile emerged as her heart filled with the happiness they'd shared.

She glanced at the tarnished alarm clock by her bedside and realized that soon moonbeams would be replaced by sunlight. Anticipating the morning, she tiptoed to her tiny closet and rummaged through the clothes. Disappointed with all her outfits, she wished the garments with tattered hems and stains could be magically swapped for a stunning wardrobe. Last week, she'd wanted to buy a fashionable dress to leave a lasting impression in Mike's mind and a smile on his face, an outfit to sustain him for his duration in the army. At Kaufmann's Department Store, she found a crisp, long-sleeved rayon dress that was simple, yet stylish, and accentuated her figure without being provocative. Regrettably, she did not have enough money to buy it. Helen complied with the rule of the house, just as her three older sisters had before they were married. She relinquished her entire paycheck to her mother in exchange for one month's streetcar and incline fare and a few dollars for essentials. The dress would have to remain in the store.

Obsessed with finding an alluring outfit, Helen frantically swiped through her clothes. She rejected every outfit until she spotted a rayon mid-calf dress in navy blue with a white eyelet collar, tucked behind her summer coat. Its fitted waistline and full, flared skirt always elicited a flattering remark from Mike. Squinting in the darkness, Helen held the outfit in front of her and scrutinized it. Although it was not the captivating fashion statement she'd coveted at Kaufmann's last week, she chose this dress to adorn her slim body. Unable to keep her eyes open, Helen carried the dress to her bed, clutched it to her chest, and fell back into an uneasy sleep.

Flo awoke before the alarm clock sounded and noticed Helen cuddling the dress. With utmost care she endeavored to remove the dress, but Helen jerked. "Flo, what are you doing? What time is it?"

"It's still early, and I didn't want your dress to get wrinkled."

"Oh, thanks."

"Looks like you couldn't sleep again last night. You're worried about Mike, aren't you?"

"Of course, I'm worried." Helen's voice rose. "Mike acts like everything's okay, but I'm scared. I'm scared of what he'll have to go through. I'm scared that if he's gone too long, I'll forget who he is and why I love him. I'm scared that this war will break us up."

"Helen, you're hysterical! Calm down and listen. I know both of you, and you have something special. You two have history and memories and love. Time and war can't destroy that."

"Maybe not, but it can destroy him. I lie awake at night, and these thoughts rush into my head, and . . . and . . . I'm . . . afraid of losing him. I think about the bombs. The fighting. What if he gets killed? That's all they talk about in the papers. All the names of the soldiers killed. And you've seen the newsreels."

"I know. Sometimes I wish they wouldn't even show that stuff."

Helen wiped her eyes. "Flo, I'm sorry for being upset. It's just . . . we just celebrated Thanksgiving, thanking God for everyone, and now Mike's leaving."

Flo handed her a hanky. "I know, Helen. It's hard to let go, but he'll be okay. You'll be okay. I promise."

Sensing her sister needed a reason to smile, Flo cajoled her. "If you keep cryin', I'm gonna get a bucket. This handkerchief won't be enough for you."

Helen grinned and playfully pushed her sister on the shoulder. "Oh, you're so funny."

"It put a smile on your face!"

"Yeah, it did." Helen hugged Flo. "Thanks for being here. When Bern leaves for boot camp, I'll be here for you, too."

"How 'bout I make some coffee?"

"That would sure hit the spot. Thanks."

After Flo left, Helen glanced at the framed picture of Mike that sat next to the lamp. She smiled and wondered why she'd initially sworn to her sister Gert she would not date Mike if he were the last man on earth. How could those words have flowed so effortlessly from her lips? After she'd relinquished her heart to Mike, her life had been transformed. She envisioned walking down the aisle and becoming his wife, having children, and making a house into a living, breathing microcosm of heaven. Now, raging, fanatical political leaders were forcing Mike to fight and confining her to solitude.

Feeling helpless, Helen reached for her tattered, worn prayer book. Falling to her knees, she passionately prayed for Mike's life and their future. After an exhaustive plea, she wiped her tears and joined her sister in the kitchen.

Flo buttered her toast at the rickety wooden table. "Coffee's ready! I put an empty cup by the stove for you."

"Thanks."

"There's still three pieces of bread left. Do you want toast, too?"

"I don't think I can eat anything right now. I'm surprised Mom and Pop aren't up yet."

"It's still early. I'm sure when they get a whiff of the coffee, they'll be down. So, are you going to wear that dress you were holding?"

Helen added cream to her cup. "Yes. Do you think the spectator shoes will look good with it?"

"Yeah, I do."

"I hope so. I just want everything to be perfect . . . It . . . What if . . . it's the last time . . . You know."

Flo searched her mind for something to say, as Helen repeatedly stirred her coffee. "Mmm, ahh. Hey, are Mike's parents going to the train station?"

"I don't know. Why?"

"I was just wondering."

"To tell you the truth, Flo, I don't think they will go because they're selfish people."

"Why would you say that?"

Helen's shoulders tightened. "I'll tell you why! Ever since they found out Mike was drafted, all they talk about is the money they'll lose that he used to give them from his paycheck. They say they will starve when he leaves. I understand they depended on the money he gave them, but they just went on and on about how awful it's going to be. Do they realize how terrible it will be for Mike? No sympathy, just complaints. Not once did I hear them say, 'We're going to miss you' or 'We'll pray for you.'"

Flo's eyebrows arched. "Wow! I'm sure they're still concerned about him, though."

"Not as much as they are about the money! They sounded like a broken record. What are we going to do? Why can't you stay here and work and give us money? If they cared, they wouldn't be talking about money all the time; they'd be worried about his life."

"I don't understand why they're so dependent on Mike anyway," Flo said.

"Me neither! You'd think he was the only one in the family. They've used him since he was a teenager. He lied about his age to get into the CCC so he could help them pay the rent. And because of that, he graduated late."

"I never knew that, but you've got to hand it to him for helping his family."

"Of course, I do! That's why I love him. But it upsets me the way they take advantage of him. And his sisters are just as bad, always asking him for something."

"What do you think his parents are gonna do?" Flo asked.

Helen shrugged. "Argh! I don't know. Maybe the rest of the family could help them for once. I know Stan helps a little, but his sisters only think about themselves. Anyway, I don't want to talk about it. Especially not today!"

Flo stood up. "Sorry. Do you want more coffee?"

"I'd love some, but we should save the rest for Mom and Pop." Helen noticed the time. "Oh, I better get cleaned up and dressed. I don't want Mike waiting for me."

"When I finish readin' the newspaper, I'll come help you."

Flo flipped through the *Pittsburgh Post-Gazette*, glanced at the headlines, and read several articles about the war overseas. None of the articles provided any hope for a swift end to the conflict. With no encouraging news, Flo slurped the last sip of coffee and scampered upstairs.

When she popped back into the room, she found Helen searching through her dresser drawer.

"What are you lookin' for?"

"A pair of silk stockings with no runners. I thought I might get lucky and find one buried in here. All that's in here are these dingy cotton ones. What should I do? I can't buy new ones today."

"I have an idea. You've read about how women are faking stockings, haven't you?" Flo asked.

"Yeah, I have. But do you think it'll look good?"

"Everyone's doin' it. Wanna give it a try? You have nothin' to lose."

"I guess."

Flo scoured the top of the dresser for the unassuming object that would create the allure of stockings. "Yes, this will do the job!" She snatched it, held it up, and approached Helen like a surgeon with a scalpel. "Step on this chair; it'll be easier for me to do this."

"Are you sure this will work?"

"All I have to do is take this eyebrow pencil and draw lines down your legs to look like the seams."

"What if the line is crooked?"

"Don't worry. I can do it. I've been drawing straight lines since grade school."

"Yeah, on paper, not on people!"

"Listen, stand still so I don't mess up."

Flo flawlessly drew thin brown lines down the backs of Helen's legs.

"There you go. All done."

Helen kicked her leg out to the side and crooked her neck to see her sister's handiwork. "Not bad. I wonder if Mike will realize I'm not wearing stockings."

"If he doesn't say anything, then I'd say it was successful."

"Thanks, Flo."

Flo stepped back and looked straight into Helen's eyes, "That's what sisters are for. Now get dressed and see your man off."

Helen slid the navy-blue dress over her head, brushed her chestnut-colored locks backward, and secured them with several bobby pins. As she slid the last pin into her hair, she heard the dog bark in the kitchen.

Her mom, Mary, shushed the dog and opened the back door. "Come on in."

"Hi, Mrs. Cypyrch. You must have been waiting for me. I didn't even knock."

"The dog barked, so I figured it must be you. Where's your suitcase?"

"In the car. My brother, Stan, drove me. He's waiting outside."

Helen listened to the voices at the bottom of the stairwell. She blurted out, "Flo, I'm not sure I'm ready."

"You look fine."

"I mean, I don't know if I'm ready to say goodbye."

Flo assured her, "It'll be okay. Take another minute and finish up. I'll go down and shoot the breeze with him for a few minutes."

Helen stood at the dresser and stared at the pallid image in the mirror reflecting the fear inside her. To disguise her true emotions, she powdered her face, dabbed her cheeks with rouge, and glided red lipstick across her lips. After blotting her lips with a tissue, she glanced at her reflection one last time. Taking in a deep breath and releasing it, she straightened her shoulders, fixed the collar of her dress, and smiled.

Flo heard Helen's footsteps on the creaky wooden stairs. To give the lovebirds privacy, Flo promptly excused herself, saying she wanted to tell Stan hello. Helen's mother hugged Mike, wished him Godspeed, and retreated to her bedroom.

Helen smiled and sauntered toward Mike. "Hi, honey," she said.

"Well, sweetheart, you ready to see me off?"

"As ready as I'll ever be."

"You look fantastic. In fact, you're the most beautiful woman I know."

"So, you want a quarter now for complimenting me?"

"No, not a quarter, just the reassurance you'll wait for me."

"Of course, I will."

Mike drew her close, and they remained entwined for several minutes. Easing away, he rested his hands on her shoulders and stared into her hazel eyes. He drank in her flawless ivory skin, her beguiling smile, and the locks of her long hair. Eyeing her up and down, he mentally engraved every detail into his memory, from her dress and shoes to the thin gold watchband around her slender wrist, the delicate earrings that sparkled like her eyes, and the imitation ruby ring on her finger, as red as her luscious lips. As he inhaled the sweet scent of White Shoulders perfume, he vowed it would forever linger in his mind. Helen focused on his dark-blue bedroom eyes that transported her to the depths of his soul. She felt safe, loved, and euphoric next to Mike and wished time would stand still.

Mike leaned forward, and they sought each other's lips like magnets drawn together by an uncontrollable force. Relaxing for a second, he whispered, "I can't let go, but we have to leave, Helen," and locked lips with her again. Her body slowly dissolved into his sheltering arms.

Flo burst through the back door, rubbing her palms together to warm them.

"Sorry to intrude, but it's getting colder outside."

Mike replied, "That's okay, Flo, we're leaving now anyway."

Helen collected her coat and hat. "Who else is in the car?"

"Just Stan," Mike said. "My mom and dad said their goodbyes this morning. Besides, they hate train stations. Bad memories from when they left Poland."

"My parents aren't too fond of them either. What about your sisters?"

"Francie and Sophie had some things to do, and Jo wasn't feeling well. Anyway, we better get going."

Flo hugged Mike and wished him well. "I'll be here when you get back, Helen," she said to her sister.

Mike opened the back door of the old Buick for Helen, hopped in the other side, and slid next to her. "Hey, Stan, thanks again for driving."

"No problem, that's the least I can do for my little brother."

As the car clunked along the cobblestone and streetcar tracks of Carson Street, Mike rested his arm around Helen. "Sitting next to you made me think about what I want you to do for me while I'm gone."

"What's that?"

"I want you to make sure nobody takes my place on the couch next to you. I want that reserved for me."

"Well, sometimes my pop likes to sit there," Helen said. "I can't say no to him."

"You know what I mean."

Helen smiled. "Oh, you think you're the only one who can be funny?"

Mike laughed and squeezed her tight. Although she joked and smiled, the car ride to Pennsylvania Train Station felt akin to riding in the funeral car behind the hearse. Mike peered into her alluring eyes. "You know what I'm going to miss the most while I'm away?"

"No, what?"

"My dog."

Helen's eyes widened. "What?"

"Oh, you know I'm kiddin'. It's home-cooked food."

As Helen smirked, the car stopped in front of the station. and Stan said, "Why don't you two get out here? I'll park the car and meet you there in a couple of minutes."

As Helen exited the car, Mike ogled her well-defined calves and whistled, "You sure look swell!"

Helen giggled. "Oh, Mike, stop that. People are staring at us."

"Hey, I can't help it if I have the best-looking gal around here."

He jerked open the oversized doors leading to the waiting area, held them open, and waved a hand toward the entrance. "Ladies first."

They both paused as the glass-and-metal doors slammed shut behind them and reverberated like prison doors sentencing them to solitude. They surveyed the crowd of men and well-wishers occupying every inch of floor space. Hundreds of soldiers, each with a satchel of personal items in one hand and a woman clinging to his other arm, stood alongside teary-eyed mothers and sisters. Only a few waited alone, lost among the crowd. Distracting clatter echoed off the marble floor and the high ceiling. The band playing cheerful songs in the background lightened the mood but added to the clamor. Mike and Helen were unwilling participants in the tense, bittersweet scene of romance: music, a cacophony of voices, train whistles, and tears. Seeking solitude, they squeezed through the crowd and found a space next to the water fountain, nestled along a wall.

Mike clasped Helen's hands. "Darling, I want you to know that with God's help, I'll do whatever's in my power to come back to you. Just keep me in your heart and prayers."

"You know I will."

"That's my girl. But don't pray for me to come back too soon."

"Oh, why would you say that?"

"I'm serious. I've told you I like to travel. Well, this is my opportunity. It gives me a chance to see different places and if they're worth a return visit. If they are, then I'll take you there someday. Wouldn't that be swell? You and me traveling."

"I'd go anywhere with you, but I still want you to come back as soon as possible."

"Yes, sirree. Your man is going to see the world, all courtesy of Uncle Sam. I'll whip myself into shape and gain more muscles. When I come back, I'll have arms like Popeye to protect you."

"Oh, Mike, I like you the way you are."

"I'm telling you, you're gonna like me a lot better, especially if I'm in my uniform. Just you wait and see."

"Hey, there you are," called Stan. "I wasn't sure if I'd find you in this mess of people. If I hadn't recognized Helen's hat, I might not have found you."

"Well, I'm glad you did. I think I heard an announcement for me."

Leaning toward Helen, Mike said, "Guess I have to board the train."

She whispered, "I know," and reached into her pocket. She placed her hand in his and released a medal of the Blessed Mother into his palm. "Mike, promise me you'll always carry this with you. I know she'll protect you, wherever you go."

He hugged her. "Thanks, sweetheart. I promise."

"Oh, I almost forgot." She removed a magazine from her purse. "I got you this. I thought you might want something to read on the train. Oh, and here's some candy."

"Thanks, you're the sweetest." The train whistle blew. "Sorry, gotta go, darling."

After one more life-sustaining kiss and final goodbye, Mike boarded the crowded steam engine train. The last few men jumped into the car, and the conductor signaled the engineer to move forward. Mike knelt on the bench seat, nudged his head through an open window, and searched frantically among the sea of women on the platform for one last glimpse of Helen. Fog swirled around their faces as people in the crowd shouted to their loved ones in the cold air outside the train. Mike easily focused on his treasure among the crowd blowing kisses, as the cars inched along the tracks. The forlorn whistle echoed, and soon Helen disappeared from sight.

On the crowded train, the men squeezed three across in a seat meant for two. Mike, crushed against the wintry pane of glass, regretted that he'd snatched the window seat. Glancing through the cabin, he noticed how young some of these "men" looked. He was only twenty, but others appeared as if they'd just left grade school and were away from their family possibly for the first time. Recalling his own lonely, anxious feelings on his initial train trip to the CCC for the summer, when he had been only sixteen, he concluded that these inexperienced men needed encouragement.

Mike, born with a microphone in one hand and a notepad of one-liners in the other, decided to do what he did best. He approached a couple of men at the head of the car, who were puffing on their cigarettes and staring out the window. "So, you fellows ready for a new haircut?"

"Not really, but we don't have a choice," one of the boys said.

Mike said, "Yeah, you're right, and I gotta tell you, I heard many of the GIs were complaining about their haircuts to the barber, and he told them, 'Don't worry. After a while, it'll grow on you.'"

Sounds of laughter erupted, and a recruit inquired, "Hey, buddy, you some kind of comedian?"

"Are you kidding? I'm not a comedian. I'm American. How about you?"

Guffawing, a young man said, "Hey, that reminds me of a joke I heard on the radio the other day," and he shared his story.

In a short time, others joined in, and an hour-long comedic fest ensued, with each man attempting to one-up the others. The jovial crowd exchanged stories about families, girlfriends, and work, as pockets of poker games started.

After dinner, a stocky man pulled out his harmonica and played a few notes. Mike approached him. "Hey, pal, do you know how to play 'You're a Grand Ole Flag'?"

"Sure, you want me to play it?"

"Yeah, go ahead."

Mike blared out the lyrics to the tune and coaxed the other recruits to join in. They continued with "Over There" and other songs from the popular movie *Yankee Doodle Dandy*. Soon the whole car burst into a melody of voices that spilled over into other cars, enticing everyone to join in the frivolity. Strangers, all with different stories, some recent immigrants to the United States, bonded over common ground: their hatred of the enemy and their patriotic devotion to their country.

Helen arrived home from the station to the sounds of her mother and Flo conversing, but their talking ceased when she walked into the kitchen. After she hung her coat on the door, she glanced at her mom and sister, waiting for them to say something. Their muteness pierced her bruised soul. She needed words, hugs, anything, no matter how trivial, to acknowledge her fear and loneliness. Her throat clogged with tension, as she tried to break the stifling silence. Unable to say anything, she turned on the radio, and Kate Smith's pleasant voice sang, "I wonder when my baby's coming home." Helen sighed and burst into tears.

Her mother slapped her hand on the table, stood up, and grabbed Helen by the shoulders. "I've had enough of your moping. Stop crying and accept the situation. You're not the only woman on the face of the earth to send a man off to war! Toughen up, or you'll become a basket case."

Helen's eyes bulged, and her muscles tightened. *Why is she always so harsh? Doesn't she understand my heartache?*

Mary, the stern matriarch of the family, never allowed ordinary human emotions to penetrate or awaken her soul. She had the facade of a stone statue, masked by a round, chubby face; short, graying hair with tight curls; rimless glasses; and a conservative smile. She had grown comfortable with her aging appearance and body and considered them a well-earned symbol of her wisdom and rank in the family.

Unlike her mother, who safeguarded her emotions inside an ice-cold vault, Helen freely unlocked her heart and allowed others into her soul. Unable to comprehend her mother's actions, she thought, *Why can't she have some compassion for once?*

Instead of being tormented by more of Mary's disparaging remarks, Helen wiped her eyes and said, "I'm sorry I'm a disappointment. I'm going for a walk."

Chapter Two

December 1942

Helen bid goodnight to her fellow workers at Donahoe's grocery store and faced the cold winter night. Pausing for a moment to button her coat, she glanced at the spot where Mike usually greeted her in his baritone voice. Only the image of his handsome face in her mind made an appearance. She had to be content with a brisk walk to the Monongahela Incline by herself, instead of enjoying Mike's companionship and pleasant conversation.

Inside the station, Helen warmed her hands by the stove. She imagined Mike holding her tightly as she waited for the vehicle to clamber up the steep metal rails on the rocky mountainside. The wooden cable car squeaked to a stop. She inserted a nickel in the fare box and sat down on the bench. Staring at the vacant seat next to her, she wondered when her loneliness would disappear.

Although the wind snapped at her skin, she leisurely strolled home from the incline. This was her time to dream about Mike. She didn't want her memories to fade. On entering the kitchen, she checked the table for a letter from Mike, as she had done for the last two weeks. She beamed at the sight of two letters from Private Wozniak. Without stopping to remove her coat, she seized a knife from the drawer, slid it through the envelope flap, and withdrew the precious note. Her only connection to Mike and the beginning of their long-distance relationship ensued via the U.S. Post

Office. Mike, no longer able to woo her with his mesmerizing blue eyes and wry smile, sweet-talked her with his scratchy, handwritten words.

December 7, 1942

Dearest Helen:

Writing to let you know that I am feeling fine, in the best of spirits and I hope you are the same.

I only stayed in Fort Meade, Maryland for two days. Left there Wednesday about 10:30 PM. We slept in a Pullman and ate our meals in a diner car. Now I ask you can you imagine me (space reserved for imagination) eating my meals in a diner and being served by a waiter. Those four days I spent on the train made me feel like one of the high class of society.

I ate the first meal, breakfast passing through Pittsburgh, at that time it was snowing so I can imagine what kind of weather you have there.

Dinner and Supper were later in the state of Ohio. Passing through Akron, Newark and Columbus. During the night we passed through the state of Indiana and found ourselves eating breakfast in the state of Missouri. Then dinner in Arkansas and finally but not least eating supper in the state of Texas. Finally arrived at Camp Maxey, Texas about 1:30 AM Saturday morning.

How do you like that for traveling Helen, not bad is it?

Do you remember that picture **Sergeant York,** *if you do then you know how the people in Arkansas live? All I seen traveling through that state were shacks, and people living in them. In a pen were several pigs, a mule, and few chickens. After I seen that I figured I wasn't so bad after all.*

Before we left Ft. Meade no one knew where we were going, to what outfit or when we would arrive. I never thought I'd get way out here in Texas and in the Medical Corp. This outfit is on non-combat service. That means we don't fight or carry a gun. This camp I'm in covers an area of about 45 square miles and contains about 18 different outfits consisting of about 30,000 men. Now you can imagine how big this camp is. As much as I've seen of the army, I think I'm going to like it.

You know you're going to laugh when I tell you this. The second day I was at Ft. Meade the Sergeant came through our barracks and told the men who needed haircuts to fall in and go over to the barbers. I was the first one to sit in the barber chair. I told the barber to give me a trim and take a little off the top. He said all right. First thing you know he ran the clippers up one side, then the other, in the back and said that's all buddy. Boy you should have seen that haircut. I just about had enough hair on my head to run a comb through lightly. And the best part of it all it only took 3 minutes. That's the fastest haircut I had in my life. Now go ahead and laugh because I did when I looked at myself in the mirror after he got through with me.

All men that arrived with me are to be quarantined for 14 days that means we have to stay in our barracks at all times. The only time we leave is when we go to eat. That's only three times a day.

Before I forget say hello to your mother, father, and Florence for me Helen. Another thing is say hello to Johnnie and the boys up in the store for me. I would have dropped them a card, but I didn't know their address.

Every night before I go to bed, I get to thinking about what it would be like if I were home with you. Now there is one thing I want to tell you if I don't write anything sentimental in my letters don't think that I've forgotten about you or that I've stopped loving you. I loved you then, I love you now and I will love you always. These are the things that keep me going.

No matter what anyone says remember what I told you before I left that they'll never be another you. May God Bless you.

Always remembering. Never forgetting. Loving you forever Mike

December 10, 1942

Dearest Helen:

I'm very sorry I can't write to you oftener than I do because they haven't been giving us much time to ourselves, but every time I get an opportunity, I'll write you even if it's only a few lines. Just this afternoon our whole detachment seen a movie pertaining to life in the Army and what we are fighting for.

Yesterday I got another shot in my arm. They intend to give us about six more. If they keep this up, I'll be immune from practically all diseases. We get shots for Typhoid, Tetanus, Pneumonia, Yellow Fever, Malaria, Tuberculosis, and other diseases.

You're probably wondering what those letters I had on the back of the envelope stands for. Well I'm going to tell you. SWAK means Sealed with a kiss and SMRLH means Soldier's mail, rush like hell. I hope that satisfies your curiosity. Do you know that I just can't wait to hear from you? Do you blame me? I'll bet when I do get a letter, I'll read it over about twenty different times or more.

I came back from a five-mile hike just about 20 minutes ago. If it isn't a lecture, drill, a hike or a first aid lesson it's an inspection or something. I've been examined about 14 times since I've arrived here.

When I was stationed at Ft. Meade I saw a moving picture on Sex Hygiene. The purpose of the film was to impress upon the minds of the men in the Army the effect syphilis; gonorrhea and the other social diseases have on the body. If you had seen that film it would have turned your stomach. Honestly it would. The film also showed how to protect yourself from these diseases and care of them. So you see the Army looks after these men.

Yesterday was the feast of the Immaculate Conception. I went to mass in the evening. Now you're probably surprised that I went to mass in the evening instead of the morning. The Army does that because very few men have time to go to the church in the morning. The best part of it all is that you can even go to communion in the evening if you refrain from solid foods for four hours and liquids for two hours before the evening mass. This privilege is only granted to the Army.

Do you know I miss the evenings we were together? I've only been here two weeks and already it seems like a lifetime. When I say this, please believe me, I'm not exaggerating. Every time I think of all this, I just don't know how to explain it, but my heart feels as if it dropped down to my feet.

There are times that I wish you were here so I could tell you how much I really love you. This idea of writing things on paper doesn't agree with me. I feel that way right now and I know I'll feel that way while you're reading this letter. There's one thing, Helen no matter how far I'm from you my heart will always be with you.

That reminds me of the song, always in my heart, though we're far apart. Helen if you don't understand some things, I say in my letters please write and tell me because I know I probably write in circles, and it may make it hard for you to understand what I mean. So there won't be any misunderstanding.

Helen there's one thing I want to ask you. Now don't think I don't have any faith in you, but do you have the same feeling toward me as you did before I left. I believe I shouldn't have asked you that question because I'm sure the answer is yes. Before I forget will you please say hello to your mother and father for me. Thanks, I knew you would.

I'll tell you plainly that I love you now and forever.

May God bless you and protect you.

Hoping to hear from you soon. Always remembering. Never forgetting. Loving you forever Mike

PS XXXXXXXXXXXXXXXXX

Just like I said before I wish these were the real thing.

Helen stared out the window and tried to imagine Mike's new army haircut, instead of his usual thick dark hair slicked down with Brylcreem to control an uncooperative cowlick. The army changed how he looked, but they could not alter his heart and mind. Helen would forever remain the core of his existence.

Eager to respond to him, she retrieved a writing pad from the kitchen drawer and scampered upstairs to her bedroom. Sitting on the bed, she stared at the blank sheet of paper. *How do I show my love in words?* Helen had not written anything besides a shopping list since ninth grade. Slowly, line by line, she revealed to Mike her heartache in his absence and her undying love. She closed the letter with "Love Always, Helen," and sprayed it with her perfume. Now she would have to wait for the mailman to deliver Mike's response, the only avenue to bridge their distance and fill the void in her life.

December 15, 1942 CAMP MAXEY, TEXAS

Dearest Helen,

Received your letter Sunday evening and boy was I certainly glad to hear from you. I mentioned in my last letter whether you felt the same toward me now as you did before I left. Please disregard that. I'm sorry I asked you that question I know now how you feel since I've received your letter. I should have known better.

Since I've been stationed at camp, I've been moved about seven times. That is not out of the camp but in different barracks. If this keeps up I ought to put a revolving door on my locker.

You know this army life is beginning to agree with me. I don't believe I've felt better in all my life, that is physically.

We've been given demonstrations on how to use our gas masks in case of a gas attack. We are supposed to get these gas masks on inside of twenty seconds. So you see we're required to work very efficiently without wasting any time. We also had a lecture on first aid, pertaining to fractures and open wounds. At another time we were given some information on the human body. This lecture included again several lessons on first aid. We were shown a chart revealing the human skeleton. Shown what fractures that were most likely to occur and how to locate a fracture in case there was one present. We have to know almost all the names of the bones in the human skeleton and how these bones are connected. Late in the afternoon we were given lectures on how to identify our aircraft from that of our enemies.

We were also shown pictures on what to do in case of an air attack. Along with these charts, diagrams were placed on the blackboard, and we were shown the different types of airplanes. Pursuit, Transports, Bombing, Recognizance and Observation. We were shown how to distinguish one from the other by the length and width of the fuselage and wingspread and on the speed and maneuverability.

Do you know Helen, we have to put up our tents inside of our barracks every night before we go to bed? Now that probably sounds very silly, but it isn't. The reason for this is because we are so crowded. The tents are to protect ourselves from the men in the barracks that happen to have colds or fevers. Another reason is so there won't be any flu epidemics going throughout the camp. The tents are placed on your bed over your head. Now you see what I mean. I hope you do because I'm apt to talk in circles.

I'm very happy to hear that I'm the only one in your heart because there is no one in my heart but you.

You know it seems my love grows stronger every day I'm away from you. Every night before I go to bed, I never fail to think about you.

I love you now always and forever. I'm always thinking of you and hoping you are doing the same.

You know I really liked that piece of paper you sent me about going to the Lord in time of need. It really made me think for a while. This Saturday I'll be going to confession so that I can go to communion on Sunday. This way I will be able to make a good Christmas. Thanks very much Helen for saying a prayer for me and you. I'm doing the same thing back here. Loving you more than ever.

I remain always yours. Love Mike
May God protect you and bless you.

Helen took a sip of coffee and smiled. Even in his absence, Mike managed to charm and captivate her with his well-written letters. For a few moments, Mike had been sitting at the table, conversing with her.

Her respite with Mike vanished when her mom marched into the kitchen like a general on a mission. She shoved a dust rag and a bucket in Helen's face. "Don't just sit there. You need to finish your chores."

Without comment, Helen accepted the cleaning tools and filled the bucket with water. Mike's correspondence had elevated her spirit, and even housework did not diminish her uplifted mood. Every time she received a letter, the distance between them waned, and his essence grew closer. Unable to hold him or make him smile, she clung to his words and sentiment as a life preserver in her empty existence.

Helen knelt and sang "Don't Sit under the Apple Tree," while she scrubbed the black-and-white linoleum floor.

"Stop that noise, Helen," her mother barked from the parlor. "I told you before, you're not a singer."

Helen halted, swallowing hard, and thrust her brush onto the floor. She completed her chores in record time.

Exhausted, she turned on the radio and settled into the threadbare, oversize chair. She closed her eyes and listened to her favorite show. After a few minutes, she heard her mother shout, "Helen!"

Helen's eyes flew open, and she saw her mother towering over her. "Helen, in all of those letters Mike sent you, has he mentioned anything about an engagement ring?"

"No, why?"

"If he's serious and wants you to wait till this war is over, he should offer you a ring."

"I'm sure he will, Mom, but he's in Texas right now."

"That doesn't matter. You need to know if he's man enough to commit. I want you to write him."

"But . . . but . . . "

"No buts! I've been telling you about this even before he left, and now I want you to ask him about a ring."

"Mom . . . he . . . "

Her mom crossed her arms and shouted, "What?"

Defeated, Helen stood up, her eyes fixed on the floor. She shuffled into the kitchen for a glass of milk and oatmeal cookies. She wanted an engagement ring from Mike more than a prisoner desired freedom, but she felt uncomfortable broaching the subject. Demanding a ring might drive a wedge between her and Mike. She searched her mind for appropriate words to express her mother's concerns in a letter to him without sounding angry or bitter. Unlike Mike, the eloquent wordsmith who had honed his skill as editor of the school newspaper and by composing poems, Helen found it burdensome to convey her thoughts. She scribbled a few words on unlined stationery, half listening to the *Amos and Andy Show* on the radio. Unsatisfied with her phrases, she snatched the paper from the pad and ripped it into tiny pieces. She grabbed the glass bottle and poured some more milk, endeavoring again to convert her emotions into a story, instead of mere words. After three laborious attempts, Helen subtly, toward the end of the letter, posed the sensitive question.

Chapter Three

December 1942

With Christmas only a few weeks away, Helen hopped onto the Number 50 streetcar and headed downtown to complete her shopping. As she exited the streetcar, she was pleasantly surprised to see a light snowfall whitening the streets. Her holiday spirit elevated more when she saw a few children tugging at their mothers' sleeves with pleas. "Hurry, Mama, we need to tell Santa what we want. Do you think he'll bring me a baby doll?"

Before entering the store, Helen stopped to admire the always-elaborate holiday displays in Kaufmann's windows. She imagined bringing her youngsters downtown to linger in the wonderland of fairytales and animated figures. Inside Kaufmann's, the lights reflected off the giant Christmas balls, and, positioned above the counters, the towering trees sparkled. Everywhere she turned, the store reflected the grandeur of the season. Passing the display of headscarves, Helen remembered her mother wanted a new babushka and purchased a red-and-blue-flowered one. Her trek through the store resulted in numerous gifts for her sisters, but deciding what to buy a war-bound man proved a more arduous task. Undeterred, she searched Boggs and Buhl, G. C. Murphy's, and several other stores. At her final stop at Kresge's, she selected a shiny pipe and tobacco for her father.

Regrettably, she was unable to find the perfect present for Mike, one that expressed her love. Instead, she settled on a collection of small, thoughtful items: a shaving kit, Lucky Strike cigarettes, a tin of ribbon candy, a writing pen, and a copy of *Life* magazine.

After arriving home, Helen carefully packed the items in a box, adding the local newspaper and clippings from Mike's favorite comic strip, *Gasoline Alley*. She slipped the last item into the box: a card she had taken an hour to choose.

The sights and sounds of the holiday inspired and motivated Helen to retrieve boxes of decorations from the basement and fill the house with Christmas glee. Even though President Roosevelt had decided not to light the National Christmas Tree for security reasons, Helen was not deterred by his decision and strung the bubble lights on the tree. Within a short time, the colorful balls and ornaments sparkled in the sunlight streaming through the windows. She stepped back to admire her handiwork and decided it needed a final touch. She threaded an ornament hanger through the top of a photo of Mike and placed it on the tree.

With several more boxes to be unpacked before dinner, Helen quickly decorated the rest of the parlor. She placed candles, Santa figures, and holly on the mantel and hung the dusty old wreath with jingle bells on the front door. Finally, she arranged the nativity set on the wooden table between the two living room windows and kissed the baby Jesus before placing him in the manger.

Satisfied the house was prepared for the holiday, she poured a cup of coffee and sat by the tree to read Mike's letter.

Friday, December 18, 1942 CAMP MAXEY, TEXAS

Dearest Helen,

You mentioned in your letter something about an engagement ring. Helen I wish this was possible. I'd be able to do this if I wasn't so far away from home because it wouldn't cost me so much money to go home, that is if I got a furlough. It would cost me about $60.00 round trip. I don't know how long it would take to save that much because I haven't got my pay as yet. I know if I do get paid, I won't get very much. They take out for bonds, insurance and laundry after that I don't know how much I'll have left. But if it's possible to send any, you can bet your life I will. I hope you understand Helen. If you don't, please write me about it.

I was certainly glad I received your letter and that Wonderful Christmas card you sent me. Helen, I'm sorry I won't be able to send you a Christmas card. I wasn't able to get away. I hope you'll forgive me Helen for not sending you a Christmas card. But I still can wish you a very Merry Christmas and May the Lord Shower his blessings upon you. I wish I was there to wish you this personally, but this will have to do for the present. Since I just got out of quarantine I decided to go to town. The nearest town is Paris, nine miles away. This town is fairly large, but it isn't big enough to accommodate all the soldiers in this camp. This camp is really big. It holds about 50 thousand men.

There are 16 areas in this camp and in every area there is a Post Exchange and a theatre. I was at the theatre last night and I seen John Wayne and Randolph Scott in a picture by the name of "Pittsburgh." It was fairly good but it doesn't show Pittsburgh as it really is.

Helen, when the army says they'll make a man out of you they really mean it. We have to go through an obstacle course about three times a week. This obstacle course consists of going over fences ranging from two feet to about nine feet, climbing trees, jumping over trenches, crawling on your stomach through tunnels etc. There's more but they're too numerous to mention. You know I've learned a lot since I've been here. I heard the Sgt. say the other day that the one who passes this course with flying colors would be sent to a medical school to further his education. And when he comes back he'll be a surgical technician. You can bet your life I'm going to try my best so I can come up on top. I'm going to try to get as much out of this Army that I can.

Helen before I forget please tell your mother and father that I wish them a Merry Christmas and I hope that the Lord will Bless and Protect them. Thanks Helen. I'll do the same for you some day, in fact any day. Loving you more than ever. I remain always yours.

Always remembering. Never forgetting. Loving you forever Mike

Chapter Four

Christmas 1942

Whiffs of baked ham with cloves; *golabki*, cabbage leaves stuffed with flavored beef and pork; and *haluski*, an aromatic and tasty dish of fried cabbage, noodles, and onions, commingled in the distinctive aura of a traditional Polish Christmas. The scent often lingered for a few days, inducing hunger even after the family had consumed massive amounts of food. In a corner of the kitchen, the dark walnut sideboard was set with dishes, utensils, and accouterments for assembling a sandwich and awaited the placement of the hot items.

Helen's older sister Gert, carrying her daughter, Mary Ann, in one arm and gifts in the other, stumbled through the door, saying, "Merry Christmas!" Her husband, Stan, followed her, juggling food and additional presents.

Flo ran into the parlor when she heard the commotion. "Gert, let me take all those goodies you brought," she said, relieving her sister of the containers.

"Thanks, Flo."

Helen reached out for her niece. "I'd be glad to hold Mary Ann while you get settled."

While Mary Ann sat on her lap, Helen removed the child's wool coat and pecked her on the cheek. Gert hung her coat on the back of the door and returned to Helen. "I can take her now."

"Oh, I don't mind," Helen said. "If she'll sit on my lap, I'd like to hold her. We can play paddy cake."

"Okay," Gert said. "I'll see if Flo needs any help."

Gert uncovered the containers of food, and the scent of hot apple pie wafted around the room. Her mother, washing her hands, remarked, "Smells like you brought your famous dessert, Gert."

"Yeah, and some of the date cookies that you and Pop like so much."

"Your father does love them. Hope he doesn't eat them all."

The commotion increased as Helen's grandparents and her eldest sister, Marie, and her family stomped through the door, overloaded with packages and food. Stan started to close the door, but Ben, Marie's husband, carrying a case of Duke beer, said, "Hey, don't close the door yet. Clara's family is right behind us."

Clara, Helen's third oldest sister, wiped her wet, snowy shoes on the small throw rug and told her husband, Ed, to put the deviled eggs on the table. While balancing their son, Eddie, on her hip, Clara lay the presents by the tree.

Marie sat her daughter, Lorraine, on the tattered couch next to Helen. "Can you keep an eye on her while I slice the bread?"

"Sure."

Mary asked the men, "Who wants a beer?"

In unison, they all replied, "Yeah, I'll take one."

"Hey, Flo, get the men a beer," ordered Mary, "and bring me a glass of ginger ale."

Flo popped open the beers and walked into the parlor, careful not to drop any bottles.

The only two rooms on the first floor erupted with babies crying, and a medley of conversations and activity, while the 1936 Philco combination phonograph and radio played Christmas tunes. Huddled in the smoke-filled living room under pictures of the Blessed Virgin Mary and the Sacred Heart of Jesus, the men discussed the war and their hatred of the Germans and the Japanese. In the kitchen, the women rattled on endlessly.

Gert grumbled, "It's bad enough I had to drink my coffee without sugar because of the rations. Now with coffee rations, I can only have coffee a couple times a week."

Clara interjected, "Have you tried adding corn syrup? It tastes a little funny, but at least it's sweet. Anyway, did you hear about what happened to Mrs.—"

Their mother interrupted the gabfest. "Helen, Flo, we should eat now. Which one of you knows where the *oplatek* are? We need to break bread before dinner."

Flo answered, "They're on the shelf by the coffee cups. I'll get them."

After retrieving the thin, unleavened wafers, Flo offered one to each family member. Helen's father reached out to his wife and carefully cracked a piece from her wafer as she broke off a corner of his. As they did, they wished each other a Merry Christmas. The Polish ritual continued around the room until everyone had shared a piece of his or her wafer. At the conclusion of their custom, Mary declared, "Merry Christmas, everybody! Now, let's eat."

Following dinner, the men retired to the parlor, while the siblings cleared the table and washed the dishes. Helen appreciated their help. Otherwise, the chore would fall to her and Flo. Ever since the sisters had been old enough to clean the dishes, their mother's hands had never again touched dish detergent. Mary relished her role as the matriarch and sat in the kitchen chair like a queen on her throne, observing her charges and barking out orders. Occasionally, she abdicated her role and participated in their chatter as they worked.

With full stomachs and the chores completed, the women joined the men in the parlor. Marie took her usual seat at the piano and played "*Dzisiaj w Betlejem.*" Helen's parents and grandparents sang the traditional Polish carol, and everyone joined in for the chorus. After a few old Christmas tunes, Clara asked, "Marie, do you know the new song 'I'm Dreaming of a White Christmas'?"

"I don't know it by heart, but I bought the sheet music a couple of weeks ago," Marie said. "Bear with me in case I make any mistakes."

Everyone gathered around the piano, and the amateur choir burst into song. The loud voices drowned out the mellow ones like Helen's, but no one noticed a few off-key notes. Stan, unfamiliar with the words, jumped to the chorus, causing confusion, but the merriment continued. As the music played, Mary Ann bopped her head and twisted her body. Helen giggled and imagined one day sitting next to Mike with their baby. Marie played several more Christmas songs until Clara announced, "It's getting late. We should open the presents."

Clara plucked a present from under the tree and handed Marie a colorfully wrapped box. "This one is from Mom and Dad to you and Ben."

Marie painstakingly removed the wrapping paper, in an attempt to save it for next year's gifts. She uncovered a milky-white knobbed vase. "Mom, Pop, I love it."

Clara grabbed the next gift on the pile. "Here, Flo, this one is from Stan and Gert."

The exchange of gifts continued, while the men gathered in the corner by the mantel, drinking beer, snacking on pretzels, and occasionally feigning interest in the festivities. Helen opened the last gift, a 78 RPM phonograph recording of one of her favorite songs: Gene Autry's "You Are My Sunshine."

Flo collected the scraps of paper scattered around the room as the clock on the mantel chimed eleven times. Mary declared, "Oh, I didn't realize it was that late already. We need to leave soon for Midnight Mass."

Weary and tipsy, the men collected the presents and, with their families, strolled home. Helen and her family departed on the heels of their guests to walk the five blocks to St. Adalbert's Church. As they turned onto Jane Street, Flo noticed snow sprinkling the coats and hats of a family and pointed. "Look, doesn't that remind you of one of the snow globes we have at home?"

Their mother scolded, "Quit gibbering, we need to walk a little faster."

"It's only 11:30," moaned Flo.

"I know," her mother said. "And that's when the choir is supposed to start singing before mass. We're already late, as far as I'm concerned."

"Okay, okay," Flo said with a sigh.

The family quickened their pace and opted for the shortcut to church through two narrow alleyways that cut through a row of houses. As Helen ascended the four concrete steps to the church, she heard the choir's piercing song through the massive doors of the turn-of-the-century brick-and-stone building. The choir's vocal intensity echoed from the high ceiling, as she heaved open the doors.

Surrounded by numerous oversize statues, Helen sat at peace amid the scent of frankincense, the radiance of the vigil candles, and the soothing voices of the choir. She focused on the impressive stories-high, white marble altar with its intricately carved crucifix of Christ, surrounded by sculptures of saints and angels. Kneeling before her savior, Helen fervently prayed to God, Jesus, the Blessed Mother, and all the saints for her family and friends. This year, her list of pleas grew as she prayed for Mike's safety and for God to follow him into battle.

She had barely finished her petitions before the altar bells rang, signaling the beginning of mass. The organist played a Polish Christmas hymn, and the congregation sang enthusiastically. Yet Helen's thoughts drifted to Mike spending Christmas with strangers and the empty seat next to her.

Chapter Five

December 31st, 1942

New Year's Eve

Helen awoke to pounding rain on the roof and howling wind whistling through the windows. She crept downstairs, plopped onto the couch, and opened the Sears catalog.

Flo strolled into the parlor and sat next to her. "Couldn't sleep either, huh?"

"No, it sounds awful out there." Helen gazed at Flo. "You look like you've been crying."

"Well, maybe," Flo admitted.

"What's wrong?"

"You know, Helen, when Mike left for the army, I felt bad for you, but I don't think I really understood what you were going through."

"What do you mean?" Helen asked.

Flo sniffled. "I tried to pretend Christmas was okay, but with the New Year coming, it's another holiday without Bern. I feel so alone and afraid. Mom acts like everything is hunky dory, but I don't think she realizes how hard it is."

Helen put her arm around Flo. "Mom will never understand, but it's gonna be okay. At least, we have each other, and we're safe."

"Yeah, you're right, but I still feel lonely."

Their mother walked into the parlor. "You two are up early."

Flo yawned. "Yeah, the wind woke me up."

"Well, since we're up now, go make some coffee, Helen, and get me one of those cookies on the buffet."

Helen brewed the coffee. As she reached for the cookie jar, she noticed a letter from

Mike.

"Mom," she asked, "why didn't you put this letter on the table like you always do?"

"Your father got the mail yesterday," her mother said. "Quit bellyaching, you have it now."

Helen snatched the letter, stormed into the parlor, and sat by the window to read it.

December 24, 1942 CAMP MAXEY, TEXAS

Dearest Helen,

Today I received that long letter you sent me. I like that poem you had in the letter it expresses my sentiments also.

Helen, you don't have to worry about me changing if you like me the way I am. I haven't done anything that I regret or will ever regret. It's pretty hard to change once you have your ways set.

Monday of this week we had some practical experience in fixing fractures and bandaging wounds on all parts of the body. During the class on bandaging the Lieutenant called me up front and used me to demonstrate the different types of bandages. You should have seen me I had my head, leg, arm, palms, and wrist bandaged. I bet I looked pretty. (Space reserved for a good laugh). After that he put a splint on my arm and then my leg. But I got even after a while because I had my chance to put on splints and bandages on one of my buddies.

That same day we seen two pictures one on Personal Hygiene and Emergency First Aid showing how to deal with sunstroke, heat exhaustion, shock, burns, different types of wounds, drowning and electrical shock.

Besides this we had our usual one-hour of exercise and close order drill. This was one of our easiest days.

Tuesday I was on KP (Kitchen Police). I never washed so many dishes in all my life. Imagine washing about 300 dishes three times a day besides setting the tables, mopping the floor. I even had to peel about half a sack of potatoes. Everyone has to do KP about twice a month. Wednesday, I went through the obstacle course and went on a 10-mile hike with a full field pack. This doesn't sound like much but when you do it in 2 hours without stopping then it is something. My buddy said if this keeps up, he's going to send home for his brother's bicycle. After walking three ten miles we rested for a while and one of the fellows took several mess kits, cups, and a helmet and really beat out some fast tunes. Think of the Hoosier Hot shots and you'll understand what I mean.

In the afternoon we went out in the woods and dug foxholes. These holes are 3 feet wide 3 feet long and about 6 feet deep. I only had a pick, so I had to shovel the dirt out with my steel helmet. The reason for these foxholes are to protect yourself from small arms fire and tanks. After we dug the fox holes, we had to camouflage them.

Then we were marched out to the woods again, and again and had to splint a fracture of the leg. Three of my buddies and I put him on a stretcher, and I had to carry him for a thousand yards. We got through at 4:30 and then marched back to camp. It's now 6:30 PM in the evening. I'm thinking of going into town tonight. They're having a Christmas party at the USO center. You know while I'm writing this letter, I'm wondering what you're doing at this time. You're probably coming home on the incline at this time.

You know there was a beautiful moon, and I was just hoping you could be there in my arms so I could tell you personally how much I really love you. You were right when you said, "Absence makes the Heart grow Fonder."

Love you more than ever. I remain always yours Mike

May God bless you and protect you Always.

AML means all my love

Helen finished reading the letter and held it tightly to her chest, absorbing Mike's adventures. For every extraordinary experience in his life, hers remained static, rote, and boring. She stood in a stagnant pool, waiting for a ripple or a wave to propel her onward. Her days consisted of an endless series of interchangeable events: go to work, worry, babysit, listen to the evening news, clean the house, worry, rinse, repeat. How could her inconsequential daily drudgery offer the slightest excitement to a man who spent his days soaking in USO shows, trekking through the woods, and learning about medicine? He wrote that he remained the same man, unaffected by the forces molding his life around him. However, Helen felt that for better or worse, things were changing.

Staring at the front door, she recalled a time when her main ambition was to spend her life healing others. Yet one unmerciful event during the summer when she turned fourteen had forever changed her fate.

Helen had answered a knock at the door. Before her stood an official from South High School, asking to speak to one of her parents. Helen called to her mother, sitting outside.

"Mom, a lady from South High wants to talk to you."

"What does she want?"

"I don't know. She didn't say."

Helen's mother greeted the woman.

"Hello, Mrs. Cypyrch, I'm here to inquire if Helen will be returning to school next year."

Perched on the couch, Helen listened intently. She wondered why the woman asked such a ridiculous question, thinking, *Of course, I'm going back to school. Why wouldn't I? I passed to the tenth grade, and I never missed one day of school in the last few years.*

Without consideration or hesitation, Mary declared to the official, "No."

Helen's head drooped toward the floor. *What? Why?*

The lady asked, "Why will she not be returning?"

"She's a girl!" her mother said, as if that were an obvious reason to curtail Helen's education. "A ninth-grade education is good enough for a woman. She can go to work now and contribute to the family, instead of learning nonsense about science and history. She'll never need any of that."

"Are you sure? Is that your final decision?"

Mary nudged her glasses up her nose. "Of course, it is. I didn't finish school, and I'm doing fine."

"Very well," the woman said. "I need you to sign this document releasing her from the educational program."

Helen's mother, using the pen as if it were a knife, instantaneously executed Helen's future dreams as she scribbled her signature. She thrust the paper back at the woman. "Is there anything else?"

"No, that's all, and have a good day, Mrs. Cypyrch."

Helen sat speechless as her mother swiftly passed by her on the couch and returned to the backyard. Her mother refused to acknowledge how the consequences of this decision impacted her daughter. For the first time in Helen's life, she wanted to scream at her mother, but she couldn't even murmur the words running through her mind. *Why? Why?* Her stomach churned, and she felt nauseous. Her skin tightened around her throat, and she gagged. *What did I do to deserve this? Does she hate me?* She had told her mother numerous times of her love for education, always eager to share her daily dose of knowledge. Now, what activity would fill the void of her future days? Helen moaned to herself, "I want to be a nurse." Suddenly, the boulder of consequences smashed down on her. "Without a high school education, I can't be a nurse, I can't be anything! I'll be useless!"

She needed to escape from the noose she felt slipping around her neck. She bolted upstairs to her room. In a short time, she exhausted every clean handkerchief she owned. Releasing her tears of resentment gave her the courage and strength to speak to her mother.

Quivering from head to toe, Helen approached her mother and begged to go back to school. She defended her position profoundly and eloquently, but beseeching did not alter her death sentence. The verdict from her mother stood firm.

Now, years later, Helen stared at Mike's letter and contemplated the magnitude of her mother's decision. *Why would Mike want me? I'm sure those girls at the USO are prettier and smarter.* If only her mother had listened to her when she'd begged to complete high school. She could have enrolled in a nursing program, and then she and Mike could trade stories of men and women on the mend. Her dismal mood morphed into anger. *Why did she take my education away from me? Mike says he loves me, but once he realizes I hardly know anything compared to him, he'll want another woman. If I were a nurse, we'd have more in common.* She shoved the letter into her pocket and trudged into the kitchen.

A booming voice from the radio announced, "The constant rain and runoff of melting snow from the hillsides has caused the river to overflow at twenty-nine feet and will possibly continue to rise. We are asking people to stay out of downtown and low-lying areas unless absolutely necessary. It looks like 1942 is going out with a rush of water and will probably cause people to change their New Year's Eve celebrations."

"Mom, did you hear that?" Flo asked. "It sounds like the rivers have flooded from this rain."

"I could have predicted that. It reminds me of the flood of '36."

Helen peered out the window. "I remember that. We had no electricity or water for days. I hope it doesn't get that bad."

"We need to be prepared," their mother said. "You two get the buckets to fill with water and see if there are any old candles in the basement. While you're down there, bring up the steel tub. We'll fill that with water, too. I'll make some coffee."

As their mother placed the kettle of water on the stove, a gust of cold air from the back door blew into the kitchen. Marie, carrying Lorraine, came in and asked, "Mom, did you hear about the flood? It sounds like it's going to be bad."

"No need to fuss. We survived the flood of '36. We can weather this one. Since you're here, you might as well stay and have a cup of coffee."

Before Marie hung up her coat, Gert stormed in behind her, carrying her daughter.

The sisters' mother declared, "What are you doing out in this rain?"

"I heard about the flood," Gert said, "and I thought the electricity might go out. I wanted to borrow some candles."

Flo stumbled into the kitchen, carrying buckets and candles. Their mother pointed at her. "You're just in time. Flo's got some."

A booming thunderclap shook the house. The back door swung open, hitting Helen in the back. She almost dropped the tub she was carrying to the sink.

"Oh, sorry, Helen," said Clara. She squeezed through the door with her son.

The girls' mother held up her hands. "You, too? I guess you want to know if we heard about the flood?"

"Well . . . yeah . . . ," Clara said.

"We heard! We're fine! Come in, you might as well have some coffee and cookies, too."

The kettle whistled. "I'll finish making the coffee," Helen said, "and then I'll fill the buckets."

While she poured boiling water into the drip coffee pot, Marie confronted her. "I didn't want to say anything on Christmas Eve because everyone was having such a good time. But I still don't understand why you took Adam's ring if you love Mike." This comment opened Pandora's box and served as the start of Helen's inquisition. Her sisters joined in to launch their accusations, talking over one another. Their questions, opinions, and suggestions blindsided Helen. She felt as if she were standing before a firing squad.

"I was thinking the same thing. You know, if it were me, I never would have even taken the ring."

"Some people never find a man. You've got two!"

"Hell, you accepted the guy's ring, and you're dating Mike?"

"If you love Mike, let the other guy go."

"Helen, what do you imagine Adam's family thinks about you taking the ring and promising to wait for Mike at the same time?"

"Adam's family! What about Mike's family? What do they think of you?"

"How can he be so understanding?"

Each statement and question flew at her with greater conviction than the last. They pierced Helen's heart and mind with their skepticism.

She grabbed her apron from the hook. "Why all the questions?" she asked. "You know why I took the ring. I didn't want to do it. Mike and Adam both understand. Why don't you?"

Talking over one another, her siblings continued to scream disparaging remarks. With each accusation, Helen felt her blood pressure rising. She exploded. "Stop it, all of you! I did nothing wrong. I don't need to prove to you that I have a good man and he loves me. Are you jealous I'm happy?"

"We're just concerned for you," Marie said. "People will start talking about you."

"Why?" shouted Helen.

"Because you're engaged to Adam and dating Mike?"

Helen stomped her foot. "For the last time, I am not engaged to him!!"

The girls' mother, who rarely defended Helen, halted the cross-examination. "Leave Helen alone! I think it's fine she has Adam's ring. Times are different now. That's all there is to it. Now pour me a cup of coffee."

Chapter Six

July 1941

Helen thought back to the months before the war started, when she hadn't even started dating Mike yet. It was the Saturday after her twentieth birthday, and she stood before the mirror, fretting like a pubescent teenager. Every time she pushed a bobby pin into her hair, she sighed louder. Flo, irritated by her grumbling, looked up from a copy of *Life* and said, "Helen, what's going on? I've read half the magazine, and you're still not ready."

"It's . . . I was thinking . . . Adam's the first fella to ask me for a date. I'm not sure how to act. He's probably been on lots of dates and will laugh at me because I don't know what to do."

"Just be yourself. And what do you mean, he's the first to ask you out? Mike asked you many times!"

"I guess so, but that's different, he . . . he's . . . "

"What? Because he's our brother-in-law? That shouldn't matter. You could have gone out with him if you wanted to."

"Well, I didn't want to. Just hand me my shoes."

Flo shook her head and flung the shoes at Helen. "I'm just happy to see you going out. Mom said you were headed to be an old maid."

"I'm not that old. I'm only twenty."

"And this is your first date! I'd have to agree with Mom."

"Listen, I don't want to talk about that. I have a question."

"What?"

"I was wondering . . . Oh, never mind . . . Well . . . you've been on a few dates, and . . ."

Flo squeaked, "What? What? Just say it!"

Helen sighed. "What if he gets fresh with me?"

"Just tell him you're a lady. Besides, you're just getting ice cream. What could happen?"

"You told me when you went out with that one fella that he kept trying to kiss you, even when you told him not to."

"I know, and I never went out with him again. It'll be okay. Just go and have fun. Oh, I think I hear him downstairs."

Flo grabbed the lipstick and handed it to Helen. "Here, put this on and get going. You know how Mom is. She's probably asking him all kinds of questions. If you keep him waiting too long, he just might leave."

"I guess I should rescue him."

Helen quickly colored her lips, snatched her purse from her bed, and apprehensively descended the stairs.

Adam jumped to his feet when she walked into the parlor. "Ah, ah . . . Helen, you look swell."

"Ahh, you do, too."

As they stared at each other, Adam played with the coins in his pocket, while Helen pushed her bobby pins tighter into her hair.

Her mother asked, "Well, are you two gonna stand there, or are you gonna get ice cream?"

"Oh, yes, ma'am," Adam said. "No problem."

"Just make sure you have her back here by five so she can help fix dinner."

As they strolled along South 19th Street, Adam commented, "Hey, Helen, it's great to see how much your mother cares about you."

"What do you mean?"

"Well, she's obviously protective of you, making sure you go out with the right man. She asked me about my nationality, if I had a job, and some other things. Although I'm surprised it wasn't your father askin' me questions."

"Oh, my pop is such a sweet man. You'd like him, but he doesn't speak English very well, so he leaves those matters to my mom," Helen explained. "Are you okay that she asked you all those questions?"

"Sure, it's okay. Anyway, I was going to take you downtown, but I don't think we'll have enough time to go there and get back here in time so you can help with dinner. Is it okay if we go to Isaly's?"

"Sure. I don't mind."

Helen ordered her favorite, a White House skyscraper cone, vanilla ice cream with bits of cordial cherries. Adam requested a strawberry ice cream soda and asked, "Do you mind where we sit? I thought we'd grab a seat in the back. It might give us a little extra privacy."

"Okay."

He led the way, and they slid into opposite sides of the red upholstered booth.

As they stared at each other, Adam tapped his toes on the floor. He pushed his ice cream into the soda and stirred it quickly. In silence, he frantically shoveled the frozen treat into his mouth. Within a few minutes, he was slurping the bottom of the strawberry soda.

Helen, slowly licking her cone, stared in amazement. "I can see you really like ice cream."

"Oh! Oh, yeah," Adam said sheepishly. "Sorry about that. Helen, I gotta tell you, I'm a little nervous."

"You? Why are you nervous?"

"I just can't believe you agreed to go out with me. I mean . . . well . . . you know . . . "

Suddenly, the song "Tea for Two" blared from the jukebox. Adam said, "Hey, isn't that a grand song? Do you like it?"

"Yeah, I do."

"What other songs do you like?"

"Oh, there's so many songs. I like all the songs from the Andrews Sisters, and I like to listen to the Glenn Miller Orchestra. I just love listening to music, and I could watch musicals all day."

"So, you'd rather watch a musical than a mystery?"

"Well, I love to dance, and the dancing in musicals is so much fun to watch, but I like mystery movies, too. I even like the radio show *The Shadow*. Even though my mother says it's stupid."

The once-shy couple chatted endlessly until Adam noticed the time. "We could stay here for a little longer before I have to take you home, or we could go for a little walk."

"It's such a beautiful day, I'd love to stretch my legs," Helen said.

As they passed the Arcade Theater, Adam turned to her. "Helen, now that we know a little more about each other, would you like to go to a movie soon? We don't have to go to the Arcade Theatre. I'll take you wherever you want to go."

Helen wavered, uncertain whether she could reciprocate Adam's affection for her. She remembered her mother's comments about her not dating. "Okay. How about the Bob Hope movie *Caught in the Draft*?" she asked.

Adam's eyes widened. "That's swell! I'll come and pick you up on Tuesday after work."

When they arrived back at her house, Adam asked, "Can I give you a hug?"

"Yeah, I guess that's okay."

Adam gently squeezed her. "I had a swell time, Helen, and I'm happy you'll go to a movie with me."

Helen smiled. "Sure. I'll see you later."

On her way into the kitchen, she strolled past her father, who was listening to music in the parlor. She bent down and pecked his cheek. "Do you need anything before I start helping with dinner?"

He smiled and shook his head no.

Silently, she tied her apron and joined Flo in cutting vegetables for soup. Flo opened her mouth to pose a question, but their mother intruded, pushing open the screen door into the kitchen.

"Well, how do you like this Adam?" their mother asked.

"Not sure," Helen said. "We had a good chat, and he wasn't fresh with me. I told him I'd go to the movies with him, so we'll see."

Mary said to her husband in Polish, "Well, it looks like Helen's finally dating."

Her father nodded. "*Który jest dobry.*"

Her mother smiled. "I guess you made your father happy. While you two finish dinner, I'll be outside reading the paper."

Flo stirred the soup. "I still want to know how come you went out with Adam, but you won't go out with Mike?"

"I don't know."

"What do you mean, you don't know? You must have a reason."

"Just don't worry your little head over it. Here, add these extra vegetables to the broth."

"Okay, don't tell me, but does Gert know you went out with Adam?" Flo asked.

"No, I didn't tell her," Helen said.

"Well, you know she's gonna ask you why you went out with this fella, and you never dated Mike. Gert's been trying to match you up even before she put you two together as partners for her wedding. You know he likes you. Come on, tell me, did Mike say something rude to you or try anything?"

"No, and that's all I'm going to say. Will you hand me the dishrag?"

As Helen wiped the crumbs from the oilcloth, she reflected on Flo's questions and thought about the first time she'd met Mike.

The men were playing catch when Gert and her sisters arrived at the park. Clara carried the tote with blankets, and Helen carted the picnic basket to the crooked wooden table. As Mike twisted to catch a glimpse of Helen sauntering past, the ball smacked him in the shoulder.

"Hey, Mike, pay attention!" said Stan. "You're gonna get yourself knocked out."

"Who's the gal carrying the picnic basket?" Mike asked.

"That's Gert's younger sister Helen. I told you about her before."

"You never told me how swell looking she is. Look at those gams."

"I told you she was a dish."

"She sure is. Look at her beautiful smile. I can't wait to meet her."

"Just let the girls get their stuff together, and you should get back to improving your pitchin' arm. We'll go over in a while."

Mike threw a couple of balls and shouted, "Hey, Stan, I think I'm done for now. There's a beautiful girl dying to meet me." He jogged toward the picnic tables. As he approached, he called out, "Hi, Gert. You going to tell me who these charming ladies are?"

Gert introduced Clara and Flo, adding, "My oldest sister, Marie, couldn't come today, and this is Helen."

Mike fixated on her appearance, her iridescent hair, her innocent soulful eyes, and her blissful smile. Without saying a word, Helen had unknowingly captured his heart.

She politely shook Mike's hand. "So you're Stan's brother?" she asked and straightened the tablecloth.

"Yep! Since the day I was born and not a minute sooner."

Helen stared at Mike and snickered. "Hah, yeah, I guess you're right."

"Is there anything I can help you with?" Mike asked her.

"No, thank you."

He grabbed the dishes from inside the picnic basket. "Let me help you set the table."

"Thanks for offering, but you can go back to your ball game if you want to. I'm fine."

"You can say that again because you sure do look fine to me."

With eyes wide as an owl's, Helen stopped setting the table and blankly stared at Mike.

The silence reverberated louder than fireworks, overpowering Mike's usual charming personality. He blurted out, "Hey, look, there's a lake. I like to swim . . . ahh, do you?"

Helen gazed at him, squinting. "Well, I really don't swim. I just like to wade in the water and cool off."

"I'm a pretty good swimmer, and if you wanted me to teach you sometime, I could. And you should know, if you need rescuing, I'm your man."

Helen anxiously looked around and started to walk backward.

Gert observed the obvious awkwardness and adjusted her matchmaker's hat, as she walked over to loosen the rigid conversation.

"Hey, Helen, when Mike said he's a good swimmer, he's not kidding. Stan told me he got a few awards."

Helen smiled. "Oh, congratulations."

"You know he runs track, too. Isn't that great?"

Helen set the glasses on the table. "It sounds like you were quite busy."

Gert searched her mind for some commonality between the two. "Helen, Mike says he loves movies with Bob Hope. You like them, too, don't you?"

Helen's eyes lit up. "Yes, I do. Which ones have you seen, Mike?"

"I think I've seen almost all of them."

Mike stared at Helen as she smiled, talking about all her favorite movies. The conversation melted her cold shoulder, and Mike jumped at the opportunity to get closer to her.

"You know, Helen, I love talking about movies but was wondering have you ever thrown a baseball?"

"When I was little, we'd throw a rubber ball, but not a baseball," Helen said.

"Well, why don't we go throw a couple of balls?"

"I don't know if I'll be any good."

Gert interrupted, "Go ahead, Helen, you go. I'll stay here and get the food ready."

After a few tosses back and forth, it was obvious Helen had never learned how to throw a straight long ball.

Mike said, "Why don't you stand by me and let me show you how to wallop a baseball like a pro?"

She slowly walked toward him, and he pressed the ball into her hand. He walked behind her, and his outstretched arm latched onto her wrist. Helen tensed and wiggled as Mike stood behind her, but she let him continue his instruction.

"Now keep your arm straight, only slightly bent at the elbow." He drew her arm back behind her ear. "Okay, bend your wrist and relax it. I'm going to push your arm forward and when I say, 'Go,' release the ball."

They both watched as the ball flew wildly, as unrestrained as Helen's previous attempts. Yet Mike had accomplished his goal of capturing her attention.

"There, that's a little better," he said. "Would you like to give it another try?"

Helen stepped backward. "I don't kn—"

Suddenly, Gert shouted, "I have all the food out! Who wants to eat?"

As they walked toward the picnic table, Mike asked, "So, are you the youngest?"

"No, Flo is. I'm the second to the youngest."

"Me, too. I have a younger sister, two older sisters, and Stan's the oldest."

"How much older are you than Flo?"

"Two years, I'm nineteen, and she's seventeen."

"That's the same as me and my younger sister Jo. We're two years apart. Hey, Helen, we have a lot in common."

"We do?"

"Yeah, like our families. We're both here at this picnic, and we like movies. We're both Catholic. You like to play ball. You know my brother, and I know your sister. See, we have lots in common."

"Yeah, I guess so."

Mike grimaced and mumbled to himself, "Ah, I could kick myself, that sounded stupid."

Helen sat on the bench, and Mike snatched the seat next to her.

Stan passed the bowl of potato salad to Mike. "You want some?"

"Sure, it looks good. Did you make this, Helen?"

"Me and Flo made it this morning."

"If you made it, then I'm taking an extra helping. Can I put some on your plate, Helen?"

"Sure. Thanks."

"You did real good throwin' the ball. If you were a boy, you'd make a great shortstop."

Flo whispered to Clara, "You'd think Helen is the only person here. Mike's hardly saying anything to us."

"Are you jealous?"

"No, I'm not jealous. I just think it's rude."

"Flo, it's obvious he likes her. Besides, Gert told me she thought Helen and Mike would be great for each other. Just let them be."

Mike grabbed a hard-boiled egg with a cracked shell and held it up. "Hey, who's telling jokes around here?"

Helen stared at Mike with a blank expression. "What do you mean?"

"Well, I thought someone told a joke because this egg cracked up."

Helen laughed. "Oh you're such a card?"

Stan jumped in. "Oh, no, don't laugh at his corny jokes, he'll be telling them for the rest of the day now that he has a new audience."

"That's okay, I like jokes."

Mike shoved a hefty spoon of potato salad into his mouth. "Hey, this food is delicious. You know what they say, the way to a man's heart is through his stomach."

Helen smiled. "Is that so?"

"I believe it. There's nothing like good home cooking and a charming gal to cook it. If you ever want to cook for me, I'm game."

"Gert cooked almost all the food," Helen said. "She's a better cook than me. She should send some food over to you and your family."

Flo piped up, "I could make chicken for you."

Disappointed Helen wasn't catching on, Mike replied, "Yeah . . . sure . . . I guess so. Can I get you anything else, Helen?"

"No, thank you."

"No wonder you're so thin, you eat like a bird. Talking about birds. Do you know why birds fly south?"

"No," replied Helen and Clara simultaneously.

"It's too far to walk."

Stan sighed. "I told you he wouldn't stop."

Helen asked, "Mike, are you always like this?"

Mike touched his head, arms, and legs. "I guess so, seems like the same body I remember from last week."

Helen laughed. "Oh, you're right, Stan. He just keeps on going."

It seemed as if the invisible wall Helen had erected between them had started to crumble, and the afternoon segued from trivial chatter to conversation.

On the way home from the picnic, Mike confessed to Stan, "I'm sure glad you're dating Gert because I'd never have met Helen. Since we left the picnic, I keep seeing this movie playing over and over in my head of Helen's face, her bubbly laugh. And that smile, that smile could melt ice. I don't know what it is, but there's something really special about her."

"Mike, that sounds like someone in love, and you just met her."

"I know. That's crazy! All I know is I really enjoyed being with her. She's so down to earth and beautiful."

"You haven't even gone out with her. How can you be so smitten?" Stan asked.

"I spent all day talking with her. It sure felt like a date. I wanted to ask her to a movie or for some ice cream, but I didn't want to seem too forward. Besides, I sorta got the feeling that she wasn't too keen on me."

"Why do you think that?"

"She's sweet and all, but she just didn't seem interested."

"Why, because she wasn't gushing with giddiness and flirting with you like all those other gals who swoon over you and chase you? Waiting for you to sweep them off their feet? Maybe she's a little shy."

"I think that's what I like about her," Mike said. "She's playful and not pushy and has a sweet innocence about her, not like some of those uppity girls. She's beautiful and doesn't even know it. Next time you see Gert, you need to find out what Helen thinks about me."

After the picnic, Gert, curious whether her matchmaking skills had worked, questioned Helen while they organized the picnic basket items in the basement.

"Helen, I didn't want to ask in front of Clara and Flo, but what did you think about Mike? Isn't he a swell fella? I bet you can't wait to see him again."

Helen folded the blanket. "Gert, I wouldn't date him if he was the last man on Earth."

Gert's eyes widened. "What?"

"Shh, don't yell," Helen said. "You heard what I said."

"Yes, I heard what you said. I'm just shocked. You seemed to have a really good time."

"I kinda had a good time, but I don't want to go out with him."

"What do you mean you 'kinda' had a good time? You were laughin' and talkin' to him almost the whole time."

"Well, I kept talkin' to him because he kept talkin' to me."

"Oh, don't kid yourself. You could have walked away. I think he really likes you. He gave you his undivided attention at the picnic, and I saw him tryin' to teach you how to throw the ball."

"I know he did, but I . . . I . . . I just don't know what to think."

"Is that what's bothering you? That he paid attention to you?"

"I don't know. I'm not used to being around a man who . . . says . . . who compliments me."

"Helen, that's what men do if they like you."

"Well, I'm tellin' you, I don't want to repeat myself, but I wouldn't go out with him if he was the last man on Earth."

"I don't get it. He's a really good fella and smart, and he was really kind to you."

"Gert, just don't worry about it. I never told you who to go out with."

"I'm older than you, and I'm just looking out for you. I don't understand why you're saying this. I think you owe me an explanation."

"Goodnight, Gert, I'm going to bed."

Gert shook her head, thinking, *Ugh, she's so naïve. She knows as well as I do that she likes him. Why won't she admit it?*

Chapter Seven

Mike, hot with sweat and his shirt drenched, placed his lunchbox on the kitchen table and headed toward the backyard. After working in the stifling warehouse as a lathe operator at Westinghouse all day, he wanted to relax before dinner. He swung open the battered screen door and noticed Gert sitting on the low brick wall.

"Hey, Gert, what are you doing here?" he asked.

"Visiting with your mom. Do you want some lemonade and cookies?"

"Sure."

Gert poured the lemonade. "Hey, Mike, did you hear the news?"

"What news?"

"You know how you've been trying to get Helen to go out with you since that picnic, and she's always making excuses?"

"Yeah, but that's nothin' new."

"Well, what is new is she decided to finally start dating someone," Gert said.

Mike felt betrayed, and his nostrils flared. "She's seeing someone?"

"Yeah, his name is Adam."

"Adam?" Mike gulped the lemonade. "What do you know about him?"

"I know they met at Donahoe's."

Mike rested on the old bench. "Gert, I know you told me Helen said she'd never go out with me after the first time we met. But later at your wedding, she seemed like she enjoyed being with me. And we get along when you invite the family to your house. I thought she was changing her mind about me. She has to know me better than some joker she met at work. I just don't understand."

"I really don't know," Gert said. "I'm as confused as you. You know I'm on your side."

"Do you think it's because he has a better job or his family has more money?"

"First, Helen doesn't care about money, and his job is no better than yours. He works in a glass factory. And you've got one up on him because Helen mentioned that he didn't finish high school."

"What? He didn't finish high school? I can sorta understand why girls don't finish school, but he's a man. How's he expect to take care of a wife and family?" Mike snatched two cookies. "You know, this really irks me. I care about her. I wish she'd given me a chance to take her on a proper date when we first met. Then if she wanted to go out with him instead of me, I'd understand."

Gert refilled his glass. "Why don't you ask her again? It's been a while. Maybe she's changed her mind about you."

"I will, but not before I check out my competition. I need to meet him, somehow."

"She's going to the county fair with him on Sunday. Maybe you'll run into them, and you can see for yourself."

Mike bellowed as he stood up and stormed into the house. "Damn right, I will! I'm not giving up because she's dating someone else, especially if he's not the right man for her."

When Sunday arrived, Helen prepared a picnic basket with sandwiches, cookies, and drinks.

She asked her mother, "Mom, are you and Pop coming to the fair?"

"No, not this year."

"Okay, I'll leave the sandwiches I made for you in the icebox. You know it's supposed to be really good this year."

"You act like an excited little schoolgirl every time the fair comes," her mother said. "I don't find it interesting."

"I do! All the exhibits and singing shows. Besides, I like walking around and stopping to talk. You used to like it."

"Maybe I'm just getting older," moaned her mother. "Or maybe because it seems like it rains every year. Who needs a weatherman? I can predict it's going to rain later today, so you better take your umbrella and sweater."

"I already have it, thanks."

"Helen, I think that's Adam knocking."

"Bye, Mom. Bye, Pop."

While she waited for the bus with Adam, it began to drizzle. "Oh, my mother was right," she said. "It's going to rain."

He added, "It's a light shower. It might stop, and anyway here comes the bus."

Helen slid into the seat. "Wow, we're so lucky we got the last two seats."

"Yeah. Maybe we'll have more luck, and it'll stop raining!"

Before the bus reached the next stop, the clouds burst and unleashed a downpour. Everyone on the bus sighed. Immediately, a jovial woman, half singing and half shouting, proclaimed, "Rain, rain, go away!" A big, burly man added, "And come again another day!" The bus exploded in giggles, as numerous passengers squeezed onto the bus, cramming into the aisle. Despite the rain, the jam-packed bus overflowed with a hubbub of loud babble and laughter.

As the bus neared South Park, the rain subsided, and the sun peeked through the hazy gray sky.

Umbrellas tucked away, Helen and Adam ambled through the crowd toward the agricultural building. Mike had arrived earlier and lingered near the bus stop, waiting for Helen. Within seconds, he spotted Helen and assumed the gangly, ordinary man behind her was Adam. Stealthily, Mike followed behind them. When they stopped, he tapped on Helen's shoulder.

She twisted around, and her eyes popped open. "Mike?"

"Hey, Helen! How you doin'? Isn't it a great fair this year?"

"Ah, we just got here. We haven't seen anything yet."

Mike noticed that Adam appeared ill at ease and confused. He stretched out his hand toward Adam. "Hi, I'm Mike."

Before Adam had a chance to respond, Helen stated, "Ah, Mike this is Adam. Adam, this is Mike, my brother-in-law."

"Hey, pal, how you doin'?" asked Adam. "Are you here with anyone?"

"Nope, just me. Enjoying the animals and exhibits. I was just headed to the ice cream stand. Want to join me?"

Adam agreed. "You bet. Helen mentioned she wanted to get some on the bus ride."

When they arrived at the ice cream cart, Adam bought one for Mike and handed it to him. "Here you go, buddy, this one's on me."

Why is he being so welcoming? Mike wondered. *Does he know I'm interested in Helen? He probably thinks I'm just her brother-in-law and has no idea I'm vying for her heart.* Taking advantage of the situation, Mike continued to hover, endeavoring to captivate Helen.

He sprinkled the conversation with flattering comments and flirtatious jokes, but Adam remained oblivious to Mike's intentions.

After scrutinizing his adversary for most of the day, Mike's confidence grew. *Helen deserves better than a third-string school dropout,* he thought. Not intent to sit on the sidelines, Mike decided to play offensive and give Helen another option.

Chapter Eight

It was Stan and Gert's first anniversary, and they invited the family to celebrate. Mike strolled into the kitchen and noticed Helen without Adam by her side. He grabbed a soda and, with the suave sophistication of a prince, approached Helen. "So, I don't see Adam."

"He had to work the late shift."

Smirking, Mike said, "Oh, that's too bad. How've you been?"

"You know, working, helping my mom and pop. How about you?"

The pockets of conversations throughout the house were deafening. Mike said, "It's pretty loud in here. Want to get away from the commotion and catch some fresh air?"

Helen took a sip of ginger ale. "Sure."

Together, they walked outside.

Mike tilted his head upward. "Wow, look at that sky. It's such a beautiful day. It should have been like this when Gert and Stan got married."

"Yeah, I know. It was a little chilly and rainy, but everything else turned out good."

Mike lit a cigarette. "You know what I liked best that day?"

"I know you like sweets, so probably the cookies," Helen said.

Before Mike could answer, Flo and Clara bolted into the yard.

"So, what are you two talking about?" asked Clara.

Helen replied, "Just remembering Stan and Gert's wedding."

"Oh, I had a great time that day," said Flo. "If I remember correctly, you two did, too. You were the star dancers that night."

Helen tilted her head. "Why do you say that?"

"You both danced to almost every song, and you looked great together."

Mike knew the time was perfect to ask Helen on a date. "Thanks, Flo, I thought we did, too. In fact, Helen, I think . . . "

Interrupting the conversation, Gert nudged her head outside the screen door and announced, "Come on in, supper's ready."

Mike sighed and stepped on his cigarette. Clara and Flo raced to the back door. As Helen started toward the house, Mike tapped her shoulder. "Helen, before we go back, can I ask you something?"

"Sure."

"I'm glad I got the chance to meet Adam, but I need to ask you. Are you serious about him?"

"What do you mean?"

"I mean, how do you feel about him? Does he mean anything to you?"

"We have a good time, but . . . why are you asking me?"

"Well, I've known you for a long time, and you know I've wanted to go out with you. I need to know if you're serious. If you are, then I'll understand that you don't want to go out with anyone else. If not, you should have the opportunity to date other men."

"I don't want to marry him right now, if that's what you're asking. We just started dating, and it's hard for us to see each other since he works different shifts."

"So that means you can date other men?"

Helen stared up at the clouds. "Yeah . . . I guess. If I want to."

"Listen, you know I'm not a bad guy, and I know you're dating Adam. Give me a chance to show you a good time."

Helen took a deep breath. "Ahhh, Mike . . . "

He inched closer to her. "Wait. Don't say anything yet. You know we're gonna see each other at these family events, and it could be awkward. If we go out one time, and you think I'm not the man for you, I'll respect your decision, and we can go on with our lives. Just give me one chance to show you who I am when it's just you and me. I'm not asking you to stop dating Adam. You can still date him. I don't mind, and I'm sure he won't either since it's not serious. Besides, think about your sister's comment. She said we looked good together. What do you say we give it another shot on the dance floor?"

Helen rolled her shoulders back and exhaled. "I do like to dance."

Mike beamed. "Does that mean you'll go?"

"Well." After a stretch of silence, she smiled and replied, "Okay, but you promise if it doesn't work out, you won't ask me again?"

"I'll be disappointed, but you have my word," Mike said.

"Just do me a favor and don't say anything when we get inside."

"Mum's the word, and I promise you won't regret this, Helen."

Her willingness to appease him unearthed new excitement and a zest for life in Mike. It fueled his determination to enthrall her. He wanted the date to be extraordinary and to prove his worthiness to carry her heart. In his eyes, Helen was a queen, and she deserved a king to show her a royal time, not a court jester like Adam.

On his journey to woo Helen, Mike's nerves twisted as taut as a tightrope. He knew this was his final chance to spotlight his charisma and expose his soul and character. To increase his odds for getting another date, he stopped at the florist. He boasted to the clerk, "These are for the most beautiful girl in the world. Please make it your best, and add a few yellow roses."

He arrived at the front door with a handful of flowers, a twinkle in his eye, and a spring in his step that withered as soon as Helen's mother answered the door.

"Ah, Michael, come in. How are your parents doing?"

"They're fine, thank you. Is Helen ready?"

"Flo, go see if your sister is ready."

Upstairs, Helen foraged through the items on top of the dresser. "Flo, I'm glad you're here. Do you know where the bobby pins are? I need them to fasten my hair."

"I put them in the box in the bottom drawer."

"Oh, thanks. You know, I can't believe how nervous I am. I've seen Mike a hundred times before."

"Maybe you're starting to think differently about him."

"What do you mean?"

"Maybe you finally see something in him you like, but you've been too stubborn to admit you might like him."

"I'm not stubborn!"

Flo rolled her eyes and handed Helen a bobby pin. "I don't understand why you're being so picky about Mike. You only knew Adam a short while before you went out with him. I think you're being bull-headed. Is it because Gert suggested you go out with him?"

"No, that has nothing to do with it."

"Then what is it?"

Helen shrugged her shoulders. "It's . . . it's like he knows everything and I'm . . . oh, ohhh, I don't know."

"That's silly. It's good he's smart. Do you want to date a dunce?"

Helen clasped her earrings. "Of course not. I just feel different when I'm around him."

Flo's eyes widened. "Ah ha, I know what it is. You felt different because of the way he made you feel, and I think you like him. But because you're stubborn, you're ignoring your feelings."

"Oh, you don't know what you're talking about. I better go. I've kept Mike waiting too long already."

Mike jumped to his feet as soon as he heard the clicking of Helen's heels on the black-and-white checkered floor.

He held out the bouquet and smiled. "Hi, Helen, these are for you."

Her eyes sparkled like snowflakes in the beam of a headlight as Mike presented the bouquet. When she spied the two yellow roses, a blanket of warmth enveloped her. Adam had never offered her one single wildflower.

"They're beautiful, especially the yellow roses. They're my favorite."

"I know," Mike said. "I overheard you tell Gert a while back."

Her smile grew, and she pressed the blossoms to her nose. "They smell wonderful, Mike. I don't want them to die. Can you wait a minute while I take care of these?"

"Sure, take your time. I'm not goin' anywhere."

Helen beamed as she meticulously arranged the flowers in the vase, inhaling the sweet scent of each one before placing it in the water.

"Okay, I'm ready."

"Great."

"Bye, Mom. Bye, Pop."

Mike looked at her parents. "Nice to see you both, and don't worry, Helen is in good hands."

He gawked at Helen in her two-piece blue dress with a wide lapel. "You look swell, Helen. Blue's my favorite color. I take it yellow's your favorite?"

"It is, and the yellow roses were very thoughtful."

"Nothing but the best for you."

She blushed. "Aww, thanks. So, where we going?"

"Someplace special. You'll just have to wait and see. Trust me."

"I guess I'll have to."

As they strolled along the sidewalk, Mike said, "Tell me about yourself, Helen."

"What do you mean?"

"We've never really talked about ourselves. We spoke about your family, neighbors, and movies, and I learned a few things. I could see you were a sweet, caring person, but I want to know about your dreams, your favorite things to do, your thoughts. I want to know everything about you."

Helen was dumbfounded. No one before had shown an interest in her likes or dislikes, her favorite color, or her inner soul. Her mother, always telling her what to do or like, rarely allowed Helen a chance to think for herself. Mike was aware of Helen's outer beauty, but he wanted to delve deeper and unlock the file cabinet of her life.

Hesitantly, she revealed each stratum of herself to Mike. In turn, she discovered his tender and honorable qualities. His sincerity overwhelmed her, and she found him more interesting and captivating than she'd remembered. By the time they arrived at the dance hall, her sense of worth had escalated, and, for the first time, her heart expanded its usual boundaries.

During the night, Helen and Mike shared intricacies of their lives and danced until their feet ached. Mike figuratively and literally swept Helen off her feet with his charismatic personality and his Fred Astaire dance maneuvers.

While walking home, he said, "Helen, I have to tell you, nobody does the jitterbug better than you."

"Oh, you think so?"

"I know so. I'm sure Adam has told you what a fantastic dancer you are."

"We've never gone dancing."

"Well, lucky for me. I could have danced till morning. I've never had so much fun in my life. Oh, you're shivering, let me give you my coat."

"Thanks."

"A man's gotta take care of his gal. Do you mind if I hold your hand while we walk?"

She extended her palm toward him.

Mike gazed upward. "You know the moonlight makes your eyes sparkle more." He crooned, "*Shine on, shine on harvest moon up in the sky. I ain't had no lovin since January, February, June, or July. Snow time, ain't no time to stay indoors and spoon. So, shine on, shine on harvest moon, for me and my gal.*"

Helen smiled and declared, "Wow, Mike you can really sing. Do you sing in church?"

"I'm not in the choir, but I do like to sing. Do you like to sing in church?"

"No."

"Why not?"

"Well, my mother insists I can't even carry a tune in a bucket, so I don't."

"Nonsense, everyone can sing, and your voice is so pleasant. Sing a song with me."

Helen, embarrassed by her perceived shortcoming, said, "No, I really don't want to. I can't."

"That's okay, maybe another time when you feel more comfortable, but I got a feeling you probably sing as well as you dance."

"That's not true, but thanks, Mike."

When they arrived at her house, Mike accompanied her inside.

"Hi, Mrs. Cypyrch, just wanted to say goodnight and let you know Helen and I had a great time tonight."

"Is that right, Helen?"

"Yes, Mom. We danced and danced."

"That's good. Since you're home, I'm going to bed. Good night, Michael."

"Good night, Mrs. Cypyrch."

After Helen's mother left the room, Mike said, "Sounds like you enjoyed yourself tonight. Does that mean you want to go out again?"

Helen cocked one eyebrow and tilted her head to the side. "Let me think."

"Oh, come on. Don't leave me in suspense. What do ya say?"

Her knees wobbled as she coyly replied, "Okay."

"Swell! How about a movie next time?"

"Okay."

"What about Adam? Are you gonna tell him about us?"

"I already told him I was going out with you tonight."

"So, he's fine with you seeing me?"

"He said that's what dating's about. He wasn't upset."

Relishing a challenge, Mike said, "That's good. You need to make up your own mind who's better for you. I'm happy you agreed to give me a chance. Since I don't have a phone, do you mind if I stop by Donahoe's in a day or two and make plans?"

"Sure."

Mike wanted to kiss Helen until he ran out of breath, but he recalled her shyness and apprehension in dating him and instead politely said, "Get a good night's sleep, Helen. I'll see you soon." He pulled her to him quickly and squeezed her tight.

"Goodnight, Mike, and thanks again," she said, hugging him back.

Chapter Nine

Several months passed, and the volleyball dating game between Mike and Adam continued. With no clear choice of a winner, Helen abstained from asking either of them to join her family for Thanksgiving, only two days away. Mike respected Helen's decision to date both of them but was discontented with the occasional date. Eager to secure additional time with her, he knocked on her door.

"Mike, what are you doing here?" she asked, surprised.

"I'm sorry to intrude, but you know I don't have a phone to call you. Do you have a few minutes?"

"Sure, come on in."

"I wanted to tell you they switched my days for work. I'm off the day after Thanksgiving, and I know you are, too. I was wondering if you wanted to spend the day together?"

"I would, Mike, but I'm going to the matinee with Adam."

"What movie are you going to see?"

"I think the new Fred Astaire movie is opening at the Senator."

"Oh, I wanted to take you, but that's okay. There's other movies we can go to. Since you'll be with Adam Friday, and I'm scheduled to work Saturday, do you mind if we go to church together on Sunday?"

"Sure, and after mass, we can come back here for breakfast."

"Great! Well, I guess I'll let you get back to your duties."

He kissed her. "Happy Thanksgiving, and I'll see you Sunday, sweetheart."

On Friday, as Helen and Adam waited for the trolley, the first snowflakes of the season twirled in the air and showered on them. Helen's black coat had turned white by the time the streetcar glided to its appointed stop. As they boarded and searched for a seat, they noticed Mike sitting by the back door.

Helen approached him. "Hey, Mike, strange seeing you here today. Where you goin'?"

"I'm headed to a movie and then a little Christmas shopping. I hate wasting a day off from work."

Adam asked, "What movie are you gonna see?"

Mike answered, "I'm going to the Senator Theater."

Helen chimed in, "Hey, so are we. Isn't that funny, Adam?"

Adam sneered. "Yeah, what a coincidence."

At the ticket booth, Adam stumbled to get out the words, "Ah, make that three," and paid for Mike's admission.

Adam handed the ticket to Mike. "Here you go, Mike."

"Well, thanks, pal." Mike thought, *What a putz. If he'd intruded on my date with her, I wouldn't buy him a ticket. I'd give him the boot.*

Inside the theater lobby, Adam bought three Coca-Colas and presented one to Mike. Helen's mouth dropped open, and she thought, *Why is Adam acting like our date doesn't matter to him? If he cared, he'd confront Mike, instead of practically inviting him to join us.*

Mike, puzzled by Adam's generosity and acceptance of his encroachment, capitalized on Adam's spinelessness.

After Helen and Adam took their seats, Mike settled in directly behind them. Adam squirmed in his seat as he kept glancing back toward Mike. He attempted to put his arm around Helen's shoulders but caught Mike's menacing stare and retracted his arm. Mike leaned back, stretched his hands behind his head, and smiled.

After the meeting at the movie theater, Mike judged, *If he didn't have the guts to persuade me to leave or to take another seat in the movie theater, how could he protect her?* Helen deserved a knight, not a commoner, and Mike was willing to wield the sharp blade of the sword between her and anyone else.

Chapter Ten

February 1942

The holidays were long over, and although Mike didn't receive the number-one wish on his Christmas list, Helen's love, he remained optimistic that she would choose him over Adam. Craving Helen's attention, Mike humbled himself on her doorstep late at night and gently knocked on the door.

"Mike, I'm happy to see you, but I wasn't expecting you," she said.

"I know, but I needed to see you." He stared at her with begging puppy dog eyes. "I haven't seen you for a few days, and I wondered if you'd like the company of a love-sick man."

Helen wanted him to stay but wavered because her parents had recently gone to bed. "It's getting late."

"It's only ten." He took his arm from behind his back to reveal a golden box. "We can't let these delicious chocolates go to waste, can we? Besides, I'd love some good conversation. I'll leave whenever you want me to."

"Oh, Mike, you're always so sweet. Sure, come on in, but be quiet. My parents are sleeping. Can I get you anything?"

"All I need is you, darling. Let's sit."

"Okay, first let me put a record on."

Before settling down, she picked out her favorite chocolate from the box and nestled close to Mike on the couch. "Mmm, thanks, Mike. You always know how to put a smile on my face."

"I try."

He wrapped his arm around her and asked, "Are you trying to tell me something, Helen?"

"What? I didn't say anything."

"Listen to the song that's playing?"

In the background, Bing Crosby crooned, "*You made me love you, but I didn't want to do it.*"

Helen almost choked on her candy and sputtered, "Oh, oh . . . I didn't even look at the title. I just grabbed a record and put it on the turntable."

"Maybe, but I think you're falling for me, Helen."

She sprang from the couch, grabbed the box of chocolates, and said, "Talking about falling, did I tell you Gabby tripped on the streetcar tracks and fell in the middle of the street?"

Mike didn't pursue the topic. He smiled and listened to her story.

Cuddled on the couch next to each other, they listened to music and talked until almost midnight. "Helen, I'm having a great time, but we both have work in the morning."

"Yes, you should get going."

"I will, but before I go, let me give you something to remember me by." He leaned over and kissed her, leaving her breathless.

During the next several weeks, Mike didn't wait until he had an official date with Helen. He seized every opportunity to be with her.

As Helen waved goodnight to her coworkers, she noticed Mike leaning against the exterior wall of the store, smoking a cigarette. When their eyes met, he tipped his hat and winked, accelerating her heart. Trying not to appear overly enthusiastic, she buttoned her coat and strolled toward him.

"Mike, you just keep showing up everywhere."

"Yeah, I'm like a jack-in-a-box, and you never know when I'm gonna pop up."

She snickered. "So, why'd you pop up here?"

"Oh, it's a cold night, and I knew you might need me to keep you warm on the way home."

Helen giggled. "Is that so?"

"Yep. If I promise to keep you warm, would you take the long way home through the park, instead of the incline?"

"Mike, that's so sweet. I do prefer to walk, but it's a little chilly tonight."

"Aww, come on. It's a gorgeous night. You and me holding hands in the moonlight under the shadows of the trees. Sounds inviting, doesn't it?"

"Oh, okay. You know, Mike, you can be pretty persuasive."

She slipped her fingers into his hand, as they strolled under the star-filled sky.

"Helen, I've been thinking about you and me and the fact that you're still dating Adam. I'm not asking you to stop seeing him. That has to be your decision. But I want you to know I love you deeply, and every second I spend with you makes me love you more. I was hoping you might feel the same way about me."

"To be honest, remember a couple of weeks ago when that Bing Crosby song was playing?"

"I knew it, you did it on purpose!"

"No, it really was accidental. But yes, I love you, Mike. I think I kept trying to deny it, but you're the one I think about all day, and when you show up unexpectedly, I feel electrified and happy and . . . please don't laugh at me, but I don't think I really understood what being in love meant."

"What do you mean?"

"You and Adam were both nice, and I had a swell time with Adam, and for a long time I was confused. But I felt different with you, and I've never been happier in my life than when I'm with you. I guess I never felt this way and just thought somehow I didn't deserve it or that I was mistaken."

"Helen, you deserve everything I can give you and more. You should have more confidence, and one of these days you will realize how special you are. Why do you think you had two guys chasing after you?"

"Nothing else better to do?"

"You're so silly. You mean the world to me, and I can't imagine my life without you."

"That's the nicest thing anyone's ever said to me. I love you, Mike."

"So, if you mean what you say, are you going to tell Adam it's over between you two?"

"Yes. You're the only one I want to be with."

"So, when are you going to tell him about your decision?"

"We were supposed to go out tomorrow. I'll tell him then. I feel bad, though. He's become a friend, and I don't want to hurt him."

"Helen, that's what I love about you. Always thinking of other people. But he's a grown man, and he knew you were dating me. He'll be okay."

"I hope so."

"I know so, but let's not worry about that. I just want to hold you in the moonlight and tell you I'm the luckiest man alive. I'll never let you down, Helen. I promise."

Mike stopped walking, and their bodies merged into one, locked into a long embrace. Releasing her, he stepped back and gazed into her eyes. "Helen, I've waited a long time for this, but you know what they say. Good things come to those who wait, and nothing could be better than having you as my gal."

She lifted her coat collar. "Brrr . . . thanks, Mike, but that wind is penetrating through my clothes."

"I'm surprised you made it this long, but I told you I'd keep you warm. You know what you need?"

"No, what?"

"An armstrong heater."

"What's that?"

"You never heard of an armstrong heater?"

"No."

"Well, let me tell you, it's something only I can give you."

She laughed shyly. "Mike, what are you talking about?"

He lifted his arm over her shoulder and squeezed her close. "Are you warmer now?"

"Yes, I am. Ah, I get it. So, you're the armstrong heater?"

Mike smiled. "Yep, that's me all right. My strong arms will always be there for you to warm you, and our love keeps the heat going."

The sentiment warmed Helen as quickly as a welder's spark, a flicker that took two lives and melded them together. She had slowly built the bridge to Mike's side, but tonight their bond created the final rivet. Mike's shower of love extinguished any embers of affection for Adam remaining in Helen's heart.

The following afternoon, Adam, eager to see her, bopped up the steps and knocked on the front door.

With sweaty palms, Helen twisted the doorknob and slowly opened the door.

"Hey, Helen, you ready to go?"

Looking past him, she said, "Adam, can you come in for a minute?"

"Sure, is everything all right?"

"Let's sit," she said, gesturing to the couch. They sat down and without preamble, she spoke. "Well . . . Adam, I need to tell you . . . "

"What is it?"

She fixed her eyes on her wringing hands in her lap and stuttered, "It . . . it's, I'm in love with Mike."

Adam's hands clenched. "What? I thought you were fallin' in love with me?"

"I never said I loved you."

"But you seemed happy with me."

"We had fun, but I'm not in love with you."

Adam sprang up. "What happened all of a sudden?"

"Mike stopped by, and we talked for a long time."

Adam's head dropped, and he grimaced at his feet. "What changed overnight?"

"It didn't change overnight. I really enjoy being with Mike, and last night I realized I'm in love with him. I want to be with Mike. I'm sorry, Adam. Please try to understand. You've always been a good friend."

Raising his hands in the air, Adam said, "A friend, is that what you think? Helen, I love you."

"You never told me you loved me."

"I assumed you knew. I guess I should've seen this coming, and I shouldn't be surprised, but I am. I need to go. Goodbye, Helen."

He shoved open the door and bolted down the steps, muttering, "A friend . . . that's all I am . . . bullshit."

Chapter Eleven

October 1942

As Adam lay sweating in his bunk at Madison Barracks in New York on an unusually hot autumn night, he daydreamed about Helen. His muscles ached from the constant maneuvers and training that had been flung at him during the last few months since Uncle Sam had invited him to join the fight. If only the rigors and constant motion of army life could exhaust the pain that lingered in his heart over his loss. Helen's scent, laughter, smile, and affectionate personality penetrated his every thought.

During his musings, Adam understood that war offers no guarantees, that every soldier has as much chance of dying as the man who stands beside him. Mike was not exempt. If Mike disappeared from the picture, Adam believed Helen would run into his arms. The gnawing emptiness in his heart and his desire to gain Helen's love impelled him to take action. With nothing to lose and everything to gain, he grabbed a pen and army stationery from his footlocker. He wrote about his military experience and activities, but his true emotions emerged as he confessed his loneliness and desire to once again experience the good times they shared. To guarantee that Helen kept his image alive, he enclosed a picture of himself in his uniform, standing with one leg perched atop an old Civil War cannon.

When Helen received the letter from him, she read it and hesitated to respond but recalled the Glenn Miller Air Force tagline: "They're doing the fighting, you do the writing." To do her part for the war, she replied, precisely selecting her words to ensure that Adam understood her commitment to Mike. She finished the note with tiny tidbits about local news and reassured Adam that she continued to pray for him.

When Adam received her response, he quickly tore it open, heart pounding in anticipation. Thrilled that Helen cared enough to correspond, his spirit rose with the belief that she still held a special place in her heart for him. He read the letter, oblivious to the platonic phrases and Helen's confirmation of her allegiance to Mike. Instead, he focused on every positive word or comment and tallied each as another stitch into his fabricated cloth of a restored relationship with Helen.

Adam sat at the desk, ready to pour his heart out to her, when his commander informed him that he'd received a notice from the Red Cross. Adam's half brother had died, and he'd been granted a furlough to go home.

After packing his duffel bag, he jumped on the next train to Pittsburgh. The conductor closed the doors, and Adam found a comfortable seat in the front car. Staring out the window, he wrestled with divergent thoughts about burying his half-brother and the possibility of reconnecting with Helen again. He hoped the door opened by their correspondence was spread wide enough for him to reenter her life as more than a friend.

During the train ride, he rehearsed several scenarios of meeting Helen one more time, but he felt unprepared when she entered the dark funeral home. As she sauntered toward his parents at the casket, a small sliver of sun peeking through the window illuminated her beautiful eyes, arousing his deep-seated emotions. Sweat rolled down his back. He quickly made a beeline toward Helen, who was conveying her sympathies to his parents. His legs quivered as he sputtered, "Ahh, Helen, it's so good to see you."

Turning toward him, Helen grabbed his hand. "Oh, I'm so sorry to hear about your brother."

"Thank you. How did you know he died?" he asked.

"My mother read the death notice and told me. But I'm surprised to see you. I didn't think the army would give you time to come home."

"Well, I guess the army isn't completely insensitive," he said. "They granted me a furlough."

"That's good. I'm sure your parents need you right now."

"Yeah, they're having a hard time."

"I see a line of people waiting to talk to you. I'm going to say a prayer at the casket. Take care of yourself, Adam. It was nice to see you."

Helen departed swiftly, and Adam, drunk on an elixir of mixed emotions, stood paralyzed, unable to stop her. Her haste left a wake of her sweet perfume, and its scent drifted toward him, sparking thoughts of past moments and fueling his love for her. Helen's charming smile, her beautiful handwritten letter, and her loving actions filled his mind and ignited a fire within his soul.

To the astonishment of the mourners, Adam bolted out the door with courage and purpose. After a short detour to help him fulfill his desire, he rushed through the chilly air toward Helen's house. Each step of the journey generated another foot of courage in his goal to face Helen one more time and resolve the concerns plaguing his mind. He knocked on the front door and prayed she would answer.

Helen opened the door, and Adam stood before her, his nerves vibrating, his face flushed and sweaty. Before she could utter a word, Adam, his mind full and his resolve absolute, stepped deliberately into her home.

Her mouth dropped open. "Adam, I wasn't expecting you," she said. "What—"

He dropped down on one knee, holding a simple, brilliant ring in his worn hands, and begged, "Helen, will you marry me?"

This out-of-left-field proposal made her head spin faster than a curveball. Heat rose up her neck, and she grasped the wall for support, then inched her way toward the couch and flopped backward onto the soft cushions. Her heart belonged to Mike, and she imagined *him* kneeling before her. She focused on her naked, unadorned finger and, with glazed eyes, stared at Adam. Thoughts swirled through her head. *Why is he asking me? I told him I love Mike. What did I do to make him think he was special in my life now? He has to know I'm going to say no.*

"Helen, you're not saying anything," Adam said, still kneeling.

Her blouse grew dark with sweat as she peered into Adam's eyes. "I told you a long time ago that I'm in love with Mike," she said. "I thought you understood. I can't marry you. I don't want to marry you."

"But I *do* understand. I understand men are being killed every day, and Mike might be one of them."

"He hasn't even been drafted. Why would you say that?" Her eyes reddened as she turned away from Adam. "I don't even want to think about that."

"What I mean is when we go overseas, death is a possibility for all of us, me included. I just want a reason to come home and for you to know that if anything happens to Mike, you'll always have me. You don't need to promise to marry me. Just say you'll keep this ring from me as an option. You can decide later."

She jerked her head back. "Adam, I can't take the ring. What would Mike say? He'd be upset if I accepted an engagement ring from you when he's promised to marry me someday."

"Helen, just think about it."

"There's nothing to think about. I can't betray Mike."

Adam reached for her hands. "I'm not asking you to betray Mike. I need you to know that if anything changes between you and Mike, I'll be here for you."

"Adam, this isn't right. Why would you possibly think I'd say yes when you know I'm serious about Mike?"

"You wrote me a letter, and you came to the funeral home the other day. You wouldn't have done that if you didn't still care about me."

She yanked her hands from his. "Adam, I do care for you as a friend. Friends write to each other and offer their sympathy when a family member passes. You were lonely, and I was trying to help you."

"As a friend, will you do me a favor and take the ring?" Adam asked.

"Adam, listen to me, I don't want to marry you," Helen said.

"Why don't you talk to your parents about this and ask them their opinion?"

"If you're giving me an engagement ring, you should be the one talking to my parents," she said firmly.

"Sure, I know I should talk to them if I was askin' you to marry me, but I'm not askin' you to say yes to marry me now, just a promise you'll keep the ring and think about me occasionally. After the war, if things change and you decide to marry me, I'll do everything the proper way and ask for your parents' blessing. Please go talk to your mother. I think she might understand what I'm askin' of you."

With stooped shoulders, Helen shuffled to her parents' bedroom and explained the situation.

"Mom, I told Mike I was committed, and Adam knows that. Why would he do this?" she sniffled.

After a long discussion and many exhausting questions, Mary declared, "You should take his ring."

"Why? What are you saying? I don't love him. What about Mike?"

"Mike hasn't bought you an engagement ring!"

"I know, but I love Mike."

"There is no guarantee of Mike's intentions without an engagement ring."

Helen hung her head, her tears falling to the carpet. "And when he finds out I took Adam's ring, he definitely won't give me one."

Mary frowned. "Why are you always so mopey? Listen, in these times, you don't know what the future holds. Sometimes a man just needs a reason to come home and to know someone is thinking about him. You're giving Adam courage. Do you want to be responsible if he decides to throw in the towel and not fight the enemy? I see no harm in accepting the ring under these circumstances. You never know what's gonna happen in a war. He understands you're with Mike now, but if Mike gets killed or . . . "

"Mom, I don't even want to think about that."

"You have to face that possibility if he goes overseas."

"What do I tell Mike?"

"Tell him the truth. Maybe this will spur him to take a trip to the jeweler."

"What if he thinks I've been dishonest with him, and he decides he doesn't want to marry me?"

"If he chooses to break it off with you, then that's his choice. Better to find out now than later."

"Mom, I don't want to take a chance."

Her mother stood, stomped her foot, and glared at Helen. "Just do the man a favor. Mike knows what this war is about. He'll understand. Now go downstairs and take the ring!"

Helen left her parents' bedroom with sweaty hands, stinging eyes, and her mind frazzled. Shaking, her blouse drenched with perspiration, she approached Adam and mumbled, "I'll take your ring."

He placed the ring in her palm. "Thank you."

"I want you to know, Adam, I'm not going to wear it," she said. "I'm waiting for Mike."

"It's okay, I'm just happy you'll keep it." Even with her hesitation, he remained confident that a seed for a future together was blossoming.

After Adam left, Helen collapsed onto the couch, grounded by the anchor thrown over her shoulders and the possible consequences of her action. *How can I explain this to Mike? What if Mike thinks I don't want him? Why did I listen to my mother? Am I obligated to Adam? I love Mike and told him whenever he went to war, I'd wait for him. How can he believe me now?*

These questions demanded a resolution, but the answers were lost.

She stared at the ring, her thoughts paralyzed by her actions.

Daylight slipped into nightfall, and Flo walked into the room. "Helen, are you okay? You look like you're going to be sick."

"I am sick. Adam was here and . . . "

"I know. Mom told me everything. What are you going to do?"

"I don't know. Mike is supposed to come over tonight, and he'll be here in a little while. But I can't face him."

"Why don't you grab a cup of tea and go upstairs? When Mike comes, I'll say you went to bed early because your stomach hurt. If I say it's a woman's thing, he won't ask any questions."

"No, I won't do that. You know I don't like to lie."

"It's not like you're lying to hurt someone. I'm just giving you time to think. Besides, do you have any other ideas? Do you want me to tell him you don't want to see him?"

Helen's muscles tensed. "No, that would make matters worse, but I don't want to lie."

"Well, if it makes it any better, I'm the one who'll be lying."

"Flo, this is wrong. I need to tell Mike the truth."

"Do ya think that's the right thing to do? It could be your secret until after the war."

"Flo, I'm surprised by you. You know when you spout one lie, you need to tell another and another. I couldn't live with myself, knowing I didn't tell Mike everything. What kind of relationship would it be? If he found out from someone else, he'd never trust me again. I want Mike to be honest with me, and I need to be honest with him."

"Well, if you're sure. Me, I'd just keep it to myself."

"Flo, I can't be here when Mike gets here. I'm going to Gert's. Just tell Mike where I went and that I'll talk to him tomorrow."

"Suit yourself."

Helen's heels echoed on the sidewalk in sync with her rapid heartbeat. An icy sweat eased down her back, and tears soaked the front of her sweater. Reaching for the handkerchief inside her pocket, she felt the engagement ring from Adam. She twirled the ring between her fingers, removed it, and clenched it in her hand. This supposed symbol of love was more analogous to a hatchet, hacking at her heart and her relationship with Mike. She wanted to throw it in the gutter and forget what had happened, but she'd made a pledge to Adam. A promise had been offered to Mike as well. The predicament tore at her gut.

Gert answered the door, wiping her hands on her apron.

"Helen, what're you doing here? Are you okay? You look awful."

"I need to talk to you."

"Sure, come on in. Stan is working, and I'm feeding Mary Ann. We can talk while I finish with her."

Helen followed Gert into the kitchen in silence. As Gert wiped cereal from Mary Ann's chin, she said, "You look awful. Tell me what's wrong." Before waiting for an answer, she gasped, "Oh, no. Did you and Mike break up?"

"No, we didn't break up," Helen said.

"Then what is it?"

Helen opened her hand and revealed the diamond engagement ring.

"Helen, did Mike propose? You should be happy."

"It's not from Mike. It's from Adam."

Gert jumped up. "What? Adam? Isn't he in the army? What the hell happened?"

"Adam came home for a couple of days to bury his half-brother."

"And out of the blue, he decides to ask you to marry him? After you broke up with him? And you accepted? I can't believe this. What were you thinking?"

"Don't yell at me. It wasn't my idea. It was Mom's."

"I'm not yelling at you. I just don't know what's going on."

Helen retold the story. At the end of her saga, Gert said, "I'm sorry I got upset earlier, but now I understand. I know how persuasive Mom can be, and if you don't do what she wants, there's hell to pay."

"Now, how do I get Mike to understand?" Helen asked. "I don't want him to change his mind about me." She pounded the table. "Ohhhh, this was a big mistake!"

"I think you need to explain the whole story just like you told me. You told Adam you wouldn't wear it; it's just a morale booster for him. Mike really loves you, and he'll understand. Besides, he knows Adam's in New York and no competition for him."

"Do you really think he'll be okay with everything?"

Gert wrapped her arms around Helen. "I do, and if he doesn't understand, Stan will talk to him."

Helen asserted, "No need for Stan to say anything, I can handle this myself. I just needed to get this off my chest and to know I didn't do anything wrong." She wiped her tears. "Thanks, Gert, for listening. I'll let you know what happens after I talk with Mike."

The next day, Helen, who usually greeted Mike with a huge smile and a hug, walked out of Donahoe's wearing a somber expression. "Mike, I'm sorry about last night."

"That's okay. Flo told me you needed to help Gert."

"Well, that's not the whole truth. I have to tell you something."

"What a coincidence. I have something to say, too, but ladies first. My news can wait."

"Okay, but please let me finish the whole story before you say anything."

"You have my undivided attention."

As they walked, Helen relayed the story and held her breath in anticipation of his reaction.

Mike stopped at the end of the pathway, stared at her, and after a pregnant pause he said, "Helen, I understand what happened, and I'm not upset with you. I'm a little steamed that Adam burdened you by his proposal. I have a mind to go and tell him how unfair this is for you, but I won't. I think he's lonely and afraid. I feel kinda sorry for the fella that he's crushed about your decision not to see him anymore and that he doesn't have a girl."

Exhaling, Helen asked, "So you're not mad at me?"

Mike clasped her hands. "No, Helen. I love you and I understand. I know in your heart you love me, darling, and I'm sorry it wasn't me proposing. You know I give money to my mom and dad, and I'm taking the class at Carnegie Tech. I don't have the money right now for a ring. Rest assured, I'll buy you a ring, and I guarantee it'll be grander than the one he gave you. Do I have your word that you'll marry me when I can buy a ring?"

Helen smiled. "Of course, and Mike, I'm sorry if I hurt you in any way."

He wiped away her tears. "I'm fine."

"You know I didn't want to take it."

"I know. That's why I'm not worried. Nothing will ever come between us."

"Thanks, Mike. You're too good for me."

She went to kiss him and then pulled back. "Oh, no, I've spent all this time talking about Adam. I almost forgot. What is your news?"

"Don't be upset, but I received notice to report to the local induction board to see if I'm fit to serve. It'll only be a matter of time before I go to boot camp."

"Oh, Mike, I don't know what to say. I feel sick."

"Helen, don't be distressed. You knew I'd be drafted eventually, and I'm proud to defend my country. You'll be proud of me serving, won't you?"

"Of course, but I don't want to lose you."

"You'll never lose me. Think of me as a boomerang. You'll toss me off to war, and I'll go away for a while, and soon I'll be right back in your arms."

"Oh, that's not funny."

"Come on, Helen. I thought it was. Besides, the sooner I go, the sooner I'll be back, and we can start our life together."

"I don't want you to leave."

"Don't think about it. Instead, think about my loving arms around you and this beautiful night. Let's just enjoy the time we have right now."

The walk ended at Helen's front door, but their time in the parlor lingered into the early morning hours. Helen's eyes slowly closed, and her head fell on Mike's shoulder as she drifted into a slumber. He pushed the hair that had fallen across her face behind her ears, ran his fingers through her curly locks, and gently kissed her forehead. Sitting in the dim light of the parlor, he listened to her soft breathing and inhaled her sweet perfume. When the clock chimed three times, he gently woke her. "Honey, I need to go, and you should go to bed, but I guarantee you I'll be back tomorrow."

Back at home, Mike lay in his bed, pondering the events of the day. He empathized with Helen and the pain she felt from accepting the ring. With a desire to ease her mind and reassure her of his love, he grabbed a pad of paper. He sketched a bouquet of roses with a flowing bow and colored the flowers with a yellow crayon. At the top of the page he wrote, "To Helen, my darling, who has the beauty and sweetness of real flowers." Adding at the bottom, "These flowers will never die and let it be a reminder of my undying love for you. Love, Mike."

The next day, as promised, Mike met Helen at Donahoe's. Smiling and with one arm held behind his back, he greeted his sweetheart. "Hi, darling. Did you have a good day?"

"Better than yesterday."

"Well, I have a surprise that might brighten your day." He slowly brought his right arm forward and presented her with a rolled-up piece of paper.

"Oh, what's this? The way you had your arm behind your back I thought it might be flowers."

"Well, unroll it and take a peek."

Helen slowly unfurled the drawing of a dozen yellow roses. She read the inscription and sniffled. "Mike, you sure do know how to make me cry. You're so sweet."

"Helen, these flowers don't need water, so don't cry too hard. You'll get the paper wet."

She playfully nudged his shoulder. "Oh, get out of here, always the jokester."

"Seriously, Helen, I didn't want you to cry. I wanted to put a smile on your face. I know you like flowers, but the real ones die. It might be a long time before I can give you fresh ones, so I drew these for you. I want you know that no matter what happens, I will always love you, and I hope you smile every time you look at the drawing."

"I am smiling, Mike. I was crying because I'm happy."

"Well, come on, Happy, let's go get some supper and see a movie."

After arriving home, Helen taped the artwork to the mirror above her dresser and spotted the ring from Adam on the doily next to her hairbrush. She snatched it, crumpled it into a handkerchief, and shoved it in a drawer. Mike hadn't delivered her a band of love. Instead, he'd presented her with a tangible portrayal of his undying dedication to cherish in his absence. Compared to the ring, the simple drawing was priceless.

Chapter Twelve

January 1943

T he floodwaters from the New Year's Eve rain had long receded, but the pain Helen endured from her siblings' inquisition about Adam's ring lingered. It had been almost three weeks since she'd asked Mike his true feelings regarding her acceptance of the ring. In her heart, she believed he was not troubled and still loved her, but each passing day without a response increased her anxiety. It would be unbearable to face the disgrace and humiliation of admitting defeat to her sisters.

She decided to bake some cookies to send to Mike and relieve her mind of worry. The timer dinged, and as she slid the cookies off the tray, she heard the mail fall through the front door slot. Eagerly, she shuffled through the bundle and found two letters from Mike.

January 20, 1943 CAMP MAXEY, TEXAS

Dearest Helen,

I want to thank you for the wonderful package you sent. You shouldn't have done that. But since you did, I want you to know I appreciate it very much. I was really happy when I received it.

The engagement ring Adam gave you doesn't mean anything to me Helen, if that's what you are worried about. If it is, you can just forget about it. I know it's tougher for you to stand up under all of this than it is for me.

I don't have anyone here to bother me about who I should go with or the kind of girl I should love or even marry. If anyone bothers you just laugh it off and don't pay any attention to them.

I read a poem in a magazine, and it expressed my thoughts of the moment, so I decided to write it to you. I hope you like it. I did.

To My Girlfriend;

When the golden sun is sinking

And the stars commence their winking

Through the cloud that sail across the blue

When the silvery moon looks down

Upon the cloud at night. I think of you.

And wish that you would wait

When I'm finished with my duty

I'm reminded of your beauty

And remember all your charms'

That you can bet

When shadows softly fall

And night birds start their call

I dream of you, I dream of you

And hope you won't forget

I changed it around a bit to suit me. I hope I didn't spoil it.

Do you know I wish there were times when I could hold you close to me and feel your warm lips pressing against mine and feel our hearts merging into one steady beat and in unison repeating, I love you, I love you, I love you.

I'm sorry I can't write you anymore my time is limited. I'll try to make up for it in my other letters.

Helen, you know I don't even have one picture of you. It would please me very much if you could send one at your earliest possible convenience.

Always Remembering. Never forgetting. Loving you more than ever. I remain yours always, Mike

May God bless and protect you always.

Helen sighed in relief. Mike had unequivocally dismissed the ring and reaffirmed his love for her. However, she wished her eternal guardsman stood next to her, wielding his shield, and repelling the negative comments from those around her.

January 22, 1943 CAMP MAXEY, TEXAS

Dearest Helen,

I was certainly surprised to receive four letters from you in two days, three yesterday, and one today, Saturday. It kinda makes me feel as if I was slipping up on my letter writing.

Today we started out at 8 am with full pack for field tactics. We hiked about five miles till we came to an open field, here we were divided into small groups and told to act as skirmishers. This means every man spreads out to a distance of about 10 feet in staggered formation advancing and taking cover until they reach an appointed objective. One group at a time would go out. The other groups were stationed at different intervals and were told to watch to see if the group acting as skirmishers kept their self properly concealed.

The reason for this was to give us instruction in how to conceal ourselves properly and with the least observation. After all the groups are assembled, we were given instructions on the use of the Lensatic Compass and how to determine the direction by the use of the watch and prevailing winds. After this series of lectures and instructions we started on our hike again traveling for about another five miles. We were again divided into small groups, and I happened to be picked as a leader of one of these groups. Not bad hey. These groups acted as advance scouts, rear guard, and reserves. The scouts went ahead to study the terrain and plan the manner of advance. The rear guard spread out and advanced under cover to the positions indicated by the scouts. The reserves just followed behind.

Each group had to follow different routes to advance to the given objective by the aid of maps sketched by the platoon leader. These maps are sketched by using the Lensatic compass to determine the direction each group is to follow. We continued to do this for the greater part of the day and then started back to camp. I was then selected to act as right guide and asst. platoon leader while hiking back to camp.

I hope this gives me an opportunity to apply for a sergeants rating. I know I'm going to try my best.

The other day we had a class on Military Courtesy. I was one of the six men picked to answer any question asked by the soldiers on the subject. It was sort of an "information please" class. You can see that I'm trying my darndest to get something out of this army.

You know I really enjoyed all of those poems you sent to me. You really know how to pick them. I didn't know you had a place in your heart for poetry. It must be one of those many hidden talents you have.

I really enjoy writing to you, but I'd like nothing better than to be there with you. Words are a cheap imitation of trying to express what one really has in his heart.

Loving you more than I can express in words. I remain. Always yours Mike

Letters from Mike came steadily. When the next one arrived, Helen unfolded it, and a square sheet slipped from inside the folds and fluttered to the floor. When she turned over the runaway paper, she beamed to see a striking photograph of Mike. The comely boy who had left for boot camp had been transformed into a distinguished man. He'd lost weight, and a chiseled, defined jaw replaced the gentle curves of his face. The muscles of his arms and shoulders showed through his army jacket. The dark pressed uniform he wore afforded him an air of authority, making her flesh tingle and her body quiver.

"Hey, Pop. Look, here's a picture of Mike in his uniform. What do you think?"

"*On wygl da dobrze,*" replied her father.

"I agree. I think he looks good, too."

Helen kissed the picture and slid it into her pocketbook.

Jan 24, 1943 Sunday Camp Maxey, Texas

Dearest Helen,

I'm sorry I haven't been keeping up my correspondence regularly. This has been a pretty full week for me.

Friday night we went out on a night demonstration. I wished you had been there that night. I looked up into the sky and found a beautiful moon staring into my face when my eyes finally rested on the horizon, which were ablaze with the most beautiful, colors you ever seen. I stood still for a minute or two and tried to picture you and I walking hand in hand together like we used to do.

The demonstration showed how audible noises and how bright small lights appear at night. A click of a bolt on a gun can be heard over 600 yards away.

A match can be seen from a distance of over 1,000 yards. That's over 3/4 of a mile.

You can tell how far away rifle fire is by counting from the time of the flash to the report. I think I'm boring you with these details.

Helen do you think you could get dressed, washed, make your bed, eat breakfast, sweep up, mop up, shine your shoes and roll a full field pack in one hour and a half?

We get up at 6:30 and have to be in line at 8:00. That sounds like we have a lot of time, but we have a lot to do in that time. Could you imagine me washing my clothes, mopping and sweeping floors, washing dishes and windows?

I better watch out or I'll be getting dishwater hands and housemaids knee. _____ (space reserved for hearty laugh)

I don't believe there's a cleaner place in any of the services. We have an inspection every day in our kitchens and barracks. Helen, every one of us had to get another haircut. My hair was fairly long and beginning to lay down nicely but now it's back again to about 1/2 tall. One of my buddies got all of his hair cut off and his head shaved. I thought I'd die laughing when I seen him. His head was as smooth as a cue ball. I asked him if he wanted to borrow any of my polish to shine his head but he just laughed.

Helen, every night before I go to sleep, I just lie awake for a while and think of all of the wonderful times we had together especially those nights I came down after work, laid my head down on your lap and both you and I talked of so many different things. I could picture all of these things in my mind but they just don't seem real. When I think of all of the times we spent together it sort of makes me look forward to the time when I'll be home again. You and I back together again. The reason I don't want to mention these things is they might be tough on you. If they are please tell me.

Helen, when I start feeling low, which is very rare, I always think that there's still tomorrow.

Helen, I believe you'll agree with me when I say it's the hardships of life that make all of us appreciate more fully the finer things of life.

I'm sorry I have to close this letter but till I write you again. I want you to know I love you with all my heart. You know my heart's pretty big. Don't you?

Loving you forever, Mike.

Helen wrapped the extra scarf around her neck and slid on her gloves. Before venturing into the night, she asked her mother to join her for the Novena at the monastery.

"Not tonight. It's too cold to go out."

"Okay, I'll be back around nine."

Helen briskly scampered to the streetcar stop through the strong winds. Even in her haste, she noticed that the blue star in the window of the corner brick house had changed to gold. She knew numerous people from South Side, but, although unacquainted with this family, her heart anguished. Another neighbor devoured by the enemy. She slowed her pace, and, as she crossed the street, the trolley slowly approached her.

The powerful wind heaved at the oversize wooden doors of the monastery, and Helen struggled to drag the doors open. On entering the church vestibule, she repositioned her headscarf and tied it tightly under her chin. She had arrived early and secured a seat in the front pew. Within a short time, the monastery overflowed, mostly with women, ready to beseech God to mitigate their sorrows. When the bell rang, signaling the beginning of the service, Helen stood and opened a booklet with a large V on the front and the words "Novena for Peace and Victory." The priest started to sing, "Hymn to Our Blessed Mother for Soldiers and Sailors" to the tune of "Mary Help Us, Help We Pray."

Helen and the entire church joined in:

"Mary help them, help we pray

Help our soldiers night and day

Bring us peace and, dearest Mother,

Bring our boys home safe, we pray."

After the hymn, the prayers for victory, peace, soldiers, and country lasted for more than an hour and ended with the congregation singing, "Holy God, We Praise Thy Name."

Helen remained in the pew after the congregants had departed and prayed to St. Michael, the patron saint of soldiers and Mike's namesake. Before leaving, she stopped at the small chapel to the left of the altar. She withdrew three nickels from her change purse and deposited them into the slot of the collection box next to numerous votive candles. The sounds of the clanging coins echoed throughout the church. In the silence of the chapel, Helen ignited the long wooden stick from a burning flame and lit three candles. She knelt and prayed that the light of the symbolic candle would bathe Mike in Christ's protection.

Jan 25, 1943 Monday

Dearest Helen,

Today, that is this morning; we went into a gas chamber. The gas chamber was filled with Chloracetophenone which is plain ordinary tear gas.

We went into the chamber with our gas masks on, after we were in there for a while we were told to take off our masks one by one and run out of the chamber. You should have seen us everyone was laughing, and tears were running down our cheeks. Honestly, I laughed till I was blue in the face because everyone was standing outside and crying and laughing at the same time.

After this we had instruction on fixing a splint on broken legs and litter drill. After we fixed the splint, we had to carry the soldier on the litter for about a thousand yards.

In our surgical technician school, we had instructions on injections. How to give hypodermics in the skin, muscles and veins. We were also shown how to make a bed with a patient in it. How to bath a patient and massage him.

Helen, if I remember all I learn here I won't be far from becoming a doctor. Wouldn't that be funny, Doctor Mike? Helen if I was to tell you in detail what subjects we have here I'd have to write a book. I'm not exaggerating either.

Boy, we certainly have a happy bunch of fellows here. We sing every morning when we get up and before going to bed. You know how much I like to sing.

Boy, I wish I could be back there with you on the cold nights sitting in a warm living room with you in my arms. You know I didn't think I had such an imagination until I came into the Army. After this war is over, I'll have the real you in my arms instead of just dreams at the present.

Thanks for all your prayers. You're in mine also.

Loving you with all my heart I remain always yours. Mike

P.S. Boy, I certainly miss you these cold nights, because if I were there with you, I'd have your love to keep me warm. Mike.

The blare of the sirens echoed through the streets. Two long, two short, and two long again. Helen and Flo leapt up from the couch. Helen lowered the volume on the radio and switched off the lights. Flo pulled down the blackout shades. Huddling in the darkness, Helen noticed the dim glow emanating from the radio tubes.

"Mom, see the light? Do you think that'll be a problem?"

"That's why we have blackout curtains. Besides, if it's a problem, the air-raid wardens will knock on our door."

Flo fidgeted. "Did you hear the story about the lady from Mt. Washington who fell down the steps during the last air raid because it was so dark? And she died."

Helen exclaimed, "Oh, no, that's terrible."

Flo continued, "I also read about a man who stopped his car in the Liberty Tunnels and fell asleep waiting for the all-clear signal. He blocked traffic until a screaming man got out of his car and woke him up."

Their mother said, "It seems every time we have an air raid, there's a crazy incident. My lady-friend's husband was downtown during a blackout, and it was so dark he walked right into a telephone pole."

Flo laughed. "Oh, I'm sorry. I guess that's not funny. Hey, at least we're safe at home."

"I just wish they'd signal the all-clear so we can turn the lights on," said Helen. "I want to read Mike's letter."

Jan 28, 1943

Thursday

Dearest Helen,

I'm writing this letter to you from the firing pit. Everyone in our detachment gets a chance to go out to the firing range as a first aid man. Today happened to be my turn. I've only had to treat two men so far and I've been here about nine hours. One for a little cut and the other just to remove a splinter.

Nothing very important has happened this week except an incident that happened to me when I was in the dispensary taking blood tests. I had the job of putting the needle in the finger to draw some blood for the test. Everything went all right until I came to the last man. I put the needle in his finger, but no blood came out. I turned around to get another sterile needle and when I turned around to put the needle in again, he was on the floor. The poor man fainted so the doctor told me to stab him while he was out. I sorta felt sorry for the guy but I did it. The funny thing about it was that it happened so suddenly. One minute he was up and the next he was on the floor.

Another thing is that everyone in our section went out on maneuvers for a night. We set up a first aid station and had hypothetical patients and worked under hypothetical battle conditions. I had the job of carrying a litter. There were three other men with me. We were going along all right when my buddy stepped on a log going across a creek.

His foot slipped and all of us fell in the creek. We got all wet, but what the heck we had fun. The Lieutenant was standing on the side laughing till his sides were about to split. That same night he was crossing the same stream with another Lieutenant, and he fell in, so we had a chance to laugh. Sending you all my love

Always remembering. Never forgetting. Love Mike.

Chapter Thirteen

February 1943

Helen entered the incline sneezing. "Achoo! Achoo!" She deposited the groceries on the seat beside her and removed a clean handkerchief from her purse. Sitting quietly, she closed her eyes until the car halted, and she got out. The winds howled, but her temperature rose with each step she made closer to home.

Trudging through the door, struggling with the bags of food, Helen called out in a hoarse voice, "Flo, can you help me? The groceries are falling out of my hands."

Flo jumped up and caught the bag before it tumbled to the floor. "Helen, you look awful."

"I feel like a truck ran over me. But I'm glad I have the next two days off. I haven't missed a day of work since I first started, and I want to keep that record."

"I don't know why you care if you skip a day or two because you're sick. I've missed a couple of days."

"That's you. I don't like missing work. Right now, though, I just need a glass of hot buttermilk, an aspirin, and a warm bed, but that'll have to wait until after I help fix dinner."

"Why don't you lie down for a while?"

"Thanks, Flo, but I'll be okay. I don't mind making dinner. I'll just go to bed early."

After drying the dinner dishes, Helen excused herself and retreated to her bedroom. She undressed, slipped into her nightgown, and knelt beside her bed. With closed eyes and folded hands, she implored, "Dear God, Blessed Mother, and all the saints, please watch over all of our boys, especially Mike. Please keep him in the States for as long as possible." She began praying the *Our Father,* but before she finished, her head plopped down on the comforter, and, still kneeling, she fell into a soft slumber.

February 2, 1943

Tuesday

Dearest Helen:

Here's hoping you feel better than the last time I heard from you.

We completed our corp. examination today with flying colors. The inspecting officers said "We are the best Med. Detachment in the whole division. That's certainly a compliment. Since we rated so high in the examination our detachment commander gave us half of the afternoon off.

Helen, you know how much I like dogs. Well, a black and white dog came in our barracks the other day, we liked him so much we decided to keep him and make him our mascot. The buddy next to me gave him a bath today. I, myself just came back from the mess hall with a big bone for him. All of the fellows are undecided about his name. Some call him Major, others Medic and still others, Double Time.

You know the dogs must like this barrack. Why? I wouldn't know. The reason I mentioned this is because one of my buddies woke up one day and found two dogs sleeping under his bunk. The guys around here wouldn't part with the dog we have now. Oh, yes, I want to tell you another thing. Every time we drill or go on a hike, we have about four or five dogs following us. One day we had as high as nine with us.

You know Helen when I say I miss you that's not saying enough. Even when I say I love you that's still not saying enough. There are things in my heart that I just can't express in words. It's that certain expression or look I get when I kiss you, the pounding of my heart and increase in temperature when I hold you in my arms and that certain feeling I get when you're with me or near me.

I really hope you understand what I'm trying to tell you. It's just like Einstein's theory. An hour with your best girl seems like a minute and a minute on a hot stove seems like an hour.

Always remembering. Never forgetting. Loving you more than ever. Love Mike.

"Glad you're feeling better, Helen. You looked awful the other day when you left work," said Gabby, as they walked to the post office.

"It's amazing what some rest will do."

"So, what are you sending your fella for Valentine's Day?"

"I didn't know what to get him, so I bought him a lighter, a box of candy, gum, and a special Valentine's card. Did you see those cards for men in the service?"

"No, I didn't."

"This one has red, white, and blue ribbons around a picture of a soldier in a frame on the front that says, '*Happy Valentine's Day to my hero.*'"

"That's sweet. I'm sure Mike will love it."

"Gabby, let me tell you what I did, but don't laugh. I took a photo of Mike and cut his face out and glued it over the one on the card, and I wrote his name below it. I also gave him a poem from a magazine since I'm not good at writing my own."

"Helen, why would I laugh? That's so thoughtful. I know he's going to like the card!"

Gabby pointed toward the street corner. "Hey, isn't that Mike's sister waiting to cross the street."

"It is. Let's go say hi."

Helen tapped Francie on the shoulder. "Hi, Francie, how you doing?"

Francie turned around. "Oh, Helen." Francie's muscles tightened. "Ahh, I'm good. Have you heard from Mike lately?"

"Yes. I just got a letter yesterday."

"Oh, so he's still writing to you?"

"Of course, he is! Why wouldn't he?"

"Oh, nothing. I gotta go. Bye."

Gabby's eyebrows raised, and she looked at Helen. "Why would she ask you if Mike was still writing to you?"

"I don't know. I don't think she likes me, and she says things that aggravate me. Like, when I was at Gert's the other day, she made me feel as if I wasn't good enough for Mike because out of the blue she comes up to me and says she's surprised Mike went out with me since I never graduated high school."

"How rude! What did you say?"

"I didn't say anything. It made me mad, but part of me believes that."

"Why would you think that? You're a good person, Helen, and as smart as anybody else I know. If it was me, I'd tell her to go pound salt."

"I don't want to cause any problems."

"I think people like her need to be put in their place, or they'll just keep doing it. But I think you should mention it to Mike, in case someday you do blow up at her. This way he can't blame you for getting angry."

Helen sighed. "Maybe."

"Anyway, let's not worry about her, and let's get that package off to Mike."

February 13, 1943

Saturday

Dearest Helen,

Helen, it certainly was nice of you to send me that box of chewing gum and the wonderful Valentine. I don't believe you ever forget anyone. I hope I'm deserving of your kindness.

Helen, all of this seems like a dream. I mean this war and everything connected with it. Sons separated from their mothers and family, husbands separated from wives and sweethearts separated from one another. All this doesn't seem possible but that's what has happened. Let's just hope that after this war is over, we'll be back together again. Taking up where we left off and forgetting everything that is happening now.

Every one of us is fighting for the same cause. That is Freedom. The word Freedom covers a lot of territory. To me it means going back home to my loved ones and doing the things I want to do and to say, living our lives as we see fit without interference from everyone. It also means that I could still go on loving you, being with you constantly, going to church on Sundays, walking through the parks and having picnics there. All this and more.

I have some good news for you. I've become a corporal technician. That's all right, isn't it?

When I'm going to come home is very uncertain. It might be next week or even next year. The men are getting furloughs now but as yet haven't heard of mine. So don't place too much hope in my coming home.

Monday of this week was the most beautiful day since I've been here.

That morning our whole detachment was sent out to find most likely places for mosquitoes to breed. You know the mosquitoes here are trained. I pulled the blanket over me when I laid down to go to sleep and they pulled it off again. They're really bothersome creatures.

The other afternoon we started out for our night problem. We set up our tents, ate supper and set out for our night problem about 8:00 PM. The night for the problem was beautiful. The moon was shining brightly through the trees casting weird life like shadows on the ground. We traveled through the woods slowly and cautiously making the least noise possible.

It was wonderful traveling through the woods with the cool night breeze blowing on your face, the wind whistling through the trees, the rustling of the leaves and the flutter of a bird flying overhead, an occasional hoot of an owl and the howl of a coyote could be heard in the deep silence of the night. I didn't think the night could hold such wonders.

I rather enjoyed traveling through the woods at night listening to the natural sounds of the woods and nothing to disturb you except perhaps the sound of an occasional footfall of your buddies when they happened to step on a twig or some leaves.

This reminded me somewhat of a camping trip, tenting outside and eating your meals in the wide-open spaces. The trees and bushes are beginning to have buds. The feeling of spring is in the air. The numbers of birds are increasing rapidly. I've seen blue birds, red birds, pheasants, crows and chicken hawks flying in and out of the woods each emanating its own distinctive sound. When I sleep out in the field I lie there and gaze up into the sky and weave the stars in a wonderful pattern. With a little imagination you can see a great many things in the stars. Now don't think I'm a stargazer. I hope not.

Boy, it's a pity that all those beautiful nights go to waste. We certainly could use them. Couldn't we? "Those bright moonlight nights out here I wish that you could be here with me."

Before I forget I want to thank you for the delicious box of candy you sent me. When I received the candy, I didn't walk no more than ten feet when I was mobbed by the fellows in the barracks. This happens every time anyone gets anything from home.

Oh, another thing I certainly was surprised to receive those pictures of yourself.

Son of a gun, I enjoyed receiving your pictures better than I did the candy. Honestly you look swell. Yes sir, the same Helen.

Loving you more than ever. I remain always yours Mike

Mike had finally received the long-awaited pictures of Helen and wondered whether time had altered his perception because she appeared exceptionally radiant. Holding the picture, he gazed at her curls resting on the shoulders of a striped, form-fitting dress that called attention to her twenty-inch waist and long, lean legs. He loved the way she pinned back the front locks of her hair, accentuating her eyes and oval face. Her contagious smile leapt from the photo and electrified him.

After absorbing all the features of his gal, he uncovered another picture, and his blood pumped through his veins at torpedo speed. He gawked at Helen posing in a two-piece bathing suit with one hand on her hip and the other behind her head. She had painstakingly cut out the figure of herself and glued it to a piece of black construction paper. Usually shy and reserved, she resembled a top-rate pin-up girl. While fellow soldiers displayed pictures of Betty Grable and Marie McDonald in their footlockers and wallets, Helen wanted Mike to post her photo.

The vision of Helen overshadowed the events of Mike's day. After lights out, he rested on the cot and stared at the photograph under the moonlight shining through the window, until his eyes closed.

Chapter Fourteen

March 1943

Helen closed the umbrella, gave it a few quick shakes, and pushed her way inside Donahoe's. "This umbrella doesn't do much to keep you dry when the wind is blowing so hard," she said.

"I know, my umbrella blew inside-out as I was walking here," complained Johnnie. "It looks like I took a shower in my clothes. But thanks for coming in early. We need to make sure we're ready for all the changes with points and ration stamps."

"Okay. I'll be right back as soon as I punch in."

Helen meandered back to the office and smiled as she read a handwritten note attached to her timecard: "Congratulations on your sixth year with Donahoe's. You're one of our best assets."

Time flew by when she worked at Donohoe's. She couldn't believe it had been six years since she'd started working there. Donohoe's became more of a leisure activity, instead of a job, and had become her second home. Her customers and coworkers shared stories about their families and appreciated Helen's concern for them, and now they had developed into her extended family. Many stopped by the store to chat or give her homemade baked goods. As she hung up her coat and collected her apron, she reflected on her start as a working girl.

It had been a warm morning in March, and Helen arrived fifteen minutes early for her first day at Donahoe's to prove she was punctual and would be an exemplary employee. Young and inexperienced, she had contracted to work forty hours for incline fare. In a few months, if she demonstrated her abilities as a stellar apprentice and diligent worker, they would pay her the usual starting wage. She had anticipated that the job would be manageable, but she prayed to God to help her perform her duties to the manager's satisfaction. She did not want to contend with her mother's wrath if she lost her job. Eager to launch her career, she pushed open the door and greeted her new boss. "Hi, Mister . . ."

Her boss held up his hand. "Hey, stop right there, Helen. No formalities here, just call me Johnnie. As soon as I finish turning the lights on and fetch the money for the cash registers, I'll show you what to do."

Helen patiently stood at attention at the front door without removing her coat or headscarf.

Johnnie walked out of the office. "Okay, Helen, let me show you where you can put your pocketbook and coat, and then I'll introduce you to everyone. I'll ask one of the girls to show you around and how to stock the shelves."

Ann, a seasoned employee, welcomed Helen and showed her the back room, lined with tall stacks of groceries. "First, you need to check the shelves and see what needs stocked, then come back here and one of the boys will carry the boxes out for you. There's a sheet on the desk with the prices of the groceries. Find out what the price is, and mark each item before you put it on the shelf. Rotate all the stock so the newer ones are in the back. Any questions?"

"No, I can do that."

Ann sensed Helen's nervousness. "Helen, I know you'll do a great job. If you're not sure of anything, just come find me, and I'll help you."

"Thanks, Ann."

"Hey, everyone calls me Gabby. I think he introduced me as Ann to sound official."

"Why do they call you Gabby?" Helen asked.

"When I was in school, everyone said I couldn't stop talking. One teacher told me to quit gabbing, and the next thing I know, everyone's calling me Gabby."

Helen laughed. "I can say no one ever said that about me."

"Then it looks like we'll get along fine. We won't be talking over each other. Oh, and grab a rag and keep it with you. They're in a box over there. You'll need to dust the shelves before restocking."

Walking the aisles, Helen created a mental note of the items that were in short supply and asked the box-boy to help her find them. Every speck of dust was obliterated as she passed the rag back and forth before resting new items on the shelves. She double-checked the prices of the groceries, tagged the stock, and, with the precision of a bricklayer, aligned each item. Each shelf reflected her organized, perfectionist touch.

At the end of the day, although exhausted from the rigors of bending and reaching, Helen glided out the door with a kick in her step. Her new job had transformed her from being an uneducated, unappreciated homebody to a vessel of worth, validated by her boss's compliments.

Now, six years later, Helen's list of duties had increased, as well as her self-esteem. She tucked the treasured note in her pocket and walked to the front of the store. "Johnnie, what did you want to tell us about the ration stamps?"

"Gabby's not here yet. As soon as she gets here, I'll go over everything."

"Hi-de-ho, Helen. Ready for a good day?" shouted Gabby as she came in the door.

Helen replied, "Always ready. How'd you stay dry in this downpour?"

"Not sure. Guess I'm just lucky."

After Gabby punched in, Johnnie discussed the procedure for the point system.

"There are a few things you should all know about the additional rationed items. If we don't do it right, the OPA will come after us. Now, canned goods, dried fruit, and frozen items are rationed. I've posted the number of points by each item. Hopefully, the customers will have the required amount ready when they check out. You can double-check the number with the ration list by the register."

Helen said, "That doesn't sound too bad. Anything else we should know?"

"Remember, just like the coffee and sugar stamps, you need to rip them out of the book. You can't take loose stamps. Also, remember there are different values for different-size cans. I don't think it'll be too difficult since each person only gets forty-eight points. There's not too much you can purchase with that amount."

Gabby pushed a pencil behind her ear. "I can handle figuring out the points, but I'll never understand the thought process behind what the government does. Too many regulations. They say it's to ensure the soldiers have enough to eat. That's gobbledygook. I think it's about control. It's wacky how they asked everybody to register the number of canned goods they had at home and made them subtract points if they were over the limit."

Johnnie said, "It was to stop people from hoarding food."

"I guess so, but are they going to send the big honchos into your house to count your cans? They should figure out how to win this war, instead of worrying about what's on people's shelves."

"Yeah, it is silly," replied Helen. "I guess they're just hoping everyone is honest."

"Did you tell them how much food you had?" asked Gabby.

"I didn't register," Helen said. "My mom took care of that."

"I have to be honest. I registered and didn't tell them I have five more cans than I should have. What they don't know can't hurt them. Besides, if there's one thing I learned, figure out what the government wants you to do and wait a few days, and it'll change. Things will be different again when meat and cheese rationing starts."

Johnnie replied, "Well, let's see what happens now. Here come a few customers."

March 15, 1943

Dearest Helen

The point system of rationing will make you somewhat of a mathematician, won't it? It isn't very easy to understand I'll tell you that.

It certainly is nice to receive your sugar reports (letters). Especially on a day like to today when it's raining outside. Rationing of food goes on back home but the army feeds us well. For instance:

We have blankets (pancakes) for breakfast, punk and dog-fat (bread and butter), cat beer (milk), sweeting compound (sugar), strawberries (prunes), java (coffee), sand (salt) and specks (pepper) and Irish grapes (potatoes). Then you'll hear some fellows ask for blood (ketchup). Dinner we usually have kennel rations (meat loaf and hash), Irish grapes, swamp seed (rice), punk and dog fat, java and dessert and china berries (peas).

When we come off our hikes, we usually drink plenty of GI lemonade (water). When we go out at nights, I usually miss my flying time (sleep). I wish I could get more blanket drill (sleep) Besides going out in the field I work one day out of every week in the butcher shop (dispensary). Here's where I see plenty of fellows with chili bowls, (GI haircuts)

Boy, one of these days I'm going to murder the windjammer (bugler) at Jubilee (reveille).

There's one thing that Paris doesn't have and that is gas houses (beer joints). I'm glad of that. The best day I like in the Army is when the eagle flies (payday).

We call our cooks slum burners and belly robbers.

This letter doesn't have much sugar attached to it, but you'll find out what's cookin later.

As always Love Mike

PS Helen all this is Army slang. I'm still waiting for my homing device (furlough).

Chapter Fifteen

Summer 1943

June 20, 1943 Camp Gruber, Oklahoma

Sunday

Dearest Helen:

It feels good to be able to sit down and write you a few lines. Haven't had much time to myself here at Camp Gruber since I arrived. I'm in charge of quarters today in the dispensary. Don't have very many patients, so have time to write. As soon as I get the rainbow insignia issued to me, I'll send you one. It's really beautiful.

The dispensary was really dirty when I got here. Everyone got together and scrubbed the walls, floors, benches, cleaned instruments, cupboard and shelves and got everything in order. We expect to paint the whole dispensary. After this the place will be neat as a pin. I've been like a washwoman these last few days. Rank doesn't mean anything now since all we have here are non-commissioned. The tap sergeant and even the Lieutenant got down and scrubbed floors. I know I'll never see this again. It's a very rare occasion.

Since we've been down here, we've been living out of barracks bags. We have everything we own in those barracks bags. If you want anything it's most likely to be at the bottom and by the time you get it your bag is a mess. I had to laugh at my buddies trying to find a pair of socks. He finally gave up after about 5 minutes dumped everything out of the bag, found the socks and then dumped everything back in again. Boy, is his bag a mess. I'll certainly be glad when we get our lockers.

In our PX here we have soundies. I believe you know what they are. It's a box built like a radio, you put a dime in the machine and see a small movie short. You actually hear and see them. First one I've seen so far. It really amazed me.

The weather out here is very much cooler than it was in Texas. We are up on a mesa and get lots of cool breezes.

The camp here is built in an oval, not very much of a chance of getting lost. The nearest town is Muskogee, nice little town. Has a population of about 35,000 people. It's 22 miles from camp. It costs 70 cents round trip to get into town. The country here is really beautiful. At least it's better than Texas.

I haven't been doing very much lately. Cleaning everything up. Building walks and getting things in good shape until the new recruits come in. I have a chance to take it easy for a change.

I'll be able to see some USO shows now since there isn't very many of us, but it will be tough when the new recruits come in. The other afternoon, I was working in the Supply Room checking equipment and clothing we will issue to the new recruits. They'll arrive here about the end of July.

When a USO show comes to camp you have to get there a few hours before time to get a seat. There are so many soldiers in the army that you have to wait in line for practically everything, especially if it's free.

So, Gert had another baby girl. If you remember I told you Gert's baby would be a girl. You asked me why. I said that, "I just had a hunch." So, you see I was right.

Now since I'm not too busy I have more time to think. I usually sit and think of all the swell times we had together. The army can take a lot of things from you, but they can't take our memories. These are the things that give you hope and the feeling of security. Once the memories are taken from you there isn't much you can rely on.

Helen, I wish I could feel the warmth of your lips on mine and feel the beat of your heart. But for the present only memories exist.

I just hope that after this war is over, we can wake up where we left off and really have some fun. Going to South Park swimming, to some dances, etc. We certainly did have some fun at South Park. We would have had more if I would have known you better.

Always remembering. Never forgetting. Loving you forever Love Mike

July 14, 1943

Wednesday Camp Gruber

Dearest Sweetheart:

Sure is good to hear from you. Glad you liked the pictures I sent you. I just have a few minutes to write so please excuse the short letter. Today is the day of the reactivation of the Rainbow Division. This morning we had a dress parade and Life, Time, Signal Corps, and some other news agencies took moving pictures of us marching and of the program. This afternoon at 4:30 PM we're going to go through the actual program. There will be present 4 generals, 500 Rainbow veterans and a lot of people form Muskogee at the Reactivation Program. Tonight at 9:30 PM we have a champagne hour. There will be fireworks. That is all I know about the program. I will tell you all about it after it's through. They'll be a lot about it in the papers and probably the news in about a little time from now, so you'll be able to read about it.

I'm writing this during the noon hour. I have to get my shoes shined, shave and get cleaned up again for this afternoon.

Thinking of you always. I remain always yours. Love Mike.

Expecting changes in the ration system, Helen arrived early at work to familiarize herself with the updates. The red stamps PQRS were valid through Saturday, July 31, and the blue stamps NPQ were good until August 7. The current #22 coffee sticker could be used for only one pound of coffee. Ordering, stocking of groceries, and cleaning took a back seat to the ever-changing world of rationed commodities of colored stamps, numbers, expiration dates, and points. When almost everyone understood the system, the OPA changed the rules, altered the magic number required, or retired a book, a number, or a color. Helen, forced to handle these government-induced obstacles daily, became an expert in the guidelines—unlike her customers, who always seemed perplexed and handed her expired stamps or the wrong color. She wondered if they feigned confusion as a ploy to deceive her to get an additional supply of allotted food. With the new regulations cemented in her mind, she exited the office, prepared to start her duties.

Johnnie approached her. "Happy Birthday," he said.

"Thanks, Johnnie. You remembered?"

"Of course! You doing anything special?"

"Me and my sister Flo are going to see the free band concert in Schenley Park this weekend. The weather should be good, so I'm looking forward to it."

"That sounds swell. You doing anything else?"

"Some of the gang wants to go swimming, but I'm not sure yet."

"Did Mike send you anything special for your birthday?"

"Not yet, but you know this mail system. It takes forever to get anything."

"Maybe you'll have a surprise when you get home."

"That'd be nice!" Helen said with a smile.

July 23, 1943

Friday

Dearest Helen:

Received both of your letters. I'm on CO again today so I'm writing to you from the Dispensary, giving typhoid and tetanus shots.

We finished our basic examinations yesterday. They were chemical warfare, military sanitation and courtesy, map and compass reading, scouting, and patrolling and physical education. Did well so far but there's more to come.

Thanks a lot for those wonderful cards you sent me. You're really on the beam, as the army would say.

I would have written sooner but I've been kept quite busy. We get up at 4:30 AM and don't quit work sometimes till about 9:30 or 10:00 o'clock. The temperature here is between 106 degrees and 100 degrees. I'm sweating to beat the band now while I'm writing this letter. Just about when it gets cool enough to sleep, we have to get up. That's life for you.

Helen, I know your birthday is this month, but I won't be able to send you anything. The little money I had I lent to a buddy of mine who went home on an emergency furlough. I hope you'll understand. I'll try to make it up to you later.

We'll certainly be a rugged crew by the time the fillers come in. Fillers are what we call recruits or replacements. Some more army talk.

They certainly did give the Rainbow Division a write up in the clipping I sent you, didn't they?

I'm sorry I have to close. There are some patients coming in now. Always yours. Love Mike.

"Hey, Flo, do you want to go shopping with me? Mike's birthday is coming up, and I want to buy him something."

"Sure, I guess so. Where you going?"

"I don't know. Thought I'd browse through the shops up the street and see what I can find. You have any ideas?"

"No. They give the soldiers everything they need, and it's not like they have spare time."

"I know. That's why I need some help."

Helen and Flo walked the few short blocks to Carson Street. As they passed each store, they tried to decide whether something special was inside to present to Mike.

"Hey, Flo, there's Del's candy shop. I bet Mike would enjoy a little chocolate candy?"

"Maybe, but it might melt in this heat."

"Yeah, you're right. What about cigarettes?"

"I guess that's okay."

Flo and Helen played the "What do you think?" game as they strolled by several stores. Suddenly, Helen spied a sign in the window that read, "Get your pictures developed here!"

"Flo, Mike loves taking pictures, so I'll buy him a few rolls of film."

"That's a great idea. You should tell him to ask someone to take pictures of him and his barracks and send them back to you."

"Let's go get the film, and what do you say we stop for a Coca Cola before going home?"

"Sure. That'd be a treat!"

August 9, 1943

Monday

Dearest Helen:

Yep, it's Mike. You're probably saying it's about time.

There are only a few of us here now and we have to do all the work. KP, Guard, CO and a lot of other details. The medics have received rifles now. This will only be for a few weeks. That is till they learn all the parts and how to shoot it fairly well. Our general said he will not be satisfied until everyman in his outfit knows how to swim, shoot, and drive a truck. Just a few days ago several hundred men completed their training as swimming instructors. In a few weeks we're supposed to take some driving lessons. I just hope they don't change their mind. I surely would like to drive a truck.

The pools in Muskogee have been restricted for soldiers. There is an epidemic of Infantile paralysis. Although the pools are closed in Muskogee, I'll still have a chance to swim. The camp has opened their training lake for swimming today. I'm going there at 3 o'clock this afternoon. I think it's going to be better than swimming in a pool.

Tomorrow we're going to be firing on the rifle range. The first day with 22's for preliminaries and Tuesday for records with the M1 rifle. I'm really going to enjoy this. Do you remember how you tried to shoot the 22 rifles up in Molders? Wasn't so easy was it. Well just imagine firing a heavier rifle with a 30-caliber bullet. You have to hold the rifle tight, or it will bounce back to your shoulder and not too easy, either.

Went to USO dance yesterday. Boy, I really had a swell time. The people are certainly friendly here. During the dancing they have a lot of different games, so you get better acquainted with the girls. After working all week, practically all-night, it certainly does one good to go into town and see something besides the barracks. In town you can see a show, go to a dance at least.

You know it actually rained here for five minutes the other day. If I would have been sweating a little more that day, I doubt whether I would have noticed it.

Glancing at the paper I find it looks a little brighter in the future then it did before. We shouldn't be too optimistic because we'll be open for a few disappointments. I just hope it won't be long till we see the conclusion of this war.

Always remembering. Never forgetting. Loving you forever Love Mike

Relaxing in the backyard under the hot August sun, Helen read Mike's letter and grew agitated, thinking about him and the girls at the USO.

Her mother took a sip of lemonade. "So, anything new with Michael?"

Fearing her mother would add her usual dose of salt to Helen's burning wounds, she omitted the details.

"Oh, just the usual training. Why?"

"Just wondering. It's such a warm day, why don't you get Flo and the cards, and we'll play gin rummy."

"Okay, sure."

Helen slid the letter into her pocket, relieved her mother hadn't pressed the issue.

August 19, 1943

Thursday

Dearest Helen:

Received your letter and birthday card. I just had to write and thank you for the very wonderful gifts you sent me. Thanks a million for remembering. You know I feel kind of guilty. I still haven't sent you anything for your birthday. I'm certainly getting forgetful and careless. This makes me feel like a heel. You'll have to forgive me.

Tuesday, I went out on the range to fire for record. I was shooting well over expert until I had 8 shots to fire in a rapid prone position. I was leading the Medical Detachment until those 8 shots.

Wednesday we still had 8 more shots to shoot. This was at 500 yards. Slow fire prone position I made 6 bulls-eye and 2 4's. That's 38 points out of a possible 40. I ended up with 177 points, three points more and I would have made expert rifleman. I did end up as high sharpshooter and second highest score in the detachment. That is so far. We have 10 more men firing today.

That same day, in the afternoon we had rifle inspection. That's the last of it. We won't be using rifles anymore. At least for a while. I certainly do hate to part with it. Somehow, I wish I had one of my own. They're certainly beauts. The weather here is hot again. No luck of it staying as cool as it was those several days

As ever. Love Mike.

September 6, 1943

Monday

Dearest Helen:

We received several thousand recruits in our division. I really do get a kick out of them. The other day one of them saluted me. All they're supposed to salute is officers. One of our fellows got lost in camp here yesterday just going to the mess hall about a block away from our barracks. I have been giving these recruits instructions on how to roll a full field pack and display a full pack with all its equipment. Boy, did I get a laugh when the fellows began rolling the packs. They did alright at the beginning but when they got to the end of the roll, they'd release the pressure and the roll with all its equipment would unroll and fly into the air. This reminded me of the time I first got into the army. I had the same trouble, that's why it seemed so funny to me.

I've had to spend most of my nights preparing lectures for the next day. I've been part of a problem put on by the infantry. Our detachment acted as the enemy. The purpose of the problem was to teach the infantry how to react under very difficult conditions. Another reason was to teach the men how to react as individuals and as separate squads.

I'm on CO today so I'm writing to you during one of my breathing spells. Just finished treating several fellows. Two with sinus trouble, one a lacerated finger with possible fracture. Another one wanted a laxative. Since these recruits have come in this CO business has become kind of rough.

We have a fellow here from Norfolk, VA that is really a riot. He tells all his jokes with that southern accent. I just about die laughing whenever I hear him.

Had another softball game last night. This time we lost 8 to 7. Too bad and only by one run. I can't believe softball games interest you. I'll have to take you to one when I get home. I say that as if we were going tomorrow.

Helen, don't think this war is going to be over right away. We've only come half way. You said it'll probably be over in six months. Don't raise your hopes too high. It's better to count on a longer war, then you are not disappointed in the end.

Saturday several of the fellows and I went to the USO dance in Muskogee. Sure did have a swell time. One of the girls invited me up her house for supper. That is for next Sunday. She sure is a nice gal but I just can't make up my mind whether I should go or not. I think I'll have to disappoint her, but a home cooked meal would sure taste good.

I'll bet you're peeved about me not writing more often and going to the USO dances with some of the gals here. You can't expect a guy to sit around in the barracks all the time and just loafing with some of the fellows. If I did that, I'd sure turn out to be a dull fellow. Believe me I've been working, and it does a fellow good to have some fun once in a while. Well, here's till then. Love Mike

Helen placed the letter from Mike on the table and filled the dog dish with leftover food. She yelled to her mother in the parlor, "I'll be in the yard if you need me."

She elbowed open the wooden screen door, laid the dog's food by the fence, and slouched onto the bench next to Flo.

Flo asked, "What's the matter with you?"

"Nothing. I was just thinking about what Mike wrote."

"What did he say?"

Helen petted the dog. "Flo, I have to tell you, this is about the fourth time Mike mentioned dancing with women at the USO. I didn't really say anything about it before, but now he wrote about a woman who asked him to dinner at her house. Then he asks me if I'm peeved about him going. I am peeved! Am I wrong?"

"What do you mean?"

"I mean, I stay at home and don't go out because I don't want to dance with just any man. I want to be with Mike, and he's out flirting with strange women. I know I shouldn't be mad at him, but it irks me a little."

Flo fanned herself with a magazine. "How do you know he's flirting?"

"He's surrounded by beautiful women, and he's always dancing with them."

"Helen, I can understand why you might think that, but it's just a dance. He needs some fun."

"I know he needs to relax. I'm just saying I really miss him, and I can't help but wonder if he likes them more than me. I still don't have an engagement ring, and you know what Mom says. If you don't have a ring, the man can do whatever he wants."

"Mom says that, but Mike is different. He's always gushing after you and telling you how much he loves you. What happens at the USO is just innocent fun."

"Oh, that's not what Francie said. She said they're all floozies, tempting the men to do things."

"Well, I'm sure some men are tempted, but the girls aren't allowed to leave with any of them."

"How do you know?"

"Well, you know Stella?" Flo asked. "Well, she was telling me about her cousin who lives near a base. She's one of the girls who dances with the men, and they have strict rules about how to act. They're not allowed to date any of the men they meet at the USO. Her cousin cuts the rug with so many men, she can't remember any of them. They go from one guy to the next, so the men all have a chance to get a break from all the training."

"That makes me feel a little better. What about Bern? Does he go to the USO dances?"

"He's never said anything about it, but I'm sure he does. They all do. Whatta you say we head downtown? The stores are open late tonight. Finding a good bargain in Gimble's basement will take your mind off this."

"Sounds good. Let's go change first."

Chapter Sixteen

Beginning of May 1944

Helen hurriedly pushed through the back door of her house, soaking wet from the rain.

Her mother shouted, "Wait there while I grab a towel. I don't want you dripping water all over the kitchen floor. What happened to your umbrella?"

"I left it at the theater," Helen said. "The weather was so nice when I left, I forgot I brought one. I was halfway home when it started to pour."

"You should be happy it's warm for May. Otherwise, you'd catch yourself a deadly cold."

"Oh, look, it stopped raining. If I knew it'd be that quick, me and Gabby could've waited in a doorway."

"Well, you never know. How was the movie?"

"We saw *Chip Off the Old Block*. I thought it was funny. Where's Flo?"

"At Gert's. Stan's working late, and Gert's not feeling well, so Flo went over to watch Mary Ann and Dolores."

"What's wrong? Is it anything serious?"

"Her stomach is upset. She was throwing up all day."

Helen rubbed the towel over her hair. "Oh, I hope she feels better."

"I'm sure she'll be fine. It's good Dolores isn't walking yet. It makes taking care of the kids a lot easier."

"I'm sure she'll be walking soon. Can you believe she'll be one next month, and Mike has never even seen her? Whenever he does come home, he'll be surprised at how big Mary Ann has gotten, too. Anyway, I'm going to get out of these wet clothes."

"The *Burns and Allen* show is starting in a few minutes. Do you want to listen to it?" her mother asked.

"Sure, I'll be right down."

The radio emitted a doorbell buzzing sound, and the distinctive high-pitched voice of Gracie Allen shouted, "Oh, George. We have company."

Helen walked into the parlor. "Do you want anything before I sit down?" she asked her parents.

"Shh, the show's starting," her mother admonished.

The family was laughing at Gracie's dimwittedness in the radio skit when Helen heard a noise.

"Mom, did you hear that?"

"Shh, I want to listen to the radio."

Helen averted her attention away from the radio and listened to the sounds in the kitchen. Tap, silence, tap tap, tap, tap, pause, and two more quick taps. *That's Mike's signature knock.* When she heard it again, she raced to the back door. With a clammy hand, she reached for the handle and flung open the door. Mike stood silhouetted in the doorway, preceded by the familiar scent of old spice and tobacco. Speechless, Helen stared at him, his face the same, striking and keen. His eyes were bluer than she remembered but somehow appeared older.

He extended his calloused hand, holding a dozen yellow roses. "Hey, darling, remember me?"

Her tears began to flow, and she squealed, "Oh, Mike . . . Mike . . . I can't believe it's you!"

He pushed the flowers closer to her. "Are you going to take these?"

"Oh, of course, darling. Thank you."

She fumbled for the flowers and shifted around to place them on the sink, but she couldn't stop blubbering and sobbing. "Oh . . . Mike . . . Ahh, ohh I . . . "

Before Helen could pivot back around to greet him properly, he reached over her shoulder, seized her arm, and spun her into an embrace. Her lips and breath resurrected him from the desolate rigors and loneliness of army life. Helen, who had been drowning in his absence, received a lifeline back to shore in the form of her man.

Her father walked into the kitchen. "*Witamy z powrotem, Mickel,*" he said.

Startled, Helen pulled back, afraid her father might comment on their affection.

Mike, trying to catch his breath, uttered, "Thanks. It's good to be back in Pittsburgh."

Helen wiped her eyes, took a couple of steps backward, and stared at Mike. "Pop, doesn't he look swell in his uniform?"

Her father smiled and nodded in agreement.

"I can't believe I'm saying this, but the army has improved you. You look . . . distinguished and older," Helen said.

"Oh, so you say. I hope people don't say I robbed the cradle."

She raised her eyebrows and cocked her head.

"Get it? I'm a year younger than you, but now that I look older, people might think you're too young for me."

"Oh, still corny as ever. I can see the army hasn't changed you."

"See, I've been writing all along that I haven't changed. Helen, we have so much to catch up with. Do you know how long it's been since we've seen each other?"

She whimpered, "I do. It's been a year and seven months, but it seems like a lifetime."

"I told you I'd be home as soon as I could. I tried to get a furlough, but this damn army only gave me twenty-four- and forty-eight-hour passes. Not enough time for a train ride home and back. I'm just glad I'm here now. Being with you is like breathing in pure oxygen, and I know what that feels like because I've done it."

Helen gushed, "I don't know what to say. There's so much to tell you. I just can't think."

"Why don't we go for a walk?" Mike asked.

"I'd love to. Just let me take care of these flowers."

Her mother walked into the kitchen. "Michael, it's been a long time," she said. "How are you getting along?"

"Now that I'm here, I couldn't be better."

"How long are you here for?"

"I'm here a week, and I plan to make good use of every second."

"Is the army treating you well?"

"Couldn't be better. I'm lucky I'm still stateside."

"Do you know when you might go overseas?"

"It's day by day. When we moved from Camp Maxey to Camp Gruber, they told us the day before, and we moved out."

"Well, we're all praying for you."

"Thanks!"

"Mike, I'm ready to go now," called Helen.

Holding hands, they sauntered along the streets of South Side. She relaxed, able to relay her thoughts in person, instead of through awkward correspondence. The conversation volleyed like a fast-paced tennis match as they shared the events of the last year and a half.

Helen stopped to tighten the strap on her shoe. "Oh, my, I think we walked a couple of miles and haven't stopped talking. I'm so happy to see you and talk to you face-to-face. It's so hard to write letters; it's not like a real conversation. I never know what to say, but when you're with me, I can't stop talking."

"Well, don't let me stop you," Mike said. "I want you to tell me everything you didn't say in your letters."

"You have no idea how much I missed you. I tried to be strong and go on like life is normal, but I thought about you every day, how you were doing, and I worried about you going overseas. My mother kept telling me to stop thinking about you and that I'm weak because I want to be with you."

"That's nonsense. You're only human, and it means you love me. Nothing wrong with that. I don't want you to worry about me, but I'm happy you're still the old Helen I fell in love with."

"What do you mean?"

"I mean, you're the sweetest, most loving person I know, and I'm glad you're mine. Helen, I'm a man, and my heart's ached since I've been away from you. I think about you when I wake up and when I go to bed and every in-between. Thinking about someone doesn't make you weak. It means you care."

"So, you don't think I'm silly for missing you so much?"

"Not at all. I'd be worried if you didn't. I've missed you like the dickens."

"I've never missed anyone more in my life, and I'm so happy you're here and safe. I love you, Mike."

"I couldn't love you more, darling."

As they ducked down the alley off the main street, Mike pulled Helen close to him and brushed his lips against hers. Instantly, the yoke she'd carried since Mike went away fell from her shoulders, but she couldn't ignore her thoughts about the USO girls.

"Mike, I need to ask you something. You've been doing so many things like going to USO dances and— "

Anticipating her question, Mike interjected, "Helen, if you're worried about the girls at the dances, don't be. Those girls mean nothing. I'll never see them again. They're just a temporary distraction. We dance a little and go back to our barracks. You're the only one for me, and I've never seen another woman more attractive than you. You're the one I want."

"Oh, it feels so good to hear you say that. I do believe you love me, but my mom keeps telling me if I don't have an engagement ring, you're not serious."

"Helen, I don't mean to be disrespectful to your mother, but she can't assume. A ring is a symbol of my dedication to you, but I can be committed to you without a ring. You have my word."

"I know, Mike, and I'm committed to you also, but you know how opinionated my mother can be."

"Helen, we probably would've been engaged and married already if it wasn't for this war. It's just a little detour. Don't worry."

"Thanks, Mike. I know that. I think I just needed to hear it from you. Some members of my family seem to think you're not serious about marrying me. Sometimes they're so negative."

"What they say doesn't matter. It's what I tell you from my heart. Right now, I promise to make this the best couple of days you've had in a while, and hopefully it holds us till I return."

When they arrived back at her house, they sat on the stoop under the streetlight. Helen shivered, and Mike removed his army coat and positioned it gently around her shoulders. Pulling the lapel to her nose, Helen inhaled his scent and snuggled closer to him.

"Thanks for sharing your coat."

"No problem. I don't want my sweetie getting sick."

"I don't know what I'd do without you."

"Hopefully, you'll never have to find out. Helen, I know you're working tomorrow. So, while you're at work, I'm going to visit with my family. I'll meet you after work, and we can do something then."

"I'm sorry I need to work. If I'd known you were coming home, I'd have requested a couple of vacation days."

"That's okay, I wanted to surprise you. Besides, I have some important things to do. Don't worry," he said. "We'll have a grand time."

Mike arrived at Donahoe's at lunchtime. As he rushed through the door, he collided with Johnnie, who was leaving the store.

"Whoa, Mike, you sure do make an entrance, you old fella. It's good to see you," said Johnnie, patting Mike on the back. "Helen told us you nearly gave her a heart attack when she saw you last night."

"She certainly was surprised."

"I gotta say, you look exceptional in your uniform."

"You can thank Uncle Sam for that."

"Hey, I'm headed to the bank, but I'll be back in a jiff. Are you gonna stick around a while?"

"Yeah, I wanted to say hi to the gang. But can I talk to you outside for a minute before you go to the bank?"

"Sure, what's cookin'?"

Standing on the sidewalk, Mike asked, "Do you think Helen could leave early? I have something special planned."

"I bet you do. I don't think that'll be a problem."

"Thanks, Johnnie! You're a pal."

"You know we all love Helen, and she hasn't seen you in ages. I'd be glad to help you two out."

Mike walked into the store and approached Gabby at the cash register. "Hey, Gabby, how you doin'?"

"I'm doing great," Gabby said. "Come here and let me give you a hug!" She hugged him. "Looks like you lost weight."

"Yeah, I think it happened when the cook lost some dough in a poker game. He didn't have bread for a while."

Gabby laughed, as Helen walked toward the register.

"So, what's so funny?"

"Oh, Mike's up to his old tricks again."

"I should have guessed."

Gabby pointed at Helen. "See that smile? She's been like that since she walked in this morning. You sure made her happy. I told her she should've said she was sick to spend additional time with you, but she said she couldn't do that."

"Yeah, good old honest Helen."

Helen asked, "Mike, what're you doing here anyway? I still have half a day of work to go."

"I know. I thought I'd stick around a while and see how everyone's doing."

While Mike made his rounds, Johnnie walked over to Helen, who was loading the pickle barrel with fresh pickles. "Helen, since Mike is here, why don't you leave early? It'll give you two lovebirds extra time with each other."

Gabby, passing by on her way to the restroom, overheard the conversation. "Johnnie, I was supposed to be off for the next two days. What do you say you give Helen the rest of the week off, and I'll work for her?"

"If you want to work, it's fine with me," Johnnie said.

"Oh, you're all so great. Are you sure?" Helen asked.

Johnnie pushed gently at Helen's back. "Yeah, now get outta here."

"Enjoy your time with Mike, and don't do anything I wouldn't do!" joked Gabby.

Walking out the door, Mike said, "It's such a gorgeous spring day, it seems like summer. Would you like to go to Schenley Park for a while?"

"I'll do anything as long as I can spend time with you, honey. By the way, Gert called last night while we were out and told my mom she wanted to have everyone over for dinner."

"What time is dinner?"

"Six-thirty."

"That's great. We'll have plenty of time to be by ourselves and still make it to dinner."

Walking through Schenley Park, they decided to visit Phipps Conservatory and see the spring flower show. The scent of hundreds of fragrant blooms and the variety of colors bursting around them awakened their senses. Soft, flutelike organ music pulsated in the air, creating the perfect romantic atmosphere as they strolled the winding paths.

As they circled back to the entrance, Mike said, "We still have some time. Let's sit for a while and relax."

Helen sat on a wooden bench. "You know, this is one of my favorite places? The flowers are so beautiful."

"They are, but you're more beautiful than all the flowers put together," Mike said.

Helen giggled. "Oh, stop that."

"No, I mean it. You're a breath of fresh air for me. But there's only one thing that would make you sparkle even more."

"What's that?" Helen asked.

"A diamond ring."

Helen gasped, and her eyes bulged. "Oh, Mike."

"Helen, you've known for a long time that I love you, and we talked about getting married. This time I mean it. Helen, will you do me the honor of being my wife, the mother of our children, and making me the happiest, luckiest man on earth? I want you to know you are and always will be the only woman for me."

She opened her mouth to answer a resounding yes, but her lips froze. She nodded her head, and as Mike stroked her hair and inched toward her lips, Helen blubbered, "Yes . . . yes! You know I'll marry you. I love you!"

They peered into each other's eyes until Mike kissed her. Her blood coursed through her veins, flushing her body with warmth. She melted into his arms.

When they slid apart from their embrace, he gently brushed back her hair. "I've wanted to ask you to marry me since our first official date. I'm sorry you had to wait so long, but I finally saved enough money for a ring. I had them put a few aside at Kaufmann's. That's what I was doing this morning. We can go today to see which one you like."

Helen rested her head on his shoulder. "I'm sure I'll like whatever you picked out, darling. We've been talking about this for so long. I can't believe we're getting engaged. My heart is still pounding."

"Well, you told me in your letters you hardly have any excitement in your life. So, I'm giving you some."

"You sure know how to do it. My family's going to be so happy."

"I hope so. I'm gonna be as nervous as a church mouse in an organ when I ask your mother for her blessing."

"Oh, Mike, you shouldn't be worried, she'll give us her blessing. She's been asking about you giving me an engagement ring for a long time. She's always liked you."

"I hope I'm able to ask her without stepping on my tongue."

Helen slowly brushed his cheek. "You'll be fine, Mike."

He stood, grasped her hand, and pulled her to her feet. "I hate to rush things, but we need to get you that ring. I don't want you waiting one more minute."

They arrived back at her house, and her mother looked at them in surprise. "Aren't you supposed to be working?" she asked Helen. "Are you sick?"

"No. Mike came by the store, and Johnnie let me leave early. He gave me tomorrow off, too, so I can spend time with Mike."

"Well, I can't believe he did that. Now you lost some pay."

An uncomfortable silence lingered until Mike said anxiously, "Uh, Mrs. Cypyrch, another reason Helen is home early is I officially asked her to marry me, and she said yes. Now I'm asking for your blessing before I give her the ring."

Mary put her hands on Mike's shoulders and looked him squarely in the eyes. "Yes, you have her father's and my blessing, and I have to say, it's about time. Congratulations!"

Helen hugged her mother and breathed an exuberant, "Thanks."

Flo walked in from the backyard, holding a bushel of dry clothes from the clothesline. "What's going on?" she asked.

Helen gushed, "Mike and I are engaged, and Mom gave us her blessing."

Flo dropped the laundry basket and hugged Helen and Mike tightly. "Congratulations! Let me see the ring."

"We're going to get it now. Mike picked it out earlier."

"Well, what are you waiting for? Go get it!"

When Mike and Helen arrived back at her house, she found a note on the kitchen table. After reading it, she said, "Looks like Flo and my mom went next door to Marie's. At least for a little while, it's just you and me."

"I'm glad no one is here. I wanted this to be our private moment together." Mike took her hand, led her into the parlor, and asked her to sit down. Reaching into his pocket, he extracted the box with a gold ring accented by two unassuming diamonds on either side of a larger diamond. Dropping to one knee, he pleaded for her love and commitment and slid the band of love on her third finger. Although modest, the diamonds sparkled as the sunlight shining through the transom window bounced off the ring's facets.

With a hundred-watt smile illuminating the room, Helen stared at the ring, twisted it, and watched it dance and glisten in the light. She kissed Mike as if her life depended on it and said, "I love you, and I promise I'll always love you and be a good wife to you."

"I know you will. Sweetheart, do you mind if we kneel before the Blessed Mother and say a prayer? I want to ask for a blessing for us and our future and that we can be dutiful parents when the time comes."

"Oh, honey, I can't think of a better way to start our life together."

They clasped hands and knelt before the statue that maintained a permanent presence in the parlor. Their mediation ended when the back door swung open to the booming voices of Helen's family.

"Helen, are you here?" bellowed her mother.

Rising from the floor, Mike and Helen answered, "We're in here."

She extended her hand with the ring as her mother walked into the parlor. "Look, Mom," she exclaimed, "it's official! Do you like it?"

Mary responded, "He did good."

Flo and Marie shoved their way forward to inspect Helen's newly decorated finger. They offered oohs and aahhs and hugs for both Helen and Mike. As the congratulations continued, the girls' father walked into the parlor and asked, "Why all excited?"

"Mike asked me to marry him, and Mom gave us your blessing." Helen lifted her hand in front of her father's face. "Look, here's the ring."

Her father nodded. "This is good. This is good," he said and gave her a peck on the cheek and a hug. He extended his hand to Mike. "You a good man. I know you take care of her."

Chapter Seventeen

Helen hopped off the incline, glancing at her engagement ring. As she turned the corner, she crashed into Adam's brother.

"Oh, Carl, I'm so sorry. I was daydreaming and wasn't watching where I was going. How are you? I haven't seen you in a month of Sundays."

"I'm fine, and I'm glad you ran into me. I saw Johnnie. Is it true what I heard?" Carl asked. "That you're engaged to Mike?"

"Yes, he gave me a ring when he was home on furlough a few weeks ago."

"I'm confused," Carl said. "Adam told us he gave you an engagement ring."

"He did. I promised to keep it till he came back. But I never said I'd marry him."

Carl looked perplexed. "Adam told us that you agreed to marry him after the war. He boasts about it in the letters he sends us."

"I'm sorry he told you that because it's not true," Helen said. "I never wore his ring, and I never promised to marry him."

Carl threw up his arms and groaned. "But Adam told us he loved you, and you were engaged to each other!"

Helen's face grew red, as she surveyed the street to see if anyone was watching. "I told him I was waiting for Mike, and I only agreed to hold onto the ring. I don't understand why he didn't tell you the whole story. Everyone knows I'm in love with Mike and committed to him."

"Helen, how was I supposed to know? I haven't seen you since you stopped at the funeral home when my brother passed. We didn't talk that day, so all I could rely on was what Adam told us. Then I learned about your news from Johnnie!"

Helen slowly backed away. "I'm sorry Adam lied to you, but don't get mad at me."

Carl pivoted abruptly, walked away from Helen, and just as quickly swung back around. "I don't know what to say, Helen. We were thrilled, you were going to be part of the family. How could you do this?"

She scowled. "I didn't do anything. I promised to keep the ring till he got back, nothing more. He can have it back if he wants. Adam's a good man, but I'm engaged to Mike. Carl, I'm sorry for any misunderstanding. I still think of Adam as a friend, and I pray for him all the time."

Carl bellowed as he darted away, "I just pray he never finds out till the war is over!"

Helen's pace quickened in sync with her agitation, as she ruminated about Adam's lies. *Why did he do that? I thought I was clear. Ughhhh.*

After work, she rushed home and burst through the back door. "Mom, Mom. I need to tell you something! Where are you?"

"Quit yelling, I'm in the basement. I'll be right up," her mother called up the stairs.

As Helen slipped her shoes off, the phone rang.

"Hello?" she answered.

"Helen . . . it's Carl . . . I need to talk to you."

"Carl, if this is about my engagement, I—"

"No . . . no . . . that's not why I called. I wanted to let you know we . . . we were notified that . . . ahh . . . my . . . that Adam is dead."

Helen gasped and dropped the phone. "Oh my God . . . "

"Helen, Helen, are you still there?"

"Oh, Carl . . . I'm so sorry."

Her mother raced into the parlor when she heard Helen weeping. "Helen, what's wrong? Who's on the phone?"

"Excuse me, Carl." Lowering the phone, Helen whimpered, "Adam is dead."

Her mother laid her hand on Helen's shoulder and slowly shook her head from side to side. "May God be with him," she said quietly.

As Helen raised the phone back to her ear, she a heard an elderly nasal voice on the other end, "Hello, Hello. I need to make a phone call."

Helen asked, "Is this Mrs. Smith?"

"Yes, I need to make a phone call."

"Mrs. Smith, I can't get off the phone right now, this is a very important call. I just found out that a good friend of mine died."

Mrs. Smith sighed. "Oh, I'm so sorry. You have my condolences. I'll try again later."

"Carl," Helen moaned, "I'm so sorry. It seems every time I get on the phone, someone else needs to make a call. These stupid party lines! I'm sorry."

"It's okay."

"Carl, when did he die? What happened?"

"My mom got the telegram about an hour before I got home. It said that he died June 2nd, and it was non–battle related."

"Do you know what happened exactly? What does it mean, non–battle related?"

"We're not sure. He could've been sick or in a car accident or, or . . . who knows what. It doesn't say much in the letter they gave her. We're really frustrated that we don't have any answers. We're all in a daze right now."

Helen wiped her eyes. "How are your parents doing?"

"My mom can't stop crying, she's hysterical. We called the doctor to see if he can do anything for her."

"I'm sorry to hear that. Is there any way I can help you or your family?"

"Not right now. Until the army sends more details, there's not much we can do. I know he loved you, and he told me before he left that if anything happened to him, he wanted me to tell you personally."

Helen's cries grew louder. As she tried to calm herself, she stammered, "I'm picturing him the last time I saw him and how happy he looked when he left my house. And now, he's gone. It's sad, and my heart aches for you and your family. I'm sorry you found out the truth about me and Adam today. I didn't mean to hurt you or your family, especially now since you're grieving his loss."

"I know, Helen. Actually, knowing the truth makes it better because we know you won't be alone."

"I just hope the truth about Mike and me getting engaged didn't upset him."

Carl's voice grew sharper. "How would he know? Did you write to him about your engagement?"

"Yes."

"Why? And why didn't you tell me earlier?"

"You took off before I could say anything. I wrote to him, so he'd understand that Mike and I are truly committed to each other now. I didn't want him to be surprised whenever he returned."

"When did you send the letter?"

"A couple of weeks ago, right after I got the ring."

Carl groaned. "Oh, Helen, he really believed you two were engaged. You gave him a reason to return! I'm sure he got the letter and read the news. It must have shattered him! Oh, my God, I hope . . . I hope that wasn't the cause. I hope he didn't do something drastic."

"Carl, what do you mean? The cause? Are you saying he . . . he . . . ?"

"Ohhh, I don't know. I can't think right now. Anyway, I just wanted you to find out from me and not read it in the paper. I need to go check on my mother."

"Yes, please go take care of her, she needs you right now. Bye, Carl, I'll pray for your family."

Helen's mother retrieved a handkerchief from her pocket. "Here, dry your eyes. Your father will be home soon, and he'll be upset if he sees you whining. Go upstairs and calm down."

"Mom, first I have to tell you what Carl said."

"I know. Adam died."

"Yes, but Carl said it was non–battle related, and I think Carl was trying to say because I sent him a letter about . . . "

Interrupting her, Mary said, "Shush, I don't want to talk now. I told you. Don't let your father see you sniveling. Now go upstairs and pull yourself together."

Helen sat on her bed, whimpering, lost in thought about Adam and the letter she'd written him. Walking over to the dresser for a new handkerchief, she glanced at the picture of the yellow roses on her dresser that Mike had presented her. Carefully removing it from the mirror, she clutched the picture to her chest and lay down on her bed.

Chapter Eighteen

Summer 1944

Helen was heating the curling iron on the gas burner when Gabby popped through the back door and shouted, "Happy Birthday."

"Thanks, but what time is it? Aren't you a little early? I'm not even done curling my hair."

"Just a little bit. I guess I'm walking faster now that the heat wave is over."

"Oh, I'm so glad it's cooler. I don't think the plants outside could have survived any more ninety-degree days."

"You're not kidding, I didn't think I'd survive!"

Helen finished curling her hair and asked, "Gabby, do you still want to go shopping before the movie?"

"You betcha. Didn't you say you have a ration stamp for a new pair of shoes?"

"Yes, and I can't wait!" Pointing to her feet, she said, "I took these shoes to the shoemaker three times. I'm not sure they can fix them anymore."

"I'd say you're definitely due for a new pair of shoes, kiddo," agreed Gabby.

"Well, I guess we should get going, but I need to find the ration stamp. I'll be down in a minute.

"Hey, Mrs. Cypyrch," Gabby said, as Mary walked into the kitchen. "I haven't seen you since Helen got engaged. Isn't it exciting?"

"Yes, but with this war, who knows when they'll get married?"

"Well, whenever it is, I'm sure it'll be another humdinger Polish wedding. I love all the homemade grub, dancing the polka, and eating the leftovers the next day."

Helen grabbed her purse from the table. "Gabby I'm ready."

"It's been nice chatting, Mrs. Cypyrch. See you later," Gabby said, waving goodbye.

Walking through the long narrow alley between the houses, Gabby asked, "Did you read the newspaper yesterday about how they tried to assassinate Hitler?"

"I did, and it said they think it was his own men."

Gabby cracked her gum. "What does that tell you if his own people want to kill him?"

"I know. They must think he's the devil, too. This may sound cruel, and you know I could never hurt a fly, but if they did kill him, this war would finally be over."

"Helen, I agree with you. Did you know he was meeting with Mussolini? If they succeeded, they could've killed two devils with one bomb. Wouldn't that be something if they got both?"

"I guess. I don't want to think about it."

"You're right, there's a lot better things we could be talking about, like whether you're going to have a summer or a winter wedding!"

"Gabby, you know I can't plan anything until Mike gets back."

"I know, but if you had a choice, what do you prefer?"

Helen opened the door to Wagner's shoe store. "Probably a summer wedding, but I guess we'll talk about it later."

The shop owner rushed toward Helen and Gabby. "I haven't seen you two lately!"

"Well, you know it makes no sense to search for shoes when the powers-that-be tell you that you can only buy two pairs a year," Gabby said with a smirk.

"Yeah, crazy ration system. If it wasn't for the extra allotment of work boots the men are allowed to buy, we'd be out of business."

Gabby popped a piece of gum into her mouth. "I don't think the government thought about how the rations would affect business owners."

The owner replied, "I don't think the government ever thinks. It is what it is; there's nothing we can do about it. Anyway, I'm glad you're here now. So, what are you two looking for today?"

Gabby replied, "Unfortunately, I'm not buying shoes, but Helen is."

"Can I help you find something special, Helen?" asked the storeowner.

"I'm not really sure. Do you mind if I just look around?"

"Sure, take your time."

Helen carefully lifted a pair of black leather shoes with dancer heels and an ankle strap and examined them like an archeologist finding a rare fossil. She turned the shoes around, then upside down, rubbing her fingers across the soft, supple leather and inhaling its earthy smell. As she placed the shoe back next to its mate, the Oxford shoes with a peep toe caught her eye, and she studied them with the same microscopic attention. This ritual continued several more times until she decided to place one of the treasured commodities on her feet. She admired them in the shin-high mirror on the floor. Entertained by trying on a variety of new shoes, Helen had drifted to shoe heaven.

"Did you make up your mind?" shouted Gabby, jolting Helen out of her daydream.

Helen held up a pair of baby doll shoes with a medium heel and a small bow on the front, "Do you like these or the ones on my feet with the Mary Jane front?"

"They're both swell, Helen. What do you like?" Gabby asked.

"Actually, I like the pumps with the peep toe the best, but I won't be able to wear them in the winter. I can't make up my mind."

"Well, I hate to rush you, but if we want to make the matinee, you need to decide," Gabby said.

After some deliberation, Helen announced, "Okay, I'm ready to put my old shoes in a box and wear the new ones." Though she preferred the open-toed shoes, she chose the more practical and comfortable baby doll style.

The clerk took the ration stamp and the shoes from Helen, "So you're planning to see *Going My Way* with Bing Crosby?" she asked.

"Yes, it should be fun."

Gabby added, "I think Bing Crosby is so dreamy."

Helen laughed. "Oh, Gabby, you're so silly. I think it's time to go."

At the streetcar stop Gabby asked, "So how do you like your new shoes?"

"Great!" Helen said, admiring her feet. "I stretched out the other ones so far, they were giving me blisters. I never realized shoes were such a luxury until they started rationing them."

"Yeah, I know. I guess you don't know how good you have it until you don't have it anymore."

Helen sighed. "You can say that again."

July 26, 1944

Wednesday

Was very pleased when I received your letter. Very interesting,

Hon, I'm sorry I couldn't send you anything on your birthday. It really slipped my mind. When I did think about it, I couldn't get out of camp to buy anything. We still have to stay in camp until August 5. I'll send you something then. It may be a little late, but at least it will get there. You know I promised myself I would not forget this time, but I did. Please accept my apology.

I'm still trying to get a pillowslip with the Rainbow on it but no go. I'll still try though.

Tell Gab that I thanked her for showing you such a swell time on your birthday. I only wish I could have been there with you. It would have made us all happy.

How's your hope chest getting along? I'm going to try my darndest to save as much as I can now to start with. I'm still thinking of that little house with the big lawn around it. A small porch in the front with a swing, with the smell of flowers in the air and you there in my arms. Maybe a few small kids running around. Ours of course. Probably two girls and a boy. Me coming home from work and you greeting me at the door with a nice supper waiting on the table. Spending all the time we want to be together. Boy that's the life. I'll have to admit that I'm dreaming now for the future but with the grace of God I'll try to make all of these dreams come true.

I'm really going to try my best so that we can have something. You really deserve the best. I know if it's a little tough you'll stick it through until things get better.

Helen, I love you with all my heart. No one could love you more than I do.

Please take care of yourself. Your future husband (hope it's soon) Love Mike

"Hey, Mom," Helen said. "Gert called and asked me to help her with her victory garden. After I clean the outhouse, I'm gonna go over."

"If you go, you'll miss another meeting at church this afternoon," her mother admonished.

"I know, but Gert needs my help. Just let me know what they need me to do, and I'll do it."

"Okay. See if Gert will give you some extra vegetables to bring home."

"I will. I'll be home for supper," Helen said. "Bye."

Mary Ann greeted Helen at the front door holding a baby doll. "Can you play?" she asked.

Helen lifted her and gave her a big hug and a kiss. "I can't play right now. I'm going to help your mommy with the garden. Are you helping, too?"

Mary Ann shrugged. "I dunno."

"I hope you've been a good girl because I brought you some Chuckles."

Mary Ann grabbed the candy. "Dankoo!" she said.

Helen carried the child into the kitchen.

"Helen, I can't believe you're dressed like that. Dresses are not for gardening!" Gert said. "Go and get a pair of my overhauls. I'll wait till you change."

When Helen returned clad in Gert's overalls, Gert handed her a pair of gloves and a basket. "Thanks for helping me," she said.

"Oh, I don't mind. You know I like being outside."

"So, I found out your future sister-in-law, Francie, sent a gift to Mike for your birthday and told him to send it to you," Gert said.

"Yeah, she did. How'd you know?"

"She wrote Stan and told him."

"Is she announcing to the world she sent me a gift? I don't understand why she sent it to Mike. She could have sent it directly to me. Instead, she sent it to him at the base and then he had to send it to me. I hate to say this, but I think Francie is playing some kind of game. I wrote Mike and told him how strange his sisters act toward me. Maybe he questioned them, and now Francie is doing this to make me look like a liar, showing Mike how nice she is."

Gert harvested the green beans. "I always think she's up to no good."

"She reminds me of one of those lying carnival barkers. Ever since we got engaged, Jo and Francie have acted differently toward me. I was walking down Carson Street last week, and Jo crossed the street just to avoid me."

"Maybe she didn't see you."

Helen brushed dirt from the tomatoes. "I know she saw me. I looked right at her and was getting ready to wave when she crossed the street."

"Can you pass me the basket so I can put these vegetables in it?" Gert asked.

"Sure, here you go. What's even worse is the letter Francie wrote to me. She told me just because Mike is engaged to me doesn't mean he'll marry me when he gets back."

"I can't believe she said that!"

"Are you saying I'm lying?"

"No, I mean I think she's out of her mind."

"Well, listen to this. She also said Mike shouldn't ask his parents to save the money he sends to them for our wedding. Instead, they should be able to use it for what they need, and that Mike's family comes first, not me."

Helen clenched her fists. "Argggh, I'm going to be his family! Why would they say that to me? Did they say anything to you about me?"

"All I know is Francie reminded Stan their parents are not doing well, money-wise, and because Mike isn't married, he shouldn't be sending any money to you."

Helen yanked the weeds forcefully. "So that's why they're mad at me? It's all about the money. It's always about the money. Don't they realize it was Mike's idea to send me money, and I deposit every penny in an account for us? I don't understand why they act this way. I want to say something, but I don't know what to say."

Gert walked over to Helen and deposited the weeds in a bag. "You're better off not saying anything. It'll just make things worse."

"It's hard to understand why they say things like that and act like I'm the enemy. It's bad enough I worry about Mike, but now I have to deal with this. When we get married, do you think they'll change?"

"I hope so, for your sake, Helen. You don't deserve this."

"They're your in-laws, too. How come they treat you okay?" Helen asked.

"Oh, not all the time, but they do seem to be extra hard on you."

"Do you think I did anything wrong? Should I be nicer?"

Gert patted Helen's knee. "You're fine, Helen. I can't explain it. Some people are just born mean."

Helen finished pulling weeds and brushed the dirt off her legs. "I want us to get along. If we can't, I know it'll cause tension between Mike and me."

"Stop letting her bother you. You and Mike love each other. That's what matters. If you let her get under your skin, she might succeed in breaking you up. You can't let her do that to you. I think you need a break. Let's get some water."

July 30, 1944

Sunday

Dearest Helen:

I'm glad to hear you miss your arm-strong heater. I feel the same way. Talking about heaters, you're no cold chicken yourself. Remember how I used to lay my head on your lap? I know I felt as comfortable, and it wasn't hard to fall off to sleep because you felt so nice and warm. Thinking of all these things make me miss you more than ever.

Helen, just forget about Frances and everyone else for that matter. I say forget it, in the respect that we won't let anyone interfere with our happiness. All I'm interested in is you and nobody will have a chance to change my mind. Let's forget about it and talk about more pleasant things. We've agreed on a lot of things, and we'll continue to do so without any one's influence or interference.

Helen, let me know some of your views about married life. What would you like to have in respect to a home etc? I know we've already agreed on children. We both love them so much, so that isn't a problem. I believe we should both make some plans for the future to find out what we'd both like to have. We should use this time to plan something at least.

The going will be tough after this war so that means we'll have to have save a lot so we can have something to start with. Darling I don't care myself how tough it'll be so long as you and I are together. What's your viewpoint?

As I mentioned in my last letter, I've been thinking seriously of getting married on my next furlough. Now don't ask me when my next furlough will be because I'll be darned if I know. So, tell me what you think about it. There are a lot of advantages and disadvantages but it's not too easy to figure out. Just think if I were at home I wouldn't have to be wondering when I'm going to get married. All I'd have to do is set the date with you. Here in the army, you run into complications. You have to worry about a furlough, how long the war will last, whether you can get your job back again and a lot of other things. So, give me your idea, honey.

While I've been writing this letter the song "San Fernando Valley" has been playing over the radio. I don't believe I'll ever forget that song because if you'll remember that song was playing while I was packing up to leave for camp after my furlough.

I still haven't forgotten that I didn't get a gift for your birthday, but I'll see to it that I do get one. You know I've got the darndest memory. Well Helen, now you know one of my weaknesses so be prepared to put up with it. I imagine you'll remind me often enough, so I'll not worry about that. You tell me not to worry about you? Heck, honey that's a little impossible. I'll worry about you till I get home when I can be near you so I can hold you in my arms again. Sorry I have to close. Always in my heart. All my love, Mike.

The National Anthem played on the radio, signaling the end of programming for the day. Helen switched it off. She picked up the *Pittsburgh Press* and tried to read, but her restlessness increased as she perused headlines about the war. Wanting to escape the morose news, she turned to the comic section for her midnight reading. She laughed as she read the comics, especially "Moon Mullins." Her mood lightened, and she relaxed until she read the cartoon depicting two GIs peering into a jewelry store window. A sign posted over engagement rings read, "Only one to a customer," and the sailor said, "What? I want one for every port!"

Helen threw the paper on the table, wondering, *Is this how all men think?*

Mike had vowed his loyalty, but the comic planted a seed of uncertainty in her mind, as had accusations from Mike's family during dinner a few weeks earlier at Gert and Stan's. His sisters commented that army men find the women around the military bases and overseas easy and inviting. Adding a cursory, "Men have needs these women can fulfill. Did you ever think Mike might be collecting his share of the crop?"

Was there any truth to their comments? Helen tapped her hand on the armchair and stared at the floor. Her petri dish of low self-esteem caused the unproved hearsay to grow exponentially. Irritated, she stormed into the kitchen and grabbed a pad of paper and a pen. After writing a few lines, she stopped. Mike always reassured Helen of his love. If she continued, her words might upset Mike, but the taunts from his family had attacked her sensibility. She needed to write him about the gossip and her fears of losing him.

She received the following letter in reply.

August 1, 1944

Darling,

In order to reassure you that women out here don't mean a thing to me or any other place in fact I'll tell you something.

In the army they are always giving lectures on venereal disease. That is syphilis, gonorrhea others. Now don't get shocked if I seem a little forward.

I'll tell you about the two diseases and then what we're told here in the army and then you'll be able to draw your own conclusion.

Both of these diseases you get from having intercourse with an infected woman. Syphilis is the worst. It gets into your blood and causes a great many things like insanity, deformity, heart attack, large open sores, paralysis, lameness or a million other things. You can get this by kissing a girl that has this sore on her lips. The disease starts with a sore on any part of your body. If you have this disease when you marry your wife and children will get it. The children will be born either deaf, dumb, blind, or deformed. The person having the disease may not even know he has it because the symptoms don't show up for several years. . . . They've showed us pictures of babies with their hands eaten away, fellows with big ugly sores on their body, including the lips, tongue, mouth and private parts. The girl may look clean, but you never can tell. I mean even if you kiss her, she might give you the disease. I wish I could tell you more about this. Just think for a minute or two of fun, a fellow loses all the happiness in his life. A person may have the disease and not know it for about ten years then he goes suddenly insane, or he can't walk. Honey, I don't fool around with any women because I want to have some healthy kids. If you'd like to ask any questions, go ahead. I'll be willing to answer them if I can. I wish I could talk these things over with you, but the mail is the only means we use now. So, you see honey why you don't have to worry. I know you're as clean as they come, and I'll be darned if I'll dirty myself just for some pleasure.

I hope I haven't been too frank. I told you this, so you'd be assured a lot more.

I'll have to close now darling.

I love you with all my heart now and always. Mike XXXXX

August 12, 1944

Saturday

Darling,

I'm really feeling up to par and hope you are the same. I was in town today as you can probably see by my enclosing the money order. I also bought you the gift I promised. You'll receive this letter before it arrives so don't let your curiosity get the best of you. I'll tell you it isn't much, but all my love goes with it. I know you'll be surprised. I also bought something for Mary Ann's birthday. It's very unusual, something you couldn't get back home. I hope Mary Ann likes it.

I'm in a very good mood now, even though we're going out on a night problem tonight. However, at every mail call during this week my spirits would drop down a few notches. You know the reason why don't you? Well, let me enlighten you a little on the subject if I may. Well as you know, I've been writing regularly to you as often as I possibly can irregardless of how busy I was. Doing all of this in hopes that you'd do the same. I'm very anxious to hear from you and from your previous letters I gather you felt the same about receiving mine. I became so peeved these past few days I decided not to write till I heard from you but tonight I decided to let you know what I think.

Helen, you've known me for quite some time now and you know that I don't beat around the bush when the occasion arises that I come to the point. I mentioned that I've been writing to you even though I was very busy. In fact, I still am so I believe it's natural for me to expect to hear from you quite regularly. I've been quite broadminded. I've taken into consideration that you might work late at night and come home tired and perhaps help your mother around the house with the chores, but I still believe you'd have time to drop a few lines that is if you really cared. I can use stronger words to let you know how I feel but I believe you've gotten the general idea. I'll be waiting to hear your side of the story. We only have one way of keeping contact with each other and expressing our opinions so why not use it as often as is possible. Here we are engaged, and I'll be darned that I've heard from you 1/3 as many times as when we were going together. After all the contact now between each other should be more intimate and close. So why kill the only means we have of hearing from each other by not writing. Helen, I love you and always will but how can I really know if you still feel the same if I don't hear from you. Sorry I have to close but I have to fall out. Still loving you as much as ever. Mike

PS Sorry I had to say what I did but that's the way I feel. Take it for what it's worth. Love Mike

"Mom, I know you said I should go to work even if I'm a little sick," Helen said, "but I keep throwing up. I don't think I'll be able to wait on customers if I have to keep running to the bathroom."

"All right then, call and tell them you can't make it," her mother said. "I guess I'll call the doc and see if he can squeeze in a house call. Maybe if you get medicine, you'll feel better."

After calling her boss, Helen retreated to her bedroom, immediately fell into a deep slumber, and slept until the doctor arrived three hours later. He instructed Helen to continue to rest and drink water. He handed her a small bottle of paregoric with instructions to take two teaspoons twice a day for the next few days. She smelled the bitter-tasting liquid and gagged.

Her mother remarked, "You're not going to get better if you don't take the medicine."

"I know. I'll take it," Helen said, "but it tastes like gasoline, and it burns."

"How do you know what gasoline tastes like?"

"Well, I don't, but I don't know how else to describe it."

"Give me the bottle. I'll add some water and sugar to make it taste better."

With a desire to recover soon, Helen took the prescribed medicine, but her stomach churned and repeatedly rejected anything more than soda crackers and ginger ale. While relaxing, she recalled a time when she had suffered from a migraine headache. In the parlor, Mike had dimmed the lights and placed a cold towel on the back of her neck while she rested her head in his lap. She wondered whether he showed this compassionate side to the soldiers he treated. Picturing him caring for the men, she realized how lucky they were to have Mike as a medic, and how fortunate she was to have him in her life. She only wished he could be with her now.

August 17, 1944

Thursday

Hello Darling.

I received your letters today. Sure was surprised to hear from you. You can disregard what I mentioned in my previous letter. I thought something must have been wrong when I didn't hear from you in quite a while. I'm really relieved now to hear that you're feeling much better. Here's hoping you stay that way. You mean to tell me you lost 10 pounds. You sure must have been sick. I guess it must be because I'm not around. You need an armstrong heater. That's my prescription.

Since I'm a surgical technician or a reasonable facsimile, I had the chance to see a few operations at the hospital. I was really close where I could see everything. If I were up closer the Doctor might have cut part of my nose off in place of the operation.

The first one I saw was a skin graft. The fellow's skin was grafted from his thigh to an ugly laceration on his anklebone. He was put to sleep by a fairly new anesthesia, sodium pentathol. Very effective, no ill effects before or after like you have in ether. There's one peculiarity of the drug that is it causes a slight convulsion of the muscle. The patients' leg vibrated every time the doc made an incision.

The next thing I saw was a hernia operation. The fellow was put to sleep with nitrous oxide, and he kept sighing and making loud noises. The doc had several nurses working with him, handing him the instruments etc. When the Doc made the incision in the stomach region he showed us the hernia sac, blood vessels, nerves, and muscle fibers. In spite of the large incision and depth of the cut there was practically no blood, if any. The patient under gas was tense and it made it quite difficult for the doc to keep his insides from coming through the opening. Finally, the patient relaxed, and everything was alright. The doc did a real good job, he sewed up each layer of muscle, fiber, and skin. Did a neat job. The man laying here might as well have been a chunk of beef as much as it affected me. I must be cold blooded. The doc also made another incision opposite the one he made and removed a fatty tumor. You know being a medic you have to have a pretty strong stomach as well as being broad-minded. The fellow was lying there completely exposed after the operation and the nurses were around. But it didn't make me feel embarrassed or out of place because the man was lying there naked. You just take those things in your stride. After this operation we watched while the anesthetist drained the patient's lungs to get rid of mucous surrounding the tubes from the gas.

An autopsy was performed on a Negro fellow who drowned about two weeks ago. They slit his stomach from his neck down to his waist, pulled out the guts and everything inside. Just like anyone would do when killing a duck or chicken. The doc slit the stomach and food inside was fermented and really stunk. It smelled like an old dirty slaughterhouse. He cut a part of each organ. The heart, lungs, stomach, intestines for laboratory tests. They do this to every soldier that dies or gets killed. This is really gruesome. One fellow passed out. I don't blame him.

Hope I didn't upset your stomach talking about such things.

I've been learning to drive a jeep on the sly. Haven't been doing bad. Maybe after all this is over, I'll be able to get a car. Beats walking any day.

Helen, I asked you to give or make a comment on the idea of getting married when and if I get a furlough. What's your idea? Do you believe in waiting till this is all over or take the chance when I come home on furlough? I won't make any comments till I hear from you.

Well, I'm glad to hear you're feeling better. You sure had me worried. Still loving you as much as ever. Always remembering. Never forgetting. Loving you forever Love Mike

The mail arrived early with a small package from Mike. Helen ripped off the brown paper and uncovered a gold-colored bracelet with a red heart-shaped stone in the center, along with a note: "Sorry this is late but I'm wishing you sincere, although late birthday wishes." She smiled broadly as she slipped the bracelet onto her wrist. It wasn't real gold or a genuine ruby, but it meant the world to her in sentiment, rather than value. She proudly displayed it to her sister and her father, boasting, "Isn't Mike the sweetest man?"

Her father nodded as he puffed on his pipe, and Flo declared, "Did you notice the color of the stone matches the ring Mom and Pop gave you?"

"Oh, it does. I bet Mike did that on purpose. I remember him commenting on the ring when I wore it."

"You're lucky, Helen, to have a man like Mike," Flo said. "You better hold on to him."

August 27, 1944

Sunday

Dearest Helen:

Received your very wonderful gift of cigarettes, and wallet. Gee thanks a million. Everyone's been swell to me. I've been besieged with packages and letters for the past few days. Seemed more like Christmas than my birthday. I also received the wonderful birthday card. My morale has been very much above par since these last few days. The receipt of all these gifts and letters had very much to do with it. It's really good to know the folks at home still remember.

Helen, I didn't know how much we had saved. Didn't bother to make an account of it because I figured you would and I trust you. Well after all I'm going to marry you and one of these days and it certainly would be funny if I couldn't trust you. So you see we're off to a good start so far.

We don't have very much money or things now but what we do have is a lot more important. The things we do have, you can't save up for or buy. These things are love, faith, hope and trust. So in reality we have a lot of things. They have a saying, "Big oaks from little acorns grow." Well, that's just like our few dollars saved now and then.

If you don't hear from me in a while it is because all next week I have to put in 58 hours of mine and booby trap training, so I'll be occupied most of the time. But I'll try to squeeze in a few lines sometime.

One of my buddies got married on his furlough recently and he told me there's nothing like married life. He said he would prescribe it for everyone.

Just thinking of how wonderful it would be being at home makes my heart miss a few beats and chills run up and down my spine. That's also the way you make me feel when I'm near you.

I'm going to church in a few minutes, so I'll have to close now till later. So long for now darling.

Thanking you again from the bottom of my heart. I remain, as always. Mike

September 14, 1944

Thursday

Dearest Darling:

I received word today that I'm going to get my furlough on October 19, that's only a month away. Not too long to wait.

Honey, I've finally made up my mind. I WANT TO MARRY YOU WHEN I COME HOME THIS TIME. Surprised you didn't I? Or did I?

If you agree, here's what I want you to do because we haven't much time. Go to your pastor and have him announce the bands in church and to notify the priest from my parish so he can do the same. Also, ask him to let you fill out a freedom to marry certificate and to send me one also. This certificate is nothing but a form stating that you weren't married before, when you were baptized and confirmed etc.

You probably will have to take a blood test because that's required before you get married. I can get mine here in just a day.

I know how much you'd like to have a big wedding but times as they are doesn't permit it. We could get married and then we can plan and save for a little house and all the things that go with it. If we wait all of this expense will come at one time and it would a lot tougher to start out. You know getting married requires quite a bit of money and if you want to establish a home at the same time you'd have quite a pile of debt. If we could get married while I'm still in the army it would cut the expense in two. I hope you can see what I mean. When we get married, we'd spend some dough and then we can save for other things while I'm still in the army. A lot of money would be saved for future use.

Helen, I sure do hope you accept because I love you with all my heart. We don't have very much money to get married but here's what I've been thinking, that is if you don't mind. You know ordinarily it costs about a hundred dollars to get a wedding dress. So I was thinking we could overcome that if you could wear one of your sisters. I know this isn't a very good policy but considering the circumstance I think it's the only thing to do. The rest wouldn't cost much. Me, I don't need a suit because Uncle Sam took care of that so that saves a little more. Helen, I know this wouldn't be the best of weddings with all the finery and splendor that it usually would be, but this isn't ordinary times. We have our love, that is the most important thing. I promise that I'll try with all the strength that's in me that I'll make it up to you.

I'd be the happiest fellow on God's green earth if you'd accept. Really, I never was more serious in all my life.

I've thought it over many times, and I think this is the best thing. You might not agree marrying during wartime. If you don't take this in consideration. Over half the fellows in the army are married and they say they are better off.

So, Helen if you accept do these things I mentioned. That isn't much is it? I'm really hoping for the best.

I've always wanted to have a large wedding with all the trimmings, but the times don't permit it. We probably could have it if we'd wait but who knows how long this thing will last. Another thing you and I will l have much more to look forward to if we do get married. We can plan for the future without the thought that we might be waiting in vain.

If I'm in the army I'll have something to look forward to always. Knowing that I'll be coming back to a sweet, lovely wife who loves me and is waiting for me to come back. You'll have the same feeling.

So, please write me as soon as possible and let me know what you think.

Just so I can help you to make your mind up just take Marie and Ben. They're married and Ben is in the service. So, think it over but not too long because I want to have your answer as soon as possible because time is short. A month isn't very long.

Remember if you accept and here's hoping you do, start on those things I mentioned as soon as possible. Gert and Stan will help you.

Darling, I love you with my whole heart. Here's hoping instead of just Love Mike I'll be writing your faithful husband Mike.

PS That poem was really lovely. I could write on the paper a million x's for kisses, but I'll settle right now for just one real one from you. Good night my sweet. Mike

Chapter Nineteen

October 1944

As the train slowed to a stop, Mike leapt up from his seat and grabbed his duffel bag. He danced down the narrow metal steps, whistling "Oh, What a Beautiful Morning." The anticipation of marrying Helen had transformed a bulky, manly being into a weightless, fluttering butterfly. Standing at the bottom of the steps, the conductor inquired, "Hey, buddy, did ya just get discharged from the army?"

"Hell, no!" Mike said. "I'm home on furlough to marry my sweetheart."

"Well, good for you. Congratulations to you and the little lady."

"Thanks, pal."

A short while later, Mike arrived at Helen's doorstop, knocked, and, without waiting, pushed open the ajar door. He picked Helen up from the couch, twirled her around, and exclaimed, "So, are all the final arrangements for the wedding done, sweetheart?"

Helen's perky face darkened. "Oh, Mike, ah, ahh . . . "

"Darling, what's wrong?"

Staring at the floor, Helen stood silent.

Mike lifted her chin. "Talk to me."

Helen whimpered, "I didn't write because I wanted to tell you in person. I decided it'd be better to wait until the war is over."

Mike's smile evaporated, and he jerked backward. He shuffled toward the couch, his lips pressed tight. "Can we sit for a minute?"

Helen grabbed his arm. "Sure, but are you alright?"

"I don't understand. Did you find someone else?"

"No! There's nobody but you," Helen said.

"Well, what the hell happened? Do you still want to marry me?"

"Of course, I want to marry you! But it's my mother."

Mike's voice grew louder. "What's she got to do with your decision?"

"Please don't be angry. She brought up a few concerns."

"About me? What's wrong with me?"

"Nothing's wrong," Helen said. "She talked about things I don't even want to think about."

"Helen, I've been waiting months for this. You can't let me guess what's going on. I deserve an explanation."

"You do," Helen agreed. "But if you knew what she said, it might make you feel bad."

Mike scoffed. "No matter what your mom said, it can't make me feel worse than I do right now. Just tell me."

Helen wanted to marry Mike, but her mother had curtailed her decision by outlining all the reasons not to marry him. Mary had declared, "What if Mike is killed? You'd be a widow, and it'd be harder to marry again. What if you became pregnant? Then you'd have to raise the child by yourself." She told Helen, "You'll get no help from me because my children are all grown, and I'm too old to help raise another child. And do I need to remind you how many men have been killed in Europe and the Pacific? No one but God knows who will return. What if he comes back a cripple, and you have to take care of him for the rest of his life? Are you ready for that? We have no time to prepare for a proper wedding anyway. Helen, don't you see it's not a good idea to get married now?"

Helen repeated her mother's words and wiped her eyes. "I'm sorry, Mike, if I've disappointed you. Please don't be mad at me."

He paused and lit a cigarette. "I'm upset we're not getting married, but I'm not mad at you. In fact, I should have thought about those things. I guess I've had a pretty positive outlook and was sure I'd come back, but there's always that possibility. I wouldn't want you to be burdened."

"I wouldn't. That's what my mom thinks."

"If you became pregnant, and I came home without legs or arms, I wouldn't be able to properly take care of you and our kids. Or even worse, if you were a widow, you'd have to raise them by yourself. I love you and want to marry you, but maybe it's better if we wait."

"I want you to know I'd take care of you if something happened," Helen said.

"You say that now, but you might change your mind," Mike said. "If I come back a cripple, and you still want to marry me, then you have a choice, instead of being obligated. Your mother might be right about this. She's just looking out for you, and it's best for both of us."

Helen squeezed his hands. "Are you sure you're okay? Because I'm not."

"Yes, I think this is for the best. I'm disappointed, but I'll get over it," Mike said. "As long as you still love me and say you'll wait for me."

"Of course, I'll wait for you! And I'm sorry if I hurt you. Maybe I should have ignored my mother, but she can be so convincing and demanding."

"I promise you it's okay, darling."

Helen inched closer to him. "I love you and can't wait till this war is over so we can get married."

"You and me both! But it's water under the bridge. Let's just forget about it and go for a walk. Today's too beautiful to worry about anything."

When they arrived at First Street, they boarded the incline to Mt. Washington to visit Grandview Park. They loved the bird's-eye view of the buildings on days when the black smoke from the steel mills did not obstruct the panorama. The soft carpet of grass, serenading birds, winding walkways, and the sweet scent of wildflowers transported them to their own sanctuary. Their courtship had blossomed here many nights, under the trees among the rustling squirrels, in the glow of the moonlight. This was more than a park. It had become a hideaway that held their thoughts, secrets, and intimacies.

As they crossed the threshold of their private parlor in the middle of the city, Mike pantomimed the opening of a nonexistent door. He motioned for Helen to go through. "Welcome home."

She giggled at his antics and played along. "Thank you. It feels like heaven to be in our own home. I wish I had some coffee to offer you."

Mike followed her and closed the imaginary door behind him, perused the park, and said, "It looks as inviting as when I left, and our couch is empty and waiting for us."

"Oh, Mike, you're so funny."

In the cool air, they lounged in each other's arms among the vibrant scarlet, burnt orange, and amber leaves. They talked about everything except the failed wedding plans. By the time moonlight snuck up on them, their love had been rekindled, with renewed anticipation for their wedding after the war.

After spending a relaxing evening with Helen, Mike returned to the tranquil surroundings of his parents' home and lay back on his bed. The cushy mattress and soft blankets, a stark contrast to the noisy, sterile environment of the barracks, offered no solace or comfort for his pain. He tossed about as if at sea, distressed that Helen had allowed her mother to change her mind.

His anticipation of the wedding before he'd arrived in Pittsburgh had improved his health better than a shot of B12 in the arm. Only a week ago, mess hall food had tasted like gourmet, mouth-watering meals, and Mike had effortlessly accomplished the monotonous menial tasks of military life like a hot knife slicing through butter. Now, the idea of peeling a potato or standing at attention felt like a Herculean undertaking. His heart sat, unmoving, like a stone in a still sea, tethered in the cold depths by Helen's pronouncement.

Lying in his bed, he imagined his beautiful bride gliding toward him, ready to say, "I do," before God and family as they embarked on their new life together. Within seconds, Helen faded from his daydream, and he saw himself standing alone at the altar in an empty church. Although he understood her reasons for waiting, he started to question their relationship. Was this an excuse to delay the inevitable? Was the pain of loneliness too much for Helen to bear? Would the lingering absence from each other and the distance create the fuse to explode this promise? He had so many unanswered questions.

Mike envisioned returning to military drudgery without the sacred gold band on his finger. The same buddies who had wished him good luck would undoubtedly convince him that Helen's delay meant she'd lost her desire. Anger, doubt, and disappointment simmered in his mind, along with love and respect for Helen's decision. Suddenly, Smokie, his dog, jumped on his stomach, disturbing his sleepless musing.

Mike ruffled Smokie's ears. "Hey, boy, how'd you know I needed someone to knock a little sense into me? I got the best gal any man could ever want, and she loves me, and instead of being grateful, I'm moping. You know that's not like me, boy."

Smokie leaped off the bed, knocking the alarm clock to the floor. Mike picked it up and noticed the time. If he hurried, he could attend the 5:15 morning mass at St. Adalbert's.

After mass, with his soul refreshed, Mike knocked at Helen's door. Mary greeted him in her robe, holding a cup of coffee. "Michael, you're here early for a Sunday morning."

"I'm sorry, Mrs. Cypyrch, but I just came from mass and thought I'd stop by to see Helen if she's awake."

"I'm the only one up. Come on in. You can wake her, but make it quick. And be sure you go to the room on the left; otherwise, you'll give my husband a heart attack."

Mike tiptoed upstairs, nudged open the bedroom door, and peeked inside to see Helen and Flo sleeping. With purpose and precision, He pranced like a cat burglar to Helen's side of the bed, bent over, and brushed his lips against her forehead. She rustled but remained asleep. He stood at her bedside, admiring her angelic face, and then knelt by her bed and kissed her lips. She gasped, her eyes flew open, and her head jerked up, knocking Mike backward.

"Mike, what're you doing here? Does my mother know you're here?" Helen asked, sleepy-eyed and confused.

"Yes, she knows I'm here. She's the one who told me to wake you."

Helen yawned. "What time is it?"

"It's time for you to rise and shine," Mike said.

Their voices woke Flo. "What's going on?" she asked.

"Mike decided to wake me up."

Flo sat up and shrieked, "What? Mike's up here?" She rotated toward Helen and spotted him kneeling by her side of the bed.

"I can't believe he's in here!"

Helen scolded Flo, "Oh, just be quiet." She turned back to Mike. "It's so early. What are you doing here?"

"I couldn't wait one more minute to see you."

"That's so sweet. How about I make your breakfast before I go to church?"

"That's great, and when you go to church, I'll go visit with Gert and Stan. I bought something for their girls. Then we can spend the rest of the day together."

"Okay. Go downstairs while I get dressed."

Mike was sitting at the table, reading the Sunday paper, when Helen arrived in the kitchen. She retrieved the flowery apron from the hook on the wall and asked, "How do you like your eggs, fried or scrambled?"

"Any way you want to make them is fine with me," he said.

"Mom and Pop like their eggs fried, so I'll make everyone fried eggs and bacon."

Mike chuckled, as he watched her place the frying pan on the stove and add the bacon.

She looked at him. "Are you reading the comics?"

"No. Why?"

"Then what are you smiling about?"

"I'm envisioning our life together. It'd be just like this. I'd wake you up in the morning and listen to the radio and read the newspaper while you cooked me breakfast. Then we'd sit and eat together and plan our day. How's it make you feel?"

Helen cracked the eggs. "It makes me wish we were married."

"Me, too, honey."

"So, what do you want to do today?"

"How about a picnic in the park?"

Flo walked into the room. "Do you know it's supposed to rain today?"

"Oh, no, I didn't," replied Helen. "Well, any suggestions from you, Mike?"

"I'd love to take you to a matinee. It's been so long since I've been to a dark movie theater with a beautiful girl."

She smiled. "Okay, we can go after church."

Later, after Helen returned from church, she and Mike settled into the theater's comfortable seats, the house lights dimmed, and the Movie Times News Reel began. Mike squeezed closer and lightly caressed her cheek. Her body tingled at this one simple gesture, rejuvenating her ardor and desire, which had been subdued by their physical distance.

Embraced in Mike's loving arms, Helen forgot her anxieties about the war and her future. Her mind regressed to a time when only their love for each other mattered, they faced a bright future together, and they made decisions based on love, instead of war. As she cuddled closer and listened to the rhythm of Mike's heart, she regretted surrendering to her mother's wishes.

Leaving the movie theater, Mike said, "After dinner with my family, I want you to put on your dancing shoes. I'm not leaving until we do the jitterbug one more time."

"I'd love that, but I hope it's not like last time. You pulled me through your legs so fast, you nearly fell over."

He laughed. "I know. I thought I was gonna fall on your head, but I managed to keep my balance. Oh, boy, it would've been something to talk about if I did fall."

"Well, I'm glad you didn't. Remember, we danced till closing time? I don't know where I got all that energy."

As they walked, Mike slid his arm around her shoulders. "I have to say it was a swell time. You know, sweetheart, I love dancing with you, but what I love more is watching you smile when you glide around the floor. I love to see you happy."

Helen wrapped her arm around his waist. "I like to dance, but I was happy because I was with you. I miss having fun with you. I hate to see you leave, honey."

"I hate to go, too, but I'm not leaving yet. We have lots to look forward to. You said Marie invited us for dinner, and then we're going to the party at your cousin Eddie's. I think we might have time for a picnic in Schenley Park, too. We'll be having so much fun, you won't have time to think about us being apart. I'm going to stick to you like glue."

Helen turned toward him, kissed his cheek, and whispered, "I hope so, Mike. I love you."

October 31, 1944

Darling,

Here it is four days since I've last seen or heard from you, but it seems ages. Coming down on the train I saw a sailor going back home to stay. He had an honorable discharge. What I wouldn't do with one of them. But, a few minutes later this beautiful picture was spoiled when I saw another soldier board the train. He was wearing crutches and had his leg cut off up to the knee. He was in combat because he had a purple heart. It was a pitiful sight. The fellow was fairly young too.

Let's talk about more pleasant things.

The weather in St. Louis and from there on was beautiful. Passing many places and several states. I noticed some beautiful homes. The kind I've always dreamed of. I was thinking of when I get back for good, I'm going to build ourselves a home to suit ourselves. If you're there with me I know it can be done.

We'll try to have a lot of things but if we don't it won't make me unhappy. As long as you're with me, no matter what we have we'll make the most of it and still enjoy ourselves and be happy. Just like my mother said, "Just as long as you're healthy don't worry."

I haven't been exactly myself since I've been back. I find my mind wandering every once in a while mostly now, thinking of you and all the swell times we spent together. I'm certainly glad that I was able to get a furlough. At least we spent a little time together.

Well, I told you before and I'll tell you again. Helen, you were the prettiest girl at that party and the best dancer. I really enjoyed myself then. I can still remember how lovely you looked. I wish I had the intelligence and the command of some very lovely words to really tell you how I feel about you. My mind at present is home with you that's why I just can't seem to write anything that might sound sensible or real.

There's one thing though Helen this last furlough has brought me closer to you than all the time I've known you. I have learned to love you like no man can. That's really good because now I'll never be able to get you out of my mind and most of all out of my heart. On this last furlough you penetrated spots in my heart that were never touched before. Yep, I've really fallen and fallen hard, but I'm really happy about it all.

Helen, no matter what may come I'll always remember you because your image has been stamped on my heart. No matter where I go or where I may be I'll always love you as I do now with my whole heart.

I'll have to close but before I do I want you to know I'm always thinking of you. You're always in my heart no matter where I may be.

Distance doesn't make our love any different.

Always remembering. Never forgetting. Loving you forever Love Mike

PART II

Going Overseas

Chapter Twenty

November 1944

Mike disembarked the train outside Camp Kilmer, New Jersey, with instructions that the Rainbow Division was leaving American soil for a destination unknown. Everyone had anticipated the trip overseas, but the expectation did not lessen the blow. Hoping to boost morale before the men risked life and limb, the army issued a twelve-hour pass to New York City for a last hurrah. While many of the men headed to bars and nightclubs for one final fling, Mike wasted no time in exploring the city. New York provided nonstop entertainment, starting with a show at Radio City Music Hall, followed by a visit to the Museum of Arts and Sciences and then a live radio program performance featuring Tony Galento. Before the day was over, Mike had enjoyed the Ice Capades show at Madison Square Garden as well. The Big Apple provided everything but the one person he wanted to share it with.

Now the clock ticked, and Mike and the Rainbow Division departed to the port to await further orders. The news of the confidential departure had leaked, prompting women and a few elderly men to gather for an impromptu celebration in honor of the brave soldiers.

Mike puffed on his cigarette deeply and exhaled into the frosty air, as he and his fellow soldiers paced the crowded shoreline, drinking coffee and eating donuts from the Red Cross. A lanky private approached Mike. "Hey, you got a light? I just used my last match."

"Sure," Mike said and tossed him the matches. "Here you go."

"Thanks. You know, by the time we board those ships, we'll both be out of cigarettes and matches."

"Yeah, it's been a long time, but I figure the longer we wait, the less time we have to spend over there."

The private's hand shook as he drew the cigarette to his lips. "You got that right. Looks like we're headed to Europe to beat the shit out of the Krauts. I wonda what's worse, fightin' the Krauts or the Japs."

"Neither one is a good option, but nothing would make me happier than to see Hitler go down after how they destroyed Poland," Mike said.

"Yeah, dem assholes gave us plenty of reasons to pull the trigger. I gotta say, part of me wants to knock out the bastards; the other half of me is scared as hell. How 'bout you, Sarge?"

"Anybody who doesn't admit they're nervous of what might happen is a fool," Mike said. "But you just can't think about it too much."

The private replied, "I think 'bout my wife and little boy. Wanna see a picture?" He snatched his wallet from his pocket. "Dis here is my wife, Sylvia, and my little boy. He'll be one year ole next week. I should've wrote her and told her I was leavin', but . . . well, you know."

Mike gazed at the picture and thought, *Maybe it's good Helen and I didn't get married.*

After waiting several hours by the dock, the commander bellowed for the men to prepare to board the ship. Mike gathered his duffel bag and flung it over his shoulder. The commander called Mike's name, and he fell in line with the men from his company. He climbed the gangplank to the *Edmund B. Alexander*, formerly an old German cruise ship, *The Amerika*, which had been captured during World War I. This temporary metal sailing barracks resembled a tin library with all the men on deck packed as close as books on a shelf. As the vessel departed the harbor, the men fought for a prime spot along the railing to gander a last glimpse of Lady Liberty.

Mike stared over the convoy at the disappearing silhouette of the Statue of Liberty and the skyline of New York, his head swirling with a tornado of emotions. As he listened to the water splash along the hull, his fears washed up from the pit of his stomach in anticipation of the inevitable encounter with enemy troops. Heartache engulfed his mind as he wondered how Helen and his family felt, with their loneliness and fear. He contemplated his own uncertainties. Would he return to America to embrace Helen, or would she be forced to endure the agony of seeing him lying in a cold, dark box?

The bitter air cleared Mike's head as he stood on the deck and gazed at thousands of stars shining in the endless sky and the soft glow of moonlight on the water. He stared at the awe-inspiring night sky as the ocean winds whisked across his cheeks. God's beauty and the experience of traveling on the sea for the first time squelched the foreboding thoughts of his journey to the gates of hell.

He lazed in the allure of the setting and daydreamed of Helen resting in his arms, listening to lapping waters on the elegant cruise line of yesteryear. Lying on a chaise lounge during the afternoon and dining and dancing in the evening. Mike imagined the once-exquisite chandeliers and furniture that had adorned this ship, along with tables set with fine china and silverware. Now, the once aristocratic vessel, stripped of all its grandeur, became a bleak, barren mover of bodies across the sea.

Suddenly, the loud voices of men arguing disrupted Mike's fantasy. The commander ordered them to clear the deck, and Mike grabbed his duffel bag and proceeded to his assigned cabin. Inside the room, the men lying on the canvas-and-iron bunks, stacked five and six high to the ceiling, resembled cargo on a shelf. With all the beds occupied, Mike was assigned to the second rotation for sleep. He didn't anticipate his eyes closing or his body relaxing and was undeterred that he needed to wait.

He heaved his canvas bag onto the mountain of personal belongings in the corner. As he turned to leave, he noticed the statement "Kilroy was here" with a picture of a cartoonish man etched on the door. Various stories had circulated about the infamous and ubiquitous, yet anonymous, Kilroy. One tale declared a shipbuilder claimed responsibility; another stated it involved an admiral, and one story told about a GI searching for his girlfriend. The origin was not as significant as what Kilroy represented: an encouraging sign of an American soldier who existed, fighting for freedom.

Walking through the corridor, Mike strolled by a poker game in progress, and a corporal shouted, "Hey, buddy, you want to play?"

"Not much else to do right now," Mike said, plopping down on a steel stool.

While the private shuffled the cards, Mike removed a pack of cigarettes from his pocket, along with a few dollars, "So, what game are you fellas playing?"

"Good old five-card stud poker."

"Deal me in."

For the next few hours, they killed time as they passed the cards around the table.

Chapter Twenty-One

It wasn't long before Mike's infatuation with cruising on the open phosphorus seas under blue skies morphed to disgust. The captain zigzagged in one direction for seven minutes and swerved in another direction for seven minutes on the roller-coaster waves, in order to evade detection. Men's guts erupted in reaction to the ship's movement. Multicolored vomit coated the inside of the latrine, as men dashed to expel the contents of their stomachs. If their legs were too weak to get them to the lavatory fast enough, they threw up their inner contents wherever they stood or in one of the vomit barrels. Hosing off the latrine and the deck did not sufficiently wash away all the debris and the lingering stench. The fishy seawater, the body odor from multitudes of men, the pungent disinfectant barrels, and uncontrolled diarrhea intensified the putrid air and irritated Mike's nostrils.

This assault on his senses, in addition to the roughness of the sea, agitated his stomach, and he, too, donated the contents of his guts to the ocean. In spite of the frosty air, Mike remained on the main deck, trying to avoid the reeking scene below. He obtained little relief, as the smell of army mess food, along with the other repulsive odors, wafted outside and infiltrated the fresh outdoor air. He gagged as two privates bolted onto the deck covered in vomit. After he stopped choking, he asked, "What the hell happened to you?"

The private retched, brushing off his clothes. "The chain holding the vomit barrel broke, and there's puke all over the place. We slipped and fell in it."

"What are you doing up here? You need a shower."

"They're all full. We came up here to get some fresh air."

"Well, get it and get the hell out of those disgusting clothes."

The two men dawdled on deck for a few minutes and then slowly ventured below.

Still feeling queasy, Mike lagged in going down the narrow steps to attend a mandatory lecture. In the middle of the class, shouts of anger and swearing, along with grunts and a thud on the door, interrupted the instructor. The lieutenant flung open the door and grabbed the men. "If you want to fight, take it to the boxing ring. You can entertain the rest of the crew." As soon as he finished reprimanding the culpable pair, he bolted through the passageway to mitigate another altercation.

The cramped quarters with six thousand men aboard, tension, seasickness, and a surplus of time created a ticking time bomb. Numerous fights culminated in the boxing ring. The men's shouts and taunts created additional turmoil, resulting in a riot between Negros and whites. After a few bloody noses and bruises, the insurgence stopped, but the animosity lingered.

Mike endeavored to find solace in the warmth of a hot shower, but the foul saltwater made his normally healthy, shiny hair feel like dry hay. As he positioned himself on his bunk, he finally grasped that there was no escape from the rigors of this crossing and his new life.

During the next few days, his sensory glands and stomach became accustomed to the rancid atmosphere, and he relinquished less and less to the sea. Now he was able to eat, read, and mentally prepare himself for his entrance into war.

Days turned into weeks, and the ship passed the Rock of Gibraltar through the strait. A few men lingered on deck, and a private asked Mike, "You think we'll land in France?"

Mike said, "Sure, looks like it."

One soldier lamented, "I remember talking to my wife, saying one day we'll go to Europe and see France. Here I am now, and it's not the feeling I imagined."

The statement silenced every man, reminding them of their own sickening, menacing thoughts.

The apprehension Mike had attempted to repress erupted violently. He felt his body twitch and his heart pound in his chest, as if struggling to escape. He resorted to his calming habit and lit a cigarette, inhaling the nicotine to anesthetize his nerves. After taking the last puff, he extinguished it and without delay lit another one to fill his body with the consoling drug.

Assuming this would be his last night at sea before heading into war, Mike roamed the halls in search of consolation. By the mess hall, he found a quiet corner and extracted a *Catholic Prayer Book for the Army and Navy* from his front pocket, flipped through it, and stopped at "Prayer before Going into Action." He read, "The Lord is my light and my salvation: whom shall I fear?" The words slowed his heart, and he continued, "The Lord is the defense of my life: of whom should I be afraid?" As he turned the pages, he found comfort in each word. After finishing his devotions, he trudged to his cabin, dove onto the canvas bunk, and tried to persuade his eyes to close and his mind to travel to a land of tranquility.

The sun rose, but instead of the ship docking, the journey continued for two more angst-filled days. Finally, after a total of fifteen days at sea, the ship decelerated, the engines stopped, and the men disembarked. Mike and the soldiers scrambled onto flat open barges waiting to take the task force ashore to the Marseilles Nautical Building. Until the remainder of the

Rainbow Division arrived, this section became officially known as Task Force Linden.

As the barges floated toward land, Mike observed the devastation of the surrounding buildings and the pier from airborne bombs. His stomach churned as he commenced his journey on the road to bloodshed and tears. He captured every detail in slow motion as if this might be his last glimpse of life. As the barge landed, he noticed hundreds of enemy prisoners walking past the dock, and a glimmer of hope arose that the Allies could win this war.

Once on shore, his rubbery legs wobbled, exaggerating his naturally bowed legs, and he hobbled along the pier like an arthritic man. It took him a while to regain his land legs, but he recovered in time to hike the six miles in soft sand and freezing torrents of snow to Command Post (CP) 2. This flat, desolate area in the middle of nowhere was waiting to be transformed into their field headquarters. The bitter howling wind ripped across the open plain, pushing against their backs as they unloaded the trucks and assembled their individual shelter tents. Darkness and fatigue enveloped the men as they dug foxholes and latrines. Shivering and with half-numb fingers, the men grabbed their shovels and whacked the frozen ground, but it was like picking at an iceberg with a toothpick.

With assignments completed, the soldiers ventured into the dark forest for wood. This normally unchallenging task transformed into a scavenger hunt because fallen branches were scarce and hidden under mounds of snow. They foraged for hours, only to be rewarded with a few armfuls of wood. Eager to find warmth, the men tossed their matches onto the pile of wood, but the wet ground and the wood's dampness halted the process. A sergeant, exasperated by the unproductive attempts, secured a scant amount of precious gasoline and poured it over the logs. Mike rubbed his ice-bitten hands over the fire and stomped his boots on a hot log, sending warmth through his body. When his fingers defrosted enough to bend freely, he plunked down on a tree stump and grabbed his K-rations of biscuits and pork. He grimaced while chewing his meager meal. "This tastes like dog food," he said.

Another medic chimed in, "I've never had dog food, but I think this could be worse."

A private huddling by the fire growled, "You know what's worse? Being in the middle of this war without our division armor and artillery. You'd think they would've sent those guys over here first and then us."

Mike took a bite. "Yeah, it doesn't make sense."

Another soldier lamented, "The commander said the other half of the division won't be here till January. If we have to fight against these bastards' artillery and tanks, we'll be dead before we even start."

Other men grumbled that they'd arrived at Fort Gruber only a few months ago and felt insecure about their insufficient training. Mike wondered how much training was enough to ensure you wouldn't get killed. He said, "My fate's in the hands of God, and I pray whatever we might lack in instruction or support, God makes up the difference." He quickly changed the subject to the home front. The men talked about blackouts, family, and how they'd probably never forget this first Christmas on foreign soil. Finally, with only a half-full belly and feeling imperceptibly warmer, Mike headed back to the cramped shelter tent. Limp with exhaustion, he fell quickly asleep, which allowed him to temporarily escape his new reality. His rest, however, was disrupted when an occasional German plane buzzed in the distance, followed by antiaircraft guns at the port, aiming to blast them away.

During the night, the freezing temperatures, wicked winds, and snow infiltrated Mike's claustrophobic tent. Before the sun rose, he awoke from a few hours of intermittent sleep, quivering in his damp uniform. He pulled the extra socks from beneath his belt and, to his disappointment, found them also damp. Struggling to bend his fingers, he peeled off his soggy, dirty socks and replaced them with his clean wet ones. He walked over to the lister bags to wash the mud and stink from his socks, but the bitter weather had frozen the water. Dry, dirty socks felt better than wet ones, so he hung the latter over the fire.

Sitting by the fire, arthritic and hungry, he opened his C-ration breakfast and laid the contents on the ground. He grabbed the stick of gum, the toilet paper, and the cigarettes and deposited them in his coat pocket for later. Wanting to warm himself, he shook the Nescafe envelope of coffee into his tin cup with hot water and added two sugar cubes. After a few sips of coffee, he quickly ate the cereal bar. Ready for the main course, he reached for the tin can of chopped pork and eggs, snapped the key from the can, and slowly turned it. An odd smell wafted from the contents. He scowled as he took the first bite and wished he had ketchup to kill the taste. Yet his empty stomach demanded food, so Mike unwillingly obliged. He shoved the remainder into his mouth. To wash away the unappealing taste, he swooshed his mouth with coffee and finished the meal with Sunshine biscuits. He needed to report to duty shortly, so he grabbed his semi-dry socks and walked back to his tent.

At the aid station, he sorted the equipment and tended to the men complaining of frostbite and minor aches and pains. After assisting the last patient, he and the other medics ferreted out some straw in a barn for their beds, along with extra wood to keep the fires burning. Mike huddled near the fire and, with stiff, clumsy hands, scribbled his thoughts to Helen by the firelight, avoiding mention of his tribulations.

Helen picked up the first correspondence from Mike since he'd left for Europe and fixed her eyes on the words "Censored by Captain Lawrence Rodgers" on the envelope. Their only means of communication had been violated and scrutinized by a stranger.

December 11, 1944

Monday Somewhere in France

Dearest Helen,

I want you to know I'm still thinking of you and loving you always. We're quite a distance apart now but my feeling for you hasn't changed. I still love you, as I did before if not more. Oh yes, I did have a very pleasant ocean voyage, though it was uneventful.

We got paid in French money several days ago so I'm sending you a 10-franc note. This is equivalent to 20 cents in American money. No kidding, do you know how much I actually got paid? Just five francs. Yep, that's only 10 cents. The reason for this is the few bucks I did have coming went to a few PX purchases. I don't need any money here, so that doesn't worry me. I could use a few airmail stamps. Not many but just a few in case I wish to make an enclosure in an envelope. You'll get mail a lot faster.

Helen, I just can't help but think of how much I long to hold you in my arms once more. I want you to know that I'll always love you.

Even though we have a great task to do over here I can't help but think of you and all the swell times we had together. Hoping to hear from you soon and often.

Always remembering, Never forgetting, Loving you forever May God Bless You. Mike

Chapter Twenty-Two

End of December 1944

While soldiers awaited their introduction into battle at CP 2, the men constructed firing ranges for additional practice and attended lectures. The topics included how to prevent trench foot, the dangers of fraternizing with their opponents, and other pertinent information. Orientation films informed them why they should fight and showed them propaganda about the enemy to help galvanize their tenacity to defend their country.

Medics manned the aid station for sick call and prepared their field bags with the required supplies. As they finished their final duty, the captain announced, "Men, even though you didn't get to clean up properly, the army has clean, dry uniforms for you. If you're done here, you can report to the supply tent."

One medic replied, "Yes, sir. I'm ready to wear anything that doesn't smell like an animal died in my pockets."

Mike grabbed his helmet. "I'm right behind you, buddy."

The clean uniforms and mail call were the only highlights during the wickedly cold days at CP 2 until an Italian shower truck arrived inside the camp. The men cheered and lined up for the sweet bouquet of soap and fresh water. Mike did not understand a word the Italians uttered, but it was inconsequential. Ahead of him lingered an opportunity to feel human again, instead of like a farm animal wallowing in filth.

While waiting in line, one man commented, "It's hard for me to trust these Italians. First, they fought with Hitler, and now they say they're on our side. Who really knows whose side they're on?"

Mike added, "Right now, it looks like they're on our side."

After the line of men waited patiently for two hours, the soap and water ran out, and the Italians shooed away the remaining men. A private turned to Mike, who was standing behind him, saying, "See, I told you, you can't trust the Italians." Doing an about-face, they walked back to camp, dejected and dirty.

After nine days of drudgery at CP 2, Task Force Linden departed to join the Third Army. The men packed their gear and marched toward the railroad in the mud. Wet snow mixed with rain pummeled them, drenching their clothes and chilling their bones. Shivering, they boarded the "forty-and-eights," boxcars.

Mike jumped into the boxcar. His nostrils flared at the stench of horse manure. Another soldier climbed aboard and moaned, "Someone should've cleaned this mess before it got here. This is nauseating. There's hardly a clean place to sit."

With all the men aboard, the door slid shut, intensifying the odor. A few morning rays filtered through a tiny window at the back of the car, barely enough for the soldiers to distinguish anything. As the silent men's eyes adjusted to the light, the train eased into motion. The men shivered as the wintry wind blew in through the open window. Despite orders not to build a fire, a corporal commandeered a bucket meant to be a makeshift toilet and threw in scraps of wood and paper before tossing in a match. The train traveled through Lyon, Dijon, and other points, occasionally stopping for the men to relieve themselves and stretch their legs. At each stop, they witnessed the havoc and destruction of the Nazi rage. The sight of this devastation roused terror in Mike, faced with the possibility that one day, he might be the direct target of the next German obliteration.

After two nights of traveling, the Task Force orders changed. The men were disengaged from the Third Army and annexed to the Seventh Army. The train headed north and had almost reached Metz when the men disembarked and maneuvered south toward Strasbourg by motor convoy. As darkness approached, they stopped at Morhange for the night and billeted in apartment houses and other buildings.

The next day, the convoy approached Bensdorf, another victim of extreme bombing. After an overnight stay, the various battalions of the task force moved forward to take positions along the Rhine River and relieve the 36th Division. The Germans wanted to regain control of the Alsace region. They anticipated a thin American line and easy recapture because most of the Allied troops were fighting the Battle of the Bulge in the Ardennes. Task Force Linden was prepared, but minus their heavy artillery, the men questioned their ability against the Germans' daunting military prowess.

The Rainbow planned to sweep the Germans farther back. The 222nd and the 242nd moved to the banks of the Rhine, while Mike's battalion waited in reserves in Hoerdt. Mike searched out a suitable building and prepared the aid station in an old agricultural office. He found housing in French barracks. On Christmas Eve, while the other factions of the 42nd Division kept vigil, lying in frozen, muddy foxholes, Mike attended a celebratory mass in a nearby church. The congregation sang in German as Mike entered the church. He'd anticipated the service being in French but realized that until recently, German troops had occupied this area for years. When the organist played "Stille Nacht," he recognized the familiar tune and sang the lyrics to "Silent Night" in his head. During the song, he noticed a small boy, about seven, pumping the old-fashioned organ. He watched in amazement and smiled, as he couldn't imagine the boy's little legs pumping any harder. After the service, he handed the boy a piece of chocolate. "Good job," Mike said. The little boy did not understand the

English words, but his eyes widened, and he snatched the rare treat from Mike's hand and ran away.

On Christmas morning, the Rainbow Division repositioned along the Rhine until the men occupied the riverbank for nineteen miles. An occasional warning shot sounded across the river, but the Germans suppressed an aggressive attack. During the next few days, the Rainbow men exploited the Germans' passiveness and extended their defensive line. They seized an additional fourteen miles, stretching the defense for thirty-three miles along the Rhine.

Preparing for an attack, the gunners and the riflemen remained at Hoerdt, while Mike traveled between the aid stations at Hoerdt and Strasbourg. During one of his trips, he spotted a shiny object on the ground and halted, careful not to inch forward another step. He bent down for a closer inspection and released his breath to discover the equivalent of $80 in German currency, instead of the explosive device he'd expected. He placed the money, almost equal to his monthly pay, in his breast pocket and buttoned it. With his anticipation of a German attack only hours away, the possibility of enjoying his find was nonexistent.

While at the aid station, Mike prepared equipment and painted the Red Cross on his helmet, praying the symbol would serve as protection on the battleground. In the absence of battle and casualties, he searched the carpentry shop for something to do and discovered an old barrel. He filled it with water and washed his face, hands, and clothes. Refreshed, he found a broken chair and sat at an old, splintering wooden desk to write a short letter to Helen.

December 29, 1944

Dearest Helen:

Oh memories, what fond memories I have of the times you and I were together. I'm more than looking forward to the time when you and I can be together again not as my fiancé but as my wife. Well, I hope this doesn't last too long. We can't make up for lost time, but we can certainly try like heck. Notice I've included a number of stamps I picked up here and there. I've been in Strasbourg and-------- (censored) and saw some really interesting sights. Wish I could tell you all about them.

You'll never know how much I miss that tender smile behind those lips divine. I've missed you since the day we had to say goodbye. I promise Helen that I'd come back to wipe those tears away. Although I've sailed so far away, you seem so close my dear. Don't worry darling, with you on my mind, there's nothing that I fear.

I have to knock off now but Always remembering, Never Forgetting, Loving you forever Mike

The men patrolled their positions on the Rhine, waiting for the Germans to open fire. The stress of anticipating the attack wreaked havoc on their nerves. Many wanted to wait as long as possible, while others wished the imminent attack would manifest quickly. As the men waited by the Rhine, the medics, the aides, and the doctors moved the aid station to a woodchopper's house and waited for the inevitable casualties.

A corporal rushed into the aid station. A lanky man, limping and bleeding from the leg, held onto the corporal's neck. "I'm sorry," the corporal said. "I shot him."

Mike darted toward them. "What? You shot a man from your own unit?"

"He gave me no choice. I asked him the password at the checkpoint, and he didn't know it. I can't let anyone pass me that doesn't know it. He kept mumbling and stuttering. It was dark. I couldn't see. If I knew who he was, I wouldn't have shot him."

"Well, help me lay him on this table." Mike cut open the wounded man's pant leg to reveal an extensive bullet wound in his thigh. Dr. Rodgers, one of the battalion doctors, told Mike to stop the bleeding while he got the instruments to withdraw the bullet. Mike's heart beat rapidly as he assisted the doctor, who extracted the bullet and sewed up the wound.

Mike wiped the blood from his hands. "Doc, can you believe our first casualty was caused by one of our own?"

"Yeah, it's a shame. It could've been avoided. But it's preparation for what we'll be seeing soon."

Mike nodded. "Unfortunately, I guess you're right."

Orders were delivered to move the aid station closer to the anticipated attack. The men packed the equipment and the supplies on a truck and transferred everything to a schoolhouse in Strasbourg about twenty minutes away. With only half the supplies unloaded, two men carried a wounded soldier toward the aid station. "We have a man unconscious, and his face is pretty torn up. He was messing with his bazooka, and it blew up in his face."

Mike dropped the supply box. "Take him into the schoolhouse!" he yelled. He frantically grabbed clean bandages and methodically sopped up blood from the soldier's destroyed face. Striving to assess the damage, he noticed that flaps of skin had been demolished, revealing the underlying tissues and muscles and the deep wounds. "Hey, doc, you need to take a look at him," Mike said. "He's gonna need surgery." The doctor administered morphine and stabilized the bleeding. Mike transfused plasma and prepared the soldier for evacuation to a field hospital.

Standing outside the schoolhouse, Dr. Rodgers commented, "Mike, you did an excellent job under pressure."

"Thanks, but I can't erase the boy's blown-up face from my mind."

"You need to stop thinking about it. You'll get used to it."

Mike thought, *What kind of man have you become if you're hardened to seeing young men destroyed?*

Chapter Twenty-Three

Beginning of January 1945

The following day, the Rainbow moved out of Strasbourg. As the convoy progressed, it was evident the French believed Germany would regain the Alsace Region by the miles-long string of refugees. Columns of bodies, mostly women and children, dragged anything movable, stuffed with their possessions, through the snow and the mud. Mothers held their tiny infants close to their chests while pushing a baby buggy bulging with household items. Some refugees used horses to move their carts, while others harnessed older children or dogs to pull the wagons. The terror in their eyes and their hopeless expressions communicated their silent feelings of anguish and defeat. As the convoy passed, several women shouted at them in French. The soldiers looked on in confusion, unsure whether the women were pleading for help or cursing them.

Sympathetically, the jeep driver spoke out, "Look at all these people escaping with no place to go. I wish we could do something for them."

Mike replied, "We can win this war, so they have a home to go back to."

"I hope so, too, Sarge, but from what I've seen, the only thing these people have left is a piece of land."

The line of refugees thinned as the convoy arrived at Neuhof, south of Strasbourg. The men broke camp for the night, anticipating German movement. Since Christmas Eve, the task force had advanced from Strasbourg to Hatten and had encountered very little hostility. Occasionally, intermittent fire crossed the Rhine from either side endeavoring to determine exact positions or ward off a scouting soldier. The Germans held back a full-fledged attack until the gloomy shadows of the morning at 0745 on the fifth of January. Then, the Panzer German Tanker division showcased its destructive reputation and military skills to the Americans. The Germans attacked Gambsheim and several other cities along the Rhine with mortar guns and howitzers and bombarded the division with 88s from the large antitank guns.

As the 88s landed around them, the American soldiers' ears vibrated from the kabooms, and the ground shook violently. A few, caught off guard as the earth rumbled under them, stumbled to the ground. With the support of the 12th Armored Division, the artillery guns blasted, grenades flew, and the infantrymen shot their BARs—Browning Automatic Rifles—and repeatedly reloaded. Across the sky, streams of light flew high, descended, and exploded. The task force's first battle and the ensuing casualties had begun.

A red cross on the medics' helmets provided no advantage as they forged through the thick smoke. They zigzagged around eruptions of black dirt spouting from the ground like oil geysers as shells exploded. In the darkness, the glow from burning trees emitted enough light for medics to discern the outlines of fallen soldiers. Trying to stay low, Mike sprinted through the spattering of light and darkness. He trembled as he stopped and knelt to assess a soldier's injuries. The young man's innards were hanging out and his blood poured like water onto the snow. Mike had been trained for this medical scenario but not for the heartache. He realized he might not be able to save the man. Yet although he'd been instructed to ignore a soldier if the outcome deemed hopeless, Mike refused to make that decision. The man cried out in gut-wrenching pain, and Mike administered morphine and covered his wounds with sulfa and bandages. After pinning the morphine syrette to the man's collar to inform other medics of the dosage, he ordered the litter squad to take the man to the aid station.

The whistling, thunderous bombs shook the ground while sirens, screams of the wounded, and darkness seemed like the decimation of the world. Smells of burning skin, the bitter taste of metal, and mutilated bodies overpowered Mike but created the impetus to persist and perform his job. He thought, *These lousy Krauts aren't going to win. If I have anything to do with it, these men are not going to die.* He shouted to the corpsmen, "Get these men out of here NOW and undercover so we can treat them!" An assembly line of treatment developed as he bolted from one soldier to another, patching them up and moving on to the next. His adrenaline surged through his veins as he attended to the soldiers.

As the day grew longer, sunlight streamed in through the dark clouds of smoke, making it easier for medics to find men needing care. The light also allowed the Germans to pursue their targets in the large open fields of farmland. The Rainbow soldiers did not recoil but fearlessly assaulted the enemy, aiming their M-1 rifles at the tanks trying to penetrate a weak spot or infiltrate a slit. The inexperienced men fought like seasoned veterans, causing immense destruction to the Germans.

The day dragged on. The chaos of bombing and never-ending shrill cries for help in the frigid temperatures challenged the medics. While attempting to treat a soldier, Mike reached into his bag with a quivering, half-dead hand. Fumbling for the needed supplies, he dropped the syrette of morphine in the snow. As he tried to retrieve the syrette, his red, ice-encrusted hand burned from the cold and stiffened. The man begged for water, but when Mike opened his canteen, not a drop could be offered. It had frozen solid.

The relentless Germans continued their intense barrage of 88s, clearing everything in sight. Tanks were tossed over as effortlessly as flipping a pancake, ripping off the runners and setting the area on fire. The Rainbow Division suffered excessive losses, and a German task commander yelled to the U.S. soldiers, "Surrender, surrender! Don't you know when you are surrounded?"

The troops refused to relinquish their first battle, and the German officer's command infuriated Private First-Class Anthony Toste. He greeted the request by firing his BAR directly into the white surrender flag, ripping the German soldier's arm off, and sending it into the wind. The American Tank Destroyers finally rolled in and ravaged the Germans, holding the line.

At nightfall, Mike was directed to move out of the field and retreat to the aid station to administer to numerous wounded and dying patients. Away from the artillery fire and with additional medical supplies and plasma, he tried to perform miracles. He witnessed men survive who appeared ready to die, while others, who had not seemed as grisly, passed in the middle of a sentence. Finally, after forty-eight exhausting, sleepless hours, Mike treated the final victim.

The front line and house-to-house fighting, in and around Weyersheim and Gambsheim, grew in intensity. Casualties streamed into the aid station in a frenetic manner. German troops advanced again, and the aid station withdrew to a beer hall, away from the artillery fire. The German tanks and gunners propelled their ammunition, but the Rainbow Division held its positions and regained two-thirds of Hatten and won Sessenheim, only after depleting its ammunition supply.

When the battle ceased, the infantrymen could finally catch their breath, but the medics continued laboring over the soldiers. After the severely wounded were patched up and evacuated, the medics tended to other soldiers. When one soldier stopped asking for help, another followed right behind him.

The Germans remained at the Rhine and intermittently threw a shell or some firepower toward the Americans, but for the next two days, the deafening sounds of bombs and cries dissipated. Instead of treating casualties, Mike attended to the deceased.

He recoiled in horror as he approached rows and rows of lifeless bodies. With each step, he proceeded more slowly. He stopped at the first man, whom he remembered treating at the aid station. If only he could have done more. Mike withdrew the dog tags from the soldier's shirt, recorded his name, and unhurriedly proceeded to the next man. Kneeling by the next soldier, he turned the man's head to reach the dog tags that had slipped to one side. Mike's throat tightened, and his muscles tensed. He had spoken to this man about his family after Christmas Eve service. Now they would mourn his departed soul, striving to survive without him.

Mike, teary eyed, refused to surrender to his emotions. His heart could not bear the loss of every man. For the sake of his own mental health, he needed to remember that war resulted in countless deaths. He quickly proceeded to the next man, tried to ignore his previous brief encounter with him, and perfunctorily recorded his statistics.

Later that evening, Mike tried to sleep, but the sounds of explosions and gunfire reverberated in his brain. When he closed his eyes, the grueling scenes of blood oozing from torn legs and missing arms and the bags of stiff soldiers filled his mind. Desperately trying to eradicate the images, he focused on Helen and his family, but the repercussions of war overpowered the wondrous memories. Although his racing heart decelerated, it still pummeled in his chest as if he were running. He pulled his jacket over his head and cupped his hands over his ears, tossing back and forth, as he wrestled with his thoughts and visions. His hands and legs quivered not only from the frigid air but from the stress on his mind and body. Dawn was a few hours away, and Mike knew he could not endure another sleepless night. He shuffled to the aid station and withdrew a little blue pill of sodium amytal from the bottle. He tossed the calming drug in his mouth and swallowed it. The tablet slid rapidly through his system but took an eternity to stall his mind and allow him to sleep.

Mike awoke rested, but the bloody remnants of war and the gruesome images still raged in his mind. Within minutes of his reporting for duty, a burly soldier, visibly quivering and shrieking, stumbled into the aid station. "I can't sleep. My head hurts. You need to help me."

As Mike analyzed the soldier's complaints, a private bolted through the door, hysterically crying, "Help! Stop the sounds in my head. Please! I beg you. Stop the whistling and explosions in my head!"

Another soldier followed behind him, flailing his arms. "I need a doctor." He grabbed Mike's arm. "Help me! They're all dead. So many dead. They're all around me. My buddy blew apart right next to me." Tugging at his uniform, he said, "Look, his blood is on my jacket."

Mike thrust him into a chair. "Pull yourself together, buddy. I know it's hard, pal, but is there anything wrong with you physically?"

"Look at my arms! I can't shoot a gun. I think they're becoming paralyzed," the man said.

The doctor and the medics spoke to the men to determine their problem. One rifleman, when questioned, sobbed, "I don't know, but I can't sleep or eat. My body aches. I don't think I can go back. Please don't make me go back. Listen! The tanks are coming. They're right outside. They're gonna kill us!"

Mike reassured him there were no tanks outside the tent and that the fighting had ceased, but the crazed soldier blabbered and screamed incessantly.

After additional questioning, the doctor told the medics, "These men are suffering from shell shock. We need to give them sodium amytal and watch them for a while. They may need to be sent to a field hospital to determine if they can go back to the front."

After Mike administered the drugs, the men quieted and fell asleep. As he sat in the room keeping vigil, his heart ached. He understood precisely how the demons of war had attacked their minds and knew he needed to remain strong to survive. Kneeling next to the men, he thanked God for giving him the strength to sustain the previous battles. He begged God to be his armor against the hellish thoughts raging in his head.

The following day, the Germans persisted in finding weak spots and forcefully hammered the troops, intent on regaining this important real estate on the Rhine. The clamorous sounds of bombing and rapid machine-gun fire vibrated throughout the aid station, amplifying the medics' anxieties. As they treated combat injuries, along with those the men suffered from crossing the occasionally waist-high streams of freezing water, a shell landed directly outside the aid station. Debris penetrated the walls. Mike covered his face and ducked, evading a large piece of shrapnel that hurtled over him and out the window.

He screamed, "Damn it!" Unharmed, he cautiously rose to his feet and asked if everyone was okay.

One soldier, waiting for treatment, screamed, "Oh, God, save me, save me!"

Mike grasped his shoulders. "Hey, buddy, you're okay. It missed us."

The soldier babbled, "I was grateful to be rescued and in the aid station, and I'm still not safe. I have to get out of here. I have to get out here. I can't take it anymore!"

"We're gonna take care of you, pal, now calm down, and we'll evacuate you as soon as it's safe," Mike said and turned to another patient.

Chapter Twenty-Four

Mid-January 1945

The 36th Division relieved the Rainbow on the front line on January 18th, as sectors from the 7th Army withdrew to locations west of Haguenau. As the men traversed the snowy mountains of the Haguenau forest, icy winds stabbed at their skin. The convoy struggled through mud and snow, progressing at a snail's pace. Mike attempted to steal some sleep while the convoy crawled along the icy roads, but his violent shivering prevented him from relaxing.

After arriving at their destination, he settled into a drafty tent. As the darkness dragged on, he yearned for daylight and the opportunity to find warmer shelter. The sun rose, and he took inventory. He readied the aid station in a schoolhouse, free from the bitter winds. While he was counting bandages, two soldiers charged in, holding a private between them, hobbling and bleeding.

"What happened?" Mike asked.

"He got shot in the foot, and it's bleeding bad."

"How'd it happen, buddy?"

The wounded soldier stared at the ground, his eyes avoiding Mike's, and hesitantly mumbled, "I shot myself, . . . but it was an accident."

Mike asked firmly, "How'd you do that?"

He screamed, "God damn it, I don't know! I was walking, and the gun went off! That's all!"

"And it was pointed at your foot?"

"Yes! How bad is it? Will they send me home?"

"After the doctor sees you, he'll let you know, but I don't think you'll be going home," Mike said.

Dejected and ashamed, the soldier said, "If you can't walk, they gotta send you home. Even if it's an accident. Right?"

"I don't know, the doc needs to look at it." Mike sneered at the soldier. "You're lucky the gun didn't 'accidentally' shoot you in the head." He bent down to sop up the blood. "So. You have a girl back home?" he asked.

"I think so. I'm not sure," the soldier replied sheepishly.

"Why aren't you sure?"

"The letters she writes me seem to say she's tired of waiting."

"Were you hoping a bad injury might send you back to her?"

The soldier said in a wrenching tone, "I just want this damn war to end! I don't want to die!"

"None of us want to die, soldier, but we got to do what we got to do."

The man lay in silence while Mike got the bleeding under control and administered morphine for the pain. Witnessing the terror in the troubled man's eyes, Mike realized the man had wanted to escape and chose the easiest way to dodge his abysmal reality. Instead of fighting until war's end and returning a proud man for serving his country, he'd be court-martialed and dishonorably discharged with a bum leg. Mike cursed the Germans for starting this war and ruining virtuous men.

The following day, commander headquarters sent word to place the 232nd in reserves in Bossendorf. As the convoy advanced, the below-freezing temperature and icy road conditions transformed the journey into a competition between man and nature. Mike trudged up the icy road a couple hundred feet to board a truck, only to fall and slide backward to his original location. Rising to his feet, he noticed the men tumbling like bowling pins as they endeavored to forge ahead. Heavy jeeps attempted to tackle the ice but lost control and crashed into trees. One jeep rolled over, breaking through the frozen creek, and injuring a few men. The horrendous struggle to Bossendorf ended several hours later. Finally arriving at their destination, the men found quarters in the bombed-out buildings. Men who had previously been crammed into foxholes like rats in a cage extended their legs on a dry, albeit dirty, floor to procure a few hours of serene sleep.

January 25, 1945

Wednesday

Dearest Helen:

Helen, I keep thinking of you all the time and keep loving you as always. There isn't a day that goes by that I don't miss you and long to hold you in my arms again.

Since I've been over here, I believe I could write volumes of what I've seen, heard or experienced. Since I'm not allowed to write all I'd like to, I'll tell you all I can. I've been in action and saw some sights. Six of our aid men have been put up for the bronze star. I'm pretty sure they'll get it. They sure do deserve it.

While coming through some of the towns I noticed a great many manure piles. It seems a person's wealth is judged by the size of the pile. At least I've seen that the wealthy people have the biggest manure piles. The barns are attached right on to the houses and extend so that it forms more or less of a patio. A yard in the middle of all the houses. A woman showed me a calf that was five days old, and I sure was surprised to find out they were so big at that age. Me being a city slicker, I wouldn't know about such things.

I got a kick out of one of my buddies. He has his pockets so loaded in his combat jacket, especially the lowest pockets, he looks like a buxom woman of the ninety's. Those with the hourglass figure. I'll be getting the same way if I don't watch out because I have my socks under my shirt around my waist to keep them dry. Looks like I've been drinking beer all my life. I'm enclosing a one-mark note, which is equivalent to 15 francs, 100 Phennings or 30 cents in American money.

I'm thinking of you constantly and loving you always.

Always remembering. Never Forgetting. Loving you forever. Mike

The few days in reserves passed as swiftly as a bird in flight, and the 232nd moved forward to Schweighausen by the Moder River. The Rainbow Division took an offensive position and attacked the Germans along several strategic points by the river. The Germans counterattacked and blasted the area with their tanks, mortar, and artillery. This assault mimicked the first attack, with heavy mortar and artillery fire, a bombardment by a slew of 88s, and numerous casualties. During the assault, Mike sprinted through the enemy fire and found the bodies of his fellow soldiers ravaged by the shells and artillery, resembling rag dolls chewed by a dog. These men could not be resurrected. Mike shifted to the next injured man, and as he hunched, a mortar shell exploded nearby. A piece of shrapnel whizzed past his ear. He reached around his neck to feel for blood or a wound but found only icy sweat. The enemy's attack bulldozed toward the Rainbow, and Mike noticed one man severely wounded ahead of the 232nd position in the middle of strong mortar fire. He directed a litter squad to the infantryman's position. While zigzagging through the smoky, burning fields, a mortar exploded not far from his position. Mike felt the vibration in his gut. Shrapnel and bullets buzzed over the heads of the medics as they treated infantryman. They risked their lives carrying the man back to safety as they dodged falling trees, lethal flying tree limbs, and enemy fire. The man on the stretcher reached for

Mike's shoulder and kept repeating, "Thank you," until the morphine caused his eyes to close. Away from the center of fire, Mike continued to bandage the man and forwarded him to an aid station.

This ugly scenario continued until the Rainbow Division destroyed two German battalions, killing eight hundred Germans and taking more than a hundred prisoners in a twenty-four-hour period. Although the fighting diminished, a bevy of casualties entered the aid station at a steady pace.

Night fell, and the troops anticipating another attack took cover in a cellar. In the frigid darkness, their tension and anxiety grew as taut as threads on a parachute. Fear overpowered their exhaustion, and not a single eye shut for even a second.

Chapter Twenty-Five

End of January 1945

More than half the men were killed, wounded, or taken prisoner as a result of the vigorous fighting forces of the German army at Strasbourg, Gambsheim, Weyersheim, and Schweighausen. The Rainbow, unable to bear further casualties, was relieved of duty and moved to Moselle on January 28th for reorganization and instruction. News circulated as the second sector of the Rainbow arrived in France on January 18th, ready to reunite with the task force to complete the entire division.

The men loaded into a convoy of trucks, and Mike settled onto a stretcher in the back of the ambulance. "I never thought I'd say riding on a stretcher on a bumpy road is comfortable, but it is," he said. "It feels damn good to be out of the cold and away from the fighting."

Another medic groaned. "I can't relax thinking about what just happened. Over half our men are gone!"

Mike wiped the dirt from his face. "I know. It's a damn shame. I thought it'd never stop."

Frantically puffing on his cigarette, the medic said, "It could've been any of us or all of us. We were right there with them. We're lucky to be alive, and it makes me wonder if our luck might run out. I picture my Ma getting news I'm dead and . . . it just kills me."

Mike pulled a blanket over his legs. "You can't think about it too long, it'll drive you nuts. I don't know if it matters, but I always envision myself returning to my gal and getting married. It's the only thing that keeps me going. You got a girl?"

"Yeah, and she's great."

"Try thinking about her and your future and not about what might happen," Mike said.

"Easier said than done. Right now, I'm just happy they're removing us from front lines."

The conversation ended, their voices drowned out by sounds of snoring from the other two men. In a short time, all the men had surrendered to exhaustion.

Several hours later, the convoy arrived at Moselle, and the men found themselves surrounded by evidence of heavy bombing by the Germans. Not a single pane of glass remained intact in any of the roofless buildings. Within hours, the troops boarded up the windows and cleared the debris to make sleeping quarters. Mike was fortunate to find an undamaged bed in an old farmhouse and claimed it for the night.

The next morning, the cooks converted the taverns into mess halls, and in less than forty-eight hours, the site was organized. During the afternoon, the men received instructions about mines and booby traps and the procedures for handling prisoners and captured enemy documents. Mike had dreaded these lectures in boot camp, but now he enjoyed the relief they provided from the rigors of combat.

Life felt normal again, safe and away from enemy fire. For the first time in weeks, the men showered at a cleansing station in Nancy, several miles from the command post at Château-Salins. The warmth of the water washed away Mike's sweat and the smell of dirt, blood, and smoke. He wished the cascading amenity could pamper his body for days, but he was soon kicked out by the next man, eager to indulge in this refreshment.

Although Mike's mood had been lifted by the shower, it quickly morphed to anger as he observed the ravages of the war on the civilians. The dazed and dirty villagers rambled along, scouring the ground for food. One woman scraped a rotten smashed apple from the cobblestone street while an old man captured a bird with a bucket. Their pride had been vanquished as they lived among the streets like rats scurrying for scraps and garbage. As Mike waited in line at the mess hall, a group of children gathered outside with pots and pans. When the men exited, the clamoring children rushed toward them, begging for their leftovers. The soldiers scraped morsels of food from their trays into the children's containers. Fights broke out as the children shoved one another, scrambling for precious bites of nourishment. Strength and size prevailed as the older ones garnered the majority of the booty. The littlest ones walked away, hungry and disappointed.

A corporal turned to Mike. "It kills me to see this. I have a wife and a baby, and I'd hate to see this happen to them."

"I know, these poor people have lost everything."

Mike thought of Helen, grateful she was safe from the effects of bombings. Pining for her love, he found an old table and, as he started to write her a letter, his creativity emerged. He folded the unlined paper into the shape of a card and decided to sketch what he desired the most. Examining Helen's photo, he slowly drew her face. With each stroke of the pencil, she came to life. Soon, her image was smiling back at him. Mike stared at the portrait for a while and then embellished it with a banner: "To My Valentine." He expressed his sentiments on the inside of the card, kissed the drawing, and tucked it into an envelope for her.

February 2, 1945 Somewhere in France

Friday

Dearest Helen:

Even though I've been gone a short time, it seems a lifetime since I've seen or heard from you and always hoping and praying that soon all this will be ended so that we can start life anew. While I'm reminiscing here now, varied thoughts and emotions overcome me. We talked of many things while I held my hand in yours. Some may have been silly, but they were our thoughts. Something you and I have to cherish. We talked of home, children, and many other things but the main thing is we both knew that we belonged to each other. We both didn't agree on whether we'd like so many girls or so many boys but we both agreed that having children was what made a house a home. I told you how much I'd like to come home from work with you waiting at the door to greet me with a smile and one of your tender kisses, with my favorite meal on the table and an easy chair nearby where I could relax afterward. We were always planning and dreaming. In fact, we still are and I'm going to see that these dreams turn into reality when this is over. I can change my darling's name to MRS. I'm still planning and making sure that all of these things were not just dreams and that they actually come true. That is if the good Lord is generous enough to bring me back. I'm sure he will. Oh, before I forget I want to tell you that I've sent some money to you. God only knows when you'll get it.

Without each other we're like flowers without sunshine, school without books and a fish without water. Now we know that one is not good without the other. Right now, I've been planning, thinking, perhaps you might even call it dreaming of the things that the future will bring us. No matter what I plan or think about, there's always you. What every man wants after the war, and I'm no different, is a place he can call home. A place to come home to, a wonderful wife, a few children. Just the thought of such things seem so far away but let's hope that in time all of our dreams and plans turn into reality. Something that we both can hold on to and really call our own. Right now it is you and I. I'm just waiting for the day it will be WE.

Oh, by the way I sure was surprised to hear that your sister Florence became engaged. I intend to write her and offer my congratulations but would you in the meantime offer her my best wishes. Thanks a million. I believe you've noticed by this time that I've enclosed a sketch I drew of you. It really doesn't do you justice but even as such I hope you like it.

I sure would appreciate it if you'd send me a recent picture of yourself. Those I have are becoming worn and faded

Always remembering. Never Forgetting. Loving you forever Mike

Chapter Twenty-Six

After mail call, an officer announced that twelve lucky soldiers would win a pass to Paris. Letters from home delivered a shot of plasma for the men. Adding the possibility of a trip provided a transfusion they all needed. The officer threw the names into a helmet and tossed them around. When he called the first name, a private jumped up, waving his arms, and hooted, "Yee haw!" The next few lucky men reacted in a similar manner while the other soldiers gazed at them, silently wishing for their own names to be called. Eleven names had been called, and with all the drama of a soap opera, the commander slowly reached into the helmet, cleared his throat, and paused. The men held their breath as he stated, "And the last lucky man is . . . Staff Sergeant Mike Wozniak." Everyone sighed. Mike threw his helmet into the air, caught it, and dashed back to his temporary housing to prepare for a short liberation.

Relaxing in the back of the jeep, Mike said, "I always wanted to see Paris. I can't believe I might actually have a little bit of fun during this war!"

"It's about time," another solider replied. "We just spent weeks in hell. We deserve this!"

After the long ride to Paris, the men eagerly hastened to the hotel the army had provided, ready to explore the town.

Mike deposited his duffel bag, with the intention to proceed directly into town. Yet when he eyed the comfortable bed begging him to lie on it, he accepted the invitation. He sunk into the mattress, closed his eyes, and imagined relaxing at home with his dog on his belly. He remarked to his buddy, "You know, I'd stay here all day if there wasn't a big city out there waiting for me to explore it."

Enticed by the soft bed, the corporal plopped down next to Mike. "Ohhh, this feels like home, but I need to get some hot coffee and chow."

"I know, me, too," Mike said, "but I noticed a bathtub that's insisting I soak my tired bones in it. Besides, I can't stand this army smell. I'll see you around, I'm sure."

Mike didn't know which he preferred, the soft bed or the hot water soothing his sore muscles. Both allowed him to feel at ease for the first time on this foreign soil.

Thoroughly clean and relaxed, he bounced down the hotel steps and headed straight toward a lieutenant's recommendation, a Red Cross facility. Dashing across the street, he negotiated numerous bicyclists barreling down the road and entered the Rainbow Corner. A volunteer greeted him and directed him to the cafeteria-style food line. Mike wanted to devour everything in sight and piled a mountain of food on his plate. He walked over to the tables and found a seat next to his buddies. "How'd you like the grub?" he asked.

The corporal replied, "Better than army mess, but the atmosphere is even better. Take a gander. This is the most women I've seen in one place for months, and some of them are really stacked." Mike turned his head, and a girl with an inviting smile tapped him on the shoulder. "Are you coming back tonight for the dance?"

"I'd sure like to hear some good music," he said, "so I just might do that."

As the attractive woman left, the corporal leaned toward his fellow soldiers. "Hey, this sure beats shooting the bull on patrol, huh?"

A private smiled. "You're damn right. The dames are beautiful and a hell of a lot better than waiting for some Kraut to come out of the woods. At least, I don't have to worry about getting killed."

Mike shoved food into his mouth. "I know what you mean. My nerves were wound so tight, I'm surprised they didn't choke off my blood supply."

His buddy chimed in. "Damn, it feels great to be here, and as far as I'm concerned, the war is over for a while. The only thing I care about is food, beer, and women."

The private added, "Damn right! Now that's the right attitude! So, Sarge what's your plan for tonight? Me and the guys here are thinkin' 'bout checking out the lovely French dames walking around the city and seein' what they have to offer."

"Sorry, buddy, that's not for me," Mike said. "I promised my fiancé to be true to her, and I intend to keep my word. Besides, these French women are nothing compared to my Helen. She's better than any of them."

"Lucky for you, but for me, well, I figure I deserve some fun. Besides, I might not make it home, so I'm enjoying myself tonight. If you know what I mean." The private winked.

"That's up to you," Mike said. "I may never have a chance to see Paris again, so I'm gonna take in some sights and come back here later for the dance."

"Suit yourself, Sarge, but I think you're making the wrong decision."

Mike, agitated by the private's judgment, retorted, "I think you're making the wrong decision! I didn't give you my opinion, so next time keep it to yourself."

"Whoa, Mike, I thought you said you were relaxed! Listen, we'll see you later."

His buddies pushed their chairs away and set out to wander the streets, searching to fulfill their fantasies.

At the table, Mike lit a cigarette, glanced around the room, and noticed the GIs from other units swooning over the women like salivating dogs waiting for a piece of meat. *If any of these men had girls back home waiting for them, why would they risk losing the women they love?* Puffing on his cigarette, he retrieved a picture of Helen and stared at it for several minutes. Excited to explore Paris, he tucked the picture in his pocket, gulped his coffee, and headed out to the city's streets.

Paris was New York's city counterpart, yet very few cars rumbled down its streets. Instead, numerous horse-drawn carriages clomped along the cobblestones. Mike stopped at the corner and imagined Paris in the late 1800s: roads bustling with carriages and women in long dresses, twirling parasols and parading along the avenues like a Claude Monet painting. He envisioned women perusing the elegant shops and relishing the slow pace of life, stopping to chat with their friends along the way.

Lost in time, he strolled the streets and, as he turned the corner, noticed an impressive square with a massive column monument towering over the area. He had discovered the Place Vendôme, hosting some of the most notable, grandest, and oldest architectural buildings of Paris. He ventured through the square and wandered past the luxurious, well-known Ritz Hotel. Continuing his walk toward the Seine River, he spied the Eiffel Tower in the distance and marveled at the iconic architectural structure. Enamored with the area, he wished he had his camera so he could share the magnificent sites with Helen when he returned home.

Unable to capture the images on film, he meandered the peaceful streets and searched for postcards as mementoes of his time in Paris. In one small shop, he stumbled upon the cards and several unique French items to send home to his parents and Helen. Before traipsing back to the Red Cross facility, he stopped at the PX center and purchased a beer and French cigarettes.

A live band played "Boogie Woogie Bugle Boy" as Mike entered, reminding him of romantic nights spent dancing with Helen. He lingered and reminisced while listening to American and French tunes until a woman asked him to dance. Mike crushed his cigarette in the ashtray, hesitantly accepted her hand, and accompanied her to the dance floor. After one dance, he tipped his hat and proceeded to the doorway. Pulling his collar around his neck, he slowly walked the few blocks back to his hotel, primed for a good night's sleep.

After experiencing the outstanding views and buildings the previous day, he awoke early and asked his buddies if they wanted to join him on a tour of the city. Yet after indulging till the wee hours of the morning, the men were too inebriated and exhausted to face Paris.

Mike swept through the city after a hot breakfast and better-than-usual coffee. He started the day by visiting regal-looking Le Madeleine church, with its numerous columns and statues. Inside, Mike felt miniscule amid the magnitude and splendor of the structure. After saying a few prayers, he ventured through Place de Concord and continued along Champs-Elysées Avenue, admiring the tall trees lining both sides of the street. At the end of the avenue, he visited the tomb of the French Unknown Soldier directly under the Arc de Triomphe. For a few minutes, he forgot about the war as he lingered in Paris's grandeur and history.

He crossed the bridge to visit Notre Dame Cathedral, tingling with goose bumps as he entered. This ugly war had given him the opportunity to stand among the statues and the architecture described in Victor Hugo's *The Hunchback of Notre Dame*. While the infamous bells rang, guilt overshadowed his pleasure as he thought about the nearby troops enduring the war.

Walking back to the hotel, Mike stopped and stared at the odd-looking cars rolling pass him. When he arrived at the Red Cross, he approached the volunteers outside. "Can you tell me about the cars with contraptions on the back that look like barrels?"

One woman replied in a French accent, "Oh, yes. Ha, ha. They are different. Because of the gas shortage, people developed new ways to run their car. That one is a wood-burning car."

Mike scratched his head. "I'll be damned. I never knew you could do that. They'll never believe me back home, especially since I can't take a photograph."

The woman replied, "You want a photograph? Today, for a few francs, we are taking photos of the soldiers. If you get it taken now, we'll have it ready for you soon, and you can send it home." Mike, in his usual form, hammed it up for the photographer and ate dinner while waiting for the prints.

After eating, on a suggestion from a fellow soldier, Mike negotiated his way among the routes and the trains of the subway to Pigalle. Although numerous people spoke English and eagerly helped him with directions, their accent and the unfamiliar French names caused Mike to board the wrong train. After several attempts, he finally arrived in Pigalle, the slums of Paris. He sneered at the bawdy, perverse sights and behavior and questioned why his buddy had suggested this raunchy location. Each block reeked of excessive perversion, and Mike searched the streets for some redeeming quality to write home about. Finally, he found a place on the outskirts established by the government to keep military men off the streets of this sordid neighborhood. He wandered in, ordered a beer, and discovered a variety show of French singers, jugglers, and other acts. After the show, Mike, a little tipsy, boarded the wrong train again. After several attempts, he finally arrived back at the hotel and collapsed onto his comfortable bed, with only a few hours remaining before he needed to head back to the front.

Chapter Twenty-Seven

February/March 1945

Mike had finished his duties as Commanding Officer at the aid station, ready to catch some sleep, when he heard cries and foreign mumbling. Peeking outside, he saw several refugees approach the aid station. The worn men and women pleaded in half Polish and half German for food and shelter. Mike greeted them, "*Jak mogę pomóc.*"

An older gentleman stated, "Ah, you speak Polish. *Wspanialy!*"

The conversation continued in Polish.

"It isn't often we find Americans who speak Polish," the man said. "Someday nobody will be speaking this language. Our country has been taken over so many times, and the Germans have been there for more than six years. Now everything is in German."

"I'm sure it's been difficult dealing with the Germans."

Mike was unaware that his statement had released a multitude of emotions locked in the old man's head. With anger in his eyes and a clenched jaw, he proceeded to tell Mike his story.

"Yes, it was hard to see the Germans destroy our land and people in a short time, and now we roam all over the place. We have no country, no home, and soon probably no language. The Germans are brutal and treated us like slaves. They took my wife and raped her while they held a gun to my head. I will never forgive myself for not fighting for her. She was so beaten, she couldn't even talk. Then they came back a couple of days later and stole her away from me. The Germans killed half of my family, and the rest who could not escape were sent to labor camps. I don't know how I escaped. Maybe they thought I was too old. When I left, everyone was starving, while the German soldiers ate like kings, stealing our crops and farm animals. I hate the Germans, and I know I will never forget. You need to win the battle we lost."

The pain and anguish on the refugees' faces and their stories pierced Mike's heart and left him speechless. He suddenly understood that all the refugees and the innocent victims depended on his service as much as the United States did, if not more. He wanted to provide anything and everything for these people: hope, a home, and food. Searching his pockets, he retrieved a roll of lifesavers, a candy bar, some crackers, and a stick of gum and handed them to the man. Realizing they needed more than the pittance he offered, he searched the aid station and grabbed an army blanket and a few ration cans. "I will pray for you and your family," he said.

Three days passed, and the respite ended. The men traveled to Wimmenau, closer to the German border, to relieve the 45th Division. The weather worsened, and the jeeps and the trucks grappled with the snow-covered terrain of the Vosges Mountains. Mike gazed in awe at the towering peaks and valleys below as he was jostled around. Stirred by the beautiful scenery, he shouted to whoever might be listening, "It's a damn shame we're traveling through such striking countryside and Hitler's hell bent on destroying it. For what?"

A soldier shouted back, "I agree with you, war is a useless waste of mankind! But just think how good it's gonna feel when we take over Germany and capture Hitler."

Mike added, "I'm a God-fearing man, but I have to admit nothing would be sweeter than to see Hitler destroyed."

Feb 20, 1945, Tuesday

Darling,

Gert wrote and told me about Mary Ann liking your ring better than Flo's. I told her she certainly has a smart daughter because she knows a good thing when she sees it.

By the way give Gabby my best regards and tell her I said hello. She'd probably break my neck if I didn't remember her, but I do, because she gave you a few breaks so you and I could have some time together.

While reading your letters I imagine I'm back home and you're telling me all of these things personally.

Here's a few lines to express how I feel. Now I'll admit right now I'm no poet. But here goes anyway.

To Be With You

It matters not where I may be

I don't care what things I see

Viewing the worlds pretended pleasures

Invokes me in still greater measure

To have you back again with me

No matter what fate tries to do

In my endless strife to rend anew

I will not falter, will not tire

I will always be inspired

In my undying hope to be with you

Overhead, I hear some airplanes now. I sure hope they're headed for Berlin. That place should be kaput by now (Kaput is broken, that's a German word).

Well, I've got to close now. Always Remembering: Those tender lips, the twinkle in your eyes, that pleasant smile and sweet embrace.

Never Forgetting: The walks through the parks, the pleasant peaceful nights, the hilarious parties, the theatre. (I remember seeing the tear in your eyes when we saw the "Song of Bernadette" and how you laughed when we saw "When Irish Eyes are Smiling"

Loving you forever for what you mean to me and for what you are.

Love Always Mike

The Rainbow aggressively patrolled the region between Wimmenau and Lichtenberg, only a day's march from the German border. The combat and reconnaissance patrols scrutinized the enemy, ready to smash their defenses and take prisoners. Engineers moved forward and combed the area, clearing sections of mines to open a route for the troops. As one engineer took a step, his ears perked up as he heard a snap. He stopped and stared at the broken twig on the ground. As he crept forward, the ground popped under him, a mine rose in the air, and slammed at his feet. There was no blast or shrapnel, simply a thud as it hit the ground.

He shouted to his fellow engineer, "Oh, my God, did you see that? For a minute I thought I was dead. If I don't get hit with a mine or sniper fire, I'm gonna die of a heart attack. I need a cigarette."

After their cigarette break, the men resumed the lethal duty of removing several more mines until nightfall, when they retreated to camp. As they crossed over an area near the camp, they heard a loud explosion followed by a man screeching in pain and hollering for a medic. The men cautiously walked toward the moaning sounds, trying to avoid the mines.

"Oh, my God, he's been hit!"

"I don't know what to do. Where's the medic?"

"We can carry him to the aid station. It's not far from here."

"How can we carry him without a litter? His leg is hanging on by a thread!"

"Where the hell is the medic? We need to stop this bleeding!"

Finally, an aide heard the cries and ran to the screaming man, applied a tourniquet, and carefully lifted him onto the litter to carry him the short distance to the aid station.

Mike leaped from his chair as the men brought in the wounded solider. Without hesitation, Mike offered him morphine while the other medics and the doctor tended to his wounds.

The private who had carried in the wounded man stared at the open wounds and the massive amount of blood dripping to the floor and began to cry.

Mike abruptly turned around. "What's wrong with you, soldier? You've never seen an injured man?"

He whimpered, "I have, but . . . that . . . could've been me. I stepped . . . on a mine today but it was a dud. . . . Oh, dear God."

"Listen, I'm glad you're all right, soldier, but pull yourself together and get out of here so we can take care of this man," ordered Mike.

Vigil patrols, vital to succeeding against the Germans, persisted along the lines. During the previous eleven days, the entire Rainbow Division lost 11 men, 11 more were missing, and 45 had been wounded. The ravages of the patrols were in the Rainbow's favor because the Germans had suffered greater fatalities and numbers of wounded. The Germans gained respect for the brave Rainbow men, along with their defenders, the 83rd Chemical Mortar Battalion. When the Germans attempted to open fire on the patrols, the 83rd identified their exact location and blasted them full force.

March 6, 1945, Tuesday

Dearest Helen:

Well here it is Tuesday. Just another day but each day that goes by brings us nearer to the end of this world conflict. Then we can be together again not for just a while but for always. Not as sweethearts but as man and wife. We can leave the past behind us and look forward to a better brighter future. A future without doubts and insecurity a future filled with hopes and plans that were dreamed of all this time. As each day goes by, we both will be fulfilling these hopes and these plans until they are no longer dreams but reality. Living in the past and dreaming of the future is man's only recompense in the time of war.

When I think of you, I think of love and life.

Things of beauty, grace and joy.

Your lustrous hair, your tender lips that never meet mine

Once your hand was pressed in mine

When we walked in Autumn flare

Now these hands are empty because I'm not there

The warmth of your heart thrilled me when you were near

But these are just memories because you are not here

There's nothing but memories left and when I think of you it brings an ache to my heart that keeps mounting inside.

I feel a little tired and probably don't make sense. Here's hoping I hear from you soon.

Always remembering. Never forgetting. Loving you forever.

With letters to family written and sick call completed, Mike and the corpsmen engaged in lengthy, intelligent conversations. They debated creation, evolution, military ethics and how war affects the mind. As the men grew tired, the discussion shifted to their current assignment, patrolling the enemy lines.

A private complained, "I know we're patrolling to gain intelligence on the Germans before we advance, but I'd rather keep moving forward and end this damn war."

Another corpsman added, "Yeah, but going forward increases our chances of getting killed. I'd just as soon stay here, watch a movie, and catch up on the news."

The private replied, "You're right about that! Hey, talking about the news, did you read the article in the *Stars and Stripes*? Frank Sinatra was classified as 4F for a punctured eardrum."

"Yeah, Walter Winchell said he paid $40,000 to earn that classification," Mike retorted.

"Unbelievable! I thought a punctured eardrum is a temporary thing. It heals eventually, doesn't it?" asked the private.

Mike barked, "It does, and that really pisses me off. Just because he's a celebrity, he believes he doesn't have to serve. What makes him any better than Joey Bishop or Jimmy Stewart, who are serving their country? He's a worthless coward, and he's using his money to save his ass. He should be here like us to see what this war is all about."

There was a quiet knock at the door, and a short, elderly woman poked her head inside. "*Entschuldigen Sie, bitte,*" she said and extended her arms, holding a freshly baked apple pie. Mike accepted the pie, nodding and saying, "*Danke. Danke.*" The old woman smiled, bowed her head, and backed out into the street.

"Well, a pie from a German refugee. That's the woman we treated the other day. What do you make of that?" Mike asked.

The corpsman replied, "I guess she's trying to say thank you, but you think it's safe to eat it?"

Mike propped his feet on the table. "She reminds me of my mother, with her dark hair and eyeglasses and flowered babushka."

"Hey, Mike, I'm sure your mother's sweet, but I don't know if I trust these Germans. It sure smells like home, though, and probably better than the crap we've been eating lately."

Suddenly, a private rushed in, pushing a sixteen-year-old German prisoner into the aid tent with the barrel of his gun.

"Hey, captured this Kraut, but his arm is bleeding from some injury. The captain says for one of you guys to fix him before I send him off."

Mike answered, "Sure, have him sit down."

The corpsman who had been doubtful about the pie laughed. "Maybe he'd like a piece of pie before he heads out. If he doesn't fall over, I guess we got us some homemade dessert."

March 12, 1945, Thursday

Dearest Helen,

I want you to give due consideration to what I have to write. Please weigh each point and think it over carefully.

Helen, you know I love you with my whole heart. I've written you countless letters of how much you mean to me. How much my heart aches and keeps mounting inside when I think of you, longing to hold you my arms again, feel the touch of your hands.

I've written as often as I could and I've written often, in spite of the fact that many of my letters were unanswered. I kept writing and sincerely hoping that the reason I didn't hear from you was due to the delay in mail but the days that I waited turned into weeks and the weeks into months and still no word from you. Not a single answer to the many letters I wrote to you.

I can't see, I can't hear you, but I can write and so can you. At least give me the satisfaction of hearing from you if you love me. I'm taking into consideration the war, the delay in mail and you not seeing me might have given you a different outlook. I know that you loved me before but how can I know if that still holds true when I don't hear from you now.

Helen, you know that it takes two to love, to have perfect harmony such that is needed for a happy married life.

If there's any doubt in your mind about how you feel toward me, please tell me instead of letting me keep thinking of how wonderful it will be to hold you in my arms again after this is over, to keep thinking of you waiting for me so that we can get married and have a home of our own and making our dreams and plans a reality.

I've been waiting anxiously to hear from you all these past weeks. You can at least drop me a few lines to let me know what the score is. I've always loved you since the first time I kissed you and I still love you with my whole heart, thinking constantly, hoping and praying that all this confusion would end so I could hold you in my arms again not as my girl but as my wife. When I don't hear from you it seems that my loving you is a hopeless thing not knowing whether you still love me as you did before. If you've changed your mind don't hesitate to write and tell me about it. If that's the way you feel, it's better that I know about it now. Why prolong the misery. If you still love me and you're willing to wait for me, well write me, not just once in great while but every opportunity you get. I keep getting mail regularly from home and Gert, that's what makes it tough, wondering why is it that you're not writing. I know if there was something wrong with you, if you were sick Gert would have written to me about it. You couldn't be that busy not being able to drop me a line. If there were some reason for you not writing and you told me about it at least I'd know that you still loved me and were waiting for me to come back.

Helen you've always been frank with me so don't hesitate in doing so now.

All that I dream of and hope for is to be with you not for just a short time but always. Sharing the joys and sorrows of married life and making all our dreams come true. Hoping I'll hear from you soon.

Always remembering. Never forgetting. Loving you forever, Mike

Mike packed his backpack and medical kit and stripped the aid station, preparing the supplies for transport, as part of Task Force Coleman.

A fellow medic packing boxes commented, "Hey, Sarge, looks like we'll be in Germany soon. What do ya think?"

"I don't give a shit. I just follow orders."

"Whoa, why are you in such a pissy mood all of a sudden?"

"This whole time we've been here when we've had time to read and write letters, I've hardly heard from my sweetheart. Cripes, to be honest," Mike said, "I'm not sure she *is* still my sweetheart."

"Why? Did she say she wants to break it off?"

"She hasn't said anything; that's the problem. I don't know if something is wrong. If she's sick, or she just doesn't want to wait anymore. And now we have to head out."

"Hey, Sarge, I'm sure it'll be okay. Just hang in there. We've got to be on target. We're supposed to drive twelve miles into the German lines, and I don't think it's gonna be easy."

Mike threw the bandages in a box. "Damn it, I know! You don't have to tell me that. No matter what's going on, I'm always on target! Let's go. We need to fall in."

The commanding officer addressed them. "Men, as you know, the other sections of the division, along with the Seventh Army, moved out and started their attack at 6:45 this morning. This will be our first battle as an entire unit. The 232nd will be outposting the entire division, moving northwest. The rest will take a different direction. We'll have a platoon of tanks and tank destroyers, engineers, and battery of armored field artillery, along with a platoon from the 42nd Reconnaissance Division. As we told you the other day, the terrain is rough, and part of the 513 Mule Pack Company has been attached to us and the other part to the rest of the division. You were instructed in how to load the equipment on the animals, so get to work!"

The pack and the soldiers persistently trudged the vertical climb through the roads of the Haardt Mountains, laden with mines, boulders, and intentionally felled trees. Marching through knee-high freezing snow and patches of boot-sucking mud drained their strength. The terrain tested the mules as well. Overburdened with heavy equipment, the mules crossed through a water-laden grassy marsh, and with each step, the weight sunk them into the mud up to their bellies. The men hustled to lighten their loads and wrenched the equipment from the animals, lugged it to dry land, and proceeded to pry them out of the mud. Five of the soldiers played tug of war with the burros until their legs were finally released. After the mules moved to stable ground, the men repacked the animals and endeavored to urge them forward, but the stubborn creatures refused. Even coaxing the four-legged soldiers with grass did not entice them. The men positioned themselves firmly behind the mules and pushed, but the animals remained steadfast. Finally, they kicked the beasts to impel them to advance, but they still rebuffed their masters. Since the defiant animals were uncooperative, one soldier suggested they back-track and attempt a different, hopefully less rocky and muddy, route. The mules found the new path amicable and forged forward.

Mike grumbled, "The asses were supposed to help us. It's more like we're babysitting these creatures."

"I know. It's taking us longer with them than without them."

The struggle lagged as another mule tried frantically to ascend the hill. Burdened by voluminous supplies, he plummeted backward and landed on his back with his legs kicking the air. Several men pushed, pulled, and rocked, while a few others tried to control the animal's erratic legs. After a lengthy scuffle, they repositioned the beast and progressed forward.

Observing the antics of the furry creatures and the men scuffling with them could have brought levity to the situation. However, the task force men battling the elements and the muddy, icy terrain studded with mines and periodic sniper fire found no humor in their circumstances.

As night fell, the wet, tired, and freezing men finally unwound. Ravaged by hunger, they chowed down on the meager K-rations but yearned for more. As they rested, one man eyed a scrawny doe in the woods, sniffing at the wet ground. The doe hobbled slowly through the trees in search of food until it stood at the edge of the woods, a few feet from the men. Slowly and quietly, one rifleman took aim at the innocent doe and supplied extra nourishment for the task force.

With full stomachs, the sleepy-eyed task force entered the city of Mauterhouse the next day. The division expected to be blasted by the Germans defending the border but, fortunately, met with only little pockets of resistance. German officers had directed their troops to the roads below the Haardt Mountains to wait for the enemy. They had not expected the Americans to navigate the challenging terrain and snow and, consequently, were bushwhacked by the troops. The 232nd gained ground from Reipertswiller to Baerenthal. Advancing swiftly, the other sections of the division captured Dambach, Neunhoffen, and Bannstein. The Rainbow was edging on the German border.

Finally, on March 18, the Rainbow Division penetrated the border into Germany, prepared to attack the primary and secondary defenses of the Siegfried line. Mike's battalion positioned in Ludwigswinkel with the 242nd and the 222nd on either side. The Germans attacked vigorously, intending to destroy enough Americans to warrant a major retreat, but the Rainbow survived their onslaught and progressed swiftly. The fighting grew in intensity as the Rainbow inched toward the Siegfried Line, Germany's impenetrable fortress of pillboxes, dragon teeth, and hundreds of mines and weapons built to frighten the enemy away from its borders. This was the end-fight for the Germans. They needed to keep the Allies out of their land. The German army had become the defender, instead of the aggressor.

The Rainbow Division's effort to progress stalled, as part of the unit defended the bridgehead, while other sections scouted for vulnerable openings into the Siegfried Line. The infantry needed additional support, and on March 21, P-47s swooped overhead at 1900 hours and fearlessly aimed their artillery to pound the pillboxes and the fortifications of the Siegfried line. Mike and the other men in their foxholes cheered the sight of bombs pummeling the Germans. After forty-five minutes of continuous bombing, the planes departed and the smoke cleared, but the attack had merely cracked the fortifications. Inside, the old men and the young boys who had been commanded to defend the concrete structure but were afraid to fight, bolted when the thunderous bombing stopped. As the Rainbow progressed, the division encountered little resistance from a handful of fanatical snipers. When the footmen entered the pillboxes, they found many nerve-shattered Germans, quivering in a corner, who readily surrendered. The Seventh Army had successfully infiltrated Germany, demoralizing the German soldiers but increasing the energy of the Americans exponentially.

Early the next morning, Rainbow Division attacked the secondary defenses of the Siegfried Line but encountered no retaliation. Frightened and disheartened, the enemy troops had abandoned their posts to escape to a safer area. The airborne division refused to allow the aggressors to flee to safety and regroup. Aircraft shells wreaked havoc on the columns of Germans, their vehicles, horses, and weapons. In a couple of swift blows, everything lay lifeless.

As U.S. troops marched forward the next day, they witnessed the destruction of the bombardment. Bloody half arms and heads with squishy exposed gray matter hung out of vehicles. Some German bodies dangled upside-down by their legs from jeeps or tanks, pools of blood beneath them. Others, thrown by their horses, lay in the middle of the road beside a random arm or leg ripped from another soldier. Wafts of smoke encircled the bodies, and bloated animal carcasses lined the narrow streets. Flies and crows picked at the bloody remains. Along pathways, the masses of dead German soldiers slowed Rainbow Division's progress. There was no alternative but to trudge over the lifeless bodies. Numerous American soldiers who had become viciously callous toward the Germans stomped with pride over the bastards.

Marching forward, the U.S. troops gained two additional notches in their belts as they seized the cities of Busenberg and Dahn. The riflemen scoured the buildings and the rubble for the enemy, and when they were discovered, the Germans dropped their arms and surrendered. German civilians hung white towels, sheets, and diapers from houses and buildings, fearful of retaliation by the Americans. At every turn, people who hours earlier had chanted, "Heil, Hitler!" now screamed, *"Nicht Nazi! Nicht Nazi!"* to avoid harm from the Americans.

The weary Allies cheered as lines of dejected, shattered prisoners holding their hands above their heads marched past them. In a short time, the Allies had killed a multitude of enemy soldiers, captured more than 3,500 prisoners, and were advancing through Hitler's homeland, charged to win the war.

After settling into the town of Dahn for a day's rest and to celebrate its invasion of Germany, the Rainbow majestically paraded the flags of the forty-eight states over German soil. The colorful signs of triumph waved in the wind.

After the procession, the Jewish chaplain, eager to celebrate a highly personal victory, appropriated the town hall to commemorate Passover. The commander, pleased with the chaplain's decision, ordered the Nazi prisoners to clear and clean the hall and prepare it for the service. The Jewish soldiers reveled at the sight of Nazis preparing the room to celebrate the heritage of the people Hitler intended to obliterate. Before the chaplain began the service, he announced the significance of the celebration. It marked the first public Jewish ceremony performed in Germany since the war had begun. The rabbi told the soldiers that the original Passover had been a victory over death, and this Passover served as a conquest over the evil Hitler had perpetrated by stripping the Jews of their identity and religion in his quest for a "master race."

March 25, 1945

Palm Sunday Somewhere in Germany

Dearest Helen:

I received beaucoup of mail today. I really hit the jackpot. I sure was glad to hear from you. The poem you wrote was really good. It also expresses how I feel. I'm sorry I couldn't write sooner but I know you'll understand the reason why because the papers are full of it. I also received a letter from your cousin Ed in the Navy. He sure does write some good letters.

Helen, I'll accept your apology for not writing oftener. I'm also glad to hear that you're feeling much better and that the mail from you will be coming more often. Your letters really mean much to me. In fact, it's my whole life. My sole concern is to see the end of the war so that you and I can look forward to a brighter and happier future together.

I've been thinking seriously, and a man has much time to think especially when life and everything he's hoped and dreamed of is balanced on a very thin string. Helen, we are still young yet and we've got a prosperous and eventful future ahead of us. Just think how lovely it will be, you and I alone together doing all the things we've planned and dreamed. That's the thing that keeps me going, knowing when this is all over you will be there waiting for me so we can pick up where we left off and start anew as husband and wife.

Being Palm Sunday, I went to Mass and Holy Communion. Sure, was a swell break for me. Didn't think I'd have time.

Always remembering. Never forgetting. Loving you forever, Mike

Before progressing farther into Germany, some of the units of the Rainbow Division backtracked to the pillboxes of the Siegfried line and searched for Germans harboring in the woods and the buildings. On reaching the pillboxes, they uncovered and captured numerous surprised Germans, along with documents from military intelligence. Several hours later, the foot soldiers granted the all-clear, and the detonation team swept in and destroyed the fortifications.

March 29, 1945

Thursday Somewhere in Germany

Darling,

I read an article recently in the Reader's Digest that made me contemplate for a while. The contents of the article dealt with the treatment of the returning soldiers by the wives and sweethearts who welcomed them home after many months of combat. From what I've gathered it seems most of the people have been treating the homecoming soldier as a mental case or neurotic. They refrained from talking about the war for fear it would bring back unpleasant memories for the soldier. Some even treated him like a child who is just starting out in life giving him all sorts of attention that an ordinary individual would never get. Civilians back home doing all these sort of things not only made the individual soldier feel out of place but also made it harder for him to readjust himself to civilian life. The proper thing, the article mentioned is to treat the homecoming soldier as a normal individual and treat him as you ordinarily would, thus better results would be achieved. The reason this article peeved me so much is that I happen to be one of the many soldiers the article refers to. So far as I know I haven't experienced any let down mentally or physically. As far as I'm concerned, I'm still the same person with the same likes and dislikes I had when I left home. There's no doubt I've matured and who doesn't as the years go by. Perhaps I'm boring you with sordid details Helen, so I'll refrain from this outburst and pursue more lighter and finer subjects of correspondence.

What subject could be more finer than the subject of love? The clutches of which you and I are in now. It's a disease of the heart, the mind and the whole body. Not affecting one individual but many. Something very contagious. It can be spread from one individual to another with ease entwining them so they seem as one, inseparable and impenetrable. Helen, that's one disease I'm affected with now. With it the pains of longing and loneliness, of countless waiting along with the joys and experiences when those who love are near, grasping life by the throat and wringing out the fullest benefits. I better stop some of this poetic nonsense before you get the idea that the war has somewhat affected me. I'm not crazy I'm just a pencil sharpener. If I start jumping around flaying my arms in the air it's not because I'm out of my mind I'm just doing my daily exercise. Oh yeah. Tell it to Sweeny.

Helen, seriously you know I feel darn good and getting along swell. You see what happens when my mind is high. This was accomplished by my receiving your letters. So, you better write or you might have one of those mental cases on your hands the article was referring to.

I'll tell you one thing, you better be prepared because when I get home, I'm going to take you in my arms, hold you tight, press my lips against yours and kiss you for dear life. You better take some breathing exercises because my lungs are darn good.

You remember those long sweet kisses. You don't? Well by gosh I'll have to refresh your memory. You don't think I can. Well, I'll take you up on that and you better be prepared to suffer the consequences.

Always thinking of you through the day and night.

Always remembering. Never forgetting.

Loving you forever Mike

On Easter Sunday, the engineers completed the bridges over the Rhine and Main rivers, and the Rainbow progressed east toward Wurzburg. Leaving Dahn at 0045, the convoy traveled 125 miles to Wurzburg and crossed the Rhine over the pontoon bridge, to arrive in Worms at 0500. While some of the units pushed forward with the motor division toward Wurzburg, the first battalion and Mike's battalion of the 232nd traveled on foot, trudging up and down the treacherous cliffs. Spring had not sprung in this mountainous region, and it reminded them of the brutal days of the Haardt Mountains. The men encountered severe German opposition at the Hassloch River but continued to advance. With fighting at a halt, Mike tried to sleep but only managed to seize bouts of naps as the frigid air woke him. Soon, the troops moved out, and in an effort to gain feeling in his feet and warm his body, Mike pounded his feet forcefully.

The 232nd continued its drive toward the Main River, marching through Erlabrunn, Oberleinach, and Hettstadt, and encountered no resistance because these towns had been captured and secured by Allied troops.

In Hettstadt, they garnered some nourishment and rest. One man said, "I'd really like some coffee. Why don't we pay a visit to one of these German families and get some hot water?"

The captain agreed and knocked on the door of a cottage with the butt of his rifle. When a wrinkled, hunchbacked German answered, the captain communicated in half German, half English, and hand gestures that they wanted to use the kitchen to boil water. The man informed his wife of the soldiers' intentions, and she placed a kettle of water on the stove. Making themselves at home, the soldiers gathered around the table. The couple stared at the sullen, dirty soldiers as they opened their packets of biscuits and meat. Although ravenous with hunger, some of the men ate their rations slowly, savoring every bite, while a few shoveled the food into their mouths. The German man stared in amazement as the captain ripped open a packet and poured brown crystals into his cup of boiling water. Without warning, the man jumped up from his chair and lunged toward the sink. A sergeant grabbed his rifle. "Stoppen, halt!" he called as he readied his finger on the trigger. The man held up his hands while his frail wife gasped in horror. Mike pulled out his German translation book. "What are you doing? What do you want?" he asked.

With his arms above his head, the man pointed with one finger toward the sink filled with cups, plates, and utensils. The lieutenant, angered, grabbed a knife and shoved it in the man's face. "Is this what you want?"

Shaking violently, the man said, "*Löffel, löffel.*" The soldier handed the spoon to the old man. While still aiming the gun, the sergeant watched the German reach the spoon toward the captain's cup. Assuming the man was offering him a spoon to stir his coffee, the captain held up his spoon, indicating he didn't need one. Unexpectedly, the man dunked the spoon in the coffee and tasted it, saying, "*Das ich gut,*" and smiled. The men burst into laughter at their mistake and the old man's curiosity about the strange drink.

One corporal, still half laughing, said, "It feels good to laugh again."

Mike said, "Since your laugh muscles are all warmed up, let me tell you this old joke I remember."

The humor alleviated their pent-up stress, and the merriment persisted until their stomachs ached from excess laughter. Revived, the soldiers bid farewell to the homeowners and forged toward the next town.

The thud of the men's boots striking the ground echoed as they lined the streets to Wurzburg. Through the tramping, the captain heard moaning and ordered the troops to stop. Four Germans trapped in the crumbled remains of a bombed-out building lay under pillars and bricks. The soldiers cleared the debris off the men, and Mike and another medic administered first aid. Their injuries were not extensive: a broken leg and arm, abrasions, and an open wound on one German's face. Mike bandaged the men, applied splints, and sent them to the POW camp.

Night fell, and the soldiers took refuge in an abandoned German barracks before progressing toward Wurzburg.

Chapter Twenty-Eight

April 1945

On April 4th, Mike and his battalion entered Wurzburg, which had once been one of the most beautiful and oldest cities in Germany. The historical city and center of art sat in ruins, having been swept clean earlier by the 222nd. Finding no enemy resistance, the men relaxed and awaited further orders. When Mike searched for a place to rest his fatigued feet amid the toppled buildings, he spotted a German in the middle of the street, groaning and mumbling. The combatant's ear was missing, and blood poured from his abdomen. Mike ripped back the German's jacket, and before he could pull the bandages from his bag, the man drew his last breath. Closing his medic bag, Mike stared at the lifeless German lying at his feet and, for the first time, felt no sorrow at losing a casualty. Feeling guilty, he glanced around and noticed the other soldiers. They leaned casually against buildings, laughing and smoking, unaffected by the dead Germans all around them. Mike sat on some broken steps next to his buddy. "When I first entered this war, men were sickened to see dead soldiers, even if they were German, and now no one gives a shit."

"If we gave it any more thought, Mike, we'd probably all go nuts," his friend said.

"I know that. It's a little unsettling to sit back and witness how hardened we've become. When this whole thing started, Dr. Rodgers said,

'You'll get used to it,' and I was sure he was wrong. I guess it happens to the best of us."

"It happens to all of us. Besides, who cares about these sons of bitches anyway? These are the assholes who started this whole thing. It's their own fault they're lying there. Here's how I figure. It's gonna be a dead Heine or American, and I'll take the dead Heine."

Mike nodded in disgust. "I agree, pal, but it's a damn shame how this war changes every man."

As the troops progressed farther into the inner city of Wurzburg, they surrounded the Germans. Now the Rainbow Division faced its worst encounter with enemy resistance as a full division. All that remained of the charming city with its grand, medieval buildings, monuments, and churches were torn roofs, missing windows, and half-erected structures. Smoking hills of brick, stone, and glass created an obstacle course that had to be navigated for U.S. troops to move forward. The destruction created an advantage for the Germans because they found numerous places to hide. Snipers lurked everywhere, and the march through Wurzburg became a building-to-building confrontation, as the Americans scoured every corner to discover the snipers before they could take aim at another victim. Police and firemen joined in the defense, along with armed civilians. It developed into a madhouse of back-and-forth fighting, playing hide-and-seek along the way. The skirmish became challenging as the tenacious enemy burrowed in and out of underground tunnels.

Mike wondered why the Germans incessantly fought in such an abysmal situation. The Allies had secured almost all the other countries and half of Germany, but then he thought, *If this were America, I would fight to the bitter end, too.*

Soon he and his unit converged on a park housing a German army hospital. Disregarding the rules of war, the Germans positioned men at the hospital windows with machine guns and cannons. Additional German units surrounded the Americans and repeatedly blasted them with machine-gun fire. The rifleman and the machine gunners engaged in a fierce attack, and the Rainbow infantry secured the building.

Although the hospital was in Allied hands, the skirmish endured. Scared and desperate, the Germans refused to surrender and continued to fire their weapons, constraining numerous men until the superfire ceased.

In previous weeks, the Rainbow had captured two or three towns a day. But here, it took several days of intense fighting to capture more than 2,500 Germans and to declare Wurzburg a victory. Proud of their win, the Rainbow painted the words "42nd Rainbow Division" and its insignia on Marienburg Castle, replacing the inscription "Heil Hitler."

As the men roamed through the streets of Wurzburg, the effects of war on civilians pierced their hearts. Small children with hollow, emotionless faces wandered among the rubble. The sights, smells, and sounds of the ongoing war had invaded their undeveloped psyches, causing irreparable damage, and transformed them into zombies walking among the ruins. Men and women who had lived their lives with pride scavenged among what little survived the bombing, hoarding it, in preparation for having nothing. An elderly man snatched a partially smoked cigarette from a dead soldier's hand, lit it, and nonchalantly strolled away. As he walked farther, he found the butt of another cigarette, picked it up, and shoved it in his pocket.

While combing the area for Germans, the 42nd discovered an overabundance of Champagne in a cellar. They commandeered cases as their reward for gaining Wurzburg and toasted with some recently released Allied prisoners. Champagne flowed as abundantly as the surrounding rivers, and the men drank it like water. Countless euphoric soldiers extravagantly brushed their teeth and washed their faces with the expensive drink.

In several rural towns the Americans had captured previously, the farmers had showered them with cheers for releasing them from the Nazi stranglehold. In contrast, as the American troops departed Wurzburg on April 7th in their march toward Schweinfurt, the townspeople who had struggled fiercely to hold onto their town assembled in the streets, sullen and scared. German propaganda described Americans as the barbarian enemy who beat and raped women and tortured their captives. Now the German townspeople were confused as they watched the exuberant Americans leaving peacefully without punishing them or taking them as prisoners. The townspeople fretted about the brutal, unrelenting SS soldiers and feared repercussions for allowing the Americans to capture the city. Many thought it might be better if the peaceful Americans had remained to defend them.

Marching toward Schweinfurt, the 232nd met superfire at Arnstein from what remained of the Wehrmacht, Germany's official army, and the Volkssturm, mostly elderly men who had been conscripted by the Nazi Party. Boys and girls from the Hitler Jugend, training for future defense, also joined in the fight. The inexperienced soldiers of the Volkssturm and the Hitler Jugend, incapable of withstanding hand-to-hand combat, served their purpose with rifles and machine guns as they stood guard over the city. If they delayed the troops or pierced any of the Americans with their bullets, they proved their worth to the German cause. The frightened soldiers, both the young and the old, inflicted heavy casualties, and the medics worked diligently to save the wounded.

Mike had barely finished treating the men when the commanding officer ordered everyone to move out immediately for Schweinfurt. Before forging forward, Mike filled his helmet with water and splashed his tired eyes to remove the dirt and sweat.

After the battle at Schweinfurt, casualties poured into the aid station, and the medics occasionally had to make painful decisions while trying to save a soldier's life. One of the unconscious soldiers was bleeding profusely from an obliterated shoulder. After assessing the injuries, the doctor determined that the man's arm needed to be amputated. Mike assisted Dr.

Rodgers, who painstakingly and sorrowfully removed the arm of the young soldier.

The injured soldier remained unconscious for several hours as the medics continued to treat the wounded. Finally, the soldier awoke, and Mike conveyed the life-changing news. The dazed amputee calmly asked Mike if they had saved his wedding ring. Without hesitation, Mike dashed outside to recover the arm and rescue the coveted band. He washed blood and dirt from the ring, sat beside the soldier, and secured the ring to his dog tags. Devastated that he no longer possessed a rightful place to wear his ring, tears rolled down the groggy soldier's face onto the ring that lay on his chest. Mike cringed. Unable to remedy the situation, he rested his hand on the soldier and asked if he could pray with him.

The stories and the wounds of the injured sucked the life from every man, especially the medics and the doctors. Their nerves on edge, Mike and two other medics clenched their fists when a newly placed air force medic accused the other medics of being insensitive and not attentive in tossing the man's arm away without removing the ring. The medics working in frenetic situations were unwilling to tolerate being second-guessed by a newbie. They grabbed the airman, threw him outdoors, and released their anger. Within a few minutes, the frazzled air force medic was being treated for a bloody nose and a black eye.

On the front line, shells, artillery, and ammunition from antitank guns crossed enemy boundaries until enough mortar fire destroyed the German defense, forcing the enemy to withdraw. The Americans flooded in and captured Schweinfurt. Reveling in the enormous win, Company E of the 232nd returned to Sommersdorf via a convoy for a few days of relaxation.

Early the next day, the sorrowful news spread about President Roosevelt's death, due to a cerebral hemorrhage. The chaplain promptly arranged for a memorial tribute for the president. Hundreds of men knelt in reverent prayer, as the chaplain prayed for the president and for peace.

One fellow soldier commented to Mike after the service, "It's a damn shame Roosevelt died now. We're probably gonna win this war soon, and he's not here to see it."

"I know. Let's just hope Truman continues this battle forward and not backward," Mike said.

April 13, 1945 Friday Somewhere in Germany

Dearest Helen:

Glad to hear that you liked the bracelet I sent you. Too bad it couldn't be something more appropriate. I'm glad to hear that you liked the postcards and perfume I sent you.

I like the selection of records you bought. Helen you just stack those sweet pieces up and both of us can sit down and enjoy listening to them. Sure would be good on an automatic record changer. Then we wouldn't be disturbed. Talking about being disturbed. The trouble you mentioned having with the children reminds me of how those kids used to snoop around when we were in the parlor. They always kept asking for Uncle Mike and Aunt Helen. I remember those happy carefree days. It seems just like yesterday.

I had to laugh when you mentioned about taking the children for a walk, so they get tired. They didn't after all. You're getting a lot of experiencing tending to children. When you have a few of your own, you'll know what to do

I'm glad to hear you're getting plenty of rest. If that's what you need to keep you in shape you better get plenty of it. I want you looking fresh and lovely when I come home.

Always remembering. Never forgetting. Loving you forever, Mike

On April 14th, the 232nd departed Sommersdorf by convoy, prepared to capture Furth, north of Nuremberg. When the U.S. troops entered the large city, they found fanatical revolutionaries of the Nazi Party poised to fight to the death to defend their home, rather than surrender.

The usually organized German troops diminished into a hodgepodge of partial units that had withdrawn from other areas and had combined forces with the Volkssturm. Similar to Wurzburg, the civilians banded with the army, helping them create roadblocks by piling up wreckage and logs to prevent the Americans from entering the city. Residents hurled tables, chairs, and mattresses from apartment windows to add to the growing mound.

German soldiers at Furth were instructed to fight until the 19th of April and then retreat to Nuremberg. The German leaders hoped the collective troops from Furth and those waiting at Nuremberg, along with the SS troops, would abolish the Americans. The Rainbow advanced quickly, and its soldiers surprised the Germans on April 18th, effortlessly clearing a large portion of the city. As the Germans attempted to escape, the 232nd accosted them and secured numerous prisoners.

The forces of the 7th Army physically and psychologically defeated the town, and the Burgermeister, the mayor of Furth, surrendered to the troops. After forcing the mayor into a jeep, the U.S. troops ordered him to admit defeat to the citizens and demand they relinquish their arms and cooperate. Somber and humiliated men, women, and children standing in the streets dropped their weapons to the ground. Families stormed out of their houses with guns, helmets, gas masks, armbands, and anything associating them with the Nazi Party and threw them down. The heap of armaments rapidly rose to several feet tall and stretched for blocks.

Unaffected and emotionless, the inhabitants of Nuremberg distanced themselves from the cause and ignored the mile-long column of prisoners trampling pass their houses and businesses. The hundreds of men taken prisoner were a small price to pay for the long years of war and suffering.

The Rainbow, now attached to the XV Corps, departed from Nuremberg and Furth as quietly as the prisoners had. On April 21, the division advanced toward the Danube River and straight toward Hitler's famous Alpenfestung ("Alpine Forest"), which the Americans referred to as the "Redoubt Area." The Alpenfestung lay on the Bavarian, Italian, and Austrian border and extended for 280 miles through a series of difficult-to-navigate mountains reaching heights of 12,000 feet. It was believed that the German fort had interconnected tunnels and an impenetrable exterior and held enough food, arms, and ammunition to replenish the troops. This was the place where the Nazis vowed Hitler would rise like a phoenix from the ashes to reorganize Nazism with a vengeance and rule forever.

The men of the Rainbow Division prepared themselves for a fiery clash and forged aggressively toward Donauwörth, the beginning of the redoubt. In a furious effort to prevent the Americans from advancing, the Germans readied the roads with mines and men. The SS forced the townsmen to fight to the death and ensured their loyalty by hiding behind the open gunners with rifles aimed at their backs. They further guaranteed the townsmen's cooperation with threats of execution if they wavered. The townspeople feared the SS more than they did the Allies, especially after hearing reports of how they had hung three civilian men in Schweinfurt for attempting to surrender to the Americans.

Traversing the difficult terrain, the Rainbow covered more than ten miles each day and conquered one small town after another, stopping only for K-ration meals and catnaps. Outside Donauwörth, the men cheered when they found a house with smoked sausages hanging from the kitchen rafters. They confiscated the much-needed protein to progress onward.

As the division approached Donauwörth, a special task force formed to launch an attack. German troops quickly dwindled in numbers, and about seven hundred Germans, consisting mostly of SS troops, were stunned by the Rainbow's lightning-fast advancement. The Germans, seeking cover, ran across the open field, and the Americans easily fired upon them, one by one, as if it were a skeet shoot. Countless German soldiers were killed, but the seasoned SS troops remained behind, determined to slaughter the Americans and impede their advancement.

The bloody onslaught began as mines destroyed American tanks within the first few minutes. Each side was hell-bent on winning the conflict, which persisted for six more hours as tanks pushed forward. The U.S. riflemen fought from building to building, slaying as many Germans as possible. The SS soldiers would have rather died than surrender, and only seventeen Germans were taken prisoner at Donauwörth.

The sleep-deprived Americans, eager to end the war, trekked forward to Munich, the birthplace of Naziism. Several units of the 7th Army raced toward the Danube River, but the Rainbow Division, after negotiating narrow uphill roads and wrestling with the enemy, arrived at the river first. To reach Munich, the Rainbow men needed to cross the Danube, but all the bridges had been destroyed by the Germans. Jumping into assault boats, the men crossed the river under the light of the moon and through enemy fire. Once safely across, they forged toward the Lech River, four miles away, while tanks, trucks, and supplies waited for the engineers to complete a bridge across the water. Under heavy shelling from the Germans, the engineers frantically constructed the bridge. The first tank safely reached the other side, but the weight of the second tank compromised the bridge, and it crashed into the river, causing further delay.

When the infantry reached the Lech, the commander realized the swift waters impeded their crossing in assault boats. Initially, it appeared as if all the bridges had been destroyed, and it would be another day before they could cross. However, the 232nd found a partly collapsed bridge that could be made passable by the engineers. In the darkness of night, the expert builders raised the underwater parts of the bridge, and the troops successfully crossed the Lech. Through the division's tenacity, its men secured enough beach head to allow the other troops to cross. The nonstop movement of the troops left the soldiers sleepless and exhausted, yet they performed their duties proficiently and held off the Germans.

Gaining speed and ground in a convoy, instead of marching, the men expected Munich to be in American hands soon.

April 27, 1945 Somewhere in Germany

Friday

Darling,

I see you've finally gotten in the groove with your correspondence. I see you had a little amusement with children when you received those wooden shoes I sent. Do you know that pair of shoes is actually the kind the kids wear here? Yep, that's the reason I sent it as a souvenir. So, you see the Dutch people aren't the only ones who wear them. That pin you were so concerned about is an insignia of an Italian officer. What rank, I wouldn't know.

When you received my cards and the picture you noticed that I looked kind of hot and bothered. Maybe so. I guess it must be the war. You know actually I haven't noticed it.

I'm glad you had a chance to go the policeman's ball and had a good time. No, I'm not worried about you cheating on me. Cripes, I don't expect you to stay home and twiddle your thumbs. Enjoy life while you have a chance. Helen, I trust you explicitly. So don't think I am worried. I know you'll be waiting for me when this over and you'll be the same gal I left behind.

I liked that poem you sent me about Hitler and the devil. Two of the same kind. I imagine everyone will agree with me on that. By the way I heard that Mussolini was captured. Maybe it's true. I don't know. There's a million rumors in the army.

You asked if I remembered the song "Honey" Why certainly. Remember how we used to play that roll on the piano. I never could pump that darn thing. When I did, I sweated like a roast pig. Yep, you got a big laugh out of it too.

All this time, how I longed to hold you in my arms, to feel your tender lips against mine, hear your voice again and look into your smiling eyes. Nothing means so much to me as all these things when I come home. Knowing I have you to come home to and our future ahead of us doing all the things together makes it easier for me over here.

Well Darling I'll have to close. God Bless.

Always remembering. Never forgetting. Loving you forever

The SS guards at Dachau Concentration Camp received word that a large troop of Americans who had recently captured Nuremberg, along with an armored division, were moving toward their camp. Rage and terror erupted in the SS soldiers and officers, who feared capture and accountability for their deeds. Before escaping, they released their anger by systematically shooting the witnesses to their atrocities. They aimed their machine guns at the prisoners, executed more than two thousand inmates, and fled the camp.

The 222nd and the 242nd marched toward the silhouette of Dachau in the distance and the stomach-wrenching smell of ash and burnt flesh. On April 29th the men cautiously approached the camp and easily resisted the fire of a thin defense, overtook the Germans, and liberated the camp. A young German lieutenant who had arrived the previous day to take command of Dachau surrendered the camp to General Linden. Unable to accept surrender, some unrelenting SS soldiers launched sniper fire. The Rainbow quickly demonstrated its superiority, and the SS soldiers dropped as quickly as dry branches struck by lightning.

Gunfire, Americans charging into the camp, and screams in German and English overwhelmed the worn, sullen prisoners. For years, they had endured the brutal Nazis, had been treated like caged and beaten dogs, had witnessed innumerable people disappear or die before their eyes, and had lost any hope of freedom. Now, the soldiers of the Rainbow Division were the arms of God awakening them from their nightmare and releasing them from hell.

Countless prisoners who were barely able to walk and had been disfigured from beatings moved about aimlessly. Some walked toward the open gates and collapsed and died, their bodies too weak to survive for one more second. Other prisoners raced for their freedom and ran blindly into the electrified fence, succumbing to the shock. With rocks and clubs, the stronger prisoners avenged their captors and dispensed their years of pent-up rage on the German soldiers. Prisoners overtook one official and killed him with his own weapon. The inmates beat another official's face so viciously, only pulp remained. Chaos reigned as hundreds of prisoners climbed to the tops of the barracks, waving their arms, cheering the Americans in different languages.

As the Rainbow men walked through the camp, the prisoners shook their hands and hugged them. The sympathetic soldiers distributed their K-rations and whatever food they carried in their packs and pockets to the emaciated men and women. A corporal noticed several prisoners huddled together eating scraps of food. They had all saved little morsels for a banquet in anticipation of their rescue. As the soldiers combed through the camp, they found a few SS men dressed in the striped uniforms of the inmates, trying to escape undetected, but their robust stature and full heads of hair revealed their true identities.

Mike's unit, a few hours behind the 222nd and the 242nd, approached the outskirts of Dachau. Mike sensed a foreboding evil, increased by the indescribable odor emanating from the camp. As the unit turned a bend, he and the other men halted in their tracks. Before them sat a row of at least fifty railroad boxcars filled with a mountain of arms, legs, and ghastly, almost nonhuman, faces with mouths gaping and lifeless black eyes. Mike, who had walked among slaughtered Germans lying in the street and treated men who resembled dissected cadavers, gagged as tears streamed down his face. Some men vomited. Several stood still and speechless, while others cried out in distress, "Oh, my God, what is this? What have they done?" Mike's stomach churned, and he groaned silently, "Dear God, how could someone do this?" The men whimpered and gasped as they stared at this abomination, unable to utter a word as they passed the boxcars. Unbelievable rumors regarding concentration camps had circulated, and Mike had initially dismissed them as lies and exaggeration. Yet what he was witnessing surpassed the inconceivable stories he had heard. *Yes, this is war,* Mike thought, *but the Geneva Convention made civil rules for the treatment of prisoners. This was the product of Godless people.*

Passing by the moat surrounding the camp, the men stared aghast at the bare, lifeless bodies floating in the water. Mike recoiled in horror at a slew of dead, naked bodies strewn to the side, like bones and flesh discarded as garbage by a butcher. His mind grew numb from the unspeakable sights.

When the unit entered the camp, its men were surrounded by countless prisoners. Mike grimaced and shuddered as he stared at them. They were nothing more than skeletons painted with skin, physically indistinguishable from one another. Men and women had shaved heads and wore the same clothes. All emaciated and pale, their eyes were glazed and emotionless and admitted defeat. The windows to their souls had been metaphysically ripped out. Women and men in their twenties looked like grandparents, their faces scarred from wounds of physical and mental abuse, malnutrition, human experiments, and torture.

Mike trembled so violently at the sight that he felt his inner core almost collapse upon itself. He heard a man cry out in Polish, "Thank you!" and tears welled up in his eyes as he realized some of these people could be relatives or friends of his family. How could the German soldiers observe and participate in this barbarism, day after day, and not be affected? Hitler had transformed his army into callous machines of destruction, and he turned the Jewish race and other sympathizers into the walking dead. The devil had been reincarnated into this fanatical leader who ruled over this hell.

Mike contemplated the events of the last few months while his brain agonized over the unfathomable scenes of the concentration camp. The bombings, the airplane assaults, the wounded, and the carnage were negligible in comparison to the atrocities of the death camp. The stench of decaying bodies, human waste, the sweat, and the dirt that accumulated on the prisoners' bodies after months or years of not bathing penetrated Mike's sensory glands. He walked away and tried to breathe, but the unsettling images chiseled into his brain haunted him. Outside the crematory ovens lay a mammoth pile of shoes on one side and another mound of clothing on the other, each piece of clothing and pair of shoes representing one of the multitude of vanquished lives. He thought about the innocent souls, their unfulfilled lives forever lost. Their families' anguish of not having the honor to provide a decent burial and a marker of their life.

There was no escape from the evil and barbarity of the Nazis. In the officers' quarters, a private drew Mike's attention to lampshades made from tattooed human skin. In the buildings where the inmates slept, they noticed bloodstained fingernail scratches on the walls and the doors and clumps of dried blood on the floors. Mike whispered to himself, "Satan must be happy. God damn him."

While the other units proceeded to Munich, Mike's company remained at the camp. The nonmedical soldiers guarded Dachau and the autobahn bridge. The medics administered typhoid shots, deloused inmates, and organized them for movement to DP (displaced persons) camps near Salzburg and Linz. As the inmates shuffled in, Mike distributed DDT powder over the survivors and gagged from the smell of uniforms stained with feces, urine, blood, and dirt. Although he felt repulsed, his heart ached at the obvious signs of torture and abuse. Several men had an eye gouged out, and all that remained was a black, infected hole. The shouts of the prisoners in line were in a cacophony of languages. Mike understood "Thank you," in Polish, German, and French but could not understand their begging cries. Almost all the prisoners required more than superficial treatment, and Mike was thankful when the medical division arrived to tend to their needs.

Relieved to be leaving Dachau, Mike's unit progressed toward Munich. Marching alongside them was a mile-long line of refugees, a conglomeration of nations walking toward DP camps, their final stop to freedom.

The 242nd and 222nd divisions marched into the war-torn town of Munich, which had been decimated by multiple bombings. The Rainbow claimed the center of the city and easily captured the Rathaus and Koenig Plaza. German soldiers passively walked toward the U.S. troops with their hands held up in the air and waving white flags. Civilians were also quick to hang surrender flags on their doors or outside windows.

Slave laborers, a large percentage of the inhabitants of the city, realized the Germans had stopped fighting, and they were free. They seized their newfound independence and looted every warehouse and cellar for food and wine, in retaliation for the torture they had suffered from the Nazis. Allied prisoners of war who had been given morsels of food while in captivity also joined in the fracas, shoving bread and sausages into their mouths. Some of the prisoners from Dachau, still in their striped garb, made their way to Munich and stuffed bottles of wine in their pants and food into their shirts. The German citizens, who had suffered from years of extreme food rationing, absconded with cases of anything they could carry. The city mutated into a madhouse of angry, starving people rambling in the rubble and speeding army vehicles. Instead of fighting the German army, the Rainbow men functioned as guardsmen to prevent looting and directed foot and vehicle traffic to restore order to the town.

When Mike's unit arrived, most of the looting had ceased, and the townspeople celebrated the end of the war. Men from the other units handed out bottles of appropriated wine to Mike and his company and encouraged them to see some of the sights before they needed to move forward. Eager to catch a glimpse of history and collect a souvenir, the men darted toward the infamous remnants of Nazism. Pushing through the crowd, they wandered into the beer cellar made famous by Hitler.

Mike entered the Bürgerbräukeller and asked the man sitting in the corner of the unfinished cellar if he spoke English. The man replied very slowly in a heavy German accent, "I can speak it *gut.*"

"Great. Can you tell us anything about what happened here to Hitler and the *putsch*?"

"*Ja, ja,* it was about five years after the end of World War I, and I just start working here when Hitler barged in while Von Kahr the Staatskomissar give a speech. He jump up on table and fired gun in air to get everyone to pay *achtung.* He say he was taking over the government, and no one could leave. He came here with hundreds of SA men, ready to defend the Nazi Party."

"What is SA?" asked one corporal.

"Oh, I no remember what it means, but it was, how you say? Like a police or soldiers of the Nazi Party. They have guns and power."

"Okay, go on," said Mike

"Hitler was trying to get everyone on his side to take charge of the government, giving speech and such, it was, ah, what is the word, like koo koo."

"You mean crazy?"

"*Ja, ja,* crazy. So much going on."

The barkeeper continued, "Many hours later, guns go off outside, and about thirteen Nazis dead and Hitler arrested with other men."

Mike interjected, "Looks like Hitler always wanted to be in power, and he'd do whatever he could to achieve it."

"*Ja, ja,* the people like him and agree with him. I no remember what he say, but the people cheer for him. *Dumkopfs,* if they only know what he get us into. One brave anti-Nazi man tried to kill him during one of his talks back in '39. He blow up the whole place, everything kaput and many people hurt, but it did nothing to Hitler. He already gone. We still try to make better, but no luck."

"Well, it's over now, buddy, and you may not have beer, but we have some wine, so let's toast to a new beginning," replied Mike.

A soldier poured wine into a dusty glass and handed it to the owner, who hesitantly toasted with the Americans, feeling slight betrayal to his country even though he hated Hitler.

After vacating the beer hall, the men maneuvered their way around the lines of German prisoners in the crowded streets. The German soldiers understood that the Americans had executed Nazism at its birthplace, and there would be no retreat and no redoubt to reorganize.

Mike walked through the Koenig Platz, where Hitler had held his rallies and paraded through the streets. Now the plaza overflowed with American soldiers, released Allied prisoners, and slave laborers celebrating the downfall of Germany. A few recently liberated POWs stormed toward the Rainbow men, shook their hands, and toasted them with a bottle of wine. Some men from Company G passed by Mike and declared, "Hey, we just saw Hitler's grand apartment, and you might want to see where he lived. It's down the road a little. You can't miss it. All I can say is it felt good to piss all over his bathroom, that bastard. One of the guys took a bath in his bathtub. Can you believe that?"

Mike asked, "Do you mean the building is still standing? I'm surprised it wasn't destroyed."

"Yep, with all this destruction around, it's hard to believe it was hardly touched."

A fellow soldier interjected, "Well, let's go, I want to see how the devil lived and then spit on his bed or something."

Mike and a few men entered the house and were amazed to see everything arranged properly and untouched, although Hitler had been absent for at least two years.

One soldier relaxed in a chair and lit a cigarette. "Look at all this fancy furniture and stuff. Could you imagine Hitler's rage if he saw Americans flicking ashes in his pristine apartment?"

A lieutenant holding a glass of wine stood on a table and said, "Now that Hitler's dead, it's no longer 'Heil Hitler.' It's more like 'To Hell, Hitler, you son of a bitch.'"

Everyone laughed, and one man added, "Even hell's too good for him."

Chapter Twenty-Nine

As the Rainbow Division progressed toward Austria to secure the borders, the men discovered several units of German soldiers ready to surrender. The convoy halted, but the commanding officer, eager to move forward, directed the Germans to the nearest collection point and instructed them to surrender. Bewildered and suspicious, the Germans waited to see if the Americans would return. Men who were afraid of being killed obeyed orders and walked directly to the collection point. Others, assuming they were free, gathered at the nearest tavern to celebrate. While guzzling a large stein of beer, a few high-ranking German commanding officers, their spirits destroyed by the ravages of the prolonged war, joined in the celebration. Their disgust with the war prompted the officials to immediately sign discharge papers for the drained soldiers and advise them to go home and avoid capture by the Americans. The German soldiers tore off their coats and weapons, gulped their beer, and fled to take advantage of their liberation.

Confident and exuberant that a full surrender was imminent, the Rainbow men sang, "Over hill, over dale, we will hit the dusty trail as the Caissons go rolling along." Their delight continued as they discussed seeing the historical sites of Munich and admitting they pilfered a pen, a book, or another trinket from Hitler's house as a souvenir. Their celebration ceased as bullets from fanatical snipers, reluctant to admit defeat, pierced a jeep and scraped a man's helmet, causing the U.S. soldiers to open fire. The Germans scattered quickly, and the convoy continued.

The next day, on May 4, the American troops crossed the Austrian border and awaited further instruction. After continuous marching and fighting as sleepwalkers, with aching, numb muscles, the men rested in their quartered beds and fed their ravenous stomachs with copious amounts of fresh eggs, meat, and Austrian food. Mike wanted to write Helen a letter about his renewed hope after capturing Munich, but his fatigued legs and bulging abdomen made his eyes heavy, and soon his body succumbed to sleep.

In the States, a stream of encouraging articles filled the newspapers. The demise of Mussolini, and Hitler; the surrender of German forces in Italy; and the capture of Berlin and more than a half million German soldiers boosted the morale of the Americans, who anticipated the official announcement of victory in Europe.

On the morning of May 8th, the employees at Donahoe's strolled in, energized and bantering about the end of the war. Johnnie announced, "Since President Truman will be broadcasting his message this morning, we'll keep the doors locked until his speech is over. I don't think anyone will be shopping this early today. I'm sure they're staying home to listen to the news."

The buzzing voices hummed with hope that their loved ones would be home soon, along with praises to God that the Allies had defeated Germany.

"Shh, shh!" Johnnie said, "It's about to start."

As President Truman stated, "Germany has surrendered unconditionally," a few of the employees hugged briefly and then continued to listen to the president's speech.

"This is a solemn but glorious hour," Truman continued. "General Eisenhower has informed me that the forces of Germany have surrendered to the United Nations. I only wish Franklin D. Roosevelt had lived to witness this day. The flags of freedom fly over all of Europe."

The employees hooted and raised their hands in victory.

Johnnie announced, "We finally got the Krauts, thank God."

Helen said, "I wonder if that means the men fighting in Europe will be sent home?"

"I don't know, Helen," Johnnie said. "I'm sure some of them will come home, but like President Truman said, the war is only half won. We still have to beat the Japs." Johnnie bellowed over the din of the employees, "It's a great day for all of us, but we need to open the front door and help the customers."

A few minutes later, people excited to share the news swarmed into the store, jabbering about the defeat of Germany.

After work, Helen walked to St. Mary's of the Mount Church on Grandview Avenue to light a candle and say a prayer of thanksgiving. There was no scheduled service, but the church overflowed with people. Helen searched up and down the aisles and finally found a seat in a front pew on the side of the church. Pews of mostly women wearing headscarves wrapped tightly around their chins and rosary beads entwined in their hands knelt before the altar and prayed fervently. Helen assumed her usual position on her knees and with hands folded. "Dear God," she prayed, "thank you for ending the war in Germany and for keeping Mike safe. I pray he is still alive. Please send him home to me soon and protect all the men fighting in Japan." An hour passed before Helen noticed the time and realized that she needed to get home for dinner.

She walked in the back door to the kitchen. Flo leapt up from her chair and hugged her. "Isn't it swell? It's finally over!"

"I know. Thank God."

Flo waved her arms above her head. "This is so exciting. We need to celebrate. The boys will be coming home!"

In Austria, shouts of joy from the 42nd Rainbow Division could be heard for miles, as news circulated about the signing of the surrender papers.

A corporal exclaimed, "It's about time!"

Another soldier howled, "Woooo hoooo, now I can get back home and see my baby boy!"

A medic declared, "Yee haw. This means we're going home. I can almost taste my mother's fried chicken."

The commanding officer blew his whistle. "Men, we're all excited the war in Europe is finally over, but you have to remember that Japan is still raging forward and is a great threat in the Pacific. We beat the Nazis, but this war will not be over until Japan surrenders."

Within seconds, exhilaration and expectations of being reunited with loved ones vanished. Home had never been closer or farther away. The news of triumph, along with the possibility of having to fight Japan, was akin to being released from years in jail and still having to endure parole. Their families would have to sustain their absence until the Eastern extremist power had been obliterated.

Chapter Thirty

After VE DAY

Billeted in an Austrian house with a commanding view of the entire town square, Mike woke up to the jingle of cowbells and children giggling. He looked out the window and stood in awe of the majestic mountains covered with snow in the distance. Below his window, people gathered around a large fountain, exchanging pleasantries and news, while barefoot boys led goats to pasture. Passing by were women pulling carts to get their daily milk, while others carried large baskets of wood attached to their backs by straps. One lady noticed Mike at the window, smiled, and waved at him. Farther down the square, old men stopped to gather cigarettes from the ground and stuff the tobacco into their foot-long pipes. Modern vehicles were absent from the roads. Instead, young and old rode bicycles, navigating around the small children playing in the streets. Mike was amazed that in spite of the war and the destruction, the people persevered in endeavoring to start anew. For a moment, he forgot there were duties of war that needed performed.

He headed to the dispensary, and after hours of administering typhoid shots to displaced refugees, he ventured outdoors. With a view of houses and church steeples against the backdrop of the mountains, Mike leaned against a church wall and wrote to Helen without the constraints of wartime regulations.

May 14, 1945 Kirchberg, Austria

Monday

Dearest Helen:

Now it can be told that I'm in Kirchberg, Austria. A few miles north of Innsbruck and a few miles west of Kitzhenbuhl, the Hollywood of Austria. The few pictures I've enclosed will give you a fairly good idea what this country looks like. Kirchberg is well known as a place for skiing. Kirchberg is situated well in the heart of the Bavarian Alps. A very beautiful place indeed. The beauty of the place is really indescribable.

Just a few days ago, our outfit had a parade and a review. It really was wonderful to see all the state flags flying and Old Glory flying above them all. When the band played the Star-Spangled Banner it made chills run up and down my spine. At the review our General gave out the citations. Bronze stars and silver stars for bravery and gallantry in action. I received a bronze star for action back in January.

Now with the war over, at least over here, my mind is slightly at ease. It will be completely at ease when the war in Japan is over, and I'm settled down at home. With such beautiful and picturesque surroundings, a fellow doesn't feel too bad. Boy what a place for a honeymoon. A baseball field is just across the way about half a block, a stream for fishing a few blocks away, a lake for swimming and rowing about two miles away. Tourist houses all up the mountains in case you love to hike. Fresh air, wonderful weather, plenty of sunshine. Boy almost like a paradise. What it lacks is the most important element. The homey atmosphere and you. I could really enjoy myself if it wasn't for the fact that all the people speak German.

I've seen things here that I hope I never see again. A lot of it is too terrible to talk about. Perhaps someday when this all over we'll sit down and have a long talk and I'll tell you all about it. At present let's talk about more pleasant things.

At present I don't have much more time than I had during the war. We still have our jobs to do besides training and going to school. Yes, going to school, it's a school run by the battalion on various subjects including German.

I saw something that surprised me immensely. Several of us fellows took the long winding path that led to the church on top of the hill overlooking the entire town. When we reached the church, we had a few minutes to spare so we watched the people file into church. The old women wear a very quaint costume to church consisting of a very long colorful dress that has a wide sash around the waist which trails down behind. Also, a high hat, similar to a man's top hat with a wide band around it with a small tassel. The color of the entire costume depends on which society you belong to.

Now here's what impressed me. The mass was said in an Austrian church attended by refugees from Poland, Russia, Yugoslavia, and Hungary, by Americans and Slovak and Hungarian soldiers and by German and Austrian people. The mass was said in Latin by an American Priest with two Hungarian soldiers as altar boys. The sermon was said in English and the singing was by Slovak soldiers in their own tongue. Now don't that beat the didily whiz out of you. That's a part of democracy. I imagine in time these people will come around to our way of life. Time will tell.

Perhaps you're wondering what's going to happen now since the war is over. That is over here in the ETO. Well, Helen I don't know myself. I do know it's one of three things. Army of Occupation over here, to the states and to the Pacific, or direct to the Pacific. No matter what way you look at it I've got a couple of years in the Army to sweat out.

I don't mind waiting if you don't mind. It seems as if I've been away a lifetime, in another year or two it will seem like an eternity. If our children can enjoy the freedom and happiness we've had all our lives, it'll be worth it. I know darn well, I don't want my children to be like these people over here in Germany. If my staying away from the things I love mean my children can grow up to be freedom loving American Citizens, I'm all for it. I've seen enough people enslaved to know what this means.

Helen you know I've been thinking, if it's not too much trouble for you, I'd sure like you to send me some candy. Some gum drops, fudge or chocolate, *anything. If it's impossible to get, don't feel as if you've discouraged me because I know rationing is getting stricter back home.*

By the way you didn't tell me what Gabby said when I sent my regards. You remember she told me she'd sure knock me down a few pegs if I forgot to mention her in any of my letters.

You know Helen, I just can't get you off my mind. That's love for you. It just haunts you day and night, but I love it never the less.

Always remembering. Never forgetting. Loving you forever Mike

Mike remained in Kirchberg for a few days and then traveled to Haar, Germany, on assignment from the army. During their travels, the soldiers entered the house and studio of Hitler's close friend the famous sculptor Professor Thorak near Haar. In this building the German army Group G signed their surrender terms to General Devers. As they canvassed the property, the U.S. soldiers uncovered hundreds of sculptures by Thorak and his students.

Mike stretched his neck backward to look at them. "Can you believe how huge these statues are? The head alone must be ten feet tall."

A fellow medic pointed to several erotic statues of naked men and women embracing each other. "Look at these. Now that's the real thing. You'd never see this in the States."

The lieutenant said, "I got to take some pictures of these things. No one back home is gonna believe this."

After searching the rest of the grounds and uncovering more statues in wooden boxes, the men commandeered a large house nearby for the night. Rummaging through magazines in the library filled with trophies of wild animals, they read stories about the owner of the house and discovered that he had been a very influential man. Now he had been relegated to sleep in the garage while the U.S. soldiers lingered in his palatial house and savored all of its elite amenities. A private stated, "I could get used to this. Comfy leather chairs, a soft big bed, and beaucoup wine."

"Yeah, too bad we have to leave. I doubt we'll find billeting better than this."

Mike said, "I was happy to find a typewriter. Wish I could fit that in my backpack."

A private said, "I'd like to take some of these cigars and books."

"Well, we can't take it with us, but we sure can indulge for the night," Mike said.

After enjoying some cigars and conversation, Mike returned to the typewriter in the den and poured out his emotions to Helen.

Near Haar Germany May 22, 1945

Dearest Helen,

Am throwing some ink your way to let you know that you're foremost in my thoughts now and always. I'll always keep loving you because you are so near and dear to me. When I say near, I'm referring to the nearness of our hearts entwined in the strands of love. When I think of you, it isn't just a passing fancy but something that has taken root and is an essential part of me. The thing I'm living, hoping and praying for not for just now, but for always. With you and all these things uppermost in my mind and in my heart is the reason that my love for you grows stronger with the passing days and weeks.

Darling, please believe me when I try to say I miss you cause I love you and I love you more each day.

I miss you more than sea would ever miss the shore

I miss you more than words can say and most times even more

I miss you more than any tree would ever miss its leaves

And even more than any ship would ever miss the seas

I miss you more than Scarlet would miss her Rhett

Or even more than Romeo would miss Juliet

I miss you more than any star would ever miss the sky

And if you ever read my mind, you'd know the reason why

There's many things a man can forget but not the longing he has for the girl he loves. There's a place reserved in my heart for you Helen. It has been there since I first met you and will continue to be there always.

Right now, I'm really feeling good but would feel that much better if I had you in my arms and was able to feel the tenderness of your embrace and the sweetness of your kisses.

Always Remembering, Never Forgetting, Loving you Forever, Mike

Chapter Thirty-One

June 1945

The blazing sun penetrated the rooftops of the row houses of South Side, heating them like an oven and forcing families outdoors to cool themselves in the breezy shade. Helen and Flo, walking to Chester's Greeting Cards, passed by neighbors sitting on their front steps, reading the newspaper, and sipping cool drinks. By the time the sisters returned home, they were soaked with perspiration. Without stopping to talk to their mother sitting on the front stoop, Flo and Helen charged through the front door and changed into their swimsuits. Helen scampered to the backyard, doused herself with water, and filled a large tub of water to soak her feet.

Flo, carrying two glasses of cold water, rushed outside. "Hey, Helen, don't hog all the water. I'm hot, too, you know."

Helen aimed the hose at Flo and drenched her in the cool water.

Flo closed her eyes as the water sprayed. "Oh, that feels so good. I'm so glad they're not rationing water."

"I know." Helen turned off the water and said, "Why don't you sit on the bench with me and put your feet in the water? It'll cool you off."

The sisters sighed as they swirled their feet in the water.

Helen scooped up the water and splashed her face and arms. "Have you heard from Bern? Does he have enough points to come home?"

"Last time he wrote he still needed a lot of points. I don't understand. If they're not fighting anymore, why don't they send the boys home and forget about the points?"

"I agree, Flo, but I guess they're keeping them until they find out if they need them in Japan."

"Well, if you ask me, they should use the new recruits to fight and send the men who've already fought back home."

"You won't get an argument from me."

Their mother yelled from the kitchen, "Hey, you two, come on in. You both got mail."

June 5, 1945 Zell am Ziller

Tuesday

Dearest Helen:

What's cookin chicken? Do you want to neck? You betcha my life I do. How about you? How am I getting along? Well, I'm still kicking. You can take that literally or figuratively.

Mail is coming in very slow but I'm keeping up my correspondence irregardless. Helen, I've been thinking of you constantly and loving you with my whole heart. I'm still waiting and hoping for the day when I can hold you in my arms not for just a few moments but for always. Helen, I'm only living half a life with you over there and me over here.

Because of this I'm sweating out your letters more every day. Helen, I can't understand why you don't write more often. I've written to you while under enemy fire, in foxholes after marching all day and night, without sleep but I still found time to write even if it were only a few lines to let you know that I was thinking of you constantly and loving you with my whole heart. If I was able to write under those conditions, I don't see why you can't write while you're safe at home with nothing to worry about. Perhaps you have other more important things to occupy your mind. I wouldn't say anything, but you didn't even give me any explanation why you weren't able to write. What do I get instead, a little note saying you're sorry you haven't written for quite some time and will make it up to me in the very near future?

While I'm writing this letter, I can't help but think of you. You with your smiling eyes, sweet tender lips, warm embraces and that unsurpassable loving a man like me needs. It's no wonder I miss you not just for now but each and every day that goes by. I've only been over here seven months, but it may as well have been seven years because that's what it feels like. I've been constantly thinking and planning for the day when I'll be out of the Army and able to pursue my dreams and ambitions without interruption. I was just wondering how it would be to be home. I know just thinking of it gives me a thrill all the way from my toes to my head. All I've done over here is engage in warfare. It sure would be a change to go back to peaceful living with only little worries like paying the gas or light bill. Yea, you'd probably say that's worry enough. OK I won't argue with you.

I'm still sweating out the Pacific. Perhaps in a few weeks or so I'll be sure whether I'm going to stay here or go to the Pacific via the states or just straight to the Pacific. How many points do I have? Only 46. I still need about 39 more to get out. That certainly is a heck of a lot. There's no doubt I'll be seeing action somewhere in the Pacific. That's only my opinion. So far, I don't know what is going to happen. I've done it before so I can do it again.

Meantime I've got my fingers crossed. I'd much rather stay here for a little while than go to the Pacific, especially since I'm attached to the infantry. Well luck has been with me so far. I just hope it stays around for quite some time.

It was too bad your mother cut off your legs in the picture you sent me but irregardless the picture was really swell. It seems as if you were trying to laugh or your mother was making some funny remarks. That's the way I like to see you, laughing and full of life. That's the way I always remember you.

Even though these things have happened I still love you with my whole heart and will continually think of you. Love and Kisses Mike

This war can't last much longer but I hope it ends sooner for all concerned.

ALWAYS REMEMBERING. LOVING YOU FOREVER, MIKE

Love and kisses Mike

June 8, 1945 Zell am Ziller

Dearest Helen:

Mein lieben fraulein. (My lovely girl). I can probably write a letter to you in German. It would take a little effort but never the less I'd do it. We have a fellow in our section that knows French, Italian, and German very well. Every day we get a few lessons in German and traveling through Germany and listening to these people talk has increased my vocabulary very much. If I stay here any longer, I'll probably be speaking this as good as English. We don't speak to these people here unless necessary but we want to know the language so we can understand what they're saying. This way they can't put anything over us.

I'm in a somewhat jovial mood today. Yes, sir I feel great in spite of the fact that it's raining cats and dogs outside. How do I know? Now isn't that just like a woman. I should know because I stepped in a "poodle". One reason I feel so good is because I received two letters from you yesterday. Oh happy day. See what you do to me. You leave me breathless and speechless all at once. I've got you down in my book as morale builder number 1, but in my heart it's life giving power.

Just think Helen if we were married and had a few kids you'd have a doctor right in your own home. Kids would get a scratch you'd probably say go and see Pap he'll fix it for you. Yep, the old doc, that's me.

Though it's raining like water coming down a drain, I'm in rather good spirits (not alcoholic either). Although I wish I did have some beer at least.

I read in the army newspaper, (yes, I can still read in spite of my lack of mental capabilities), that the combat medics are at least getting some recognition. Congress passed a law giving us a ten-dollar increase per month. This isn't too bad, because the pay is retroactive. That means we will get paid from the first time we entered combat. We were authorized the combat medics badge prior to this but those extra ten bucks means a lot. We were also authorized to wear two bronze stars on our ribbon. This will help to increase my somewhat depleted points a little.

You've probably read in the papers where the critical score has been dropped to 78, I still need beaucoup points in spite of that drop of seven points. I imagine I'll get out of this army eventually. Let's hope for the best.

Life still goes on but mine seemed to stop the moment I left you. I know it will start again once we meet again and our fondest dreams will be able to blossom.

Yes, I admit I've lost weight. About 20 to 25 pounds to be exact, but nevertheless I feel like a million dollars. At present I'm getting some good fresh air, sunshine and rest so no doubt I'll gain a few pounds back. But what difference does it make as long as I am healthy. Right. I knew you'd agree with me. I may be wrong but not all the time.

By the way I ran in the regiment and won, but was disqualified for cutting two men off at the corners.

Sorry I have to close but I was just called to go out on duty.

Always Remembering. Never Forgetting. Loving you forever.

Always faithful, love and kisses Mike

While fighting the enemy, Mike tried to appreciate the beauty of nature, but now, without that burden, he breathed in every moment and scene that Mother Nature offered. He viewed his travels across Austria with the Rainbow men, performing his duties, as an outdoor exploration. As they crossed the plains and the valleys, the road twisted and turned through gorges and canyons to the top of the Alps. Occasionally, they observed a cascading waterfall along the side of a mountain, with torrents of water whipping over the rocks and throwing a thick spray of water into the air.

He wished he could capture the colorful rainbow shining through the misty water with his camera, but it soon disappeared. At one spot, he persuaded the men to stop and linger by the stream where the fish wiggled back and forth through the rocks and shot out of the swift current. Mountain goats climbed up the side of the cliff while cows grazed in the valley. Small, quaint houses constructed of colored stone with artistically carved wooden porches jutted from the sides of the mountain. Absent any visible roads, Mike wondered how people traveled to their houses.

His ears popped as they continued upward, and in the distance, he noticed wintry white tufts of flowers growing from the rocky crevices in the hillside. When he reached the flowers, he plucked a few. The plant had a yellow center, and each individual blossom resembled a star. As he caressed the velvety petals, the flower's fragrant, enticing scent tickled his nose. Closing his eyes, he imagined Helen's perfume as sweet as the flower and her soft supple skin against his arm. Curious about the blossom, Mike walked toward the men relaxing on the grass. "Have any of you seen this flower before?" he asked.

One sergeant said, "Hell, I'm not sure I know what a daisy is. I grew up in the city, and besides, I'm sure these flowers are different from back home."

Another soldier took a drag on his cigarette. "I just want to know, though, are you getting soft on us, Sarge? Picking flowers?"

"What are you talking about, soft? Just because a fellow enjoys the wonders of Mother Nature doesn't make him soft. I've seen too many horrible things since we came over here, and it's refreshing to find some beauty."

A private, who'd gained the reputation as the dunce of the group, walked over to Mike. "It's called Edelweiss."

The men turned toward him with raised eyebrows.

"Why you all lookin' at me like that? One day I was in town and saw a postcard with the flower. It said it was Edelweiss."

A corporal responded, "Well, I'll be. I just learned something from this buck private."

Mike added, "Me, too. Thanks, pal."

He smelled the flower and tucked it into his pocket.

Chapter Thirty-Two

July 1945

July 17, 1945 Tuesday Salzburg, Austria

Dearest Helen:

I was more than pleased to receive several letters from you today. You've made me happy knowing you haven't forgotten.

Yesterday I had a treat, at least it was for me. I had a scoop of ice cream for supper. First I've had in all the time I've been over here. Now I know what I'm missing back home.

July 14, was the birthday of our division, two years old. I'm one of the remaining few of those men who came as a cadre to activate it. I'll tell you I was lucky and still am for that matter. I'm sure it was your prayers that had a very great part in it.

As far as I know we may be here for a little while anyway. How long that will be, only God knows. If I hear anything definite, I'll let you know. Thanks for the clipping of Pittsburgh. No, I haven't forgotten how appealing and homelike the place is. That's one thing I never hope to forget. I've got too many things back there to come home to. You're the first and main one. You mentioned talking to Stan and Gert about information on homes. Well, the army Bill of Rights has a good deal for the returning veterans. I'm still hoping for a lovely home. That's my first step when I get home. I'm sure we can do it together. It may mean a little work but at least we'll know after it's all over we'll have something to show for it. Don't you agree? I'm sure you do. That's one thing I know I can depend on you for. In fact, I know I *can depend on you always. It'll be a little hard at first but at least we'll be doing it together. That's what really counts. I'm really looking forward to it.*

We have so much to look forward to. Just think we still have each other after so long a time.

Darling, I wish you knew how I feel toward you. I want you to know that there is not a single doubt in my mind about my deep and sincere love for you. That's why I've tried and succeeded so far, not to have anything to do with any kind of woman while I'm away from you. As far as I'm concerned, I won't have anything to do with them. It certainly is a tough job, but thinking of you and a lovely home with a few children of our own, helps me a lot. Believe me, I know you understand. Helen, I think too much of you and I want to get married and when I get married, I don't want to have my children born with a disease, blind or crippled. I hope I made you understand how I feel and sincerely hope I've cleared your mind and made you feel more at ease.

Helen, I'm as clean as when I left, perhaps a lot wiser and I intend to come back the same way. I'm in a little serious mood tonight so I'm telling you this straight from my shoulder. I'm doing this so you needn't worry about me mixing in with any of these women, and to let you know that my love for you has not changed in the least.

Loving you more than ever, ever faithful, love and kisses Mike

Helen folded the letter, closed her eyes, and tilted her head toward the sky, absorbing the hot rays. In her solitude, she lazed in the warmth of the sun and daydreamed of times spent with Mike at the North Park Lake on hot summer days. How she longed to be in his arms, as their feet dangled in the water, occasionally tickled by a fish. Without warning, the backyard door banged against the fence, and her family yelled, "Happy Birthday!" Helen screamed, and her legs jerked.

"Dear God, you scared the bejebers out of me!" she said, her hand to her chest.

Gert laughed. "Nothing like a good jumpstart for a new year. Maybe these presents will make up for scaring you."

Helen's siblings laid their boxes on the bench, and Clara said, "Before you open these, I'm going to get the tub and fill it with water. This way, the kids can splash around while we talk."

Flo said, "I'll get us some ginger ale and nuts."

The married sisters stripped their children down to their underwear and deposited them in the water.

Marie lit a cigarette and said, "You know, if you don't get married soon, they'll be calling you a spinster."

Helen scowled. "I'm engaged, and the war in Europe is over. We'll be married soon."

"Oh, Helen, I'm just kidding you," Marie said, laughing. "Open your presents."

Flo picked up a present and handed it to Helen. "Here, I think you could use this today."

Helen opened the box. "Oh, you're right. It's a perfect day for a new bathing suit. Thanks, Flo."

Gert stood up. "Since you're getting married soon, I got you some things for your hope chest."

Helen unwrapped some cookie cutters, Gert's recipes, and a hand mixer.

"Thanks, Gert, I hope I'm as good a baker as you. You've taught me everything I know."

"If Mike is anything like Stan, he'll want some goodies."

"I'm sure you're right."

After opening all the presents, Marie said, "Well, it's not official unless we sing 'Happy Birthday' so let's go inside." She played "Happy Birthday" on the piano, and everyone joined in, adding a few verses of "May our dear Lord bless you." They finished with the traditional Polish song "*Sto lat, sto lat, niech żyje, żyje nam,*" which means, "Hope you live to be a hundred."

Helen beamed. "Thanks. You made my day."

Mary glared at Flo. "Don't forget, Flo, since it's Helen's birthday, you have to do the dishes by yourself today. The breakfast dishes are still in the sink, plus all these glasses. You better get started."

Flo slowly rose from the chair. "I know, Mom."

"Hey, Helen," Gert said, "wanna take a walk with me and the girls? Stan's working the late shift and won't be home until eleven."

"Sure, it's a beautiful day."

Gert dried Dolores and Mary Ann and dressed them while Helen slipped on her shoes and freshened her lipstick.

As they walked toward Sarah Street, Gert said, "I know you're happy about your birthday, but what's on your mind?"

"What do you mean?" Helen asked.

"I can tell something's bothering you. Spill the beans."

"Well . . . ," Helen began, "you know, Gert, I didn't want to say anything, but when the war ended in Europe, I really thought Mike would've been home by now. At least given a furlough. I've thanked God so many times that he's still alive but . . . I've been waiting three years. I want to start my life with him and have babies. I'm twenty-four years old!"

"You still have plenty of time, and he'll be home soon," Gert reassured her. "It's been hard for everyone. My neighbor told me the other day that she's so lonely without her husband, she cries every night before she goes to bed. She's afraid her husband's gonna run off with another woman, like her brother-in-law who decided to stay in Paris because he found a French woman to take care of him."

"See, that's my point," Helen said. "What if I'm waiting for nothing?"

"Oh, I don't think Mike would do that. I'm just saying everyone is tired of waiting and worrying. It shouldn't be long now." Gert stopped walking, gently placed her arm around Helen's shoulder, and looked her sister straight in the eyes. "Let me ask you, do you still love Mike?"

"Of course, I do!"

"Then just wait and have faith. You're stronger than you think, Helen, and if you can survive this, you'll be able to survive anything. I know Mike, and I just know you'll both be fine."

"Thanks, Gert. Anyway, I guess we should head back. Your little ones look tired."

Monday, July 23, 1945 Salzburg, Austria

Dearest Helen:

I believe I'll start the day off right by dropping you a few lines. While I'm writing this letter, you are no doubt sleeping peacefully and dreaming, I hope of me. You notice how selfish I am I want you all to myself. I don't think you'll blame me.

I'm firmly convinced that we have some wonderful times ahead of us having so much to talk over, planning for our home, experiencing life anew and most of all being together. We will share our joys and sorrows, share the new experiences, and share our love together. We're really lucky. We still have each other even if it is over such an expanse of space. Some others were not so fortunate. Their hopes and dreams were shattered just by one little telegram from the war department. Another reason why we're lucky is that we still have our health along with our never-ending love.

All this time I've been away from you I've been promising myself that when the time comes when we're together again I'm going to try my darnedest to make you happy. Just being with you would make me happy enough but I've got to think of what would make you happy.

Today we started an intensive training program in preparation for the Pacific theatre of operations. This will continue for some five weeks or so, but this doesn't mean we will go direct to the Pacific. We're still slated to come home for a 30-day furlough. We're unfortunate in that we're taking our training over here instead of in the states but lucky in that we're not going direct and taking our training on some remote and isolated island in the great expanse of the Pacific Ocean. It takes some time to redeploy an outfit to a different theatre of operations. If we were to leave today. The trip would take about six months or more. So far, we've been lucky. I just hope it continues. The longer we stay here the better the chance becomes of the war ending in the Pacific.

In my spare time, the little I do have, I'm still studying German and Algebra. Just today I enrolled in a course for Mechanical Engineer. All this will keep me very busy, and no doubt keep me out of trouble. The more time I spend studying and training, the less time I'll have to go out.

I've been wondering what your plans for the future were. In all of the letters from you I've never heard you mention more than once what you'd like to do when we're able to be together after all this is over. Me? I've thought a great deal about what I intend to do. There are several things I want to do first. Get married to you of course, get a fairly good job, preferably the one I had before, build or buy a home of our own and going to night school so that I may be able to hold down my job and perhaps get a better position in my particular field of work. At present I'm enrolled in an army self-teaching course taking up machine shop practice and advanced mathematics. I'm very sure this will help me a great deal in the job I intend to get after the war. I believe the more I learn in that particular job the better chance I have of holding down a job, thus making it a lot more secure in future years. You as well as I know that a depression great or small always follows a war. I myself am going to make sure that I'm prepared for such an event once it does come. Marriage I know is no easy task, especially the first few years trying to get settled and getting a number of things accomplished. The situation as it is makes things still more difficult because of so much uncertainty. I sincerely believe that we can get along very well because you are not afraid to work to get many things done. Helen, let me know how you feel about the entire situation so that we may plan a little. We want to do our planning now and not afterward when things may be quite different. I love you and I want to do all in my power to make you happy and your days a lot more pleasant.

One of the fellows from our battalion, Sergeant Vito Bertoldo, is being honored for a congressional medal of honor for brave action against the enemy. We treated him at our aid station. While wounded, under fire and lying submerged in a creek he directed mortar and artillery fire on the enemy and repulsed an attack. He was wounded in the stomach and his guts were hanging down as far as his knees. It may sound incredible and fantastic, but the man is still living and getting along splendidly. I've seen many men cheat death. Some so badly wounded you wondered how they could stay alive, but never the less they pulled through with flying colors.

So, here's hoping you are in the best of health. Loving you with my whole heart. Ever faithful. Mike

Helen walked into the kitchen, "Hey, Mom, since I'm on vacation this week, I have some extra time. Do you need me to do anything for you?"

"Of course, I do," her mother replied. "Did you think you were just going to lie around all week?"

"No, I . . ."

"You can start with the outhouse. It needs a good cleaning, and then you can paint the kitchen."

"Sure, no problem, but Gabby wanted to do some things, too."

"You'll have plenty of time for that after you finish everything."

Over the next few days, Helen finished her housework and was free to go shopping with Gabby. Helen arrived at Gabby's house and found her pulling bits of weeds and grass from the brick sidewalk.

"Hi, Gabby," she greeted her friend. "Are you ready?"

Gabby brushed the dirt from her hands. "I was just cleaning up the sidewalk while I waited for you. Give me a second to wash my hands, and I'll be right back."

A moment later, Gabby pushed through the screen door to the front sidewalk. "So, how you enjoying your vacation so far?" she asked.

"It's better now that I'm done with all my chores at home."

"You know, Helen, sometimes I think your mother treats you and Flo like Cinderella in the story we read as kids."

"Maybe, but it doesn't bother me. I like to help out."

"Well, I'm glad you're done helping out because now it's time to have fun," Gabby said. "I was thinking, do you want to go to Kaufmann's and check out the new kitchen items? We could pick out some things for your hope chest."

"I don't have a lot of extra money right now. I spent most of my money on a gift for Mike."

"We don't have to buy anything. It'll be fun just to see what they have."

"That sounds good," Helen agreed. "I haven't even thought about what we're gonna need. Unless my parents give us some things, I guess we need everything."

Gabby stopped to drop a letter into a mailbox. "You'll get some of the things as wedding presents. And talking about wedding presents, show me what you really like, and I just might get that for you after you set a date."

"Oh, yeah, the wedding date. I can't really set the date till Mike comes home."

"I think he's gonna be coming home soon. Have you read the papers? It looks like we're bombing the heck out of Japan. Who knows? This war could be over tomorrow, and then they *have* to send him home. He could be home in time for the holidays, and soon wedding bells will be ringing!"

"That's music to my ears."

"Actually, Helen, we should be shopping for wedding gowns. I know you wanted to pick out a gown with your mother, but why don't we do a look-see and see if you like anything?"

"Sure, I guess there's no harm in that," Helen said.

While waiting for the streetcar to arrive, Gabby asked, "Have you heard from Mike lately?"

"Yes, I've gotten a letter from him almost every day," Helen said. "Sometimes I get two in a day. When he was fighting, his letters were short, and he didn't say too much about what he was doing. Now he writes these really long letters."

"Well, he probably has more time now."

Helen took a seat on the trolley. "Yeah, I know. I really enjoy his letters. It's like reading a storybook, and sometimes I read them two or three times. In one letter, he described a Ty-ty rolll—e—in. Oh, I don't really know how to say it, but a show in Austria where the people were dressed in their native costumes, singing and dancing and yodeling. He told me about a Corpus Christi celebration. He said the whole town participated, and the little girls wore white dresses and carried flowers, and the men and women were all dressed up, and some carried the Eucharist. He said the whole thing lasted about two hours."

"No wonder you find his letters interesting! Sounds like he's learning a lot about the culture and having loads of fun."

"Mike told me he was gonna make the most of his time in the army, and he sure is. He's gone to a few classical and opera music shows. In his last letter, he said he even saw a Russian show. He does more in one week than I do all year!"

"I think that's great. Maybe after you're hitched, he'll take you back to some places and be your personal tour guide."

"It'd be fun to travel, but I guess it all depends on how much money we have."

"That's for sure. Nothing's free unless you're in the army," Gabby said. "What else did he have to say?"

"He's traveling a lot. Almost every other letter, he's in a different city. I'm not sure how to say some of the names. He told me he stays in houses that they take from people, and while they were at one of the houses, they found women's clothes and thought it'd be fun to try them on. He sent me a picture."

"Oh, what a hoot. You'll have to show me when we get back home."

"Sure. Remind me when we get back. Oh, and he's going to school."

"That's good. For what?"

"I'm not really sure. He's learning German and sometimes writes a few German words to me and then tells me what they mean. He's taking a mathematics class, too. Oh, here's our stop."

Gabby stood up. "I'm surprised they're teaching him German. If they had plans to send

him to the Pacific, I think they'd be teaching him Japanese."

"Yeah, I never thought about that. Maybe you're right," Helen said.

Sunday July 29, 1945 Salzburg, Austria

Dearest Helen:

I don't have much time to write due to the fact that we are moving again. Where or why, I don't know. I'll know as soon as I get there. Here's a little poem that a few of us single fellows whipped up. It expresses my sentiments to the greatest degree.

I MUST BE SURE

When I have put away my gun

And victory is true

I want to see you dearest one

As I remember you

I want to find you waiting there

Beside your open door

Prepared to understand and share

The aftermath of war

I know there will be many tears

For time to turn aside and there will be silent fears

That laughter cannot hide

But dearest one, I must be sure that you will welcome me

With words of love that will endure

For all eternity

I want to build my life anew around your loving charms

And I must know for sure that you

Still want me in your arms

To all indications, just a rumor, we may stay over here till the end of this year.

Waiting I know is a very difficult and wearisome task. I wish there were something I could do to make this period of waiting a lot more pleasant for you. It makes me feel wonderful to have someone as lovely and understanding as you waiting for me when I come home for always.

Always remembering. Never forgetting. Loving you forever Love Mike

Chapter Thirty-Three

hile Helen was stocking the shelves at Donahoe's, one of the regular patrol officers greeted her. "Any word from Mike about when he might be back home?" he asked.

"I got a letter last week, and he seems pretty sure that he'll be in Austria until the end of the year."

"That's great news. If it's true. He could be home by Christmas!"

"That would be the best Christmas present ever!" Helen said. "If he does come home, I'm hoping he has enough points to stay here."

"Me, too. We all miss that fella."

"Can you excuse me? I need to go to the back office to check on the rest of this order. We'll talk later, okay?"

"Sure, I need to get to my patrol anyway," the officer said.

Helen walked into the office where Johnnie was scowling as he fumbled with the radio. "This darn radio doesn't want to cooperate. It was playing music a minute ago, and now it's all static."

Gabby retrieved coins from the safe. "Maybe it's time you bought a new one. How long have you—"

"Aha, I got it," Johnnie said.

The song ended, and an announcer said, "We have interrupted this program to bring you a special broadcast—"

"Wow, that was good timing." Johnnie waved his hand to Gabby. "Come here, listen."

Gabby pushed the safe door closed and huddled next to Johnnie and Helen.

The radio remained silent for a few seconds, and then President Truman began to speak. "A short time ago, an American airplane dropped one bomb on Hiroshima and destroyed its usefulness to the enemy. That bomb has more power than 20,000 tons of TNT. The Japanese began the war from the air at Pearl Harbor. They have been repaid many fold. And the end is not yet. With this bomb we have now added a new and revolutionary increase in destruction to supplement the growing power of our armed forces. In their present form, these bombs are now in production and even more powerful forms are in development. It is an atomic bomb. It is a harnessing of the basic power of the universe. The force from which the sun draws its power has been loosed against those who brought war to the Far East."[1]

"What? What is he saying?" asked Gabby

Johnnie tapped on the desk. "Shh! Listen!"

Gabby hovered over the radio and listened intently.

When the speech ended, she commented, "I listened to the whole speech, but I'm still not sure what he meant. Did we beat Japan? Did Japan surrender?"

Johnnie shrugged. "I'm not sure, exactly. It sounds like the government has a new powerful weapon, and they bombed the Japs."

Helen blurted out, "Does that mean the war is over?"

---

[1] Https://www.c-span.org/video/?294914-1/president-truman-speech-bombing-hiroshima.

Johnnie responded, "I don't know, but if not, it sounds like it'll be over soon, that's for damn sure. We need to tell the rest of the employees. This could be the news we've been waiting for."

"Gabby, I'm not sure what to say. He said something about the sun and ana . . . anamonic or something," Helen said.

Gabby sighed. "We don't have to talk about the details, just that we bombed the Japs, and it sounds hopeful."

After work, Helen rushed through the back door of her house. "Mom, Pop, did you hear the announcement on the radio about the Japanese?" There was no response.

"Mom, Pop, are you home?"

She started toward the back door on her way to Marie's house, but she stopped when she noticed a newspaper on the kitchen chair. Eager for information about the new bomb, she snatched it up and scoured the pages. The scientific words *uranium*, *U-235*, and *atomic weight* were foreign to her, but the reports of the magnitude of the bomb and its implications were clear. The Japanese were doomed if they didn't surrender, and the war that had snatched Mike from her life could be over.

A few days later, on August 9, the headlines in the *Pittsburgh Post-Gazette* proclaimed, "Nagasaki Atom-bombed: Russians Attack Japs." It provided encouragement that the war in Japan would soon end. Each day, people rushed to read the newspaper and listen to the radio. The Russians advanced into Manchuria, and President Truman declared the only way to stop the dropping of more atom bombs was an unconditional surrender. The president's terms confirmed the imminent end of the war.

Office workers who were prepared to pop their bottles of champagne on the morning of August 10 were disappointed when the president announced that the United States was still at war. Japan wanted Hirohito to remain as the sovereign ruler, and the United States found this demand unacceptable. Celebrations halted, but as days passed, the credible rumors incited an explosion of emotions that had been suppressed for years. Early on August 14, shop girls, businessmen, and store patrons crowded the streets of downtown Pittsburgh. Conga lines formed, weaving along Fifth Avenue, and a snowstorm of confetti and streamers fell from towering buildings onto the revelers.

Helen and Gabby heard some whistling and hoots outside of Donahoe's, and a customer ran into the store, shouting, "The war is over! You should be celebrating!"

Gabby said, "We haven't heard anything official."

Jumping and waving his hands, he replied, "It doesn't matter, it's going to happen. What are you waiting for? We won! We won!"

Johnnie realized his customer was right. The store was empty, and the boisterous sounds of the celebrants outside grew louder. "Damn it, this is what we've been waiting for. When you've cleaned up everything, go home. The war is over! It's time to celebrate!"

Gabby and Helen hugged each other, and Helen said, "Do you think it's true? Is it really over?"

Gabby wiped her eyes. "It has to be, Helen! Oh, happy happy day! The boys are coming home!"

Helen lost her footing as she stormed through the back door. She stumbled into the kitchen. "Mom! Mom! It's over. The war is over! Everyone's celebrating. Isn't it great?"

"It is," her mother said, her tone measured. "But I've been listening to the radio all day, and they haven't said anything for sure."

Finally, at 7 p.m., President Truman announced that Japan had agreed to the Potsdam surrender and declared the next two days a holiday. The floodgates of excitement burst, and people stormed from their houses. Helen and her family ran into the street and hugged their neighbors. Men clinked their beer bottles together, toasting the great news. Church bells rang, and people banged on pots and pans, blew whistles, and shouted. Hands and arms flailed out of the windows of honking cars. Teenage boys attached streamers to their bicycles and joined in the celebration. Emotions escalated as people cried, laughed, and shouted. Helen and Flo ran to Carson Street and watched as hundreds of people lined the streets. They noticed the manager of the Arcade Theater changing the marquee to read "WAR ENDS."

Cars and people from all over the city and the suburbs descended upon downtown Pittsburgh as rapidly as ants coming out of hiding to consume a piece of candy. Soon the entire area brimmed with wall-to-wall people, eager to celebrate. Cars, streetcars, and buses came to a stop. Bellboys waited outside the William Penn Hotel, then ran to catch pillows and sheets their guests flung from the windows in celebration. Policemen stood guard on the street corners, ready to halt any excessive behavior or violence, while shop owners boarded up their windows. People passed bottles of Tech and Duquesne beer around in a toast to the sailors and the soldiers who had fought bravely for their country. Bottles of champagne were popped, squirting people who were hugging and kissing each other. In the midst of the reverie, pockets of people knelt in the street to offer prayers of thanksgiving.

The people of Pittsburgh reveled in the celebratory outdoor party, which continued until their lungs could no longer shout and their legs grew weary.

The next day, Helen attended the Catholic Holy Day of the Feast of Assumption. She normally stopped in at the early service before work, but since all the stores were closed for the national holiday, she went to the late mass. Reminiscent of VE Day, the church overflowed with people, not only celebrating the feast day but giving thanks for the end of the war.

Although Helen and her family considered going to a movie or to Kennywood Amusement Park, they all converged at Gert and Stan's to celebrate the victory instead.

Thunderous celebratory sounds at Gert's house drifted into the streets, and no one cared when neighbors barged into the party. Helen's mother, who rarely displayed extreme happiness, was positively giddy with exhilaration. Gert fetched a bottle of hoarded whisky and some ginger ale and prepared highball drinks for the adults and soda for the children.

During the gathering, Stan stood on a chair and shouted, "I want to make a toast!"

Everyone raised a glass, including, Helen who rarely drank alcoholic beverages.

"In praise to God for ending the war and cheers to Ben, Bern, and my brother Mike who will be coming home soon."

They clinked their glasses. "*Na zdrowie!*"

Gert exclaimed, "Let's toast to Helen and Flo, too. They'll be tying the knot soon."

Flo raised her glass. "I can't wait. I just hope Bern hasn't changed his mind."

Helen took a sip. "I feel like I lost ten pounds, knowing Mike doesn't have to fight anymore. They must be going crazy celebrating."

"They're probably getting drunk!" Stan shouted.

Flo hiccupped. "I don't blame them. They've been fighting for a long time. If Gert has more whiskey, I think I might make myself another victory drink."

Chapter Thirty-Four

September 1945

Gentle winds whistled through the tall pine trees and gently brushed Mike's cheeks as he strolled out of the barracks. With three hours before sunset and dinner, he ventured out for a hike on the sunny, crisp autumn day. The fallen branches and pinecones crunched under his boots as he ascended the mountain. With each step he took, the air cooled a few degrees. When he reached the plateau, he stood at the edge, drinking in the pleasing view of sunrays streaming through puffy clouds. The small town below reminded him of home, set against a background of tall pines interspersed with autumn-hued maple and oak trees dotting the hillside. Under the bright sun, his tense muscles relaxed, and his body seemed to dissolve into the landscape.

He ambled away from the perimeter of the cliff and rested under the towering branches of a tree. There, he could unwind and treasure the landscape of the Austrian Alps and the valley below. Alone at the top of this precipice, he listened to the warble of birds and the rustle of small animals and savored the cooling breeze. Reposing in the peacefulness, he watched a large bird flying free and unencumbered above him, and he contemplated his journey. He thought about all that had transpired from the day he'd left the States to this tranquil moment. For months, Mike's life had been absent the luxury to unwind and soak up his surroundings. During the war, his ears reverberated with sounds of explosions. They stifled his mind, charged his nerves, and made him anxious and defensive, even when the battle raged only in the distance. When he wanted to luxuriate in the defeat of Germany, the threat of Japan always loomed in the background. Now, with all the enemies defeated, his dreams of returning home safely had become a reality.

For the first time since Mike had left New York, he allowed his mind to roam free and reckon with the events of war. He thought about his fellow soldiers, who had defended him while he attempted to treat a fallen man. Remorse filled his heart for never thanking them. The faces of countless slain men flashed through his mind. Soldiers with wives and children waiting for them to come home had lost their precious future. Some had never been afforded the opportunity to see their sons or daughters. Why had his heart been allowed to continue to beat? He was no more worthy of being saved than any other man on the battlefield. Mike wanted answers but none existed. Every day, he lauded praise to his savior, but offering thanks was insufficient for the miracle of life he had been granted. He vowed to live a life to exemplify his faith and to never forget the value of freedom and the men who died fighting for it.

Glancing across the valley, he reflected on the striking countryside he had marched through, marred with the blood of thousands of men. Once-grand buildings had been demolished and renounced to history. Millions of Jews had been eradicated, their families consigned to carry the burden of the memory of their destruction. Mike realized that through his experiences, he had accumulated more knowledge and pain than a normal man would in a lifetime. He wanted to remember, and he desperately wanted to forget.

His thoughts drifted to Helen, and he anguished over her sporadic correspondence. He feared the accumulated weight of distance and loneliness had tipped the scales, tumbling her into someone else's arms to fill the void. Worrying about her love, Mike wished she would write and disclose who possessed her heart. He had witnessed distraught men receive the infamous "Dear John" letters, crushing the soldiers' souls. The pain would be unbearable if Mike became another victim of a long war and uncertainty, but knowing was better than clinging to a meaningless dream. He had survived the near-death encounter of bullets inches from his body and shrapnel bursting at every turn. Now, on the verge of stepping foot on American soil, he questioned whether he could survive if Helen abandoned him. Various scenarios played out in his head. He cursed the Germans and the Japanese for taking away the future he had planned with Helen.

Suddenly, a black falcon swooped down before him, disturbing his contemplation. As the falcon soared away, Mike followed it with his eyes until it landed on a high tree in the distance. He stared at it for a few seconds, removed his pack of Lucky Strike cigarettes, and lit one. After a couple of long puffs, he reached into his front jacket pocket and retrieved a wrinkled, bloodstained, dirty piece of paper: a letter he had written after the first battle, intended to be mailed to Helen if the enemy took his life. While removing the dog tags from the deceased, Mike often discovered the soldiers' final written words, meant to comfort their families.

He unfolded the letter, and tears of gratitude and sorrow dripped onto the paper as he read. When he finished, he held the butt of his cigarette to the paper and watched it burn in his hand, ashes flying to the wind. As the sun dipped low on the horizon, he pulled some paper from his pocket to write to Helen.

September 1, 1945 St. Michael, Austria

Dearest Helen:

I've been fairly busy the past few days but never the less I still sweated out mail call with anxious anticipation and hope. Waiting to hear from you as I've done for the past nine months that I've been overseas. It seems though that it is useless and hopeless procedure because your letters keep coming few and further between.

I've been writing to you regularly in hopes that perhaps this situation might change as times went by, but alas it became worse. My patience Helen has finally reached a very low ebb.

I believe I loved you enough for two men all this time. No doubt that's my reason for putting up with the very inadequate correspondence on your side. I've come to the conclusion that you can't love me as much as you say, because if you did your letters would have come a lot more often and regularly.

My buddies receive an average of 6 to 7 letters a week from their girls. Me, I've only received an average of three or four a month. Why cripes, there is no comparison. You can see the reason I'm so peeved.

Many of my buddies have remarked and I've disagreed with them for months, that my girl has forgotten about me, otherwise she'd write. After such a long time I can't help but agree with them whole heartily that perhaps that's the reason.

Another reason might be is that you probably figured I'd keep on writing just like I have been regardless whether you wrote or not. If that's what you've been thinking, you might as well dismiss it from your mind. From here on out I'm only going to answer the letters you send to me and not write six or seven letters or perhaps more to your one. I love you Helen, but that love can't last forever if it is not returned. If you had any reasonable excuse for not writing it wouldn't be so bad, but when you attribute this lack of writing to laziness, then there is no excuse.

All I can say is if you really cared for me as much as you say you do, you'd write more often regardless of what you were doing. I've done it in the most trying conditions so I know.

I haven't complained very much but cripes, I'm only human.

I can't keep telling myself that well perhaps she's sick or tired or hungry. Not anymore because I've been doing that for the past nine months it just doesn't make sense anymore. You've always told me that if I loved you I would show it. Well I've shown you in the only possible way at this time through correspondence. I've written you as regularly as I could and that was very often. So, since letters are the only means of expressing our love at this time, you'd figure that if the love was true and firm the letters would keep coming in streams. Right? Well? Think it over.

I could tell you a lot more, but I have neither the time or patience. Helen, I still love you as much as I did before. So, if you still care, get on the ball, and write, write, write. If you do, I'll answer everyone with pleasure.

Ever faithful. Love Mike

Chapter Thirty-Five

Fall/Winter 1945

Surrounded by colorful leaves of autumn, Helen walked to Gert's house to help preserve the harvest from the victory garden. The rationing of canned commodities had ended, but not the ritual of canning. This year Gert and Clara's garden had produced an abundance of vegetables, and all the sisters had agreed to help. Helen arrived at Gert's kitchen, overflowing with conversation and Mason jars.

"Gert, what do you want me to do?" asked Helen.

"You can get the beans out of the icebox and wash them. Oh, and Flo, can you get the pot ready to sterilize the jars and lids?"

"Sure."

Gert asked, "Marie, can you chop the tomatoes?"

Clara said, "I'll put some coffee on, and then I'll wash the jars."

Flo filled the large pot with water, and Clara asked her, "Have you heard any news from Bern about when he's coming home?"

"No, but the sooner he gets home, the sooner we can get married."

"Yeah, that'll be good. How about you, Helen, any word about Mike?"

"No, not at all. He hasn't written me in a while."

Clara asked, "Why? Did something happen? Is he in the hospital?"

"I don't know!"

Marie shook her knife at Helen. "What do you mean, you don't know? If he's not writing you, does that mean you two are not together anymore? Are you two still together or not? Do you still love him?"

Helen slammed the icebox door. "Stop it with all of the questions. Yes, I still love him, I'm just not sure what's going on!"

Clara retrieved the coffee cups from the cupboard. "What did he say in his last letter? Did he say anything that made you think something was wrong?"

"Well . . . not really," Helen said. "He was upset that I wasn't writing him as much as he writes me and said he wouldn't write me anymore until I sent him a letter."

Marie said, "Then just send him a letter. He's gonna think you don't want him. Do you want him? Did you find someone else?"

Helen drove her knife into the beans. "No. I mean, yes, I *want* him, and, no, I didn't find someone else."

Clara placed the jars in the soapy water. "Well, if he doesn't hear from you, he's going to give up on you and find someone else. You'll lose him if you don't send him a letter. I don't understand why you won't just write him. What happened?"

"It's hard to explain . . . ," Helen said.

Marie quickly turned around. "Are you sure there isn't someone else? You're pretty friendly with those patrol cops."

"What's that supposed to mean? I'm telling you, there's no one else. Mike's the best thing that ever happened to me. I love him."

Clara dried her hands and stood over Helen. "Something's going on, Helen. What is it?"

Gert rescued Helen from the rapidly flying questions, "Just let her be. You don't know what's been going on."

"Do you know what's going on, Gert?" asked Clara.

Gert retied her apron. "Never mind, I shouldn't have said anything."

Marie said, "Okay, you two, now you've got my tail up, spill the beans."

"Please, I don't want to talk about it," Helen said.

Gert looked at Helen. "They should know, and Mike should know."

Marie stopped cutting tomatoes and slammed the knife on the table. "What? Mike should know what? Okay, this is ridiculous. I'm telling you right now, I'm not leaving until I find out what's going on."

"Yeah, me, too," agreed Flo and Clara.

Gert's eyes pierced Helen's. "Helen? Tell them."

Helen sat down at the table. "Okay, but I don't want you to think badly about Mike."

Everyone gathered around the table, waiting for Helen to divulge her story. After taking a deep breath, she spoke. "A while ago, Francie saw me on Carson Street and told me to break up with Mike for my own good. She said he'd found another woman, and I shouldn't wait around for him. I told her I didn't believe her and wasn't going to stop waiting for him. I love him, and he tells me in his letters how much he loves me, and he talks about our future."

Clara asked, "What did she say?"

"She said Mike's just stringing me along because he felt sorry for me, and I'll see what happens if I stop writing him. He doesn't care, and I should get on with my life."

Marie said, "Helen, that doesn't sound like Mike at all."

Gert chimed in, "That's what I told her."

Marie asked, "Is that when you stopped writing?"

"No," Helen said. "I still wrote to him because I loved him and didn't really believe what she said, but I didn't do it as often as I usually do because I kept thinking about what she said. What if he did have someone else? He kept asking me why I wasn't writing to him as often, and I didn't know what to say."

Clara asked, "What did you tell him?"

"I told him I was lazy, but that just made him mad. Then in his last letter he said he wouldn't write me until I wrote him."

Marie took a sip of coffee. "That's when you stopped writing to him?"

"Yes, I was just so confused. I thought maybe he was a little peeved at me, and he would start writing again when he cooled off, but he never did. Then I thought she was right that Mike didn't care. I didn't know what to do. And I wouldn't blame him if he found someone else. Other women have more to offer Mike than I do. Why would he want me when I never even graduated from high school, and he's so smart?"

Marie put her hand on Helen's shoulders. "Helen, it sounds like you're the one giving up on Mike, already deciding for him that he should have someone else. So what if you don't have an education? A lot of women don't have an education. You need to make up your mind whether you want him or not. Did he ever say he was better than you or that he doesn't want you?"

"No."

"Then you're just making assumptions, and you need to get this cleared up. If you want him, you have to tell him you still love him."

"But what if his sister is right? I'm so confused."

Marie said, "You're confused? Mike is probably more confused since you haven't written him."

Clara asked, "When you were writing to him, did you ever tell him about what his sister said?"

"No," Helen answered. "In the past I mentioned some of the things she said or did, and he told me to ignore them. I don't think he understood everything, or maybe I didn't explain it good. Besides, I didn't want to upset him."

Marie said, "Poor man, he's in the middle of this and doesn't even know what's going on. When he asked you why you weren't writing, that's when you should have told him."

"I guess so, but it's so hard to explain everything in a letter. I thought it might cause problems between us. For Pete's sake, it's his sister. He might not have believed me."

Marie said sympathetically, "Helen, you poor girl. You have been manipulated like a puppet by his sister."

"What do you mean?"

"You always said his sister didn't like you, and she probably never wanted you two to get married. She couldn't manipulate Mike, but she knew she could do it with you."

Marie said, "You should have told us sooner. You need to write to him and work out this mess. For your sake, let's just hope it's not too late."

"It's been so long, I'm not sure what to say. How could I let this happen?" Helen wailed.

Gert put her arm around her. "Let me help you write the letter."

Helen pulled away. "Thanks but no thanks! I'm tired of people telling me what to do and think. It's about time I tell Mike about my doubts and find out if he still loves me. I should have done this a long time ago, but I didn't want to cause any problems. All I know is this is the last time I am going to let anyone or anything interfere with my life. I'm going home."

On her walk home, she stopped at the store to buy Mike some candy and cigarettes. After returning home, she wrote a long letter, sprayed it with perfume, and tucked it inside the care package.

Monday November 12, 1945 Radstadt, Austria

Dearest Helen:

Received your very impressive letter of the 30th of October, yesterday. I told you in my last letter several months ago that if you did write I wouldn't promise you an answer. I'm making an exception in this case to clear up a lot of misunderstanding and false impressions you have on your mind.

The reason my decision was made is your failure to write and not because of any outward influence by others. By failing to write you just as much told me you didn't care.

You mentioned that because you did not write, doesn't necessarily mean you don't love me. Now that's preposterous. If you really love me you would write, as often as was possible regardless of what someone said or what you had to do. Since we're so far apart the only way to show our love was through correspondence. Failing to write in this case is like refusing my kisses or embraces if I were at home. Only in this case it is worse. I kept telling myself over and over again that you still loved me, but I couldn't get myself to believe it after not hearing from you in such a long time.

You tell me I should have a mind of my own and why don't I use it. That's right I should use my mind, all the other times I was using my heart instead of my mind in answer to all these things. I'd still be writing to you and as usual tearing and eating my heart out because I didn't hear from you and know where I stood.

If anyone is undecided Helen, it's you. No one has been saying anything to me. It's your imagination. You mentioned not knowing what to think because of so much talk. That goes to show you that you're not positive you love me. You let your mind do the thinking not your heart. If you would have written to me regularly and told me of your love, plans, etc., we'd still be writing to each other and planning our marriage and our dreams.

You mentioned also of people influencing me and changing my mind. I told you no one has influenced me. You said you believed me, but actually you didn't because you mentioned another reason in your letter to me. If you didn't believe me, how could you possibly know how you stand with me?

Nine long months, since this war ended here, I told you of my plans, dreams and my love for you. There was proof but I didn't get anything in return. Now that I haven't written to you for some time, you ask me for proof of my love. How do you think I felt when you didn't answer? Answer that one if you can.

Now let's see if you practice what you preach. Maybe I should say like you did in your last letter, because I didn't write doesn't mean I stopped loving you. Do you think you'd believe it if I said it? Why certainly not. How do you expect me to believe it then? I loved you and because I did, I wrote to you as often as possible. That's reasonable and sound, isn't it? When I kept writing to you, you had no doubts in your mind but when I stopped writing you began to wonder if I really loved you. Now you see what predicament I was in.

Nobody has influenced me, you practically destroyed everything yourself.

You say you had plenty of patience with everything. What do you think I had for all this time? Months of hell. Sleepless nights, hungry, tired, scared, frozen, discouraged, but I continued to write in spite of all this hell. You've been thinking of yourself all this time. Think of me once in a while. Do you think for one minute I'm enjoying myself over here? You congratulated me on the fact that I didn't complain. Perhaps I was too considerate because I thought of you all these times. I figured you had it tough so why make life more miserable than it was.

You asked me if I'm man enough to go through with what I planned. Yes, I'm man enough but are you woman enough, that's what I want to know. Helen, why don't you wise up, that's putting it bluntly, but I want to impress this upon you.

When I said I loved you and wanted to marry you. What more did you want to know? There was no more positive proof than that. But did you cooperate? No. So don't blame me. If you didn't believe it well then I'm not going to convince you.

Helen, I love you, still do right at this moment and I intend to marry you. If you still persist in having doubts in your mind and not believing me.

Well, I'll call it quits. I'd still go on loving you, but I'd give up because we'd never be happy together.

If you want to see a marriage between the two of us. SHOW me you still Love me by writing more often and start believing what I have to say instead of what other people have to say. Let your heart be your guide and not your mind. Expecting to hear from you very soon.

Love Mike

PS I received your very lovely package and appreciate it immensely. Thanks a million. I regret that the package was opened when I received it. No doubt it was looted. Love Mike

Flo walked into the bedroom. "Helen, why are you crying?"

Helen whimpered and stared at the letter in her hands, unable to answer.

Flo handed her a handkerchief. "What's wrong? Talk to me."

"Mike's upset with me."

"About what?"

"Instead of telling him exactly what Francie said, I asked him if she was trying to influence him, and I asked him about his feelings for me. I think I may have made matters worse. I'm not good at communicating on paper."

"What did he say?"

"He said no matter what, if I loved him, I would have written him."

"Well, I do have to side with him on that one. Did he call the wedding off?"

"No, in fact, he says he still wants to marry me and loves me."

"That's good. He probably was just letting off some steam and to let you know you hurt him, and he doesn't want you to do it again. In the end, he says he still loves you."

"I am happy about that, but I don't want him to be angry with me, and I never wanted to upset him. I'm so mad at myself for not having the gumption to confront his sister or think for myself."

"Don't be so hard on yourself. It sounds like you still have a chance."

"I hope so. I'm going to write him again and let him know I'm sorry and that I love him."

Thursday. December 13, 1945 Radstadt, Austria

Dearest Helen:

Received your letter today and was very delighted to hear from you.

You looked sharp as a tack in that photograph you sent to me. I'm hurrying home as fast as I can. No doubt you'll get a surprise on the 29th of December. It's very unusual and you'll wonder how I was able to do it. I did it myself so that's what makes it much more unusual. Yep, I'm still full of surprises.

So, you like that photo I sent home. Well, I hope you don't have to wait very long for the real thing. Now don't expect to find a good-looking man coming home. That picture was touched up and it's only the technique of the photographer that makes it look so swell. I'm telling you this, so you won't be disappointed.

No, I'm not in a hospital and never was, so don't worry. I'm as healthy and happy as I ever was. But I'd be happier home with you. Don't worry I'm still the clean-cut guy that left the states and I intend to stay that way.

It's quite somewhat of a task to explain these things to you because we haven't been corresponding regularly. If we would have, we'd both know what each other's opinions were on these matters I intend to discuss now.

You asked me if I intended to marry you. Why yes. I never had any other intentions. Now you'll see why I said this is going to be difficult.

I intend to go to school when I get back home. Full time or part time depending of course on how my job in Westinghouse will turn out.

This may sound a bit far-fetched, but my decision has been thought over and many possibilities taken in consideration. It's the man with a very good schooling background who will venture further in business and industry. I've been out of contact with my trade and line of work that I've become stale. I need to brush up a little so that I'll be able to continue in this line of work. Something that pays well and that I enjoy doing. I've been overseas now for over a year, and I don't have the slightest idea of how civilian life will be like when I get back. That's why any plans I make can't be made with the assumption that they will be able to be carried out.

The three years that I've been in the army are considered as far as I'm concerned nothing but lost time. Just another three years off my life.

I intend to marry you and any plans you or I make can be talked over and the best possible course taken. If we do agree on certain things, we can carry them out no matter how difficult they may seem at the time. Hoping to hear from you soon.

Love Mike

It was two hours before Helen needed to be at work, but she slipped on her coat, put Mike's letter in her purse, and headed for the incline. At the top of the hill she detoured to Grandview Park, placed a newspaper on the cold bench, and reread Mike's letter. His declaration of his intent to marry her reassured her of his love and his forgiveness for her not writing. She leaned back, breathed in the cool fresh air, and surveyed the park, relieved he didn't address the misunderstandings or chastise her. Although she was content with his response, she wondered how long it would be before she and Mike would sit in the park together. Clutching the letter, she stared at the words *Love Mike* and questioned why he hadn't ended his letter with his usual closing. Her heart started to pound as she wondered whether they could love each other as they did before the war. She knew she'd sabotaged their relationship by not writing, but it was family, time, and distance that fueled their discord. As she watched the squirrels chase each other through the trees, she laughed, remembering how she and Mike had enjoyed watching their antics. A soft breeze caressed her face, and she closed her eyes and imagined lying in Mike's arms. If only he could be home for Christmas, then their life could finally return to normal.

At the mess hall, Mike took his tin plate of food and sat down at the table. "You know, this food isn't the greatest, but it sure beats the hell out of the K-rations we were eating in the trenches last year."

"Anything would be better than that," said a medic. "Can you believe, it's gonna be Christmas in a week, and we're still stuck over here? I thought for sure we'd all be home in time for Christmas. I don't understand what the hell is taking this army so long to get us back home."

"You should know by now that when it comes to paperwork, the army is as slow as those donkeys in the Haardt Mountains."

"I don't understand their logic either. A friend of mine who was back in the States on furlough got discharged last week, and he didn't even have as many points as I do."

The company clerk interjected, "Yeah, ain't that the shit? The same thing happened to a buddy of mine, and my wife wrote me and thinks I'm lying about not getting orders to go home. She can't understand why he's home and I'm not."

Mike shoved another spoonful in his mouth. "Not only are we stuck here, I'm pissed about the fact that they told us we won't be getting mail now until after Christmas. If we can't be home for Christmas, the least they could do is get us our mail."

Another medic added, "Yeah, I was hoping my Ma would send me her nut bread she used to bake every Christmas."

The clerk leaned back in his chair. "You know, when I was back home, my married brothers and sisters would come over to my parents' house, and I hardly gave a second thought to everything my mom did to make the holiday special. Now I can't stop thinking about all the delicious Italian dishes she made and the spiked eggnog."

Mike chimed in, "Yeah, we didn't always have much food to eat, but I sure do miss kielbasa and singing Christmas songs at midnight mass."

"I think about my wife and son," the medic added. "I got married on furlough a couple of months before they shipped us over here. I never spent Christmas with my wife, and I never saw my son. I hope I can make it up to them when I go back."

Mike slurped his coffee. "Yeah, that's a tough one, buddy. I was supposed to get married before coming over here, but she wanted to wait."

The clerk said, "At Christmas in my hometown, the girls from the local church would go around on Christmas Eve, caroling. I was going to ask out this gal who looked like Lana Turner, but I chickened out. A few weeks later, I'm in the army. I think about her once in a while and wonder what happened to her."

"Well, if we ever get the hell out of here, you can always look her up."

"Yeah, I could, but I'm sure some guy scooped her up by now."

As the men exited the mess hall, Mike sang along to "I'll Be Home for Christmas," blaring from the P.A. system, and the other soldiers quickly joined in.

When they passed a large pine tree on the return to their quarters, Mike said, "Hey, fellows, look at this huge pine tree just dying for us to decorate it. What do you say we make it happy?" He dug into his pockets and pulled out a piece of gum. He twisted the wrapper into an icicle and attached it to the tree. While singing, the soldiers rummaged through their pockets for cigarette and candy wrappers to make impromptu decorations. Mike found a comb in his pocket, wrapped paper around it, and, holding it between his lips, played some musical notes to accompany the Christmas songs. Inspired by the homemade instrument, a few men contributed to the impromptu ensemble. The lieutenant pounded out some beats on his mess kit, while two medics snapped their fingers, and a private mimicked a trumpet with his mouth.

The musical assembly intrigued other soldiers as they passed by, and they joined in the merriment and donated more handmade ornaments. In a short while, the pine tree was festooned from top to bottom, temporarily easing their pain of being separated from their loved ones.

Chapter Thirty-Six

Six long months had passed since VJ day, and now Mike and the other men of the Rainbow Division boarded their vessel of freedom, headed back to the States. Unlike their journey to Europe, they spread their wings on the *Coaldale Victory* ship and relaxed on the outside deck without the threat of a bombing. Theatrical movies replaced instructional films, and manuals were switched out for literary books. Miles out to sea, Mike leaned on the railing and took a deep breath. The scent of the salty air awakened his senses, which had been previously overwhelmed by feelings of anguish aboard the SS *Amerika*. A sapphire sky with quill-like clouds tickled the wind around him. Cradled in the sun's warmth, he listened to the melodic swoosh of the waves serenading him. Nothing could be better than the grandeur of nature and going home to Helen.

His buddy walked over and said, "Whatta you smiling about, Mike?"

"I'm thinking about everything good and that as soon as they hand me my discharge papers, I'm boarding the first train home, straight into the arms of my sweetheart."

His buddy threw his cigarette into the ocean. "I'm happy for you, Sarge. Me? I'm not so sure. The last letter I got from my gal sounded like she might be having reservations about our future." He paused and added,

"You know, Mike, we may have won the war, but a lotta us lost our own battles."

Mike nodded. "Whether we realize it or not, we all lost something."

After eight days of cruising the sea, the captain announced that New York Harbor was minutes away. Men quit their poker games, stopped reading, and left conversations in mid-sentence to see the land they'd left more than a year ago. They whooped and hollered to glimpse the torch of freedom on the Statue of Liberty. Mike cheered and then bowed his head and silently offered thanks to God.

As the ship docked, Mike surveyed the area. For a while after the war had ended, crowds of people and bands had gathered at the pier to welcome the men home. Now, eight months after the peace treaties had been signed and millions of men were back home, the docks were quiet. After a multitude of announcements and instructions, the captain issued the all-clear to disembark. Mike grabbed his duffle bag, flung it over his shoulder, and dashed off the ship.

Home was only hours away. He could almost reach out and touch it, but the men were ordered onto a train for Fort Dix, New Jersey, for the final phases and paperwork. The discharge procedure was completed in a day, but it felt like a week. Signing the last paper, Mike took the $165 in mustering-out pay and remarked to the clerk, "I'm using this to buy me a ticket back to Pittsburgh."

His buddy in line overheard him. "Hey, Mike, a couple of the guys are going back to New York to celebrate. Instead of heading home right away, why don't you join us?"

"Sorry, not me," Mike said. "I've been waiting three years to make my sweetheart my wife, and nothing's going to stop me now."

"You sure? You know we'll have a swell time."

"I bet you will, but it wouldn't be a celebration without my gal. I'm heading home." Mike shook the soldier's hand. "Good luck, buddy, and I hope you have a good life."

At the train station, Mike paused in front a phone booth, ready to call Helen and relay the good news of his homecoming. He picked up the receiver and started to dial but stopped. Helen's intermittent correspondence had caused Mike to wonder if she really wanted to travel through life with him. He decided that seeing her expression when he jumped back into her life would truly reveal whether her heart still belonged to him.

Minutes out of Pittsburgh, the train passed by the steel mills as the whistles tooted, signaling the end of a shift. Grinning, Mike bounced in his seat to see the familiar rolling mountains, the winding green river, and the smoke from the mills. The mountains stood small, compared to the grandeur of the Alps in Europe, and the air had a stale scent, instead of the crisp bouquet of the forest, but it was home. A place where he planned to live a happy life with Helen and fulfill his dreams.

The train glided to a stop, and although Mike was exhausted and ravenous, he leapt to his feet and sprinted down the steel steps. He darted across the street toward the bus, waving his arms as oncoming cars screeched to avoid him. Although there were plenty of available seats, he stood at the front of the bus, eager to exit.

Within minutes, he'd arrived at his stop, crossed the crowded street to the incline, and rushed into the cable car. Beads of sweat trickled down his face as he fidgeted in his seat. An elderly woman next to him asked, "Are you okay, soldier? It's cold outside, and you look like you're working at the mill."

"Thanks for asking, ma'am, but I'm better than okay. I just got into town, and I'm going to see my gal for the first time in years."

She patted him on knee. "Well, that's good news, sonny. She's a lucky lady."

The doors of the car opened, and Mike pushed past the other passengers. He ran the few blocks to Donahue's. Barely able to breathe, he burst into the store and slammed the door against a stack of boxes, which tumbled to the floor. At the sound of the clamor, cashiers and customers gazed toward the door. When people recognized Mike, they started chattering, welcoming him back home. He smiled and waved, but their silhouettes and voices faded to the background as he searched for Helen. Within seconds, he homed in on her at the back of the store and called her name. Helen gasped as she recognized his voice. She spun around, and her heart stalled when her eyes met Mike's baby blue bedroom eyes. Struggling to breathe and unsteady, she grasped a shelf, knocking cans to the floor. Everything inside her wanted to race to Mike, but her knees grew weak and her feet refused to move.

Mike, released from his emotional jail, scrambled toward Helen. Without hesitation, he lifted her, squeezed her tight to his chest, and pressed his lips against hers. Helen tightened her arms around Mike and entwined her leg around his. The customers, observing the love story unfolding before their eyes, cheered and cried. Two old ladies pulled out handkerchiefs to dry their eyes as Johnnie, sniffling, walked over to the happy couple.

Johnnie looked sternly at Helen and said, "I want you to go home."

Her stomach sank, and her face turned red. How could she explain her behavior while at work?

Johnnie broke into a smile and patted her on the back. "And enjoy the evening with this wonderful man you've been waiting for."

Helen sighed. "You're not mad at me. You're not firing me?"

"No!" Johnnie said. "What kind of fool would I be to fire someone whose man just got back from war? You two need time together. Go, get out of here! I can handle the closing of the registers."

Mike stretched out his hand toward Johnnie. "Thanks, Johnnie, you're a pal. We'll make it up to you somehow."

"Just make sure you invite me to the wedding."

"You bet we will, and we'll have a few beers to celebrate."

Helen, sobbing and trembling, hugged Johnnie. "Thanks, and sorry. I don't know what I was thinking. Seeing Mike . . . here . . . alive . . . my brain stopped. I don't how to thank you."

Johnnie quipped, "Get out of here before I change my mind. And Mike, you take good care of her."

"You're damn right I'll take care of her," Mike said. "I'm not letting her out of my sight!"

Helen snatched her coat and purse, and customers and employees clapped and cheered as she and Mike rushed out the door.

With a duffle bag over one shoulder, Mike placed his free arm around her shoulders and pulled her to him. He could feel her shaking as they walked toward the park.

After a few steps, he stopped and wiped her face with his handkerchief. "Darling, are you alright? You look like Niagara Falls."

Helen blubbered, "I wasn't sure if I'd ever see you again, and . . . and . . . now you're here." She touched his face and ran her hands down his arms. "Look at you. I mean . . . Oh . . . you're alive and in one piece. People kept saying that maybe you weren't coming home right away because you were recovering in a hospital or maybe you lost a limb and were afraid to come home and tell me."

"That's nonsense, I've always been honest with you, and you can see there's nothing wrong with me."

"Sweetheart, I prayed for you every day, sometimes a couple times a day, but never knew for sure if you were okay."

"Well, God must have heard you. Your worries are over now, darling. It's just you and me from now on. I know that after going through this war, whatever comes our way, we'll be able to handle it. We've sacrificed and waited and worried. But you know what I say, whatever doesn't kill you makes you stronger."

"Oh, Mike, I hope that's true. It's been a long three years."

"Yes, but we have the rest of our lives ahead."

He stroked her hair and planted a huge kiss on her lips. They remained locked in an embrace for several minutes before he released his hold. "Darling, it feels so good to be back in your arms. I want you to know that you're the reason, along with God's grace, that I'm back here. Every time I struggled, the thought of you renewed me. You gave me the strength to survive."

"But I didn't do anything."

"You loved me from a distance and promised to marry me. You wrote to me and sent me pictures and gave me hope. I needed you, Helen, more than you may realize. I needed your letters and love, and I need you now."

"Oh, Mike. I'm so sorry."

"Sorry for what?"

Helen rattled off her thoughts like a machine gun. "For not writing more, for that time I stopped writing, for . . . making you mad. For not marrying you. For anything I did to hurt you. You needed me, and I failed you. I let people influence me . . . and . . . I was alone and confused. Your sister said . . . Oh, I thought you didn't want me anymore and . . . and you were angry and I . . . ."

Mike clasped her hands and whispered, "Shhh, darling, relax. None of that matters now. If you want, we can talk about that later. Right now, I only have one question that matters. Do you still want to marry me?"

PART III

Never-Ending Love

Chapter Thirty-Seven

Helen yawned and squinted in the glow of the refrigerator light as she gathered meats, vegetables, and condiments. In her habitual meticulous manner, she assembled the ingredients into camera-ready sandwiches. Shivering in the dimly lit and lonely kitchen, she stood by the gas space heater and waited for the water to boil. Once sufficiently warmed, she retrieved the worn construction-worker lunch pail from the sink and placed the sandwiches and an apple inside. The tarnished kettle whistled, and she poured the water into the drip coffee pot. She reached for the tall plaid thermos and yelped when she turned around and saw her husband smiling at her.

"Are you trying to give me a heart attack? I didn't even hear you coming down the steps."

"I'm just trying to keep you on your toes."

"I'm going to be lying on the floor if you keep doing that."

Mike kissed her. "Happy anniversary, darling."

"Happy anniversary, Mike. It's hard to believe it's been twenty-five years."

"I know, especially since it feels like forty."

"Oh, you'll never change. Here, sit down. I'll make you an egg and toast."

She removed a plate from the built-in wooden cupboard in the corner and placed it on the table in front of him. "I'm so happy everyone's coming for dinner tonight to help us celebrate."

"Me, too. Especially Michael and his family. It seems like ages since we saw them. What time are they coming?"

"Michael said they're leaving Philadelphia around ten, so they should be here just in time for dinner."

Mike gathered his shoes from behind the kitchen door and sat at the worn chrome table. Helen slid the egg onto his plate, and he pecked her cheek. "Thanks, honey. What would I do without you?"

"I don't know, but you're not going to have a lunch if I don't finish it."

She filled the thermos with coffee and then withdrew an anniversary card she'd hidden behind the dishes. Trying to disguise it, she covered it with a dishtowel and secretly slipped it into the lunch box.

She kissed him and handed him his lunch. "You better get going."

"Thanks, sweetheart, and happy anniversary."

Mike glanced at his watch; he lagged five minutes behind schedule. He quickened his pace to walk the eight blocks to J & L, a miles-long steel mill on the South Side. After punching the time clock, he donned his heavy protective green canvas uniform and collected his torch and tools, ready to tackle the assigned welding jobs. Working at the Steel Mill was not his first choice of a job. After the war, he had planned to further his education and acquire a position more applicable to his intelligence. He'd completed several courses at Carnegie Tech, but roadblocks caused him to veer from his chosen path. The bulk of his paycheck he'd sent to his parents during the war, earmarked for living expenses while he attended school, had been commandeered by his parents. Helen secured the funds Mike had sent her, but they were quickly depleted for necessities. When she became pregnant three months later with their son Michael, Mike insisted that she quit Donahoe's and stay home to take care of the baby. He assumed the role as sole financial provider for his family and lacked the time to go back to school, working double shifts as often as he could. As his family grew from two to six over the years, education took a back seat to providing for the necessities of his growing family.

After Mike left for work, Helen woke Kenny and Jerry, twenty-year-old twins who looked as opposite as Mutt and Jeff, and her youngest and only daughter, Kathy. As they dressed for the day, Helen prepared three more lunches, placed them in brown paper bags, and set the table. Jerry, the first in the kitchen, noticed the cereal bowls on the table and said, "Sorry, Mom, I don't have time for breakfast this morning. I need to get to work early, but thanks anyway, and happy anniversary."

"Here, don't forget your lunch," Helen said, handing it to him.

"Thanks. I should be home by four-thirty."

As the back screen door slammed shut on Jerry's heels, Kenny descended upon the kitchen. "Hey, Mom, happy anniversary."

Helen pointed to the cereal bowls. "You better eat quick and leave. You can't afford to be late for work another day."

Ken wolfed down the entire bowl in record time. "Gotta go, see you tonight."

Kathy, a pre-teenage, skinny girl who had inherited her father's eyes and her mother's cheeks, smile, and innocence, bounced into the kitchen. "Hey, Mom, this is a big day. Silver anniversary. Did you buy Daddy something silver?"

"Daddy and I bought something together. We saved up a little and splurged on silver anniversary rings for each of us."

"Can I see them?"

"Not now. We'll show you at dinner."

Kathy ate a few spoonfuls of Corn Flakes and picked up her books. "Bye, Mom, I gotta go. Sharon's probably waiting for me."

Helen sang to the tune on the radio while she cleared and washed the dishes. Her voice had remained silent for years, stifled by her mother's condescending comments, but Mike encouraged Helen to awaken her love of music. A few songs later, the kitchen was spotless, and she collected her coupons and list of errands. Helen always walked to the stores because she'd never learned to drive. She enjoyed the exercise and the opportunity to stop along the way and chat with neighbors and friends.

As she approached the bank, she noticed a man hobbling alongside her with a cane. The sight of the man reminded her of Mike's struggle to walk after an injury at the steel mill years ago. Unaware of a gas leak, he had switched on a light, triggering an explosion. He flew several feet into the air, and his head had crashed into the concrete, knocking him unconscious, the flames burning his body.

Helen's legs felt weak as she remembered the day she had received the phone call informing her of the accident. She'd dropped the phone to the floor and collapsed in the kitchen chair, struggling to breathe. As the room seemed to whirl, she prayed to God to save Mike and calm her from the thoughts that bombarded her mind. *Could he die? Is he already dead? Would he be disabled? The boys are young and need their father.* After a few minutes, she mustered the strength to rush to the emergency room. At the hospital, the nurse assured her that Mike had survived, but his recovery would take months. She led Helen toward a row of chairs. "Wait here," the nurse said. "I'll come and get you as soon as the doctors stabilize your husband."

Helen quivered alone in the uninviting, sterile waiting room. The cold metal chair caused her tense muscles to tighten even further and sent a chill up her back. She stared at the large clock, watching the minutes pass. Each tick of the second hand echoed louder, exacerbating her pounding headache and racing heart. Mike's life lay in the balance, and Helen felt helpless. With rosary beads in hand, she prayed quietly, waiting for the verdict on her husband's life.

After what seemed like an eternity of Helen's suffering in purgatory, the nurse accompanied her to Mike's room. Sedated, he lay still on the bed, his face, arms, and legs bandaged, with IVs hanging by his side. She imagined his pain and her eyes watered, but she controlled her emotions. She took Mike's left hand, held it gently, and whispered, "I love you, Mike. You'll be okay. I'm here for you and praying for you. God allowed you to survive, and now I'll take care of you."

After months of recovery, therapy, and Helen's love, Mike returned to normal, but the memory of his pain remained with her.

Suppressing the thoughts of that day, she blew her nose and greeted the bank clerk with a smile. After stops at the fruit and vegetable stand, the grocery store, and the post office, she returned home.

She swung open the door of the small white fridge, filled with groceries, and remembered a time when it had resembled Mother Hubbard's cupboard. The union had initiated a strike, the twins were newborns, and they had exhausted every last crumb of food in the house. Helen had anguished over the lack of milk for the boys. She assured God that she could survive without food, but her boys needed to be fed. Minutes after finishing her plea to God, a neighbor knocked on the door and asked Mike to repair her cement steps. She couldn't afford contractor prices and offered Mike $10 for the job. Without hesitation, Mike grabbed his tools and bolted out the door.

During the strike, their financial woes increased, but they were grateful for small blessings. The bank extended a courtesy and agreed to accept only the interest on their mortgage, and vendors consented to a running tab.

Despite roadblocks, the children were fed and content, and Helen was grateful that God stood beside them.

As she prepared dinner, recollecting the previous twenty-five years, the hours melted away, and soon Kathy burst through the back door.

"Hey, Mom, it smells so good, I can taste it! When are we going to eat?"

"Not for a while. Do you have homework?"

Kathy frowned. "Yeah, lots."

"Well, go finish it before everyone gets here."

The whistle blew, signaling the end of shift at the steel mill. Throngs of men rushed out the main gate and headed to the local bar. Mike's buddies knew not to ask him if he wanted to join them for a drink. They had stopped asking long ago after his repeated refusals.

Spending time with family or tending to faults in their century-old house that constantly needed attention took precedence over anything else. If nothing required fixing, he created projects. Mike's mind and hands were never idle. One evening a week, he volunteered as a scoutmaster for the Boy Scouts, instructing them about survival skills and providing firsthand experience from the war. Other evenings, he volunteered at church or indulged his pastimes of reading or updating his stamp collection.

Mike arrived home with a bouquet of yellow roses hidden behind his back. As Helen stood at the kitchen sink, he kissed her cheek and whispered, "Happy anniversary, honey!" He presented her with the flowers. "After all these years, you're still more beautiful than any flowers."

"Oh, Mike, you're so sweet," she said. "You haven't changed. I remember you bringing me flowers for no reason, and my sisters told you to stop because it made their husbands look bad."

"That wasn't going to stop me. What their husbands did was their business. All I cared about was taking care of you."

"I always said I got the best husband of the bunch."

She opened the card attached to the flowers and beamed as she read the familiar "Always Remembering. Never Forgetting. Loving you forever, Mike."

She kissed him. "Thanks, Mike! You know I love you more each day."

"Why wouldn't you?"

"Oh, never mind. Would you like a glass of wine before dinner?"

"Sure."

Helen poured a small glass of port. "Here, why don't you sit outside? It's a lot cooler out there."

The tightness of the row houses created an incubator in warm weather, and Helen wiped sweat from her brow as she prepared the roast beef and mashed potatoes. Kathy bopped down the steps. "Do you want me to set the table?"

"As soon as I'm done making the salad, you can wipe off the table and set it," Helen said.

"How many plates?"

"Well, there's all of us, and Uncle Stan and Aunt Gertie and Bernice and Michael and his family will be here, so we need ten plates."

"I'm so excited. I can't wait to see how big Little Mike is."

"Me, too! Your brother said he keeps outgrowing his clothes."

"Mom, how am I supposed to set ten plates around this table?" Kathy asked, eyeing the table critically.

"I guess you better get the card table and chairs, but you'll have to wait to do it until dinner is ready. If you do it now, I won't be able to open the oven door."

Kathy ran to the top of the stairs and lugged the card table and chairs down the steps, then leaned them against the kitchen table. She noticed the yellow-padded chairs covered with towels to camouflage the padding that had escaped from tears in the fabric. "Should I take the towels off?" she asked.

"Oh, I don't know. It looks bad either way. Go get some clean white towels and replace them. That should be better."

After Kathy fixed the chairs, she asked, "Can we watch the old home movies tonight? I bet everyone would love to see them."

"Ask your dad. He's the one who takes care of that."

Kathy scampered outside to the small twelve-by-twelve cement yard with a cyclone fence at the back, a brick wall to the left, and the side of a neighbor's house on the right. Several webbed folding chairs replaced a large plastic pool that normally occupied the middle of the yard. Kathy sat on her dad's lap while he read the newspaper. "Hey, Dad can we watch some home movies after dinner tonight?"

"I don't know if we'll have time," Mike said.

"Please, please, I'll help you set it up. Pleeeease! It's so much fun to watch them."

Mike's face softened, and he laughed at her enthusiasm. "Okay, I give in, but just a few."

"Awwww, I wanna watch them all! Can we at least watch the one of my birthdays . . . or us playing in the snow or Michael and Toni's wedding . . . ?"

"Okay, okay. Go see if your mother needs any help."

Satisfied, Kathy pulled open the squeaky wooden screen door and strolled back into the cramped kitchen.

The card table and the chairs were arranged, and within a short time, Michael and his wife, Toni, paraded in, carrying their son Michael, followed by Jerry and Kenny. Holding up the rear were Gert and her family.

Gert commented, "Looks like you have a full house, Helen. Do you have room for everyone?"

Helen smiled. "I always have room for my family. Let me take that apple pie off your hands, and go sit down. We're ready to eat."

Helen placed the food on the table, and everyone plunged into the array of dishes. Above the clanging of plates, Mike said, "Before we start, let's say Grace."

After his father said, "Amen," Jerry, the taller of the twins, stood up, towering over the table, and said, "I'd like to make a toast." He held up his glass of iced tea, "To Mom and Dad, for always being there for us. For loving each other and us unconditionally and for raising us to be responsible adults." Smiling down at Kathy, he said, "Well, except for Kathy. The verdict is still out on her. Rumor has it she still can't tie her shoes."

Everyone laughed and clinked glasses together.

After the toast, Kathy glared at Jerry. "Oh very funny, Jer." She glanced at Michael, her oldest brother, for compassion, but he replied, "Hey, Jer, that was a good one, and you should add that she just finished potty training last year."

Kathy snapped back, "Oh yeah, well, who's the only one who got straight A's? It was never you guys."

Helen interjected, "Okay, quit the teasing and settle down. I'm proud of all my kids. Now let's eat before the food gets cold."

The kitchen exploded with a cacophony of voices that penetrated the paper-thin walls of the row houses. Stan and Mike discussed the steel mill and politics. Gert preoccupied Little Mike as Toni tried to feed him, while the brothers bantered about the Pirates' team and their jobs. Helen paused in her chair and surveyed the crowded kitchen, overflowing with her family. She caught Mike's eye and smiled as he nodded and winked. The last twenty-five years, although meager, had been fruitful, providing the treasure of a loving family and a foundation of love more formidable than the pyramids of Egypt. As the chatter rattled on, Helen stood and refilled everyone's plate without asking if they wanted more. Toni waved her hand. "No, thanks, Mom, I'm good."

"You hardly ate anything. Here, at least have some meat."

Gradually, the voices quieted. Kathy took advantage of the silence to ask, "Hey, Mom, after all these years, what do you think was the best thing that ever happened?"

Kenny quickly snapped, "We know it wasn't Kathy."

Helen replied, "Don't say that. We were happy to get a girl."

Kathy wrinkled her nose. "Yeah, and I'm the only one. There are three of you, so that makes me special."

"Oh, you're special all right, but we won't talk about that," said Kenny.

"Stop it, you two," exclaimed Mike. "Let your mother talk."

"Sorry, go ahead, Mom," said Kenny. "What's the best thing?"

Everyone remained silent as Helen paused, slowly turning her head, and focusing on everyone around the table. "You know a lot has happened, plenty of good times and some rough times, but the best part," she said, looking each person in the eye, "is all of you, especially Dad. You know, some people have called us poor, but we are very, very rich and have things money can't buy." Her grin widened. "We have love and good memories. Nothing else matters."

Toni's eyes turned red, "Oh, that's so sweet, Mom."

"I really mean it. The best present I could ever receive from any of you is *you*. I'm really happy you're here."

Kenny interjected, "Even Kathy?"

"When are you boys going to stop teasing her?" Helen asked.

Kathy muttered, "It's okay, Mom, at least they recognize me. There was a time they didn't even know I was in the room."

Helen, not knowing what to say, asked, "Who wants pie and coffee?"

Stan patted his stomach. "Oh, not me."

Kathy put her fork down. "I can't eat another bite."

Gert responded, "I think we're all full now, Helen. Can we have it later?"

"Sure, why don't all of you go into the living room while I clear the dishes?"

Jerry said, "Oh, no, Mom, it's your anniversary. We'll take care of everything."

"That's okay, you know I don't mind."

"Mom, just go and enjoy your company."

Mike carried the folding chairs into the modest living room that held a couch, an upholstered chair, a floor lamp, a television, and a wooden bookcase.

The siblings cleared the dishes quickly. Before they covered the last leftover with plastic wrap, Kathy ran into the living room. "Can we watch movies now?"

"I guess so," Mike said.

Kathy bolted upstairs, found the reels, and staggered into the living room, her arms overflowing with film canisters. She placed them on the carpet and searched through the titles until she found the reel from her first communion.

"Can we watch this one?" she asked.

"Wait a minute, I have to set up everything." Mike placed the projector on a wobbly aluminum tray table and threaded film through the feeder.

The film flickered in the dark, drawing each of them back through the past. As one reel ended, another film was threaded through the projector. The memories melted together into an amalgamation of life, love, and laughter. There, the best times of their lives had been captured on celluloid through the lens of Mike's Super 8 camera. In that moment, bathed in the brilliance of an abundance of achievements and milestones, all the pain, illness, heartbreak, and obstacles they had endured over the years evaporated. Huddled together in the cramped room, they watched the scenes passing before them for hours: Kenny and Jerry at camp, Kathy's first communion, their grandson Little Mike's first birthday, his face covered in frosting. Mike fed numerous events through the projector of Kenny at the piano, Jerry playing basketball, Kathy's dance recitals, Michael dressed to the nines in his naval uniform. The pictures rolled on, showing the kids running through a park, Kathy on her toes smelling flowers at the conservatory, Helen watching kids splash and laugh in the small plastic pool, presents piled under the Christmas tree, and Thanksgiving dinner. Mike had recorded voluminous milestones of their life. The movies could have run till morning, but, feeling tired, Mike pronounced, "That's all, folks," and turned on the light switch, illuminating the room.

Helen stood. "Not yet! Nobody's going home till we have pie and coffee."

After dessert, one by one the family members departed until Kathy and her parents remained in the living room.

"Kathy, you better go to bed. It's getting late," said her mother.

"I know. Good night." Kathy hugged her mom and dad. "Thanks for letting us watch movies, Dad. I wish they had these cameras when you were a kid. I'd love to see what you both were like at my age."

"I don't know. It'd probably be boring."

"I don't think so. You know I love looking at the old pictures of you and Mom, but there's so few."

"It was a different time. I guess you'll just have our stories. Anyway, listen to your mother and get to bed," Mike said.

"Good night, I love you."

Helen started washing dishes, and Mike put his hands around her waist. "Honey, why don't you let those dishes go for now? We can take care of that tomorrow. Let's sit on the couch and relax."

"Okay. Just give me a minute." She dried her hands, hung up her apron, and poured two small glasses of wine.

She snuggled next to Mike on the aqua-colored couch, disguised by a burnt-orange slipcover to match the rug and prevent stains. They cuddled tighter as a cool breeze traveled through the transom over the old wooden door.

"Helen, you outdid yourself again. Dinner was great. You know roast beef is my favorite, and the best way to a man's heart is through his stomach."

"Yes, you always said that."

"Watching the movies and reminiscing made me a little sentimental. I want you to know I'm really grateful for everything that has happened, and I'm especially happy I married you."

"Me, too. I don't know what I would do without you! I'm so glad you never gave up on me, especially when I wouldn't go out with you."

"I know a gem when I find one, and I wasn't about to let you go. You just needed a little coaxing."

"Remember when you took me dancing on our first date?"

"How could I forget?"

"I wish our record player hadn't broken. I'd love to listen to some of those old dance songs."

"Well, we can improvise." He took her hand, pulled her up from the couch to dance, and in a velvety voice sang, "Gonna take a sentimental journey." After finishing the song, they cuddled on the couch, and Mike asked, "What do you think? Does it make you feel like we're young'uns again in your mom's parlor?"

"My heart says yes, but my legs aren't too sure," she said. "I think we're getting old, honey."

She turned and looked at him. "Mike, I know you didn't travel as much as you wanted, and we didn't get everything we dreamed about . . . and, well . . . do you have any regrets?"

"Hell, no! We did what we had to do, and I got more than I bargained for: you, the kids and now a grandchild, our own house. My mother told me I almost died when I was born, and I've had one too many close calls. As far as I'm concerned, as long as you're by my side, I'm the luckiest man on earth. Like Jackie Gleason says on *The Honeymooners*, 'Baby, you're the greatest.'"

Helen clasped his hand in hers and rested her head on his shoulder as moonlight peeking through the window washed over their faces.

Chapter Thirty-Eight

July 1984

Mike gulped his iced tea and yelled through the screen door to Helen, who was washing dishes. "I'm going to pull the weeds on the side of the house and fertilize the flowers. If I have time before dinner, I might paint this outside cellar door."

She walked outside. "Mike, you don't always have to keep doing something. You're working harder now than before you retired."

"Well, I have more time now."

"Seriously, you need to slow down, or you're going to have another heart attack. You know what you always said: sometimes you have to stop and smell the roses. You should heed your own advice."

"Okay, I won't paint the door, but I'm going to pull these weeds before they take over the yard."

Mike had been forced to retire from the steel mill after several heart attacks and groundbreaking open-heart surgery, as well as kidney stones and numerous invasive operations. The doctors had informed him that the caustic, strenuous conditions of the unbearably hot steel mill had compromised his health. At Helen's and his family's insistence, Mike applied for disability and hung up his welder's mask and torch permanently. Yet being unable to perform the daunting tasks at the mill did not stop him from mowing the lawn, painting, or fixing the plumbing around the house.

Early retirement afforded Helen the reward of having breakfasts and lunches with Mike and his constant companionship. From grocery shopping to weekend excursions with the senior citizens group, weekly Yahtzee games, and quiet time listening to old music, they reverted to being a young dating couple.

Mike grabbed an old garbage can to collect the weeds and knelt on the cement walkway to extract invasive plants. Halfway down the patch of dirt, he heard footsteps coming up the front steps. He rose with a huge smile to see Kathy carrying her daughter Kristin and her husband, Norm, lugging a small suitcase and a diaper bag.

"Oh, my God, Kathy, what are you doing here?" Mike exclaimed.

"I thought I'd surprise you and come for a visit."

"Well, I'm glad you're here!"

Kathy squeezed her dad and pecked his cheek. "I missed you, Daddy."

Helen ran outside when she heard the voices.

"Oh, my goodness, what a surprise. How come you didn't tell us you were coming in from Chicago?"

"If I did, then it wouldn't be a surprise," Kathy said. "You always said we have a room to stay here when we come to visit, so here we are!"

"Of course, you always have a place to stay. How long are you going to be here?"

"Only the weekend. We were missing home and decided to drive through the night to see you."

Helen hugged Kathy and Norm long and tight. "I've missed all of you, especially Kristin."

Helen reached out her arms toward Kristin. "Here, let me hold her. She's gotten so big since I saw her last time." Helen squeezed the child and kissed her cheeks.

"Mom, she has a surprise for you. We've been practicing."

Kathy poked Kristin in the stomach as she relaxed into Helen's arms. "Right, Kristin? Say, 'Hi, Grandma.'"

Kristin softly uttered, "Gum-ball."

Helen didn't notice that Kristin had mispronounced her name. It was close enough.

Mike put his arm around Norm's shoulder. "Well, let's not just stand here. Put the suitcase in the house, Norm, and all of you come sit down."

Mike retrieved two outdoor folding chairs, and Kathy set Kristin on his lap as soon as he sat down. He gave Kristin a peck on her cheek and sang, "I love you. I love you, a bushel and a peck and a hug around the neck." Kristin giggled and smiled, and Mike, not wanting to disappoint his audience of one, decided to sing "Edelweiss," one of his favorite songs.

Kathy smiled. "That reminds me of when I was little. I loved it when you sang me a bedtime song."

"Oh, you remember those times, huh?"

"How could I forget?"

"Oh, I dropped a few lines to you in the mail this morning, so I guess you can ignore it since I'll catch you up," Mike said.

"Oh, Dad, I'll still read it. You know, I have to tell you something. After work, there's two things I look forward to: seeing Kristin and Norm, and getting a letter from you. I've been in Chicago for three years, but I still get homesick. I miss all the kids' birthdays and family get-togethers. The way you write, it feels like I'm right back here with you and everyone. If you could send Mom's pork chops along, it'd be heaven."

Helen said, "Talking about pork chops, I bought some last week. They were on sale. I can take them out of the freezer and make them."

"Would you? I'd love that."

Norm's eyes widened. "Me, too, Mom, you make the best pork chops!"

Kathy suddenly remembered the slew of photos in her purse. "Oh, I want to you show you some pictures of Kristin."

Helen and Mike listened intently as Kathy and Norm passed the photos around and explained each image. When she finished, Mike retrieved a box from the dining room table. "I have pictures to show you, too."

Kathy and Norm flipped through the photos of the family events they had missed.

"Oh, Norm look at this one; it's Jeremy and Timmy in the backyard with Dad. How cute."

"Is this one with Stevie and Nikki from Father's Day this year?"

"Oh, here's Sarah's birthday party."

"See, this is what I mean. We miss so much. It's amazing how much you miss in a couple of months." Kathy continued flipping through the photos. "What are these doing in here?"

"Which ones?" Mike asked.

"These old pictures of us in the backyard at our old house. We're all so young."

"Mom found those in an old book, and I just threw them in the pile. I need to put them in an album."

"Wow, it takes me back. Do you miss the old house?"

"Yes and no. I mean, all those years in South Side."

For Mike's and Helen's entire lives, the grid of streets and houses of South Side, friends, and family had become an integral part of their existence. How could they leave? Although they were content, Jerry had known that if he could find his parents their perfect dream house, they might be persuaded. His parents had endured many obstacles over the years. After the war, a deluge of men returned to the States and married, created a shortage of rooms. Mike and Helen's only option was to move in with Helen's parents and rent her old bedroom. Eventually, they rented the apartment next to her parents, but with three boys, they quickly outgrew the one bedroom. Mike's parents offered their larger house with the stipulation that he handle the maintenance and bills. Unfortunately, Mike's parents reneged on their promise, and he and Helen were forced to move out. Having exhausted all their funds on the old house, little money remained to invest, and they settled on a small, four-room house. Although not ideal, they finally had their own place.

After eighteen years of his parents living in the small, cramped house, Jerry knew they deserved something better. He searched for months until he discovered the perfect home, a free-standing brick house just miles up the hill in Bon Air. After Mike had seen it, with its large porch surrounded by grass and a fence, he admitted that Jerry found the place Mike had always imagined. Eager to give this gift to Helen, Mike hesitated because he didn't have the down payment. Jerry provided the bulldozer to remove the obstacle standing between Mike and his dream and supplied the money.

Kathy said, "You don't regret moving? Do you, Dad?"

"Absolutely not. It was a good decision. I love the trees and grass and flowers. And your mother has room to have all of you over for dinner."

Helen, juggling a tray of iced tea, asked, "So, what about dinner?"

"Oh, we're just talking about how much bigger this house is than Larkins Way."

Helen handed Kathy a glass of iced tea. "It is. I'm glad we did it; otherwise, where would you stay when you visit?"

"I know. This is better than a hotel room. And the price is right, too!"

Kathy resumed scanning the pictures. "What's this one, Daddy?"

"It's from the Rainbow reunion they held in Pittsburgh."

"Didn't you attend that years ago? Did they have another one?"

"No, those are from '79."

"Oh, some more old pictures. You better get on the ball and organize these. You know, I never talked to you about the reunion. Was it good to meet up with your old army buddies?"

"Yeah, it was a long time since we'd seen each other, and it felt good to be with a group of guys who really understood what it was like."

"I guess everybody still remembers everything?"

"Yep, we remembered, but there's plenty of things we'd like to forget. We talked more about what happened after the war."

"Are you going to another reunion?"

"I don't know. I think the next one is in California. If I had the money, I'd rather take your mother back to Austria. I've always wanted to show her the beautiful mountains and countryside."

"I hope you both get there someday, Dad. Life is meant to be enjoyed."

Chapter Thirty-Nine

April 9, 1992

Helen retrieved the comb from the table, strolled to the monster of a hospital bed at the edge of the dining room, and combed Mike's hair. After straightening the blankets and kissing his forehead, she rested in the recliner next to his bed. She had accepted the role of twenty-four-hour caregiver and instinctively tended to her soulmate like a skilled nurse. Almost a year ago, Mike had received the diagnosis of brain cancer from a rapidly growing, tenacious tumor. The glioblastoma multi-forme had reached its tentacles deep into the core of his brain, robbing him of his physical and mental abilities. As his health declined, Helen became his eyes to read the newspaper, his mind to make decisions, and his mighty hands to feed him. Her needs remained secondary, and her life revolved around her husband.

She unrelentingly forged through every day. When she could not undertake another task, she reached down into her inner being and drew forth additional courage and strength. However, her sleepless eyes and staggering walk revealed the toll it had taken on her. To ease her burden, Jerry and Kenny alternated night vigils over Mike's bed and tended to him. On the evenings when Jerry or Kenny slept in the recliner next to Mike's bed, Helen rejuvenated herself with a little undisturbed sleep. Kathy, as well as Helen's daughter-in-law, Colleen, the day keepers, assisted with food preparation and watched Mike to allow Helen some time by herself. The family administered each deed with love, in return for everything Mike had bestowed upon them.

Helen rested at the edge of the bed, holding Mike's hands, and recounted stories about their life. Mike, the documenter and custodian of family history via his still and movie cameras, could no longer remember them. Memories had become his life preserver during the war and a way of holding onto the people he loved and treasured. Now his recollections had withered and fallen away like the bright leaves of autumn into the gusty wind. When his eyelids shut, she remained by his side. Closing her eyes, Helen absorbed Mike's spirit and breathed in sync with him. She stroked his face and threaded her fingers through his hair, recollecting the young, handsome, vibrant man he had once been.

Jerry knocked at the door several times.

"Hey, Mom, how's Dad doing?" he asked.

"I wish he was better. He's not responding."

She ignored the reality that her husband stood at death's door, and she remained ever faithful, praying for a miracle. God had previously bestowed several miracles upon them, and Helen prayed for God to shine down upon them one more time.

Standing by the bed, Jerry brushed back Mike's hair. "Hey, Dad, you ready for another day?" Jerry's stomach wrenched. For months, he'd watched the tumor transform his virile, charismatic father and master of dominating a discussion into a shell of his former self. His condition had progressed from his confusing simple words to muttering encrypted conversations that needed translation, to being unable to recognize family members. If only the Grim Reaper had stood vigil while Mike laughed and joked, instead of waiting until his personality and dignity had disappeared.

Jerry, knowing how much his dad loved the Easter season, perched on the recliner and reminded Mike of the upcoming celebration of Palm Sunday and the events of Holy Week. His throat tightened and his eyes watered. The solemn tradition of mass and visiting churches on Holy Thursday, Good Friday services, and the blessing of the food basket on Saturday would proceed without Mike. Jerry recalled fond moments from past holiday family celebrations and retold the stories until Mike's eyes forever closed, and he slipped into a coma.

Soon, the dining room overflowed with family, prepared to shower him with love. Silence, whimpers, and hearts burdened with grief surrounded the bed. An occasional light-hearted remark filtered through the somber atmosphere to mask the grimness of the situation.

As they waited for the inevitable, everyone waded through the uncharted waters of a vanishing life. Helen mechanically prepared coffee and offered cookies while Colleen washed the dishes. In between duties or conversations, the family members privately offered their final farewell to Mike, all except for Helen. To say goodbye would acknowledge Mike's imminent demise, and she refused to relinquish him and admit that he had lost his battle.

Kathy also prayed for a miracle, but if God wanted him home, she trusted in His decision. As a child, while her much older brothers were occupied with girls and work, she had reaped the preciousness of Mike's time and attention. On weekends, they explored the numerous hidden gems of Pittsburgh, and Kathy discovered insight into her dad's soul and personality. Mike became an integral part of her life as her hero and role model. In relinquishing him, a part of herself perished. With a heavy heart, she laid her head on her father's chest, held his hand, gently kissed him on the cheek, and lowered her lips to his ear. "I love you, Daddy, and will always be your little girl. I don't want to let you go, but if God can ease your pain, it's okay to let go. You gave it a good fight, and I'll see you in heaven someday." Her effort to be strong and convince her dad that her life would be okay came to a halt as she glanced at her own children. His departure meant his influence, strength, and wisdom would evaporate from their lives. Tears erupted from her eyes and cascaded down her cheeks.

Releasing his hand, she silently dragged herself away, her legs wrapped with weights from the force of grief.

Even though Mike lay silent, his spirit still survived. Eric, almost two years old, sat on his stomach. In his innocence, he responded to the familiar face, expecting a response. He called, "Grand-pap, Grand-pap?"

As his youngest grandchild sat upon his belly, Mike drew his last breath. Noticing that his breathing had stopped and in a voice oozing pain, Kathy screamed, "Daddy!" Helen stormed toward the bed. Quivering and bawling, she embraced her husband and yelled, "Mike, Mike, Mike, no! Don't go, please, Mike, don't go, I love you!" She kissed him again and again. As his soul departed, it carried away the bedrock of Helen's life.

Silence hit as quickly as a runner out of the blocks, and a deluge of salty tears followed. The reality of Mike's death descended from the heavens, crashing into their world with an exploding force. Darkness lingered in the room; a fog enveloped everything in sight. No words were spoken, only incessant cries. Some cried silently, other cries penetrated the walls, and the little ones, unable to comprehend the gravity of the situation, cried in response to the heartache in the room. When Mike's last gasp of breath escaped, even the house felt anguish as the air grew thin. It seemed as if the room darkened, and walls hemmed in around them. It felt as if the foundation crumbled under their feet, making the floors like quicksand, ready to suck them into the depths and shadows of the earth. Even the hands of the clock seemed to stand still in response to the family's immense grief. After the illusion of hours of silence, Jerry put his arms around his mother. As tears soaked his shirt, he said, "We need to call the doctor and the funeral home."

Kathy, her throat swollen, barely able to talk, stuttered, "We'll have to make funeral arrangements, too."

Helen's paralyzed mind awoke, and she whimpered, "Yes, we do, but I can't do this. Mike . . . Mike . . . what am I supposed to do?"

A short time later, the hearse arrived. When they laid the sheets and the body bag on the gurney and lifted Mike's lifeless body, Kathy bolted out the back door. Jerry ran after his sister and held her, but his hugs and concern could not erase her torment.

After everyone departed, Kathy and Helen slowly prepared for bed. Helen settled in, and Kathy snuggled next to her mom. Helen clung to Kathy and wept, "I wish it were Dad's arms around me. I'll never . . . feel his arms . . . again."

"I know, Mom, I wish . . . I could hug him, too . . . it's going to be hard."

Helen's voice cracked as she struggled to say, "Kathy, what am I going to do without him?"

Kathy nodded and closed her eyes. "I know, Mom, I know. It'll never . . . never be the same."

No more words could be spoken, and in the dark room, in each other's arms, they cried every last tear.

Chapter Forty

Helen ambled into the bedroom, stood before the closet, and rested her hand on the door handle. With closed eyes, she took a deep breath and opened the louvered doors. Mike's best suit hung prominently before her in the plastic covering. The suit she had sent to the cleaners only a few days ago in anticipation of better times, not for his funeral. Minutes passed before she removed the suit from the metal pole and laid it on the bed. She pivoted back to the line of clothes, methodically dragged a shirt out, and inspected it like a forensic examiner. *No, this one is too old. Not this one, it's not a good color.* After numerous attempts, she found Mike's favorite, a white-on-white striped shirt, and placed it next to the suit. She felt déjà vu, remembering the day Mike had left for boot camp. But instead of preparing herself for his temporary absence, she prepared for Mike's final departure.

She took another quick glance at the shirt, and although it looked crisp and clean, it was not perfect. It needed her loving touch.

Over the decades, Helen had ironed mountains of clothes, always searching for the last wrinkle. When she finished, the shirts and the pants always looked brand new. To outsiders, it appeared to be a precise ironing job, but her family knew the perfectly crisp articles reflected Helen's deep love. Today would be no different, except this would be the last time she would display her love to Mike in this way.

She stood by the ironing board, pressing the shirt repeatedly. Her hands moved across the board, and her mind drifted to the past. Thoughts of their first encounter, their marriage, her knight in shining armor shielding her from harm, and her "arm-strong heater" warming her on cold nights.

Would she freeze now without him? Would she be safe? What would she do without him? How would she survive? Helen never fathomed Mike leaving her; he was supposed to be there forever. Now, these questions and more whirled around her head. She fluctuated from reverie to anger, then back to remembering, and splashed down in an ocean of sorrow.

Kathy walked into the room. "Mom, I found Dad's shoes. Mom, Mom! Mom! Can you hear me?" When she received no answer to her repeated entreaties, Kathy physically shook her mother. "Mom! Look at me. Are you okay?"

"I'm sorry. I'm okay. Did you get Dad's shoes?"

"Yes, what else do you need?"

Helen stared at the ironing board. Her list of desires was endless. She needed Mike back. She needed support and assurance that everything would be all right. She needed everything to be perfect for this funeral. She quietly responded, "I want you to get the Holy Spirit pin Dad always wore and the Rainbow Division pin. I want him to be buried with them."

The two pins used to lie side by side on the dresser, but the Holy Spirit pin was missing. Kathy frantically searched the room. She crawled on the carpet, reached her hand under the bed, and flung open the dresser drawers. Finally, she opened the nightstand drawer and discovered the pin. Next to it, she found a letter addressed to "My Family."

The emotional piece of prose had been written almost a year ago and had remained unnoticed. Mike, through his faith, knew God would reveal his thoughts at the appropriate time. Mike wanted to convey his sentiments intelligently to his family before the ravenous disease overtook his mind and body. In numerous conversations or decisions, he always commanded the last word; this time was no different. But instead of bidding farewell in his gregarious voice, he said goodbye softly in a letter.

Kathy's hand trembled as she reached for the pin and the letter. Her eyes fixed on her father's handwriting. She tried to shout that she'd found the pin and an unexpected treasure, but anguish clogged her throat.

Helen walked into the room and noticed Kathy's teary eyes and puzzled expression. "What's wrong?" she asked.

"Mom," Kathy said with trembling lips, "I found the pin in the drawer . . . and . . . and . . . next to it was a letter . . . from Daddy."

Helen's nerves, already fraying, were on the verge of breaking down. "What do you mean, a letter from Daddy? I don't understand."

"I haven't read it, but it's dated a year ago, and it says, 'To my family.'"

Helen lowered herself slowly onto the bed in a daze.

"Mom, are you okay? You're not saying anything! Say something"

Kathy knelt by her mother. "We have to read it, Mom. Obviously, Daddy wanted to say something to us." She handed the letter to her mother.

Helen stared at it briefly and surrendered it to Kathy. "I don't think I can read this right now."

"I know it's hard, Mom, but obviously Daddy wanted us to find the letter. It was right next to the pin. You should be the one to read it."

Helen's lips quivered. "No, I'm telling you I can't. I want . . . you to read it to me. I just want to listen."

Kathy slowly unfolded the letter and started to read, but the words blurred through her glassy eyes, and her throat tightened. "I can't," she said.

Helen grabbed Kathy's hand and squeezed it tightly. "Please."

Kathy gazed into her mother's begging eyes and inhaled deeply. Calmness entered her body as she sensed her father's presence giving her courage to continue. She slowly read the letter and heard the words in her father's voice:

Dear Family, April 29, 1991

While I'm still under control of most of my faculties I decided to express some of my thoughts and feelings.

I'm not going to give you any advice or tell you how to live your lives or even expound upon the theories of life. I just want to tell you how much I love you each and every one of you. I couldn't have made a better choice than The Good Lord when you were born. I constantly prayed to the Good Lord that He would give me the strength, courage, and wisdom to bring up my family properly. A family with true sense of purpose, honesty, and integrity. A sense of values that I've constantly cherished and still do.

I know that I never achieved all that I decided on or set out to accomplish but I have no regrets knowing that I did my best and accepting nothing less. I have no problem accepting what happened to me. I've had a full enjoyable life and feel much at peace with myself.

So, don't weep for me. Remember me as someone who hopefully had a sense of humor, even if it was a bit corny. Someone who enjoyed the simple wonders of nature, a beautiful sunset, the smell of new mown grass, the glistening dew on a sweet smelling rose, the rustling of autumn leaves on the ground and the clear crisp chill of new fallen snow on the ground. All the wonderful wonders of the four seasons. Also remember me as one who loved his family very much and enjoyed being with them and sharing their joy and sorrow.

So put a smile on your face, a song in your heart, and a snap in your step and continue with your lives.

If it's at all possible I'll be looking down on all of you and watching out for you. I'm extremely proud to have been a part of your lives.

All my love--God Bless you all. Love Dad

The two women seized each other for support. Sorrowful sobs reverberated through the room for minutes, halted by knocking on the back door. Kathy slowly pulled away from Helen. "Mom, I need to answer the door. It's probably Jerry."

"Hey. Bad night?" Jerry asked when Kathy opened the door.

Still clutching the letter in her hands, she stared into Jerry's eyes. "Yes, but . . . it's a . . ." Exhaling quickly, Kathy extended the paper to her brother. "Jer, we found a letter from Daddy to us he wrote a year ago."

Jerry froze, and the color disappeared from his face. "What do you mean, a letter from Dad? How?"

"We found it while looking for the Holy Spirit pin. It was next to it."

"I don't think I can read that now." Jerry had been a constant presence during the last year, bathing Mike, doing chores, and doing the tasks Mike used to preside over before the tumor. The thought of his death had barely become a reality, and reading his final sentiments would be too overwhelming.

"You have to read it. It was hard for me to read it, too." Handing the letter to Jerry, she sobbed, "Take it. Daddy left it for us because he loves us. It's a gift."

Jerry sat down, and as he read, tears fell upon the letter. The pain and loss choked his throat, and when he was finished, he said, "Yeah, that's Dad. That's Dad."

Kathy nodded. "Yeah, you're right."

Chapter Forty-One

Spring 1992

Helen rambled from one room to another like a lost puzzle piece searching for the rest of the picture. During Mike's illness, she had developed the strength and commitment of a battleship during war. Now, the war had ceased and consigned her to having no purpose in life, no one to care for, no one to keep her warm at night, no one to converse with, and nothing to do. She opened a dresser drawer, withdrew Mike's favorite pajamas, and held them to her nose, clinging to his scent. Folding them carefully, she returned the pajamas to the drawer and removed a pair of thinning socks and slid them onto her cold feet. Dragging her feet toward the closet, she rustled through his clothes on the hangers. She pulled out a shirt with a soup stain, recalling the story behind it, and the corners of her mouth lifted in a smile. One by one, she stroked each piece of clothing, lost in time and stories.

Helen stared at the shoes at the bottom of the wardrobe and glimpsed a few worn and long-forgotten boxes. Kneeling on the carpet, she withdrew the top box. Under the flaps, she found Mike's high school play program, in which he had played the lead role, and his yearbook, along with postcards and pictures from his days in the CCC and the CMTC. As she searched deeper, she discovered the school newspaper he'd edited, a photo of him as a track star, and another with the swim team. Nothing had seemed impossible for Mike.

She shuffled through the next box and discovered his medals and insignia from the army, his enlistment papers, a Rainbow Division yearbook, and other memorabilia from his time away from Helen. One box remained. Helen raised the lid and gasped when she recognized the yellow, faded letters addressed to her from Mike during the war. She reached for the envelopes and jerked back her hand when she heard the high-pitched trill of the train whistle. The sound sent shivers up her back and carried images of the day Mike had left for boot camp. Now it reminded her of his absence. The fresh wounds in her heart forced her to shut the lid and return the treasure back to the closet.

Weeks passed, and the precious correspondence remained hidden beneath the wardrobe. Helen, searching for her shoes one day, stopped when the box tumbled out, and the contents spread before her. To the beat of the ticking clock on the nightstand, she arranged the letters in the carton, one by one. When she picked up the last envelope, she clutched it to her chest and closed her eyes. Would Mike's words heal her broken heart or overwhelm her with grief? With trembling hands, she released the letter. She read the greeting and then shoved it back into the envelope and threw it in the box. A few days later, she withdrew the letters. Again, they were returned unread. This ritual continued for a few months until she was emotionally ready to walk down the sentimental lane.

On Mike's birthday, she gathered several letters, strolled to the recliner in the corner, and placed them on her lap. Her shoulders tightened as she slowly removed the correspondence from its envelope. The sweat from her brow commingled with her tears as she read. One mechanical motion unleashed an onslaught of memories of young love and times long gone but not forgotten.

She smiled at the distinctive scratchy handwriting. With each word she read, his voice grew louder, and his face became clearer. The exuberant, handsome young man who had gained her heart lingered in the empty room with her. For a second, she smelled his aftershave.

Helen, who had initially been hesitant to embark on this journey, yielded to the onslaught of memories. With each letter, the reassurance of Mike's undying love grew, and she knew that even in his absence, he would forever remain with her.

Until Helen would see him again, she would always be remembering, never forgetting, and loving him forever.

Author's Note

For those of you wondering what happened to Adam, let me explain. While stationed in Persia (modern-day Iran), Adam committed suicide by hanging himself, but Helen was unaware of how he died. His family had been informed it was non–battle related but was never given an explanation. Through my research, I obtained Adam's records and discovered his cause of death. Helen lost touch with Adam's family, and perhaps they eventually uncovered the truth, but Helen died without knowing the real story. I am unaware of any suicide note or reason for his decision, but Helen did write to Adam to let him know of her engagement to Mike. Shortly after he received the news, he took his own life, and one assumption is that he could not bear the pain of having lost Helen forever.

Made in the USA
Middletown, DE
12 November 2023

42306876R00213